WHEN HE WAS WICKED

Also by Julia Quinn
in Large Print:

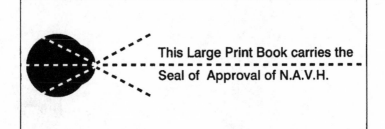

This Large Print Book carries the
Seal of Approval of N.A.V.H.

WHEN HE WAS WICKED

JULIA QUINN

Thorndike Press • Waterville, Maine

Published in 2004 by arrangement with Avon Books, an imprint of HarperCollins Publishers Inc.

Thorndike Press® Large Print Basic.

The tree indicium is a trademark of Thorndike Press.

The text of this Large Print edition is unabridged.
Other aspects of the book may vary from the original edition.

Set in 16 pt. Plantin by Carleen Stearns.

Printed in the United States on permanent paper.

Library of Congress Cataloging-in-Publication Data

Quinn, Julia.
    When he was wicked / Julia Quinn.
        p. cm.
    ISBN 0-7862-7083-7 (lg. print : hc : alk. paper)
    1. Large type books.   2. London (England) — Fiction.
    I. Title.
    PS3617.U57W47 2004
    813'.6—dc22   2004046235

For B.B.,
who kept me company
throughout the writing of this book.
The best things come to those who wait!

And also for Paul,
even though he wanted to call it
Love in the Time of Malaria.

As the Founder/CEO of NAVH, the only national health agency solely devoted to those who, although not totally blind, have an eye disease which could lead to serious visual impairment, I am pleased to recognize Thorndike Press* as one of the leading publishers in the large print field.

Founded in 1954 in San Francisco to prepare large print textbooks for partially seeing children, NAVH became the pioneer and standard setting agency in the preparation of large type.

Today, those publishers who meet our standards carry the prestigious "Seal of Approval" indicating high quality large print. We are delighted that Thorndike Press is one of the publishers whose titles meet these standards. We are also pleased to recognize the significant contribution Thorndike Press is making in this important and growing field.

Lorraine H. Marchi, L.H.D.
Founder/CEO
NAVH

* Thorndike Press encompasses the following imprints: Thorndike, Wheeler, Walker and Large Print Press.

Acknowledgments

The author wishes to thank Paul Pottinger, MD, and Philip Yarnell, MD, for their expertise in the fields of, respectively, infectious diseases and neurology.

Bridgerton
FAMILY TREE

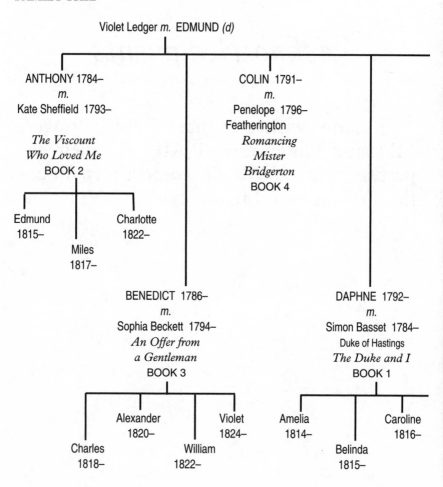

Violet Ledger *m.* EDMUND *(d)*

ANTHONY 1784–
m.
Kate Sheffield 1793–

*The Viscount
Who Loved Me*
BOOK 2

Edmund
1815–

Miles
1817–

Charlotte
1822–

COLIN 1791–
m.
Penelope 1796–
Featherington
*Romancing
Mister
Bridgerton*
BOOK 4

BENEDICT 1786–
m.
Sophia Beckett 1794–
*An Offer from
a Gentleman*
BOOK 3

Charles
1818–

Alexander
1820–

William
1822–

Violet
1824–

DAPHNE 1792–
m.
Simon Basset 1784–
Duke of Hastings
The Duke and I
BOOK 1

Amelia
1814–

Belinda
1815–

Caroline
1816–

to see the expanded f‹

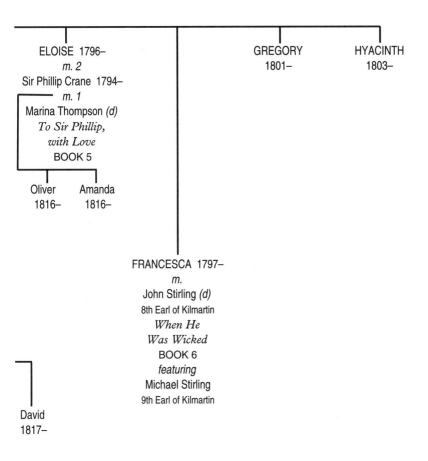

ELOISE 1796–
m. 2
Sir Phillip Crane 1794–
m. 1
Marina Thompson *(d)*
To Sir Phillip,
with Love
BOOK 5

Oliver
1816–

Amanda
1816–

GREGORY
1801–

HYACINTH
1803–

FRANCESCA 1797–
m.
John Stirling *(d)*
8th Earl of Kilmartin
When He
Was Wicked
BOOK 6
featuring
Michael Stirling
9th Earl of Kilmartin

David
1817–

amily tree, please visit www.juliaquinn.com

Part One

March, 1820
London, England

 *Chapter 1*

. . . I wouldn't call it a jolly good time, but it's not as bad as that. There are women, after all, and where there are women, I'm bound to make merry.

— from Michael Stirling to his cousin John, the Earl of Kilmartin, posted from the 52nd Foot Guards during the Napoleonic Wars

In every life there is a turning point. A moment so tremendous, so sharp and clear that one feels as if one's been hit in the chest, all the breath knocked out, and one knows, absolutely *knows* without the merest hint of a shadow of a doubt that one's life will never be the same.

For Michael Stirling, that moment came the first time he laid eyes on Francesca Bridgerton.

After a lifetime of chasing women, of smiling slyly as they chased him, of allowing himself to be caught and then turning the tables until he was the victor, of caressing and kissing and making love to them but never actually allowing his heart to become engaged, he took one look at Francesca Bridgerton and fell so fast and so hard into love it was a wonder he managed to remain standing.

Unfortunately for Michael, however, Francesca's surname was to remain Bridgerton a mere thirty-six hours longer; the occasion of their meeting was, lamentably, a supper celebrating her imminent wedding to his cousin.

Life was ironic that way, Michael liked to think in his more polite moods.

In his less polite moods, he used a different adjective entirely.

And his moods, since falling in love with his first cousin's wife, were not often polite.

Oh, he hid it well. It wouldn't do to be visibly out of sorts. Then some annoyingly perceptive soul might actually take notice, and — God forbid — *inquire* as to his welfare. And while Michael Stirling held a not unsubstantiated pride in his ability to dissemble and deceive (he had, after all, seduced more women than anyone cared to count, and had somehow managed to do it all without ever once being challenged to a duel) — Well, the sodding truth of it was that he'd never been in love before, and if ever there was a time that a man might lose his ability to maintain a façade under direct questioning, this was probably it.

And so he laughed, and was very merry, and he continued to seduce women, trying not to notice that he tended to close his eyes when he had them in bed, and he stopped going to church entirely, because there seemed no point now in even contemplating prayer for his soul. Besides, the parish church near Kilmartin dated to 1432, and the crumbling stones certainly couldn't take a direct strike of lightning.

And if God ever wanted to smite a sinner, he couldn't do better than Michael Stirling.

Michael Stirling, Sinner.

He could see it on a calling card. He'd have had it printed up, even — his was just that sort of black sense of humor — if he weren't convinced it would kill his mother on the spot.

Rake he might be, but there was no need to torture the woman who'd borne him.

Funny how he'd never seen all those other women as a sin. He still didn't. They'd all been willing, of course; you couldn't seduce an unwilling woman, at least not if you took seduction at the true sense of the word and took care not to confuse it with rape. They had to actually want it, and if they didn't — if Michael sensed even a hint of unease, he turned and walked away. His passions were never so out of control that he couldn't manage a quick and decisive departure.

And besides, he'd never seduced a virgin, and he'd never slept with a married woman. Oh very well, one ought to remain true to oneself, even while living a lie — he'd slept with married women, plenty of them, but only the ones whose husbands were rotters, and even then, not unless she'd already produced two male offspring; three, if one of the boys seemed a little sickly.

A man had to have rules of conduct, after all.

But this . . . This was beyond the pale. Entirely unacceptable. This was the one transgression (and he'd had many) that was finally going to blacken his soul, or at the very least — and this was assuming he maintained the strength never to act upon his desires — make it a rather deep shade of charcoal. Because this . . . this —

He coveted his cousin's wife.

He coveted John's wife.

John.

John, who, damn it all, was more of a brother to him than one of his own could ever have been. John, whose family had taken him in when his father had died. John, whose father had raised him and taught him to be a man. John, with whom —

Ah, bloody hell. Did he really need to do this to himself? He could spend a sennight cataloguing all the reasons why he was going straight to hell for having chosen John's wife with whom to fall in love. And none of it was ever going to change one simple fact.

He couldn't have her.

He could never have Francesca Bridgerton Stirling.

But, he thought with a snort as he slouched into the sofa and propped his ankle over his knee, watching them across their drawing room, laughing and smiling, and making nauseating eyes at each other, he *could* have another drink.

"I think I will," he announced, downing it in one gulp.

"What was that, Michael?" John asked, his hearing superb, as always, damn it.

Michael produced an excellent forgery

of a smile and lifted his glass aloft. "Just thirsty," he said, maintaining the perfect picture of a bon vivant.

They were at Kilmartin House, in London, as opposed to Kilmartin (no House, no Castle, just Kilmartin), up in Scotland, where the boys had grown up, or the other Kilmartin House, in Edinburgh — not a creative soul among his forbearers, Michael had often reflected; there was also a Kilmartin Cottage (if one could call twenty-two rooms a cottage), Kilmartin Abbey, and, of course, Kilmartin Hall. Michael had no idea why no one had thought to offer their surname to one of the residences; "Stirling House" had a perfectly respectful ring to it, in his opinion. He supposed that the ambitious — and unimaginative — Stirlings of old had been so damned besotted with their newfound earldom that they couldn't think to put any other name on anything.

He snorted into his glass of whisky. It was a wonder he didn't drink Kilmartin Tea and sit on a Kilmartin-style chair. In fact, he probably would be doing just that if his grandmother had found a way to manage it without actually taking the family into trade. The old martinet had been so proud one would have thought she'd been born a Stirling rather than simply married into the name. As far as she'd been concerned, the Countess of Kilmartin (herself) was just as important as any loftier personage, and she'd more than once sniffed her displeasure when being led into supper after an upstart marchioness or duchess.

The Queen, Michael thought dispassionately. He supposed his grandmother had knelt before the Queen, but he certainly couldn't imagine her offering deference to any other female.

She would have approved of Francesca Bridgerton. Grandmother Stirling would surely have turned her nose up upon learning that Francesca's father was a mere viscount, but the Bridgertons were an old and immensely popular — and, when the fancy took them, powerful — family. Plus, Francesca's spine was straight and her manner was proud, and her sense of humor was sly and subversive. If she'd been fifty years older and not nearly so attractive, she would have made quite a fine companion for Grandmother Stirling.

And now Francesca was the Countess of Kilmartin, married to his cousin John, who was one year his junior but in the Stirling household always treated with the deference due the elder; he was the heir, after all. Their fathers had been twins, but John's had entered the world seven minutes before Michael's.

The most critical seven minutes in Michael Stirling's life, and he hadn't even been alive for them.

"What shall we do for our second anniversary?" Francesca asked as she crossed the room and seated herself at the pianoforte.

"Whatever you want," John answered.

Francesca turned to Michael, her eyes startlingly blue, even in the candlelight. Or maybe it was just that he knew how blue they were. He seemed to dream in blue these days. Francesca blue, the color ought to be called.

"Michael?" she said, her tone indicating that the word was a repetition.

"Sorry," he said, offering her the lopsided smile he so frequently affixed to his face. No one ever took him seriously when he smiled like that, which was, of course, the point. "Wasn't listening."

"Do you have any ideas?" she asked.

"For what?"

"For our anniversary."

If she'd had an arrow, she couldn't have jammed it into his heart any harder. But he just shrugged, since he was appallingly good at faking it. "It's not my anniversary," he reminded her.

"I know," she said. He wasn't looking at her, but she sounded like she rolled her eyes.

But she hadn't. Michael was certain of that. He'd come to know Francesca agonizingly well in the past two years, and he knew she didn't roll her eyes. When she was feeling sarcastic, or ironic, or sly, it was all there in her voice and the curious tip of her mouth. She didn't need to roll her eyes. She just looked at you with that direct stare, her lips curving ever so slightly, and —

Michael swallowed reflexively, then covered it with a sip of his drink. It didn't really speak well of him that he'd spent so much time analyzing the curve of his cousin's wife's lips.

"I assure you," Francesca continued, idly trailing the pads of her fingertips along the surface of the piano keys without actually pressing any into sound, "I'm well aware of whom I married."

"I'm sure you are," he muttered.

"Beg pardon?"

"Continue," he said.

Her lips pursed in a peevish crease. He'd

seen her with that expression quite frequently, usually in her dealings with her brothers. "I was asking your advice," she said, "because you are so often merry."

"I'm so often merry?" he repeated, knowing that was how the world saw him — they called him the Merry Rake, after all — but hating the word on her lips. It made him feel frivolous, without substance.

And then he felt even worse, because it was probably true.

"You disagree?" she inquired.

"Of course not," he murmured. "I'm simply unused to being asked for advice regarding anniversary celebrations, as it is clear I have no talent for marriage."

"That's not clear at all," she said.

"You're in for it now," John said with a chuckle, settling back in his seat with that morning's copy of the *Times*.

"You have never tried marriage," Francesca pointed out. "How could you possibly know you have no talent for it?"

Michael managed a smirk. "I think it's fairly clear to all who know me. Besides, what need have I? I have no title, no property —"

"You have property," John interjected, demonstrating that he was still listening from behind his newspaper.

"Only a small bit of property," Michael corrected, "which I am more than happy to leave for your children, since it was given to me by John, anyway."

Francesca looked at her husband, and Michael knew exactly what she was thinking — that John had given him the property because John wanted him to feel he had something, a purpose, really. Michael had been at loose ends since decommissioning from the army several years back. And although John had never said so, Michael knew that he felt guilty for having not fought for England on the Continent, for remaining behind while Michael faced danger alone.

But John had been heir to an earldom. He had a duty to marry, be fruitful and multiply. No one had expected him to go to war.

Michael had often wondered if the property — a rather lovely and comfortable manor house with twenty acres — was John's form of penance. And he rather suspected that Francesca wondered the same.

But she would never ask. Francesca understood men with remarkable clarity — probably from growing up with all of those brothers. Francesca knew exactly what not to ask a man.

Which always left Michael a little worried. He thought he hid his feelings well, but what if she *knew?* She would never speak of it, of course, never even allude to it. He rather suspected they were, ironically, alike that way; if Francesca suspected he was in love with her, she would *never* alter her manner in any way.

"I think you should go to Kilmartin," Michael said abruptly.

"To Scotland?" Francesca asked, pressing gently against B-flat on the pianoforte. "With the season so close?"

Michael stood, suddenly rather eager to depart. He shouldn't have come over in any case. "Why not?" he asked, his tone careless. "You love it there. John loves it there. It's not such a long journey if your carriage is well sprung."

"Will you come?" John asked.

"I think not," Michael said sharply. As if he cared to witness their anniversary celebration. Truly, all it would do was remind him of what he could never have. Which would then remind him of the guilt. Or amplify it. Reminders were rather unnecessary; he lived with it every day.

Thou Shalt Not Covet Thy Cousin's Wife.

Moses must have forgotten to write that one down.

"I have much to do here," Michael said.

"You do?" Francesca asked, her eyes lighting with interest. "What?"

"Oh, you know," he said wryly, "all those things I have to do to prepare for a life of dissolution and aimlessness."

Francesca stood.

Oh God, she stood, and she was walking to him. This was the worst — when she actually touched him.

She laid her hand on his upper arm. Michael did his best not to flinch.

"I wish you wouldn't speak that way," she said.

Michael looked past her shoulder to John, who had raised his newspaper just high enough so that he could pretend he wasn't listening.

"Am I to become your project, then?" Michael asked, a bit unkindly.

She drew back. "We care about you."

We. *We*. Not *I*, not *John*. We. A subtle reminder that they were a unit. John and Francesca. Lord and Lady Kilmartin. She hadn't meant it that way, of course, but it was how he heard it all the same.

"And I care for you," Michael said, waiting for a plague of locusts to stream through the room.

"I know," she said, oblivious to his distress. "I could never ask for a better cousin. But I want you to be happy."

Michael glanced over at John, giving him a look that clearly said: *Save me.*

John gave up his pretense of reading and set the paper down. "Francesca, darling, Michael is a grown man. He'll find his happiness as he sees fit. *When* he sees fit."

Francesca's lips pursed, and Michael could tell she was irritated. She didn't like to be thwarted, and she certainly did not enjoy admitting that she might not be able to arrange her world — and the people inhabiting it — to her satisfaction.

"I should introduce you to my sister," she said.

Good God. "I've met your sister," Michael said quickly. "All of them, in fact. Even the one still in leading strings."

"She's not in —" She cut herself off, grinding her teeth together. "I grant you that Hyacinth is not suitable, but Eloise is —"

"I'm not marrying Eloise," Michael said sharply.

"I didn't say you had to marry her," Francesca said. "Just dance with her once or twice."

"I've done so," he reminded her. "And that is all I am going to do."

"But —"

"Francesca," John said. His voice was gentle, but his meaning was clear. *Stop*.

Michael could have kissed him for his interference. John of course just thought that he was saving his cousin from needless feminine nagging; there was no way he could know the truth — that Michael was trying to compute the level of guilt one might feel for being in love with one's cousin's wife *and* one's wife's sister.

Good God, married to Eloise Bridgerton. Was Francesca trying to *kill* him?

"We should all go for a walk," Francesca said suddenly.

Michael glanced out the window. All vestiges of daylight had left the sky. "Isn't it a bit late for that?" he asked.

"Not with two strong men as escorts," she said, "and besides, the streets in Mayfair are well lit. We shall be perfectly safe." She turned to her husband. "What do you say, darling?"

"I have an appointment this evening," John said, consulting his pocket watch, "but you should go with Michael."

More proof that John had no idea of Michael's feelings.

"The two of you always have such a fine time together," John added.

Francesca turned to Michael and smiled, worming her way another inch into his heart. "Will you?" she asked. "I'm desperate for a spot of fresh air now that the rain has stopped. And I've been feeling rather odd all day, I must say."

"Of course," Michael replied, since they all knew that he had no appointments. His was a life of carefully cultivated dissolution.

Besides, he couldn't resist her. He knew he should stay away, knew he should never allow himself to be alone in her company. He would never act upon his desires, but truly, did he really need to subject himself to this sort of agony? He'd just end the day alone in bed, wracked by guilt and desire, in almost equal measures.

But when she smiled at him he couldn't say no. And he certainly wasn't strong enough to deny himself an hour in her presence.

Because her presence was all he was ever going to get. There would never be a kiss, never a meaningful glance or touch. There would be no whispered words of love, no moans of passion.

All he could have was her smile and her

company, and pathetic idiot that he was, he was willing to take it.

"Just give me a moment," she said, pausing in the doorway. "I need to get my coat."

"Be quick about it," John said. "It's already after seven."

"I'll be safe enough with Michael to protect me," she said with a jaunty smile, "but don't worry, I'll be quick." And then she offered her husband a wicked smile. "I'm always quick."

Michael averted his eyes as his cousin actually blushed. Lord above, but he *truly* did not want to know the meaning behind *I'll be quick*. Unfortunately, it could have been any number of things, all of them deliciously sexual. And he was likely to spend the next hour cataloguing them all in his mind, imagining them being done to him.

He tugged at his cravat. Maybe he could get out of this jaunt with Francesca. Maybe he could go home and draw a cold bath. Or better yet, find himself a willing woman with long chestnut hair. And if he was lucky, blue eyes as well.

"I'm sorry about that," John said, once Francesca had left.

Michael's eyes flew to his face. Surely

John would never mention Francesca's innuendo.

"Her nagging," John added. "You're young enough. You don't need to be married yet."

"You're younger than I," Michael said, mostly to be contrary.

"Yes, but I met Francesca." John shrugged helplessly, as if that ought to be explanation enough. And of course it was.

"I don't mind her nagging," Michael said.

"Of course you do. I can see it in your eyes."

And that was the problem. John *could* see it in his eyes. There was no one in the world who knew him better. If something was bothering him, John would always be able to tell. The miracle was that John didn't realize *why* Michael was distressed.

"I will tell her to leave you alone," John said, "although you should know that she only nags because she loves you."

Michael managed a tight smile. He certainly couldn't manage words.

"Thank you for taking her for a walk," John said, standing up. "She's been a bit peckish all day, with the rain. Said she's been feeling uncommonly closed in."

"When is your appointment?" Michael asked.

"Nine o'clock," John replied as they walked out into the hall. "I'm meeting Lord Liverpool."

"Parliamentary business?"

John nodded. He took his position in the House of Lords very seriously. Michael had often wondered if he'd have approached the duty with as much gravity, had he been born a lord.

Probably not. But then again, it didn't much matter, did it?

Michael watched as John rubbed his left temple. "Are you all right?" he asked. "You look a little . . ." He didn't finish the sentence, since he wasn't quite certain how John looked. Not right. That was all he knew.

And he knew John. Inside and out. Probably better than Francesca did.

"Devil of a headache," John muttered. "I've had it all day."

"Do you want me to call for some laudanum?"

John shook his head. "Hate the stuff. It makes my mind fuzzy, and I need my wits about me for the meeting with Liverpool."

Michael nodded. "You look pale," he said. Why, he didn't know. It wasn't as if it was going to change John's mind about the laudanum.

"Do I?" John asked, wincing as he pressed his fingers harder into the skin of his temple. "I think I'll lie down, if you don't mind. I don't need to leave for an hour."

"Right," Michael murmured. "Do you want me to have someone wake you?"

John shook his head. "I'll ask my valet myself."

Just then, Francesca descended the stairs, wrapped in a long velvet cloak of midnight blue. "Good evening, gentlemen," she said, clearly basking in the undivided male attention. But as she reached the bottom, she frowned. "Is something wrong, darling?" she asked John.

"Just a headache," John said. "It's nothing."

"You should lie down," she said.

John managed a smile. "I'd just finished telling Michael that I was planning to do that very thing. I'll have Simons wake me in time for my meeting."

"With Lord Liverpool?" Francesca queried.

"Yes. At nine."

"Is it about the Six Acts?"

John nodded. "Yes, and the return to the

gold standard. I told you about it at breakfast, if you recall."

"Make sure you —" She stopped, smiling as she shook her head. "Well, you know how I feel."

John smiled, then leaned down and dropped a tender kiss on her lips. "I always know how you feel, darling."

Michael pretended to look the other way.

"Not always," she said, her voice warm and teasing.

"Always when it matters," John said.

"Well, *that* is true," she admitted. "So much for my attempts to be a lady of mystery."

He kissed her again. "I prefer you as an open book, myself."

Michael cleared his throat. This shouldn't be so difficult; it wasn't as if John and Francesca were acting any differently than was normal. They were, as so much of society had commented, like two peas in a pod, marvelously in accord, and splendidly in love.

"It's growing late," Francesca said. "I should go if I want that spot of fresh air."

John nodded, closing his eyes for a moment.

"Are you sure you're well?"

"I'm fine," he said. "Just a headache."

Francesca looped her hand into the crook of Michael's elbow. "Be sure to take some laudanum when you return from your meeting," she said over her shoulder, once they'd reached the door, "since I know you won't do it now."

John nodded, his expression weary, then headed up the stairs.

"Poor John," Francesca said, stepping outside into the brisk night air. She took a deep inhale, then let out a sigh. "I detest headaches. They always seem to lay me especially low."

"Never get them myself," Michael admitted, leading her down the steps to the pavement.

"Really?" She looked up at him, one corner of her mouth quirking in that achingly familiar way. "Lucky you."

It almost made Michael laugh. Here he was, strolling through the night with the woman he loved.

Lucky him.

Chapter 2

. . . and if it were as bad as that, I suspect you would not tell me. As for the women, do at least try to make sure they are clean and free of disease. Beyond that, do what you must to make your time bearable. And please, try not to get yourself killed. At the risk of sounding maudlin, I don't know what I would do without you.

> — *from the Earl of Kilmartin*
> *to his cousin Michael Stirling,*
> *sent in care of the 52nd Foot Guards*
> *during the Napoleonic Wars*

For all his faults — and Francesca was willing to allow that Michael Stirling had many — he really was the *dearest* man.

He was a horrible flirt (she'd seen him in action, and even she had to admit that otherwise intelligent women lost all measure of sense when he chose to be charming), and he certainly didn't approach his life with the gravity that she and John would have liked him to, but even with all that, she couldn't help but love him.

He was the best friend John had ever had — until he'd married *her*, of course — and over the last two years, he'd become her close confidant as well.

It was a funny thing, that. Who would have thought she'd have counted a man as one of her closest friends? She was not uncomfortable around men; four brothers tended to wring the delicacy out of even the most feminine of creatures. But she was not like her sisters. Daphne and Eloise — and Hyacinth, too, she supposed, although she was still a bit young to know for sure — were so open and sunny. They were the sorts of females who excelled at hunting and shooting — the kinds of pursuits that tended to get them labeled as "jolly good sports." Men always felt comfortable in their presence, and the feeling was, Francesca had observed, entirely mutual.

But she was different. She'd always felt a little different from the rest of her family. She loved them fiercely, and would have laid down her life for any one of them, but even though she looked like a Bridgerton, on the inside she always felt like a bit of a changeling.

Where the rest of her family was outgoing, she was . . . not shy, precisely, but a bit more reserved, more careful with her words. She'd developed a reputation for irony and wit, and she had to admit, she could rarely resist the opportunity to needle her siblings with a dry remark. It was done out of love, of course, and perhaps a touch of the desperation that comes from having spent far too much time with one's family, but they teased Francesca right back, so all was fair.

It was the way of her family. They laughed, they teased, they bickered. Francesca's contributions to the din were simply a touch quieter than the rest, a bit more sly and subversive.

She often wondered if part of her attraction to John had been the simple fact that he removed her from the chaos that was so often the Bridgerton household. Not that she didn't love him; she did. She adored him with every last breath in her body. He was her kindred spirit, so like her in so many ways. But it had, in a strange sort of fashion, been a relief to exit her mother's home, to escape to a more serene existence with John, whose sense of humor was precisely like hers.

He understood her, he anticipated her.

He completed her.

It had been the oddest sensation when she'd met him, almost as if she were a jagged puzzle piece finally finding its mate. Their first meeting hadn't been one of overwhelming love or passion, but rather filled with the most bizarre sense that she'd finally found the one person with whom she could completely be herself.

It had been instant. It had been sudden. She couldn't remember just what it was he'd said to her, but from the moment words first left his lips, she had felt at home.

And with him had come Michael, his cousin — although truth be told, the two men were much more like brothers. They'd been raised together, and they were so close in age that they'd shared everything.

Well, almost everything. John was the heir to an earldom, and Michael was just his cousin, and so it was only natural that the two boys would not be treated quite the same. But from what Francesca had heard, and from what she knew of the Stirling family now, they had been loved in equal measure, and she rather thought that was the key to Michael's good humor.

Because even though John had inherited

the title and the wealth, and well, everything, Michael didn't seem to envy him.

He didn't envy him. It was amazing to her. He'd been raised as John's brother — John's older brother, even — and yet he'd never once begrudged John any of his blessings.

And it was for that reason that Francesca loved him best. Michael would surely scoff if she tried to praise him for it, and she was quite certain that he would point to his many misdeeds (none of which, she feared, were exaggerated) to prove that his soul was black and he was a scoundrel through and through — but the truth of the matter was that Michael Stirling possessed a generosity of spirit and a capability for love that was unmatched among men.

And if she didn't find a wife for him soon, she was going to go mad.

"What," she said, aware that her voice was quite suddenly piercing the silence of the night, "is wrong with my sister?"

"Francesca," he said, and she could hear irritation — and, thankfully, a bit of amusement as well — in his voice, "I'm not going to marry your sister."

"I didn't say you had to marry her."

"You didn't have to. Your face is an open book."

She looked up at him, twisting her lips. "You weren't even looking at me."

"Of course I was, and anyway, it wouldn't matter if I weren't. I know what you're about."

He was right, and it scared her. Sometimes she worried that he understood her as well as John did.

"You need a wife," she said.

"Didn't you just promise your husband that you would stop pestering me about this?"

"I did not, actually," she said, giving him a rather superior glance. "He asked, of course —"

"Of course," Michael muttered.

She laughed. He could always make her laugh.

"I thought wives were supposed to accede to their husbands' wishes," Michael said, quirking his right brow. "In fact, I'm quite certain it's right there in the marriage vows."

"I'd be doing you a grave disservice if I found you a wife like *that*," she said, punctuating the sentiment with a well-timed and extremely disdainful snort.

He turned and gazed down at her with a vaguely paternalistic expression. He should have been a nobleman, Francesca thought.

He was far too irresponsible for the duties of a title, but when he looked at a person like that, all superciliousness and certitude, he might as well have been a royal duke.

"Your responsibilities as Countess of Kilmartin do not include finding me a wife," he said.

"They should."

He laughed, which delighted her. She could always make him laugh.

"Very well," she said, giving up for now. "Tell me about something wicked, then. Something John would not approve of."

It was a game they played, even in John's presence, although John always made at least the pretense of discouraging them. But Francesca suspected that John enjoyed Michael's tales as much as she did. Once he'd finished with his obligatory admonitions, he was always all ears.

Not that Michael ever told them much. He was far too discreet for that. But he dropped hints and innuendo, and Francesca and John were always thoroughly entertained. They wouldn't trade their wedded bliss for anything, but who didn't like to be regaled with tales of debauchery and spice?

"I'm afraid I've done nothing wicked this week," Michael said, steering her around the corner to King Street.

"You? Impossible."

"It's only Tuesday," he reminded her.

"Yes, but not counting Sunday, which I'm sure you would not desecrate" — she shot him a look that said she was quite certain he'd already sinned in every way possible, Sunday or no — "that does leave you Monday, and a man can do quite a bit on a Monday."

"Not this man. Not this Monday."

"What did you do, then?"

He thought about that, then said, "Nothing, really."

"That's impossible," she teased. "I'm quite certain I saw you awake for at least an hour."

He didn't say anything, and then he shrugged in a way she found oddly disturbing and said, "I did nothing. I walked, I spoke, I ate, but at the end of the day, there was nothing."

Francesca impulsively squeezed his arm. "We shall have to find you something," she said softly.

He turned and looked at her, his strange, silvery eyes catching hers with an intensity she knew he didn't often allow to rise to the fore.

And then it was gone, and he was himself again, except she suspected that Michael Stirling wasn't at all the man he wished people to believe him to be.

Even, sometimes, her.

"We should return home," he said. "It's growing late, and John will have my head if I let you catch a chill."

"John would blame *me* for my foolishness, and well you know it," Francesca said. "This is just your way of telling me you have a woman waiting for you, probably draped in nothing but the sheets on her bed."

He turned to her and grinned. It was wicked and devilish, and she understood why half the *ton* — the female half, that was — fancied themselves in love with him, even with no title or fortune to his name.

"You said you wanted something wicked, didn't you?" he asked. "Did you want more detail? The color of the sheets, perhaps?"

She blushed, drat it all. She *hated* that she blushed, but at least the reaction was covered by the night. "Not yellow, I hope," she said, because she couldn't bear to let the conversation end on her embarrassment. "It makes you look sallow."

"I won't be wearing the sheets," he drawled.

"Nevertheless."

43

He chuckled, and she knew that he knew that she'd said it just to have the last word. And she thought he was going to allow her the small victory, but then, just when she was beginning to find relief in the silence, he said, "Red."

"I beg your pardon?" But of course she knew what he meant.

"Red sheets, I think."

"I can't believe you told me that."

"You asked, Francesca Stirling." He looked down at her, and one lock of midnight black hair fell onto his forehead. "You're just lucky I don't tell your husband on you."

"John would never worry over me," she said.

For a moment she didn't think he would reply, but then he said, "I know," and his voice was oddly grave and serious. "It's the only reason I tease you."

She'd been watching the pavement, looking for rough spots, but his tone was so serious she had to look up.

"You're the only woman I know who would never stray," he said, touching her chin. "You have no idea how much I admire you for that."

"I love your cousin," she whispered. "I would never betray him."

He brought his hand back to his side. "I know."

He looked so handsome in the moonlight, and so unbearably in need of love, that her heart nearly broke. Surely there was no woman who could resist him, not with that perfect face and tall, muscular body. And anyone who took the time to explore what was underneath would come to know him as she did — as a kindhearted man, loyal and true.

With a hint of the devil, of course, but Francesca supposed that was what would attract the ladies in the first place.

"Shall we?" Michael said, suddenly all charm. He tilted his head back in the direction of home, and she sighed and turned around.

"Thank you for taking me out," she said, after a few minutes of companionable silence. "I wasn't exaggerating when I said I was going mad with the rain."

"You didn't say that," he said, immediately giving himself a mental kick. She'd said that she'd been feeling a bit odd, not that she'd been going mad, but only an idiot savant or a lovesick fool would have noticed the difference.

"Didn't I?" She scrunched her brow together. "Well, I was certainly thinking it.

I've been rather sluggish, if you must know. The fresh air did me a great deal of good."

"Then I'm happy to have helped," he said gallantly.

She smiled as they ascended the front steps to Kilmartin House. The door opened as their feet touched the top stair — the butler must have been watching for them — and then Michael waited as Francesca was divested of her cloak in the front hall.

"Will you stay for another drink, or must you leave immediately for your appointment?" she inquired, her eyes glinting with the devil.

He glanced at the clock at the end of the hall. It was half eight, and while he had no place to be — there was no lady waiting for him, although he could certainly find one at the drop of a hat, and he rather thought he would — he didn't much feel like remaining here at Kilmartin House.

"I must go," he said. "I've much to do."

"You've nothing to do, and you know it," she said. "You just wish to be wicked."

"It's an admirable pastime," he murmured.

She opened her mouth to offer a retort, but just then Simons, John's recently hired valet, came down the stairs.

"My lady?" he inquired.

Francesca turned to him and inclined her head, indicating that he should proceed.

"I've rapped on his lordship's door and called his name — twice — but he seems to be sleeping quite soundly. Do you still wish me to wake him?"

Francesca nodded. "Yes. I'd love to let him sleep. He's been working so hard lately" — she directed this last bit at Michael — "but I know that this meeting with Lord Liverpool is very important. You should — No, wait, I'll rouse him myself. It will be better that way."

She turned to Michael. "I shall see you tomorrow?"

"Actually, if John hasn't yet left, I'll wait," he replied. "I came on foot, so I might as well avail myself of his carriage once he's done with it."

She nodded and hurried up the stairs, leaving Michael with nothing to do but hum under his breath as he idly examined the paintings in the hall.

And then she screamed.

Michael had no recollection of running up the stairs, but somehow there he was, in John's and Francesca's bedchamber, the one room in the house he never invaded.

"Francesca?" he gasped. "Frannie, Frannie, what is —"

She was sitting next to the bed, clutching John's forearm, which was dangling over the side. "Wake him up, Michael," she cried. "Wake him up. Do it for me. Wake him up!"

Michael felt his world slip away. The bed was across the room, a good twelve feet away, but he *knew.*

No one knew John as well as he did. No one.

And John wasn't there in the room. He was gone. What was on the bed —

It wasn't John.

"Francesca," he whispered, moving slowly toward her. His limbs felt strange and funny and gruesomely sluggish. "Francesca."

She looked up at him with huge, stricken eyes. "Wake him up, Michael."

"Francesca, I —"

"Now!" she screamed, launching herself at him. "Wake him up! You can do it. Wake him up! Wake him up!"

And all he could do was stand there as she beat her fists against his chest, stand there as she grabbed his cravat and shook and yanked until he was gasping for breath. He couldn't even embrace her, couldn't offer her comfort, because he was every bit as devastated and confused.

And then suddenly the fire left her, and she collapsed in his arms, her tears soaking his shirt. "He had a headache," she whimpered. "That's all. He just had a headache. It was just a headache." She looked up at him, her eyes searching his face, looking for answers he'd never be able to give her. "It was just a headache," she said again.

And she looked broken.

"I know," he said, even though he knew it wasn't enough.

"Oh, Michael," she sobbed. "What am I to do?"

"I don't know," he said, because he didn't. Between Eton, Cambridge, and the army, he'd been trained for everything that the life of an English gentleman was supposed to offer. But he hadn't been trained for *this*.

"I don't understand," she was saying, and he supposed she was saying a lot of things, but none of it made any sense to his ears. He didn't even have the strength to stand, and together the two of them sank to the carpet, leaning against the side of the bed.

He stared sightlessly at the far wall, wondering why he wasn't crying. He was numb, and his body felt heavy, and he couldn't shake the feeling that his very soul had been ripped from his body.

Not John.

Why?

Why?

And as he sat there, dimly aware of the servants gathering just outside the open door, it occurred to him that Francesca was whimpering those very same words.

"Not John.

"Why?

"*Why?*"

"Do you think she might be with child?"

Michael stared at Lord Winston, a new and apparently overeager appointee to the Committee for Privileges of the House of Lords, trying to make sense of his words. John had been dead barely a day. It was still hard to make sense of anything. And now here was this puffy little man, demanding an audience, prattling on about some sacred duty to the crown.

"Her ladyship," Lord Winston said. "If she's carrying, it will complicate everything."

"I don't know," Michael said. "I didn't ask her."

"You need to. I'm sure you're eager to assume control of your new holdings, but we really must determine if she's carrying. Furthermore, if she *is* pregnant, a member of our committee will need to be present at the birth."

Michael felt his face go slack. "I beg your pardon?" he somehow managed to say.

"Baby switching," Lord Winston said grimly. "There have been instances —"

"For God's sake —"

"It's for your protection as much as anyone's," Lord Winston cut in. "If her ladyship gives birth to a girl, and there is no one present to witness it, what is to stop her from switching the babe with a boy?"

Michael couldn't even bring himself to dignify this with an answer.

"You need to find out if she is carrying," Lord Winston pressed. "Arrangements will need to be made."

"She was widowed yesterday," Michael said sharply. "I will not burden her with such intrusive questions."

"There is more at stake here than her ladyship's feelings," Lord Winston returned. "We cannot properly transfer the earldom while there is doubt as to the succession."

"The devil take the earldom," Michael snapped.

Lord Winston gasped, drawing back in visible horror. "You forget yourself, my lord."

"I'm not your lord," Michael bit off. "I'm not anyone's —" He halted his words, sinking into a chair, trying very hard to get past the fact that he was perilously close to tears. Right here, in John's study, with this damnable little man who didn't seem to understand that a man had died, not just an earl, but a man, Michael wanted to cry.

And he would, he suspected. As soon as Lord Winston left, and Michael could lock the door and make sure that no one could see him, he would probably bury his face in his hands and cry.

"Someone has to ask her," Lord Winston said.

"It won't be me," Michael said in a low voice.

"I will do it, then."

Michael leapt from his seat and pinned Lord Winston against the wall. "You will not approach Lady Kilmartin," he growled. "You will not even breathe the same air. Do I make myself clear?"

"Quite," the smaller man gurgled.

Michael let go, dimly aware that Lord

52

Winston's face was beginning to turn purple. "Get out," he said.

"You will need —"

"Get out!" he roared.

"I will come back tomorrow," Lord Winston said, skittering out the door. "We will speak when you are in a calmer frame of mind."

Michael leaned against the wall, staring at the open doorway. Good God, how had it all come to this? John hadn't even been thirty. He was the picture of health. Michael might have been second in line for the earldom as long as John and Francesca's marriage remained childless, but no one had truly thought he'd ever inherit.

Already he'd heard that men in the clubs were calling him the luckiest man in Britain. Overnight, he'd gone from the fringe of aristocracy to its very epicenter. No one seemed to understand that Michael had never wanted this. Never.

He didn't want an earldom. He wanted his cousin back. And no one seemed to understand that.

Except, perhaps, Francesca, but she was so wrapped in her own grief that she could not quite comprehend the pain in Michael's heart.

And he would never ask her to. Not

when she was so wrecked by her own.

Michael wrapped his arms against his chest as he thought of her. For the rest of his life, he would not forget the sight of Francesca's face once the truth had finally sunk in. John was not sleeping. He was not going to wake up.

And Francesca Bridgerton Stirling was, at the tender age of two and twenty, the saddest thing imaginable.

Alone.

Michael understood her despair better than anyone could ever imagine.

They'd put her to bed that night, he and her mother, who had hurried over at Michael's urgent summons. And she'd slept like a baby, with nary even a whimper, her body worn out from the shock of it all.

But when she'd awakened the next morning, she'd acquired the proverbial stiff upper lip, determined to remain strong and steadfast, handling the myriad details that had showered down upon the house at John's death.

The problem was, neither one of them had a clue what those details were. They were young; they had been carefree. They had never thought to deal with death.

Who knew, for example, that the Committee for Privileges would get involved?

And demand a box seat at what ought to be a private moment for Francesca?

If indeed she was even carrying.

But bloody hell, *he* wasn't going to ask her.

"We need to tell his mother," Francesca had said earlier that morning. It was the first thing she'd said, actually. There was no preamble, no greeting, just, "We need to tell his mother."

Michael had nodded, since of course she was right.

"We need to tell your mother, too. They're both in Scotland; they won't know yet."

He nodded again. It was all he could manage.

"I'll write the notes."

And he nodded a third time, wondering what *he* was supposed to do.

That question had been answered when Lord Winston had come to call, but Michael couldn't bear to think about all that now. It seemed so distasteful. He didn't want to think of all he would gain at John's death. How could anyone possibly speak as if something *good* had come of all this?

Michael felt himself sinking down, down, sliding against the wall until he was sitting on the floor, his legs bent in front of him, his head resting on his knees. He hadn't wanted this. Had he?

He'd wanted Francesca. That was all. But not like this. Not at this cost.

He'd never begrudged John his good fortune. He'd never coveted the title, the money, or the power.

He'd merely coveted his wife.

Now he was meant to assume John's title, step into his shoes. And guilt was squeezing its merciless fist right around his heart.

Had he somehow wished for this? No, he couldn't have. He hadn't.

Had he?

"Michael?"

He looked up. It was Francesca, still wearing that hollow look, her face a blank mask that tore at his heart far more than her wailing sorrow ever could have done.

"I sent for Janet."

He nodded. John's mother. She would be devastated.

"And your mother as well."

She would be equally bereft.

"Is there anyone else you think —"

He shook his head, aware that he should get up, aware that propriety dictated that he rise, but he just couldn't find the strength. He didn't want Francesca to see him so weak, but he couldn't help it.

"You should sit down," he finally said. "You need to rest."

"I can't," she said. "I need to . . . If I stop, even for a moment, I will . . ."

Her words trailed off, but it didn't matter. He understood.

He looked up at her. Her chestnut hair was pulled back into a simple queue, and her face was pale. She looked young, barely out of the schoolroom, certainly too young for this sort of heartbreak. "Francesca," he said, his word not quite a question, more of a sigh, really.

And then she said it. She said it without his having to ask.

"I'm pregnant."

Chapter 3

. . . I love him madly. Madly! Truly, I would die without him.

> — *from the Countess of Kilmartin to her sister Eloise Bridgerton, one week after Francesca's wedding*

"I declare, Francesca, you are the healthiest expectant mother I have ever laid eyes upon."

Francesca smiled at her mother-in-law, who had just entered the garden of the St. James's mansion they now shared. Overnight, it seemed, Kilmartin House had become a household of women. First Janet had taken up residence, and then Helen, Michael's mother. It was a house full of Stirling females, or at least those who had acquired the name in marriage.

And it all felt so different.

It was strange. She would have thought that she'd sense John's presence, feel him in the air, see him in the surroundings they'd shared for two years. But instead, he was simply gone, and the influx of women had changed the tone of the house entirely. Francesca supposed that was a good thing; she needed the support of women right now.

But it was odd, living among women. There were more flowers now — vases everywhere, it seemed. And there was no longer any lingering smell of John's cheroot, or the sandalwood soap he'd favored.

Kilmartin House now smelled of lavender and rosewater, and every whiff of it broke Francesca's heart.

Even Michael had been strangely distant. Oh, he came to call — several times a week, if one cared to count, which Francesca had to admit she did. But he wasn't *there*, not in the way he had been before John's death. He wasn't the same, and she supposed she ought not to castigate him for that, even if only in her mind.

He was hurting, too.

She knew that. She reminded herself of it when she saw him, and his eyes were distant. She reminded herself of it when she didn't know what to say to him, and when he didn't tease her.

And she reminded herself of it when

they sat together in the drawing room and had nothing to say.

She'd lost John, and now it seemed she'd lost Michael, too. And even with two mother hens fussing over her — three, if she counted her own, who came to call every single day — she was so lonely.

And sad.

No one had ever told her how sad she'd be. Who would have *thought* to tell her? And even if someone had, even if her mother, who had also been widowed young, had explained the pain, how could she have understood?

It was one of those things that had to be experienced to be understood. And oh, how Francesca wished she didn't belong to this melancholy club.

And where was Michael? Why couldn't he comfort her? Why didn't he realize how very much she needed him? Him, not his mother. Not anyone's mother.

She needed Michael, the one person who had known John the way she had, the only person who had loved him as fully. Michael was her one link to the husband she had lost, and she hated him for staying away.

Even when he was here at Kilmartin House, in the same dashed room as her, it

60

wasn't the same. They didn't joke, and they didn't tease. They just sat there and looked sad and grief stricken, and when they spoke, there was an awkwardness that had never been there before.

Couldn't *anything* remain as it was before John had died? It had never occurred to her that her friendship with Michael might be killed off as well.

"How are you feeling, dear?"

Francesca looked up at Janet, belatedly realizing that her mother-in-law had asked her a question. Several, probably, and she'd forgotten to answer, lost in her own thoughts. She did that a lot lately.

"Fine," she said. "No different than I ever have done."

Janet shook her head in wonder. "It's remarkable. I've never heard of such a thing."

Francesca shrugged. "If it weren't for the loss of my courses, I'd never know anything was different."

And it was true. She wasn't sick, she wasn't hungry, she wasn't anything. A trifle more tired than usual, she supposed, but that could be the grief as well. Her mother told her that she'd been tired for a year after her father had died.

Of course her mother had had eight children to look after. Francesca just had herself, with a small army of servants treating her like an invalid queen.

"You're very fortunate," Janet said, sitting down on the chair opposite Francesca's. "When I was carrying John, I was sick every single morning. And most afternoons as well."

Francesca nodded and smiled. Janet had told this to her before, several times. John's death had turned his mother into a magpie, constantly chattering on, trying to fill the silence that was Francesca's grief. Francesca adored her for it, for trying, but she suspected the only thing that would assuage her pain was time.

"I'm so pleased you're carrying," Janet said, leaning forward and impulsively squeezing Francesca's hand. "It makes it all a bit more bearable. Or I suppose a bit less unbearable," she added, not really smiling, but looking like she was trying to.

Francesca just nodded, afraid that speaking would loosen the tears in her eyes.

"I'd always wanted more children," Janet confessed. "But it wasn't to be. And when John died, I — Well, let's just say that no grandchild shall ever be loved more than the one you're carrying." She stopped, pretending to dab her handkerchief against her nose but really aiming for her eyes. "Don't tell anyone, but I don't care whether it's a boy or a girl. It's a piece of him. That's all that matters."

"I know," Francesca said softly, placing her hand on her belly. She wished there was some sign of the baby within. She knew it was too soon to feel movement; she wasn't even three months along, by her carefully calculated estimation. But all her dresses still fit perfectly, and her food still tasted just as it always had, and she simply wasn't experiencing any of the quirks and illnesses that other women had told her about.

She'd have been happy to have been casting up her accounts each morning, if only so that she could imagine the baby was waving its hand with a cheerful, "I'm here!"

"Have you seen Michael recently?" Janet asked.

"Not since Monday," Francesca said. "He doesn't come to call very often anymore."

"He misses John," Janet said softly.

"So do I," Francesca replied, and she was horrified by the sharp edge to her voice.

"It must be very difficult for him," Janet mused.

Francesca just stared at her, her lips parting with surprise.

"I do not mean to say it is not difficult for you, too," Janet said quickly, "but think of the tenuousness of his position. He won't know if he's to be the earl for six more months."

"There is nothing I can do about that."

"No, of course not," Janet assured her, "but it does put him in awkward straits. I've heard more than one matron say that they simply can't consider him as a potential suitor for their daughters until and unless you give birth to a girl. It's one thing to marry the Earl of Kilmartin. It's quite another when it's his impoverished cousin. And no one knows which he will be."

"Michael isn't impoverished," Francesca said peevishly, "and besides, he would never marry while in mourning for John."

"No, I suppose not, but I do hope he starts looking," Janet said. "I do so want him to be happy. And of course if he is to be the earl, he shall have to beget an heir. Otherwise the title shall go to that awful Debenham side of the family." Janet shuddered at the thought.

"Michael will do what he must," Francesca said, although she wasn't so sure. It was difficult to imagine him marrying. It

64

had always been difficult — Michael wasn't the sort to stay true to any woman for very long — but now it just seemed strange. For years, she had had John, and Michael had been their companion. Could she bear it if he married, and then she was the third wheel? Was her heart big enough to be happy for him while she was alone?

She rubbed her eyes. She felt very tired, and in truth a bit weak. A good sign, she supposed; she'd heard that pregnant women were supposed to be more tired than she usually was. She looked over at Janet. "I think I shall go upstairs and take a nap."

"An excellent idea," Janet said approvingly. "You need your rest."

Francesca nodded and stood, then grabbed the arm of the chair to steady herself when she swayed. "I don't know what is wrong with me," she said, attempting a wobbly smile. "I feel very unsteady. I —"

Janet's gasp cut her off.

"Janet?" Francesca looked at her mother-in-law with concern. She'd gone quite pale, and one shaking hand rose to meet her lips.

"What is it?" Francesca asked, and then she realized that Janet wasn't looking at her. She was looking at her chair.

With slowly dawning horror, Francesca looked down, forcing herself to look at the seat she'd just vacated.

There, in the middle of the cushion, was a small patch of red.

Blood.

Life would have been easier, Michael thought wryly, if he'd been given to drink. If ever there was a time to overindulge, to drown one's sorrows in the bottle, this was it.

But no, he'd been cursed with a robust constitution and a marvelous ability to hold his liquor with dignity and flair. Which meant that if he wanted to reach any sort of mind-numbing oblivion, he'd have to down the entire bottle of whisky sitting on his desk, and maybe even then some.

He looked out the window. It wasn't yet dark. Even he, dissolute rake that he tried to be, couldn't bring himself to drink an entire bottle of whisky before the sun went down.

Michael tapped his fingers against his desk, wishing he knew what to do with himself. John had been dead for six weeks now, but he was still living in his modest apartments in the Albany. He couldn't quite bring himself to take up residence in

Kilmartin House. It was the residence of the earl, and that wouldn't be him for at least another six months.

Or maybe not ever.

According to Lord Winston, whose lectures Michael had eventually been forced to tolerate, the title would go into abeyance until Francesca delivered. And if she gave birth to a boy, Michael would remain in the same position he'd always been in — cousin to the earl.

But it wasn't Michael's peculiar situation that was keeping him away. He'd have been reticent to move into Kilmartin House even if Francesca hadn't been pregnant. She was still *there*.

She was still there, and she was still the Countess of Kilmartin, and even if he was the earl, with no questions attached to the title, she wouldn't be *his* countess, and he just didn't know if he could take the irony of it.

He'd thought that his grief might finally overtake his longing for her, that he might finally be with her and *not* want her, but no, his breath still caught every time she walked into the room, and his body tightened when she brushed past him, and his heart still ached with the pain of loving her.

Except now it was all wrapped in an extra layer of guilt — as if he hadn't had enough of *that* while John was alive. She was in pain, and she was grieving, and he ought to be comforting her, not lusting after her. Good God, John wasn't even cold in his grave. What kind of monster would lust after his wife?

His pregnant wife.

He was already stepping into John's shoes in so many ways. He would not complete the betrayal by taking his place with Francesca as well.

And so he stayed away. Not completely; that would have been too obvious, and besides, he couldn't do that, not with his mother and John's in residence at Kilmartin House. Plus, everyone was looking to him to manage the affairs of the earl, even though the title wasn't potentially to be his for another six months.

He did it, though. He didn't mind the details, didn't care that he was spending several hours per day looking after a fortune that might go to another. It was the least he could do for John.

And for Francesca. He couldn't bring himself to be a friend to her, not the way he ought, but he could make sure that her financial affairs were in order.

But he knew she didn't understand. She often came to visit him while he was working in John's study at Kilmartin House, poring over reports from various land stewards and solicitors. And he could tell that she was looking for their old camaraderie, but he just couldn't do it.

Call him weak, call him shallow. But he just couldn't be her friend. Not just yet, anyway.

"Mr. Stirling?"

Michael looked up. His valet was at the door, accompanied by a footman dressed in the unmistakable green and gold livery of Kilmartin House.

"A message for you," the footman said. "From your mother."

Michael held out his hand as the footman crossed the room, wondering what it was this time. His mother summoned him to Kilmartin House every other day, it seemed.

"She said it was urgent," the footman added as he placed the envelope in Michael's hand.

Urgent, eh? That was new. Michael glanced up at the footman and valet, his steady gaze a clear dismissal, and then, once the room had been emptied, slid his letter-opener under the flap.

Come quickly, was all it said. *Francesca has lost the baby.*

Michael nearly killed himself rushing to Kilmartin House, racing on horseback at a breakneck pace, ignoring the shouts from the angry pedestrians he'd nearly decapitated in his haste.

But now that he was here, standing in the hall, he had no idea what to do with himself.

Miscarriage? It seemed such a womanly thing. What was he meant to do? It was a tragedy, and he felt horrible for Francesca, but what did they think he could say? Why did they want him here?

And then it hit him. He was the earl now. It was done. Slowly but surely, he was assuming John's life, filling every corner of the world that had once belonged to his cousin.

"Oh, Michael," his mother said, rushing into the hall. "I'm so glad you're here."

He embraced her, his arms awkwardly coming around her. And he said something utterly meaningless like, "Such a tragedy," but mostly he just stood there, feeling foolish and out of place.

"How is she?" he finally asked, once his mother stepped back.

"In shock," she replied. "She's been cry-ing."

He swallowed, wanting desperately to loosen his cravat. "Well, that's to be ex-pected," he said. "I — I —"

"She can't seem to stop," Helen inter-rupted.

"Crying?" Michael asked.

Helen nodded. "I don't know what to do."

Michael measured his breaths. Even. Slow. In and out.

"Michael?" His mother was looking up to him for a response. Maybe for guidance.

As if *he* would know what to do.

"Her mother came by," Helen said, when it became apparent that Michael was not going to speak. "She wants Francesca to go back to Bridgerton House."

"Does Francesca want to?"

Helen shrugged sadly. "I don't think she knows. It's all such a shock."

"Yes," Michael said, swallowing again. He didn't want to be here. He wanted to get out.

"The doctor said we're not to move her for several days, in any case," Helen added.

He nodded.

"Naturally, we called for you."

Naturally? There was nothing natural

about it. He'd never felt so out of place, so completely at a loss for words or action.

"You're Kilmartin now," his mother said quietly.

He nodded again. Just once. It was as much of an acknowledgment as he could muster.

"I must say I —" Helen stopped, her lips pursing in an odd, jerky manner. "Well, a mother wants the world for her children, but I didn't — I never would have —"

"Don't say it," Michael said hoarsely. He wasn't ready for anyone to say this was a good thing. And by God, if anyone offered his congratulations . . .

Well, he wouldn't be responsible for the violence.

"She asked for you," his mother said.

"Francesca?" he asked, his eyes flying open with surprise.

Helen nodded. "She said she wanted you."

"I can't," he said.

"You have to."

"I can't." He shook his head, panic making his movements too quick. "I can't go in there."

"You can't abandon her," his mother said.

"She was never mine to abandon."

"Michael!" Helen gasped. "How can you say such a thing?"

"Mother," he said, desperately trying to redirect the conversation, "she needs a woman. What can I do?"

"You can be her friend," Helen said softly, and he felt eight again, scolded for a thoughtless transgression.

"No," he said, and his voice horrified him. He sounded like a wounded animal, pained and confused. But there was one thing he knew for certain. He couldn't see her. Not now. Not yet.

"Michael," his mother said.

"No," he said again. "I will . . . Tomorrow, I'll . . ." And he strode for the door with nothing more than a "Give her my best."

And then he fled, coward that he was.

Chapter 4

. . . I am sure it is not worth such high drama. I do not profess to know or understand romantic love between husband and wife, but surely it is not so all-encompassing that the loss of one would destroy the other. You are stronger than you think, dear sister. You would survive quite handily without him, moot point though it may be.

— from Eloise Bridgerton
to her sister, the Countess of Kilmartin,
three weeks after Francesca's wedding

The following month was, Michael was certain, the best approximation of hell on earth that any human being was likely to experience.

With every new ceremony, each and every document he found himself signing as Kilmartin, or "my lord" he was forced to endure, it was as if John's spirit was being pushed farther away.

Soon, Michael thought dispassionately, it would be as if he'd never existed. Even the baby — who was to have been the last piece of John Stirling left on earth — was gone.

And everything that had been John's was now Michael's.

Except Francesca.

And Michael intended to keep it that way. He would not — no, he *could* not offer his cousin that last insult.

He'd had to see her, of course, and he'd offered his best words of comfort, but whatever he'd said, it wasn't the right thing, and she'd just turned her head and looked at the wall.

He didn't know what to say. Frankly, he was more relieved that she was not injured than he was upset that the baby had been lost. The mothers — his, John's, and Francesca's — had felt compelled to describe the gore to him in appalling detail, and one of the maids had even trotted out the bloody sheets, which someone had saved to offer as proof that Francesca had miscarried.

Lord Winston had nodded approvingly but had then added that he would have to keep an eye on the countess, just to be sure that the sheets were truly hers, and that she wasn't actually increasing. This wouldn't be the first time someone had tried to circumvent the sacred laws of primogeniture, he'd added.

Michael had wanted to hurl the yappy little man out the window, but instead he'd merely shown him the door. He no longer had energy for that kind of anger, it seemed.

He still hadn't moved into Kilmartin House. He wasn't quite ready for it, and the thought of living there with all those women was suffocating. He'd have to do so soon, he knew; it was expected of the earl. But for now, he was content enough in his small suite of apartments.

And that was where he was, avoiding his duties, when Francesca finally sought him out.

"Michael?" she said, once his valet had shown her to his small sitting room.

"Francesca," he replied, shocked at her appearance. She'd never come here before. Not when John had been alive, and certainly not after. "What are you doing here?"

"I wanted to see you," she said.

The unspoken message being: *You're avoiding me.*

It was the truth, of course, but all he said was, "Sit down." And then belatedly: "Please."

Was this improper? Her being here in his apartments? He wasn't sure. The circumstances of their position were so odd, so completely out of order that he had no idea which rules of etiquette were currently governing them.

She sat, and did nothing but fiddle her fingers against her skirts for a full minute, and then she looked up at him, her eyes meeting his with heartbreaking intensity, and said, "I miss you."

The walls began to close in around him. "Francesca, I —"

"You were my friend," she said accusingly. "Besides John, you were my closest friend, and I don't know who you are any longer."

"I —" Oh, he felt like a fool, utterly impotent and brought down by a pair of blue eyes and a mountain of guilt.

Guilt for what, he wasn't even certain any longer. It seemed to come from so many sources, from such a variety of directions, that he couldn't quite keep track of it.

"What is wrong with you?" she asked. "Why do you avoid me?"

"I don't know," he replied, since he couldn't lie to her and say that he wasn't. She was too smart for that. But neither could he tell her the truth.

Her lips quivered, and then the lower one caught between her teeth. He stared at it, unable to take his eyes off her mouth, hating himself for the rush of longing that swept over him.

"You were supposed to be my friend, too," she whispered.

"Francesca, don't."

"I needed you," she said softly. "I still do."

"No you don't," he replied. "You have the mothers, and all your sisters as well."

"I don't want to talk to my sisters," she said, her voice growing impassioned. "They don't understand."

"Well, *I* certainly don't understand," he shot back, desperation lending an unpleasant edge to his voice.

She just stared at him, condemnation coloring her eyes.

"Francesca, you —" He wanted to throw up his arms but instead he just crossed them. "You — you *miscarried.*"

"I am aware of that," she said tightly.

"What do I know of such things? You need to talk to a woman."

"Can't you say you're sorry?"

"I *did* say I was sorry!"

"Can't you mean it?"

What did she *want* from him? "Francesca, I *did* mean it."

"I'm just so angry," she said, her voice rising in intensity, "and I'm sad, and I'm upset, and I look at you and I don't understand why you're *not*."

For a moment he didn't move. "Don't you ever say that," he whispered.

Her eyes flashed with anger. "Well, you've a funny way of showing it. You never call, and you never speak to me, and you don't understand —"

"What do you want me to understand?" he burst out. "What *can* I understand? For the love of —" He stopped himself before he blasphemed and turned away from her, leaning heavily on the windowsill.

Behind him Francesca just sat quietly, still as death. And then, finally, she said, "I don't know why I came. I'll go."

"Don't go," he said hoarsely. But he didn't turn around.

She said nothing; she wasn't sure what he meant.

"You only just arrived," he said, his voice halting and awkward. "You should have a cup of tea, at least."

Francesca nodded, even though he still wasn't looking at her.

And they remained thus for several minutes, for far too long, until she could not bear the silence any longer. The clock ticked in the corner, and her only company was Michael's back, and all she could do was sit there and think and think and wonder why she'd come here.

What did she want from him?

And wouldn't her life be easier if she actually knew.

"Michael," she said, his name leaving her lips before she realized it.

He turned around. He didn't speak, but he acknowledged her with his eyes.

"I . . ." Why had she called out to him? What did she want? "I . . ."

Still, he didn't speak. Just stood there and waited for her to collect her thoughts, which made everything so much harder.

And then, to her horror, it spilled out. "I don't know what I'm supposed to do now," she said, hearing her voice break. "And I'm so angry, and . . ." She stopped, gasped — anything to halt the tears.

Across from her, Michael opened his mouth, but only barely, and even then, nothing came out.

"I don't know why this is happening,"

she whimpered. "What did I do? What did I ever do?"

"Nothing," he assured her.

"He's gone, and he isn't coming back, and I'm so . . . so . . ." She looked up at him, feeling the grief and the anger etching themselves into her face. "It isn't fair. It isn't fair that it's me and not someone else, and it isn't fair that it should be anyone, and it isn't fair that I lost the —" And then she choked, and the gasps became sobs, and all she could do was cry.

"Francesca," Michael said, kneeling at her feet. "I'm sorry. I'm so sorry."

"I know," she sobbed, "but it doesn't make it better."

"No," he murmured.

"And it doesn't make it fair."

"No," he said again.

"And it doesn't — It doesn't —"

He didn't try to finish the sentence for her. She wished he had; for years she wished he had, because maybe then he would have said the wrong thing, and maybe then she wouldn't have leaned into him, and maybe then she wouldn't have allowed him to hold her.

But oh, God, how she missed being held.

"Why did you go?" she cried. "Why can't you help me?"

"I want to — You don't —" And then finally he just said, "I don't know what to say."

She was asking too much of him. She knew it, but she didn't care. She was just so sick of being alone.

But right then, at least for a moment, she wasn't alone. Michael was there, and he was holding her, and she felt warm and safe for the first time in weeks. And she just cried. She cried weeks of tears. She cried for John and she cried for the baby she'd never know.

But most of all she cried for herself.

"Michael," she said, once she'd recovered enough to speak. Her voice was still shaky, but she managed his name, and she knew she was going to have to manage more.

"Yes?"

"We can't go on like this."

She felt something change in him. His embrace tightened, or maybe it loosened, but something was not quite the same. "Like what?" he asked, his voice hoarse and hesitant.

She drew back so she could see him, relieved when his arms fell away, and she didn't have to wriggle free. "Like this," she said, even though she knew he didn't understand. Or if he did, that he was going to pretend otherwise. "With you ignoring me," she continued.

"Francesca, I —"

"The baby was to have been yours in a way, too," she blurted out.

He went pale, deathly pale. So much so that for a moment she couldn't breathe.

"What do you mean?" he whispered.

"It would have needed a father," she said, shrugging helplessly. "I — You — It would have had to be you."

"You have brothers," he choked out.

"They didn't know John. Not the way you did."

He moved away, stood, and then, as if that weren't enough, backed up as far as he could, all the way to the window. His eyes flared slightly, and for a moment she could have sworn that he resembled a trapped animal, cornered and terrified, waiting for the finality of the kill.

"Why are you telling me this?" he said, his voice flat and low.

"I don't know," she said, swallowing uncomfortably. But she did know. She wanted him to grieve as she grieved. She wanted him to hurt in every way she hurt. It wasn't fair, and it wasn't nice, but she couldn't help it and she didn't feel like apologizing for it, either.

"Francesca," he said, and his tone was strange, hollow and sharp, and like nothing she'd ever heard.

She looked at him, but she moved her head slowly, scared by what she might see in his face.

"I'm not John," he said.

"I know that."

"I'm not John," he said again, louder, and she wondered if he'd even heard her.

"I know."

His eyes narrowed and focused on her with dangerous intensity. "It wasn't my baby, and I can't be what you need."

And inside of her, something started to die. "Michael, I —"

"I won't take his place," he said, and he wasn't shouting, but it sounded like maybe he wanted to.

"No, you couldn't. You —"

And then, in a startling flash of motion, he was at her side, and he'd grabbed her shoulders and hauled her to her feet. "I won't do it," he yelled, and he was shaking her, and then holding her still, and then shaking her again. "I can't be him. I won't be him."

She couldn't speak, couldn't form words, didn't know what to do.

Didn't know who he was.

He stopped shaking her, but his fingers bit into her shoulders as he stared down at her, his quicksilver eyes afire with something terrifying and sad. "You can't ask this of me," he gasped. "I can't do it."

"Michael?" she whispered, hearing something awful in her voice. Fear. "Michael, please let me go."

He didn't, but she wasn't even sure he'd heard her. His eyes were lost, and he seemed beyond her, unreachable.

"Michael!" she said again, and her voice was louder, panicked.

And then, abruptly, he did as she asked, and he stumbled back, his face a portrait of self-loathing. "I'm sorry," he whispered, staring at his hands as if they were foreign bodies. "I'm so sorry."

Francesca edged toward the door. "I'd better go," she said.

He nodded. "Yes."

"I think —" She stopped, choking on the word as she grasped the doorknob, clutching it like her salvation. "I think we had better not see each other for a while."

He nodded jerkily.

"Maybe . . ." But she didn't say anything more. She didn't know what *to* say. If she'd known what had just happened between them she might have found some words, but for now she was too bewildered and scared to figure it all out.

Scared, but why? She certainly wasn't scared of *him*. Michael would never hurt her. He'd lay down his life for her if the opportunity forced itself; she was quite sure of that.

Maybe she was just scared of tomorrow. And the day after that. She'd lost everything, and now it appeared she'd lost Michael as well, and she just wasn't sure how she was supposed to bear it all.

"I'm going to go," she said, giving him one last chance to stop her, to say something, to say *any*thing that might make it all go away.

But he didn't. He didn't even nod. He just looked at her, his eyes silent in their agreement.

And Francesca left. She walked out the door and out of his house. And then she climbed into her carriage and went home.

And she didn't say a word. She climbed up her stairs and she climbed into her bed.

But she didn't cry. She kept thinking she should, kept feeling like she might like to.

But all she did was stare at the ceiling.

The ceiling, at least, didn't mind her regard.

Back in his apartments in the Albany, Michael grabbed his bottle of whisky and poured himself a tall glass, even though a glance at the clock revealed the day to be still younger than noon.

He'd sunk to a new low, that much was clear.

But try as he might, he couldn't figure out what else he could have done. It wasn't as if he'd meant to hurt her, and he certainly hadn't stopped, pondered, and decided *Oh, yes, I do believe I shall act like an ass,* but even though his reactions had been swift and unconsidered, he didn't see how he might have behaved any other way.

He knew himself. He didn't always — or these days even often — like himself, but he knew himself. And when Francesca had turned to him with those bottomless blue eyes and said, "The baby was to have been yours in a way, too," she'd shattered him to his very soul.

She didn't know.

She had no idea.

And as long as she remained in the dark about his feelings for her, as long as she couldn't understand why he had no choice but to hate himself for every step he took in John's shoes, he couldn't be near her.

Because she was going to keep saying things like that.

And he simply didn't know how much he could take.

And so, as he stood in his study, his body taut with misery and guilt, he realized two things.

The first was easy. The whisky was doing nothing to ease his pain, and if twenty-five-year-old whisky, straight from Speyside, didn't make him feel any better, nothing in the British Isles was going to do so.

Which led him to the second, which wasn't easy at all. But he had to do it. Rarely had the choices in his life been so clear. Painful, but painfully clear.

And so he set down his glass, two fingers of the amber liquid remaining, and he walked down the hall to his bedchamber.

"Reivers," he said, upon finding his valet standing at the wardrobe, carefully folding a cravat, "what do you think of India?"

Part Two

March, 1824
Four years later

Chapter 5

. . . you would enjoy it here. Not the heat, I should think; no one seems to enjoy the heat. But the rest would enchant you. The colors, the spices, the scent of the air — they can place one in a strange, sensuous haze that is at turns unsettling and intoxicating. Most of all, I think you would enjoy the pleasure gardens. They are rather like our London parks, except far more green and lush, and full of the most remarkable flowers you have ever seen. You have always loved to be out among nature; this you would adore, I am quite sure of it.

— from Michael Stirling
(the new Earl of Kilmartin)
to the Countess of Kilmartin,
one month after his arrival in India

Francesca wanted a baby.

She had for quite some time, but it was only in recent months that she'd been able to admit as much to herself, to finally put words to the sense of longing that seemed to accompany her wherever she went.

It had started innocently enough, with a little pang in her heart upon reading a letter from her brother's wife Kate, the missive filled with news of their little girl Charlotte, soon to turn two and already incorrigible.

But the pang had grown worse, into something more akin to an ache, when her sister Daphne had arrived in Scotland for a visit, all four of her children in tow. It hadn't occurred to Francesca just how completely a gaggle of children could transform a home. The Hastings children had altered the very essence of Kilmartin, brought to it life and laughter that Francesca realized had been sadly lacking for years.

And then they left, and all was quiet, but it wasn't peaceful.

Just empty.

From that moment on, Francesca was different. She saw a nursemaid pushing a pram, and her heart ached. She spied a rabbit hopping across a field and couldn't help but think that she ought to be pointing it out to someone else, someone small. She traveled to Kent to spend Christmas with her family, but when night fell, and all of her nieces and nephews were tucked into bed, she felt too alone.

And all she could think was that her life was passing her by, and if she didn't do something soon, she'd die this way.

Alone.

Not unhappy — she wasn't that. Strangely enough, she'd grown into her widowhood and found a comfortable and contented pattern to her life. It was something she never would have believed possible during the awful months immediately following John's death, but she had, a bit through trial and error, found a place for herself in the world. And with it, a small measure of peace.

She enjoyed her life as Countess of Kilmartin — Michael had never married, so she retained the duties as well as the title. She loved Kilmartin, and she ran it with no interference from Michael; his instructions upon leaving the country four years earlier had been that she should manage the earldom as she saw fit, and once the shock of his departure had worn off, she'd realized that that had been the most precious gift he could have bestowed upon her.

It had given her something to do, something to work toward.

A reason to stop staring at the ceiling.

She had friends, and she had family, both Stirling and Bridgerton, and she had a full life, in Scotland and London, where she spent several months of each year.

So she should have been happy. And she was, mostly.

She just wanted a baby.

It had taken some time to admit this to herself. It was a desire that seemed somewhat disloyal to John; it wouldn't be *his* baby, after all, and even now, with him gone four years, it was difficult to imagine a child without his features woven across its face.

And it meant, first and foremost, that she'd have to remarry. She'd have to change her name and pledge her troth to another man, to vow to make him first in her heart and her loyalties, and while the thought of that no longer struck pain in her heart, it seemed . . . well . . . strange.

But she supposed there were some things a woman simply had to get past, and one cold February day, as she was staring out a window at Kilmartin, watching the snow slowly wrap a shroud around the tree branches, she realized that this was one of them.

There were a lot of things in life to be afraid of, but strangeness ought not be among them.

And so she decided to pack her things and head down to London a bit early this year. She generally spent the season in town, enjoying time with her family, shopping and attending musicales, taking in plays and doing all the things that simply weren't available in the Scottish countryside. But this season would be different. She needed a new wardrobe, for one. She'd been out of mourning for some time, but she hadn't completely shrugged off the grays and lavenders of half-mourning, and she certainly hadn't paid the attention to fashion that a woman in her new position ought.

It was time to wear blue. Bright, beautiful, cornflower blue. It had been her favorite color years ago, and she'd been vain enough that she'd worn it fully expecting people to comment on how it matched her eyes.

She'd buy blue, and yes, pink and yellow as well, and maybe even — something in her heart shivered with anticipation at the thought — crimson.

She wasn't an unmarried miss this time

around. She was an eligible widow, and the rules were different.

But the aspirations were the same.

She was going to London to find herself a husband.

It had been too long.

Michael knew that his return to Britain was well overdue, but it had been one of those things that was appallingly easy to put off. According to his mother's letters, which had found him with remarkable regularity, the earldom was thriving under Francesca's stewardship. He had no dependents who might accuse him of neglect, and by all accounts, everyone he'd left behind was faring rather better in his absence than they had when he'd been around to cheer them on.

So there was nothing to feel guilty about.

But a man could only run from his destiny for so long, and as he marked his third year in the tropics, he had to admit that the novelty of an exotic life had worn off, and to be completely frank, he was growing rather sick of the climate. India had given him a purpose, a place in life that went beyond the only two things at which he'd ever excelled — soldiering and making merry. He'd boarded a ship with nothing but the name of an army friend who'd moved to Madras three years earlier. Within a month he'd obtained a governmental post and found himself making decisions that mattered, implementing laws and policies that actually shaped the lives of men.

For the first time, Michael finally understood why John had been so enamored of his work in the British Parliament.

But India hadn't made him happy. It had given him a small measure of peace, which seemed rather paradoxical, since in the past few years he'd nearly met his demise three times, four if one counted that run-in with the knife-wielding Indian princess (Michael still maintained that he could have disarmed her without injury, but she did, he had to admit, have a rather murderous look in her eye, and he'd long since learned that one should never ever underestimate a woman who believes — however erroneously — herself scorned.)

Life-threatening episodes aside, however, his time in India had brought him a certain sense of balance. He'd finally done something for himself, made something *of* himself.

But most of all, India had brought him peace because he didn't have to live with the constant knowledge that Francesca was just around the corner.

Life wasn't necessarily better with thousands of miles between him and Francesca, but it certainly was easier.

It was past time, however, to face up to the rigors of having her in close proximity, and so he'd packed up his belongings, informed his rather relieved valet that they were going back to England, booked a luxurious starboard suite on the *Princess Amelia*, and headed home.

He'd have to face her, of course. There was no escaping that. He would have to look into the blue eyes that had haunted him relentlessly and try to be her friend. It was the one thing she'd wanted during the dark days after John's death, and it had been the only thing he had been completely unable to do for her.

But maybe now, with the benefit of time and the healing power of distance, he could manage it. He wasn't stupid enough to hope that she'd changed, that he'd see her and discover he no longer loved her — *that*, he was quite certain, would never happen. But Michael had finally grown used to hearing the words "Earl of Kilmartin" without looking over his shoulder for his cousin. And maybe now, with the grief no longer so raw, he could be with Francesca in friendship, without feeling as if he were a thief, plotting to steal what he'd coveted for so long.

And hopefully she, too, had moved on, and wouldn't ask him to fulfill John's duties in every way but one.

But all the same, he was glad that it would be March when he disembarked in London, too early in the year for Francesca to have arrived for the season.

He was a brave man; he'd proven that countless times, on and off the battlefield. But he was an honest man, too, honest enough to admit that the prospect of facing Francesca was terrifying in a way that no French battlefield or toothy tiger could ever be.

Maybe, if he was lucky, she'd choose not to come down to London for the season at all.

Wouldn't that be a boon.

It was dark, and she couldn't sleep, and the house was miserably cold, and the worst of it was, it was all her fault.

Oh, very well, not the dark. Francesca supposed she couldn't take the blame for that. Night was night, after all, and she was rather overreaching to think that she had anything to do with the sun going down. But it was her fault that the household hadn't been given adequate time to prepare for her arrival. She'd forgotten to send notice that she was planning to come down to London a month early, and as a result, Kilmartin House was still running with a skeleton staff, and the stores of coal and beeswax candles were perilously low.

All would be better on the morrow, after the housekeeper and butler made a mad dash to the Bond Street shops, but for now Francesca was shivering in her bed. It had been a miserably freezing day, with a blustery wind that made it far colder than was normal for early March. The housekeeper had attempted to move all the available coal to Francesca's grate, but countess or no, she couldn't allow the rest of the household to freeze at her expense. Besides, the countess's bedchamber was immense, and it had always been difficult to heat properly unless the rest of the house was warm as well.

The library. That was it. It was small and cozy, and if Francesca shut the door, a fire in its grate would keep the room nice and toasty. Furthermore, there was a settee on which she could lie. It was small, but then again, so was she, and it couldn't possibly be any worse than freezing to death in her bedroom.

Her decision made, Francesca leapt out of bed and dashed through the cold night air to her nightrobe, which was lying across the back of a chair. It wasn't nearly warm enough — Francesca hadn't thought to need anything bulkier — but it was better than nothing, and, she thought rather stoically, beggars couldn't be choosers, especially when their toes were falling off with cold.

She hurried downstairs, her heavy wool socks slipping and sliding on the polished steps. She tumbled down the last two, thankfully landing on her feet, then ran along the runner carpet to the library.

"Fire fire fire," she mumbled to herself. She'd ring for someone just as soon as she got to the library. They'd have a blaze roaring in no time. She'd regain feeling in her nose, her fingertips would lose that sickly blue color and —

She pushed open the door.

A short, staccato scream hurled itself across her lips. There was already a fire in the grate, and a man standing in front of it, idly warming his hands.

Francesca reached wildly for something — anything — that she might use as a weapon.

And then he turned.

"Michael?"

He hadn't known she'd be in London. Damn it, he hadn't even considered that she might be in London. Not that it would have made any difference, but at least he'd have been prepared. He might have schooled his features into a saturnine smirk, or at the very least made sure that he was impeccably dressed and whole-heartedly immersed in his role as the un-recoverable rake.

But no, there he was, just gaping at her, trying not to notice that she was wearing nothing but a dark crimson nightgown and dressing robe, so thin and sheer that he could see the outline of —

He gulped. Don't look. Do *not* look.

"Michael?" she whispered again.

"Francesca," he said, since he had to say something. "What are you doing here?"

And that seemed to snap her into thought and motion. "What am I doing here?" she echoed. "I'm not the one who's meant to be in India. What are *you* doing here?"

He shrugged carelessly. "Thought it was

time to come home."

"Couldn't you have written?"

"To you?" he asked, quirking a brow. It was, and was meant to be, a direct hit. She hadn't penned him a single letter during his travels. He had sent her three letters, but once it became apparent that she didn't plan to answer, he'd conducted the rest of his correspondence through his mother and John's.

"To anyone," she replied. "Someone would have been here to greet you."

"You're here," he pointed out.

She scowled at him. "If we'd known you were coming, we would have readied the house for you."

He shrugged again. The motion seemed to embody the image he desperately needed to convey. "It's ready enough."

She hugged her arms to her body, effectively blocking his view of her breasts, which, he had to concede, was probably for the best. "Well, you might have written," she finally said, her voice hanging sharp in the night air. "It would only have been courteous."

"Francesca," he said, turning slightly away from her so that he could continue to rub his hands together by the fire, "do you have any idea how long it takes for mail to reach London from India?"

"Five months," she answered promptly. "Four, if the winds are kind."

Damn it, she was right. "Be that as it may," he said peevishly, "by the time I decided to return, there was little use in attempting forward notice. The letter would have gone out on the same ship I did."

"Really? I thought the passenger vessels were slower than the ones that take the mail."

He sighed, glancing at her over his shoulder. "They all take the mail. And besides, does it really matter?"

For a moment he thought she would answer in the affirmative, but then she said quietly, "No, of course not. The important thing is that you're home. Your mother will be thrilled."

He turned away so that she wouldn't see his humorless smile. "Yes," he murmured, "of course."

"And I —" She stopped, cleared her throat. "I am delighted to have you back as well."

She sounded as if she were trying very hard to convince herself of this, but Michael decided to play the gentleman for once and not point it out. "Are you cold?" he asked instead.

"Not very," she said.

"You're lying."

"Just a little."

He stepped to the side, making room for her closer to the fire. When he didn't hear her move toward him, he motioned toward the empty space with his hand.

"I should go back to my room," she said.

"For God's sake, Francesca, if you're cold, just come to the fire. I won't bite."

She gritted her teeth and stepped forward, joining him near the blaze. But she kept herself somewhat off to the side, maintaining a bit of distance between them. "You look well," she said.

"As do you."

"It's been a long time."

"I know. Four years, I believe."

Francesca swallowed, wishing this weren't so difficult. This was Michael, for heaven's sake. It wasn't supposed to be difficult. Yes, they'd parted badly, but that had been in the dark days immediately following John's death. They'd all been in pain then, wounded animals lashing out at anyone in their way. It was supposed to be different now. Heaven knew she'd thought of this moment often enough. Michael couldn't stay away forever, they'd all known that. But once her initial anger had passed, she'd rather hoped that when he did return, they'd be able to forget that anything unpleasant had ever passed between them.

And be friends again. She needed that, more than she'd ever realized.

"Do you have any plans?" she asked, mostly because the silence was too awful.

"For now, all I can think about is getting warm," he muttered.

She smiled in spite of herself. "It *is* exceptionally chilly for this time of year."

"I'd forgotten how damnably cold it can be here," he grumbled, rubbing his hands together briskly.

"One would think you'd never escape the memory of a Scottish winter," Francesca murmured.

He turned to her then, a wry smile tilting one corner of his mouth. He'd changed, she realized. Oh, there were the obvious differences — the ones everyone would notice. He was tan, quite scandalously so, and his hair, always midnight black, now sported a few odd strands of silver.

But there was more. He held his mouth differently, more tightly, if that made any sense, and his smooth, lanky grace seemed to have gone missing. He had always seemed so at ease, so comfortable in his skin, but now he was . . . taut.

Strained.

"You'd think," he murmured, and she just looked at him blankly, having quite forgotten what he was replying to until he added, "I came home because I couldn't stand the heat any longer, and now here I am, ready to perish from the cold."

"It will be spring soon," she said.

"Ah yes, spring. With its merely frigid winds, as opposed to the icy ones of winter."

She laughed at that, absurdly pleased to have anything to laugh about in his presence. "The house will be better tomorrow," she said. "I only just arrived this evening, and like you, I neglected to send advance notice. Mrs. Parrish assures me that the house will be restocked tomorrow."

He nodded, then turned around to warm his back. "What are you doing here?"

"Me?"

He motioned to the empty room, as if to make a point.

"I live here," she said.

"You usually don't come down until April."

"You know that?"

For a moment, he looked almost embarrassed. "My mother's letters are remarkably detailed," he said.

She shrugged, then inched a little closer to the fire. She ought not stand so near to him, but dash it, she was still rather cold, and her thin nightrobe did little to ward off the chill.

"Is that an answer?" he drawled.

"I just felt like it," she said insolently. "Isn't that a lady's prerogative?"

He turned again, presumably to warm his side, and then he was facing her.

And he seemed terribly close.

She moved, just an inch or so; she didn't want him to realize she'd been made uncomfortable by his nearness.

Nor did she want to admit the very same thing to herself.

"I thought it was a lady's prerogative to change her mind," he said.

"It's a lady's prerogative to do anything she wants," Francesca said pertly.

"Touché," Michael murmured. He looked at her again, more closely this time. "You haven't changed."

Her lips parted. "How can you say that?"

"Because you look exactly as I remembered you." And then, devilishly, he motioned toward her revealing nightwear. "Aside from your attire, of course."

She gasped and stepped back, wrapping her arms more tightly around her body.

It was a bit sick of him, but he was rather pleased with himself for having offended her. He'd needed her to step away, to move out of his reach. She was going to have to set the boundaries.

Because he wasn't sure he'd prove up to the task.

He'd been lying when he'd said she hadn't changed. There was something different about her, something entirely unexpected.

Something that shook him down to his very soul.

It was a sense about her — all in his mind, really, but no less devastating. There was an air of availability, a horrible, torturous knowledge that John was gone, really, truly gone, and the only thing stopping Michael from reaching out and touching her was his own conscience.

It was almost funny.

Almost.

And there she was, still without a clue, still completely unaware that the man standing next to her wanted nothing so much than to peel every layer of silk from her body and lay her down in front of the fire. He wanted to nudge her thighs apart, sink himself into her, and —

He laughed grimly. Four years, it seemed, had done little to cool his inappropriate ardor.

"Michael?"

He looked over at her.

"What's so funny?"

Her question, that's what. "You wouldn't understand."

"Try me," she dared.

"Oh, I think not."

"Michael," she prodded.

He turned to her and said with deliberate coolness, "Francesca, there are some things you will never understand."

Her lips parted, and for a moment she looked as if she'd been struck.

And he felt as horrid as if he'd done so.

"That was a terrible thing to say," she whispered.

He shrugged.

"You've changed," she said.

The sad thing was, he hadn't. Not in any of the ways that might have made his life easier to bear. He sighed, hating himself because he couldn't bear to have her hate him. "Forgive me," he said, running his hand through his hair. "I'm tired, and I'm cold, and I'm an ass."

She grinned at that, and for a moment

they were transported back in time. "It's all right," she said kindly, touching his upper arm. "You've had a long journey."

He sucked in his breath. She used to do this all the time — touch his arm in friendship. Never in public, of course, and rarely even when it had just been the two of them. John would have been there; John was always there. And it had always — *always* — shaken him.

But never so much as now.

"I need to go to bed," he mumbled. He was usually a master at hiding his unease, but he just hadn't been prepared to see her this evening, and beyond that, he was damned tired.

She withdrew her hand. "There won't be a room ready for you. You should take mine. I'll sleep here."

"No," he said, with far more force than he'd intended. "I'll sleep here, or . . . hell," he muttered, striding across the room to yank on the bellpull. What the devil was the point of being the bloody Earl of Kilmartin if you couldn't have a bedchamber readied at any hour of the night?

Besides, ringing the bell would mean that a servant would arrive within minutes, which would mean that he would no longer be standing here alone with Francesca.

It wasn't as if they hadn't been alone together before, but never at night, and never with her in her nightgown, and —

He yanked the cord again.

"Michael," she said, sounding almost amused. "I'm sure they heard you the first time."

"Yes, well, it's been a long day," he said. "Storm in the Channel and all that."

"You'll have to tell me of your travels soon," she said gently.

He looked over at her, lifting a brow. "I would have written to you of them."

Her lips pursed for a moment. It was an expression he'd seen countless times on her face. She was choosing her words, deciding whether or not to spear him with her legendary wit.

And apparently she decided against it, because instead she said, "I was rather angry with you for leaving."

He sucked in his breath. Trust Francesca to choose stark honesty over a scathing retort.

"I'm sorry," he said, and he meant it, even though he wouldn't have changed any of his actions. He'd needed to leave. He'd *had* to leave. Maybe it meant he was a coward; maybe it meant he'd been less of a man. But he hadn't been ready to be the earl. He wasn't John, could never be John. And that was the one thing everyone had seemed to want of him.

Even Francesca, in her own halfway sort of manner.

He looked at her. He was quite sure she still didn't understand why he'd left. She probably thought she did, but how could she? She didn't know that he loved her, couldn't possibly understand how damned guilty he felt at assuming John's life.

But none of that was her fault. And as he looked at her, standing fragile and proud as she stared at the fire, he said it again.

"I'm sorry."

She acknowledged his apology with the barest hint of a nod. "I should have written to you," she said. She turned to him then, her eyes filled with sorrow and perhaps a hint of their own apology. "But the truth was, I just didn't feel like it. Thinking of you made me think of John, and I suppose I needed not to think of him so much just then."

Michael didn't pretend to understand, but he nodded nonetheless.

She smiled wistfully. "We had such fun, the three of us, didn't we?"

He nodded again. "I miss him," he said,

and he was surprised by how good it felt to voice that.

"I always thought it would be so lovely when you finally married," Francesca added. "You would have chosen someone brilliant and fun, I'm sure. What grand times the four of us would have had."

Michael coughed. It seemed the best course of action.

She looked up, broken from her reverie. "Are you catching a chill?"

"Probably. I'll be at death's door by Saturday, I'm sure."

She arched a brow. "I hope you don't expect me to nurse you."

Just the opening he needed to move their banter back to where he felt most comfortable. "Not necessary," he said with a wave of his hand. "I shouldn't need more than three days to attract a bevy of unsuitable women to attend to my every need."

Her lips pinched slightly, but she was clearly amused. "The same as ever, I see."

He gave her a lopsided grin. "No one ever really changes, Francesca."

She cocked her head to the side, motioning to the hall, where they could hear someone moving toward them on swift feet. The footman arrived, and Francesca took care of everything, allowing Michael to do nothing but stand by the fire, looking vaguely imperial as he nodded his agreement.

"Good night, Michael," she said, once the footman had left to do her bidding.

"Good night, Francesca," he said softly.

"It's good to see you again," she said. And then, as if she needed to convince one of them of it — he wasn't sure which, she added, "It truly is."

Chapter 6

. . . I'm sorry I haven't written. No, that's not true. I'm not sorry. I don't wish to write. I don't wish to think of —

> — *from the Countess of Kilmartin*
> *to the new Earl of Kilmartin,*
> *one day after the receipt*
> *of his first missive to her,*
> *torn to bits, then soaked with tears*

By the time Michael arose the next morning, Kilmartin House seemed to be back up and running as befitted the home of an earl. There were fires in every grate, and a splendid breakfast had been laid out in the informal dining room, with coddled eggs, ham, bacon, sausage, toast with butter and marmalade, and his own personal favorite, broiled mackerel.

Francesca, however, was nowhere to be found.

When he inquired after her, he was given a folded note she'd left for him earlier that morning. It seemed she felt that tongues might wag at their living alone together at Kilmartin House, and so she had removed herself to her mother's residence at Number Five, Bruton Street, until either Janet or Helen arrived down from Scotland. She did, however, invite him to call upon her that day, as she was certain they had much to discuss.

And Michael supposed she was right, so once he'd finished with his breakfast (finding, much to his great surprise, that he rather missed the yogurts and dosas of his Indian morning meal), he stepped outside and made his way to Number Five.

He elected to walk; it wasn't very far, and the air had warmed appreciably since the icy gusts of the day before. But mostly, he just wanted to take in the cityscape, to remind himself of the rhythms of London. He'd never noticed the particular smells and sounds of the capital before, how the clip-clop of horses' hooves combined with the festive shout of the flower seller and low rumble of cultured voices. There was the sound of his feet on the pavement, and smell of roasting nuts, and the vague heft of soot

117

in the air, all combining to make something that was uniquely London.

It was almost overpowering, which was strange, because he remembered feeling precisely the same way upon landing in India four years earlier. The humid air, redolent with spice and flowers, had shocked his every sense. It had felt almost like an assault, leaving him drowsy and disoriented. And while his reaction to London wasn't quite that dramatic, he still felt rather like the odd man out, his senses buffeted by smells and sounds that shouldn't have felt so unfamiliar.

Had he become a stranger in his own land? It seemed almost bizarre, and yet, as he walked along the crowded streets of London's most exclusive shopping district, he couldn't help but think that he stood out, that anyone glancing upon him must instantly know that he was different, removed from their very British existence.

Or, he allowed, as he caught sight of his reflection in a shop window, it could be the tan.

It would take weeks to fade. Months, maybe.

His mother was going to be scandalized.

The thought of it made him grin. He rather enjoyed scandalizing his mother.

He'd never be so grown up that *that* ceased to be fun.

He turned on Bruton Street and walked past the last few homes to Number Five. He'd been there before, of course. Francesca's mother had always defined the word "family" in the widest of all possible manners, so Michael had found himself invited along with John and Francesca to any number of Bridgerton family events.

When he arrived, Lady Bridgerton was already in the green-and-cream drawing room, taking a cup of tea at her writing desk under the window. "Michael!" she exclaimed, rising to her feet with obvious affection. "How good to see you!"

"Lady Bridgerton," he said, taking her hand and gracing it with a gallant kiss.

"No one does that like you," she said approvingly.

"One has to cultivate one's best maneuvers," he murmured.

"And I can't tell you how much we ladies of a certain age appreciate your doing so."

"A certain age being . . ." He smiled devilishly. ". . . one and thirty?"

Lady Bridgerton was the sort of woman who grew lovelier with age, but the smile she gave him made her positively radiant.

"You are *always* welcome in this house, Michael Stirling."

He grinned and sat in a high-backed chair when she motioned for him to do so.

"Oh, dear," she said with a slight frown. "I must apologize. I suppose I should be calling you Kilmartin now."

" 'Michael' is just fine," he assured her.

"I know that it's been four years," she continued, "but as I haven't seen you . . ."

"You may call me anything you wish," he said smoothly. It was strange. He'd finally grown used to being called Kilmartin, adapted to the way his title had overtaken his surname. But that had been in India, where no one had known him as plain Mr. Stirling, and perhaps more importantly, no one had known John as the earl. Hearing his title on Violet Bridgerton's lips was a little unnerving, especially since she had, as was the custom for many mothers-in-law, habitually referred to John as her son.

But if she sensed any of his inner discomfort, she gave no indication. "If you are going to be so accommodating," she said, "then I must be as well. Please do call me Violet. It's well past time that you did."

"Oh, I couldn't," he said quickly. And he meant it. This was Lady Bridgerton. She was . . . Well, he didn't know what she was, but she couldn't possibly be *Violet* to him.

"I insist, Michael," she said, "and I'm certain you're already aware that I usually get my way."

There was no way he was going to win the argument, so he just sighed and said, "I don't know if I can kiss the hand of a Violet. It seems rather scandalously intimate, don't you think?"

"Don't you dare stop."

"Tongues will wag," he warned her.

"I believe my reputation can withstand it."

"Ah, but can mine?"

She laughed. "You are a rascal."

He leaned back in his chair. "It serves me well."

"Would you care for tea?" She motioned to the delicate china pot on the desk across the room. "Mine has gone cold, but I would be happy to ring for more."

"I'd love some," he admitted.

"I suppose you're spoiled for it now, after so many years in India," she said, standing and crossing the room to ring the bellpull.

"It's just not the same," he said, quickly rising to his feet as well. "I can't explain it, but nothing tastes quite like tea in England."

"The quality of the water, do you think?"

He smiled stealthily. "The quality of the woman pouring."

She laughed. "You, my lord, need a wife. Immediately."

"Oh, really? And why is that?"

"Because in your present state, you are clearly a danger to unmarried women everywhere."

He couldn't resist one last flirtation. "I hope you are including yourself in those ranks, Violet."

And then a voice from the door: "Are you flirting with my *mother?*"

It was Francesca, of course, impeccably turned out in a lavender morning dress adorned with a rather intricate stretch of Belgian lace. She looked as if she were very much trying to be stern with him.

And not entirely succeeding.

Michael allowed his lips to curve into a mysterious smile as he watched the two ladies take their seats. "I have traveled the world over, Francesca, and can say without qualification that there are few women with whom I'd rather flirt than your mother."

"I am inviting you to supper right now," Violet announced, "and I will not accept no for an answer."

Michael chuckled. "I'd be honored."

Across from him, Francesca murmured, "You are incorrigible."

He just flashed her a lanky grin. This was good, he decided. The morning was proceeding exactly as he'd hoped, with he and Francesca falling into their old roles and habits. He was once again the reckless charmer and she was pretending to scold him, and all was as it had been back before John had died.

He'd been surprised last night. He hadn't expected to see her. And he hadn't been able to make sure that his public persona was firmly in place.

And it wasn't as if it *all* was an act. He'd always been a bit reckless, and he probably *was* an irredeemable flirt. His mother certainly liked to say that he'd been charming the ladies since the age of four.

It was just that when he was with Francesca it was vitally important that that aspect of his personality remained at the forefront, so that she never suspected what lay underneath.

"What are your plans now that you are returned?" Violet asked.

Michael turned to her with what he knew had to be a blank expression. "I'm not certain, actually," he said, ashamed to admit to himself that that was true. "I imagine it will take me some time to understand just what exactly is expected of me in my new role."

"I'm sure Francesca can be of help in that quarter," Violet said.

"Only if she wishes it," Michael said quietly.

"Of course," Francesca said, moving slightly to the side when a maid came in with a tea tray. "I will assist you in any way you need."

"That was rather quick," Michael murmured.

"I'm mad for tea," Violet explained. "Drink it all day long. The maids keep water to near boiling on the stove at all times now."

"Will you have some?" Francesca asked, since she had taken charge of pouring.

"Yes, thank you," Michael replied.

"No one knows Kilmartin as Francesca does," Violet said, with all the pride of a mother hen. "She will prove invaluable to you."

"I am quite sure that you are correct," Michael said, accepting a cup from Francesca. She had remembered how he took it — milk, no sugar. For some reason this pleased him immensely. "She has been the countess for six years, and for four of them, she has had to be the earl as well." At Francesca's startled glance, he added, "In every way but in name. Oh, come now, Francesca, you must realize that it is true."

"I —"

"*And*," he added, "that it is a compliment. I owe you a greater debt than I could ever repay. I could not have stayed away so long had I not known that the earldom was in such capable hands."

Francesca actually blushed, which surprised him. In all the years he'd known her, he could count on one hand the times he had seen her cheeks go pink.

"Thank you," she mumbled. "It was no difficulty, I assure you."

"Perhaps, but it is appreciated all the same." He lifted his teacup to his lips, allowing the ladies to direct the conversation from there.

Which they did. Violet asked him about his time in India, and before he knew it he was telling them of palaces and princesses, caravans and curries. He left out the marauders and malaria, deciding they weren't quite the thing for a drawing-room conversation.

After a while he realized that he was enjoying himself immensely. Maybe, he thought, reflecting on the moment as Violet said something about an Indian-themed ball she'd attended the year before, just maybe he'd made the right decision.

It might actually be good to be home.

An hour later, Francesca found herself on Michael's arm, strolling through Hyde Park. The sun had broken through the clouds, and when she had declared that she could not resist the fine weather, Michael had had no choice but to offer to accompany her for a walk.

"It's rather like old times," she said, tilting her face up toward the sun. She'd most likely end up with a ghastly tan, or at the very least freckles, but she supposed she'd always look like pale porcelain next to Michael, whose skin marked him immediately as a recent returnee from the tropics.

"Walking, you mean?" he asked. "Or your expertly maneuvering me into accompanying you?"

She tried to maintain a straight face. "Both, of course. You used to take me out a great deal. Whenever John was busy."

"So I did."

They walked on in silence for a few moments, and then he said, "I was a bit surprised to find you gone this morning."

"I hope you understand why I had to leave," she said. "I didn't want to, of course; returning to my mother's home makes me feel as if I'm stepping right back into childhood." She felt her lips pinching together in distaste. "I adore her, of course, but I've grown rather used to maintaining my own household."

"Would you like me to take up residence elsewhere?"

"No, of course not," she said quickly. "You are the earl. Kilmartin House belongs to you. Besides, Helen and Janet are only a week behind me; they should arrive soon, and then I will be able to move back in."

"Chin up, Francesca. I'm sure you will endure."

She shot him a sideways glance. "It is nothing that you — or any man, for that matter — will understand, but I much prefer my status as a married woman to that of a debutante. When I'm at Number Five, with both Eloise and Hyacinth in residence, I feel as if I'm back in my first season, with all the attendant rules and regulations."

"Not all of them," he pointed out. "If

that were true, you'd not be allowed out with me right now."

"True," she acceded. "Especially with you, I imagine."

"And just what is that supposed to mean?"

She laughed. "Oh, come now, Michael. Did you really think that your reputation would find itself whitewashed just because you left the country for four years?"

"Francesca —"

"You're a *legend*."

He looked aghast.

"It's true," she said, wondering why he was so surprised. "Goodness, women are still talking about you."

"Not to you, I hope," he muttered.

"Oh, to me above all others." She grinned wickedly. "They all want to know when you plan to return. And it's sure to be worse once word gets out that you're back. I must say, it's rather an odd role — confidante to London's most notorious rake."

"Confidante, eh?"

"What else would you call it?"

"No, no, confidante is a perfectly appropriate word. It's just that if you think I've confided *everything* in you . . ."

Francesca shot him a cross expression.

128

This was so like him, letting his words trail off meaningfully, leaving her imagination feverish with questions. "I take it then," she muttered, "that you did not share with us all the news from India."

He just smiled. Devilishly.

"Very well. Allow me, then, to move the conversation to more respectable areas. What *do* you plan to do now that you are back? Will you take up your seat in Parliament?"

He appeared not to have considered that.

"It is what John would have wanted," she said, knowing that she was being fiendishly manipulative.

Michael looked at her grimly, and his eyes told her that he did not appreciate her tactics.

"You will have to marry as well," Francesca said.

"Do you plan to take on the role of my matchmaker?" he asked peevishly.

She shrugged. "If you desire it. I'm sure I couldn't possibly do a worse job of it than you."

"Good God," he grumbled, "I've been back one day. Do we need to address this now?"

"No, of course not," she allowed. "But

soon. You're not getting any younger."

Michael just stared at her in shock. "I can't imagine permitting anyone else to speak to me in such a manner."

"Don't forget your mother," she said with a satisfied smile.

"You," he said rather forcefully, "are *not* my mother."

"Thank heavens for that," she returned. "I'd have expired of heart failure years ago. I don't know how she does it."

He actually halted in his tracks. "I'm not *that* bad."

She shrugged delicately. "Aren't you?"

And he was speechless. Absolutely speechless. It was a conversation they'd had countless times, but something was different now. There was an edge to her voice, a jab to her words that had never quite been there before.

Or maybe it was just that he'd never noticed it.

"Oh, don't look so shocked, Michael," she said, reaching across her body and patting him lightly on the arm. "Of course you have a terrible reputation. But you are endlessly charming, and so you are always forgiven."

Was this how she saw him, he wondered. And why was he surprised? It was exactly the image he'd cultivated.

"And now that you are the earl," she continued, "the mamas shall be falling all over themselves to pair you with their precious daughters."

"I feel afraid," he said under his breath. "Very afraid."

"You should," she said, with no sympathy whatsoever. "It will be a feeding frenzy, I assure you. You are fortunate that I took my mother aside this morning and made her swear not to throw Eloise or Hyacinth in your path. She would do it, too," she added, clearly relishing the conversation.

"I seem to recall that you used to find joy in throwing your sisters in my path."

Her lips twisted slightly. "That was years ago," she said, swishing her hand through the air as if she could wave his words away on the wind. "You would never suit."

He'd never had any desire to court either of her sisters, but nor could he resist the chance to give Francesca a wee verbal poke. "Eloise," he queried, "or Hyacinth?"

"Neither," she replied, with enough testiness to make him smile. "But I shall find you someone, do not fret."

"Was I fretting?"

She went on as if he hadn't spoken. "I think I shall introduce you to Eloise's friend Penelope."

"Miss Featherington?" he asked, vaguely recalling a slightly pudgy girl who never spoke.

"She's my friend as well, of course," Francesca added. "I believe you might like her."

"Has she learned to speak?"

She glared at him. "I'm going to ignore that comment. Penelope is a perfectly lovely and highly intelligent lady once one gets past her initial shyness."

"And how long does *that* take?" he muttered.

"I think she would balance you quite nicely," Francesca declared.

"Francesca," he said, somewhat forcefully, "you will not play matchmaker for me. Is that understood?"

"Well, some —"

"And don't you say that someone has to," he cut in. Really, she was the same open book she'd been years ago. She'd always wanted to manage his life.

"Michael," she said, the word coming out as a sigh that was far more long-suffering than she had a right to be.

"I have been back in town for one day,"

132

he said. "One day. I am tired, and I don't care if the sun is out — I'm still bloody cold, and my belongings haven't even been unpacked. Pray give me at least a week before you start planning my wedding."

"A week, then?" she said slyly.

"Francesca," he said, his voice laced with warning.

"Very well," she said dismissively. "But don't you dare say I didn't warn you. Once you are out in society, and the young ladies have you backed into a corner with their mamas coming in for the kill —"

He shuddered at the image. And at the knowledge that her prediction was probably correct.

"— you will be begging for my help," she finished, looking up at him with a rather annoyingly satisfied expression.

"I'm sure I will," he said, giving her a paternalistic smile that he knew she'd detest. "And when that happens, I promise you that I shall be duly prostrate with regretfulness, atonement, shamefacedness, and any other unpleasant emotion you care to assign to me."

And then she laughed, which warmed his heart far more than he should have let it. He could always make her laugh.

She turned to him and smiled, then

patted his arm. "It's good to have you back."

"It's good to be back," he said. He'd said the words automatically, but he realized he'd meant them. It *was* good. Difficult, but good. But even difficult wasn't worth complaining over. It was certainly nothing he wasn't used to.

They were fairly deep in Hyde Park now, and the grounds were growing a bit more crowded. The trees were only just beginning to bud, but the air was still nippy enough that the people out strolling weren't looking for shade.

"I should have brought bread for the birds," Francesca murmured.

"At the Serpentine?" Michael asked with surprise. He'd often walked in Hyde Park with Francesca, and they had tended to avoid that area of the Serpentine's banks like the plague. It was always full of nursemaids and children, shrieking like little savages (often the nursemaids more so than the children) and Michael had at least one acquaintance who had found himself pelted in the head with a loaf of bread.

Seems no one had told the budding little cricket player that one was supposed to break the bread into more manageable — and less hazardous — segments.

"I like to toss bread in for the birds," Francesca said, a touch defensively. "Besides, there won't be too many children about today. It's still a bit cold yet."

"Never stopped John and me," Michael offered gamely.

"Yes, well, you're Scottish," she returned. "Your blood circulates quite well half frozen."

He grinned. "A hearty lot, we Scots." It was a bit of a joke, that. With so much intermarriage, the family was at least as much English as it was Scottish, perhaps even more so, but with Kilmartin firmly situated in the border counties, the Stirlings clung to their Scottish heritage like a badge of honor.

They found a bench not too far from the Serpentine and sat, idly watching the ducks on the water.

"You'd think they'd find a warmer spot," Michael said. "France, maybe."

"And miss out on all the food the children toss at them?" Francesca smiled wryly. "They're not stupid."

He just shrugged. Far be it from him to pretend any great knowledge of avian behavior.

"How did you find the climate in India?" Francesca queried. "Is it as hot as they say?"

"More so," he replied. "Or maybe not. I don't know. I imagine the descriptions are perfectly accurate. The problem is, no Englishman can truly understand what they mean until he gets there."

She looked at him quizzically.

"It's hotter than you could ever imagine," he said, spelling it out.

"It sounds . . . Well, I don't know how it sounds," she admitted.

"The heat isn't nearly so difficult as the insects."

"It sounds dreadful," Francesca decided.

"You probably wouldn't like it. Not for an extended stay, anyway."

"I'd like to travel, though," she said softly. "I'd always planned to."

She fell silent, nodding in a rather absentminded manner, her chin tilting up and down for so long that he was quite sure she'd forgotten she was doing it. Then he realized that her eyes were fixed off in the distance. She was watching something, but for the life of him he couldn't imagine what. There was nothing interesting in the vista, just a pinchfaced nursemaid pushing a pram.

"What are you looking at?" he finally asked.

She said nothing, just continued to stare.

"Francesca?"

She turned to him. "I want a baby."

Chapter 7

. . . had hoped to have received a note from you by now, but of course the post is notoriously unreliable when it must travel so far. Just last week I heard tale of the arrival of a mail pouch that was a full two years old; many of the recipients had already returned to England. My mother writes that you are well and fully recovered from your ordeal; I am glad to hear of it. My work here continues to challenge and fulfill. I have taken up residence outside the city proper, as do most Europeans here in Madras. Nonetheless, I enjoy visiting the city; it is rather Grecian in appearance; or rather, what I must imagine is Grecian, having never visited that country myself. The sky is blue, so blue it is nearly blinding, almost the bluest thing I have ever seen.

— from the Earl of Kilmartin
to the Countess of Kilmartin,

"I beg your pardon?"

She'd shocked him. He was sputtering, even. She hadn't made her announcement to elicit this sort of reaction, but now that he was sitting there, his mouth hanging open and slack, she couldn't help but take a small amount of pleasure from the moment.

"I want a baby," she said with a shrug. "Is there something surprising in that?"

His lips moved before he actually made sound. "Well . . . no . . . but . . ."

"I'm twenty-six."

"I know how old you are," he said, a little testily.

"I'll be twenty-seven at the end of April. I don't think it's so odd that I might want a child."

His eyes still held a vaguely glazed sort of quality. "No, of course not, but —"

"And I shouldn't have to explain myself to you!"

"I wasn't asking you to," he said, staring at her as if she'd grown two heads.

"I'm sorry," she mumbled. "I overreacted."

He said nothing, which irritated her. At the very least, he could have contradicted her. It would have been a lie, but it was still the kind and courteous thing to do.

Finally, because the silence was simply unbearable, she muttered, "A lot of women want children."

"Right," he said, coughing on the word. "Of course. But . . . don't you think you might want a husband first?"

"Of course." She speared him with an aggravated glare. "Why do you think I came down to London early?"

He looked at her blankly.

"I am shopping for a husband," she said, speaking to him as if he were a halfwit.

"How mercenarily put," he murmured.

She pursed her lips. "It's what it is. And you had probably best get used to it for your own sake. It's precisely how the ladies will soon be talking about *you*."

He ignored the latter part of her statement. "Do you have a particular gentleman in mind?"

She shook her head. "Not yet. I imagine someone will pop to the forefront once I start looking, though." She was trying to sound jolly about it, but the truth was, her voice was dropping in both tone and volume. "I'm sure my brothers have friends," she finally mumbled.

He looked at her, then slumped back slightly and stared at the water.

"I've shocked you," she said.

"Well . . . yes."

"Normally, I'd take great pleasure in that," she said, her lips twisting ironically.

He didn't reply, but he did roll his eyes slightly.

"I can't mourn John forever," she said. "I mean, I can, and I will, but . . ." She stopped, hating that she was near tears. "And the worst part of it is, maybe I can't even *have* children. It took me two years to conceive with John, and look how I mucked that up."

"Francesca," he said fiercely, "you mustn't blame yourself for the miscarriage."

She let out a bitter laugh. "Can you imagine? Marrying someone just so I could have a baby and then not having one?"

"It happens to people all the time," he said softly.

It was true, but it didn't make her feel any better. *She* had a choice. She didn't have to marry; she would be quite well provided for — and blessedly independent — if she remained a widow. If she married — no, *when* she married — she had to mentally commit to the idea — it wouldn't be for love. She wasn't going to have a marriage like the one she'd shared with John; a woman simply didn't find love like that twice in a lifetime.

She was going to marry for a baby, and there was no guarantee that she would get one.

"Francesca?"

She didn't look at him, just sat there and blinked, desperately trying to ignore the tears burning at the corners of her eyes.

Michael held out a handkerchief, but she didn't want to acknowledge the gesture. If she took the cloth, then she'd *have* to cry. There would be nothing stopping her.

"I must move on," she said defiantly. "I must. John is gone, and I —"

And then the strangest thing happened. Except *strange* wasn't really the right word. Shocking, perhaps, or altering, or maybe there wasn't a word for the type of surprise that stole the pulse from one's body, leaving one immobile, unable to breathe.

She turned to him. It should have been a simple thing. She'd certainly turned to Michael before, hundreds . . . no, thousands of times. He might have spent the last four years in India, but she knew his face, and she knew his smile. In truth, she knew everything about him —

Except this time was different. She turned to him, but she hadn't expected him to have already turned to her. And she hadn't expected him to be so close that she'd see the charcoal flecks in his eyes.

But most of all, she hadn't expected her gaze to drop to his lips. They were full, and lush, and finely molded, and she knew the shape as well as the shape of her own, except never before had she really *looked* at them, noticed the way they weren't quite uniform in color, or how the curve of his lower lip was really quite sensual, and —

She stood. So quickly that she nearly lost her balance. "I have to go," she said, stunned that her voice sounded like her own and not some freakish demon. "I have an appointment. I'd forgotten."

"Of course," he said, standing beside her.

"With the dressmaker," she added, as if details would make her lie more convincing. "All my clothes are in half-mourning colors."

He nodded. "They don't suit you."

"Kind of you to point it out," she said testily.

"You should wear blue," he said.

She nodded jerkily, still off balance and out of sorts.

"Are you all right?" he asked.

"I'm fine," she bit off. And then, because no one would ever have been fooled by her tone, she added, more carefully, "I'm fine. I assure you. I simply detest being tardy." That much was true, and he knew it of her, so hopefully he'd accept it as reason for her snappishness.

"Very well," he said collegially, and Francesca chattered all the way back to Number Five. She had to put up a good front, she realized rather feverishly. She couldn't possibly allow him to guess what had really transpired within her on the bench by the Serpentine.

She had known, of course, that Michael was handsome, even startlingly so. But it had all been an abstract sort of knowledge. Michael was handsome, just as her brother Benedict was tall, and her mother had beautiful eyes.

But suddenly . . . But now . . .

She'd looked at him, and she'd seen something entirely new.

She'd seen a *man*.

And it scared the very devil out of her.

Francesca tended to subscribe to the notion that the best course of action was more action, so when she returned to Number Five after her stroll, she sought out her mother and informed her that she needed to visit the modiste immediately. Best to make truth out of her lie as soon as possible, after all.

Her mother was only too delighted to see Francesca out of her half-mourning grays and lavenders, and so barely an hour passed before the two of them were comfortably ensconced in Violet's elegant carriage, on their way to the exclusive shops on Bond Street. Normally, Francesca would have bristled at Violet's interference; she was perfectly capable of picking out her own wardrobe, thank you very much, but today she found her mother's presence oddly comforting.

Not that her mother wasn't usually a comfort. Just that Francesca tended to favor her independent streak more often than not, and she rather preferred not to be thought of as "one of those Bridgerton girls." And in a very strange way, this trip to the dressmaker was rather discomfiting. It would have required full-fledged torture to get her to admit it, but Francesca was, quite simply, terrified.

Even if she hadn't decided it was time to

remarry, shrugging off her widow's weeds signaled a huge change, and not one she was entirely sure she was ready for.

She looked down at her sleeve as she sat in the carriage. She couldn't see the fabric of her dress — it was covered by her coat — but she knew that it was lavender. And there was something comforting in that, something solid and dependable. She'd worn that color, or gray in its place, for three years now. And unrelenting black for a year before that. It had been a bit of a badge, she realized, a uniform of sorts. One never had to worry about who one was when one's clothing proclaimed it so loudly.

"Mother?" she said, before she even realized that she had a question to ask.

Violet turned to her with a smile. "Yes, dear?"

"Why did you never remarry?"

Violet's lips parted slightly, and to Francesca's great surprise, her eyes grew bright. "Do you know," Violet said softly, "this is the first time any of you has asked me that?"

"That can't be true," Francesca said. "Are you certain?"

Violet nodded. "None of my children has asked me. I would have remembered."

"No, no, of course you would," Francesca said quickly. But it was all so . . . odd. And unthinking, really. Why would no one have asked Violet about this? It seemed to Francesca quite the most burning question imaginable. And even if none of Violet's children had cared about the answer for their own personal curiosity, didn't they realize how important it was to Violet?

Didn't they want to *know* their mother? Truly know her?

"When your father died . . ." Violet said. "Well, I don't know how much you recall, but it was very sudden. None of us expected it." She gave a sad little laugh, and Francesca wondered if she'd ever be able to laugh about John's death, even if it was tinged with grief.

"A bee sting," Violet continued, and Francesca realized that even now, more than twenty years after Edmund Bridgerton's death, her mother still sounded surprised when she talked about it.

"Who would have thought it possible?" Violet said, shaking her head. "I don't know how well you remember him, but your father was a very large man. As tall as Benedict and perhaps even broader in the shoulders. You just wouldn't think that a bee . . ." She stopped, pulling out a crisp, white handkerchief and holding it to her lips as she cleared her throat. "Well, it was unexpected. I don't really know what else to say, except . . ." She turned to her daughter with achingly wise eyes. "Except I imagine you understand better than anyone."

Francesca nodded, not even trying to stem the burning sensation behind her eyes.

"Anyway," Violet said briskly, obviously eager to move forward, "after his death, I was just so . . . stunned. I felt as if I were walking in a haze. I'm not at all certain how I functioned that first year. Or even the ones directly thereafter. So I couldn't possibly even think of marriage."

"I know," Francesca said softly. And she did.

"And after that . . . well, I don't know what happened. Maybe I just didn't meet anyone with whom I cared to share my life. Maybe I loved your father too much." She shrugged. "Maybe I just never saw the need. I was in a very different position from you, after all. I was older, don't forget, and already the mother of eight children. And your father left our affairs in very good order. I knew we would never want for anything."

"John left Kilmartin in excellent order," Francesca said quickly.

"Of course he did," Violet said, patting her hand. "Forgive me. I did not mean to imply otherwise. But you don't have eight children, Francesca." Her eyes changed somehow, grew an even deeper blue. "And you've quite a lot of time ahead of you to spend it all alone."

Francesca nodded jerkily. "I know," she said. "I know. I know, but I can't quite . . . I can't . . ."

"You can't what?" Violet asked gently.

"I can't . . ." Francesca looked down. She didn't know why, but for some reason she couldn't take her eyes off the floor. "I can't rid myself of the feeling that I'm doing something wrong, that I'm dishonoring John, dishonoring our marriage."

"John would have wanted you to be happy."

"I know. I know. Of course he would. But don't you see —" She looked up again, her eyes searching her mother's face for something, she wasn't sure what — maybe approval, maybe just love, since there was something comforting in looking for something she already knew she'd find. "I'm not even looking for that," she added. "I'm not going to find someone like John. I've accepted that. And it feels so wrong to marry with less."

"You won't find someone like John, that is true," Violet said. "But you might find a man who will suit you equally well, just in a different way."

"You didn't."

"No, I didn't," she agreed, "but I didn't look very hard. I didn't look at all."

"Do you wish you had?"

Violet opened her mouth, but not a sound came out, not even breath. Finally she said, "I don't know, Francesca. I honestly don't know." And then, because the moment almost certainly needed a bit of laughter, she added, "I certainly didn't want any more children!"

Francesca couldn't help but smile. "I do," she said softly. "I want a baby."

"I thought that you did."

"Why did you never ask me about it?"

Violet tilted her head to the side. "Why did you never ask me about why I never remarried?"

Francesca felt her lips part. She shouldn't have been so surprised by her mother's perceptiveness.

"If you had been Eloise, I think I would have said something," Violet added. "Or any of your sisters, for that matter. But you —" She smiled nostalgically. "You're not the same. You never have been. Even as a child you set yourself apart. And you needed your distance."

Impulsively, Francesca reached out and squeezed her mother's hand. "I love you, did you know that?"

Violet smiled. "I rather suspected it."

"Mother!"

"Very well, of course I knew it. How could you not love me when I love you so very, very much?"

"I haven't said it," Francesca said, feeling rather horrified by her omission. "Not recently, anyway."

"It's quite all right." Violet squeezed her hand back. "You've had other things on your mind."

And for some reason that made Francesca giggle under her breath. "A bit of an understatement, I should say."

Violet just grinned.

"Mother?" Francesca blurted out. "May I ask you one more question?"

"Of course."

"If I don't find someone — not like John, of course, but still not equally suited to me. If I don't find someone like that, and I marry someone whom I rather like, but perhaps don't love . . . is that all right?"

Violet was silent for several moments before she answered. "I'm afraid only you will know the answer to that," she finally said. "I would never say no, of course. Half the *ton* — more than half, in truth — has marriages like that, and quite a few of them are perfectly content. But you will have to make your judgments for yourself when they arise. Everyone is different, Francesca. I suspect you know that better than most. And when a man asks for your hand, you will have to judge him on his merits and not by some arbitrary standard you have set out ahead of time."

She was right, of course, but Francesca was so sick of life being messy and complicated that it wasn't the answer she'd been seeking.

And none of it addressed the problem that lay most deeply within her heart. What would happen if she actually did meet someone who made her feel the way she'd felt with John? She couldn't imagine that she would; truly, it seemed wildly improbable.

But what if she did? How could she live with herself then?

There was something rather satisfying

about a foul mood, so Michael decided to indulge his completely.

He kicked a pebble all the way home.

He snarled at anyone who jostled him on the street.

He yanked open his front door with such ferocity that it slammed into the stone wall behind it. Or rather he would have done, if his sodding butler hadn't been so on his toes and had the door open before Michael's fingers could even touch the handle.

But he *thought* about slamming it open, which provided some satisfaction in and of itself.

And then he stomped up the stairs to his room — which still felt too bloody much like John's room, not that there was anything he could do about that just then — and yanked off his boots.

Or tried to.

Bloody hell.

"Reivers!" he bellowed.

His valet appeared — or really, it seemed rather more like he apparated — in the doorway.

"Yes, my lord?"

"Would you help me with my boots?" Michael ground out, feeling rather infantile. Three years in the army and four in India, and he couldn't remove his own damned boots? What was it about London that reduced a man to a sniveling idiot? He seemed to recall that Reivers had had to remove his boots for him the last time he'd lived in London as well.

He looked down. They *were* different boots. Different styles, he supposed, for different situations, and Reivers had always taken a stunningly ridiculous pride in his work. Of course he'd have wanted to outfit Michael in the very best of London fashion. He'd have —

"Reivers?" Michael said in a low voice. "Where did you get these boots?"

"My lord?"

"These boots. I do not recognize them."

"We have not yet received all of your trunks from the ship, my lord. You didn't have anything suitable for London, so I located these among the previous earl's belong—"

"*Jesus.*"

"My lord? I'm terribly sorry if these don't suit you. I remembered that the two of you were of a size, and I thought you'd want —"

"Just get them off. Now." Michael closed his eyes and sat in a leather chair — *John's* leather chair — marveling at the irony of it. His worst nightmare coming true, in the most literal of fashions.

"Of course, my lord." Reivers looked pained, but he quickly went to work removing the boots.

Michael pinched the bridge of his nose with his thumb and forefinger and let out a long breath before speaking again. "I would prefer not to use any items from the previous earl's wardrobe," he said wearily. Truly, he had no idea why John's clothing was still here; the lot of it should have been given to the servants or donated to charity years ago. But he supposed that was Francesca's decision to make, not his.

"Of course, my lord. I shall see to it immediately."

"Good," Michael grunted.

"Shall I have it locked away?"

Locked? Good God, it wasn't as if the stuff were toxic. "I'm sure it is all just fine where it is," Michael said. "Just don't use any of it for me."

"Right." Reivers swallowed, and his Adam's apple bobbed uncomfortably.

"What is it now, Reivers?"

"It's just that all of the previous Lord Kilmartin's accouterments are still here."

"Here?" Michael asked blankly.

"Here," Reivers confirmed, glancing about the room.

Michael sagged in his chair. It wasn't that he wanted to wipe every last reminder of his cousin off the face of this earth; *no one* missed John as much as he did, no one.

Well, except maybe Francesca, he allowed, but that was different.

But he just didn't know how he was meant to lead his life so completely and smotheringly surrounded by John's belongings. He held his title, spent his money, lived in his house. Was he meant to wear his damned shoes as well?

"Pack it all up," he said to Reivers. "Tomorrow. I don't wish to be disturbed this evening."

And besides, he probably ought to alert Francesca of his intentions.

Francesca.

He sighed, rising to his feet once the valet had departed. Christ, Reivers had forgotten to take the boots with him. Michael picked them up and deposited them outside the door. He was probably overreacting, but hell, he just didn't want to stare at John's boots for the next six hours.

After shutting the door with a decisive click, he padded aimlessly over to the window. The sill was wide and deep, and he leaned heavily against it, gazing through the sheer curtains at the blurry streetscape below. He pushed the thin fabric aside, his lips twisting into a bitter smile as he watched a nursemaid tugging a small child along the pavement.

Francesca. She wanted a baby.

He didn't know why he was so surprised. If he thought about it rationally, he really shouldn't have been. She was a woman, for God's sake; of course she'd want children. Didn't they all? And while he'd never consciously sat down and told himself that she'd pine away for John forever, he'd also never considered the idea that she might actually care to remarry one day.

Francesca and John. John and Francesca. They were a unit, or at least they had been, and although John's death had made it sadly easy to envision one without the other, it was quite something else entirely to think of one with another.

And then of course there was the small matter of his skin crawling, which was his general reaction to the thought of Francesca with another man.

He shuddered. Or was that a shiver? Damn, he hoped it wasn't a shiver.

He supposed he was simply going to have to get used to the notion. If Francesca wanted children, then Francesca needed a husband, and there wasn't a damned thing he could do about it. It would have been rather nice, he supposed, if she had come to this decision and taken care of the whole odious matter last year, sparing him the nausea of having to witness the entire courtship unfold. If she'd just gone and gotten herself married *last* year, then it would have been over and done with, and that would have been that.

End of story.

But now he was going to have to *watch*. Maybe even advise.

Bloody hell.

He shivered again. Damn. Maybe he was just cold. It was March, after all, and a chilly one at that, even with a fire in the grate.

He tugged at his cravat, which was starting to feel unaccountably tight, then yanked it off altogether. Christ, he felt like the very devil, all hot and cold, and queerly off balance.

He sat down. It seemed the best course of action.

And then he just gave up all pretense of being well, stripping off the rest of his clothing and crawling into bed.

It was going to be a long night.

 *Chapter 8*

. . . ~~wonderful lovely nice~~ good to hear from you. I am glad you are faring well. John would have been proud. ~~I miss you.~~ I miss him. ~~I miss you.~~ Some of the flowers are still out. Isn't it nice that some of the flowers are still out?

> — *from the Countess of Kilmartin to the Earl of Kilmartin, one week after the receipt of his second missive to her, first draft, never finished, never sent*

"Didn't Michael say that he would be joining us for supper this evening?"

Francesca looked up at her mother, who was standing before her with concerned eyes. She had been thinking the exact same thing, actually, wondering what was keeping him.

She'd spent the better part of the day dreading his arrival, even though he had absolutely no idea that she had been so distressed by that moment in the park. Good heavens, he probably didn't even realize there *had* been a "moment."

It was the first time in her life that Francesca was thankful for the general obtuseness of men.

"Yes, he did say that he would come," she replied, shifting slightly in her chair. She had been waiting for some time now in the drawing room with her mother and two of her sisters, idly passing the time until their supper guest arrived.

"Didn't we give him the time?" Violet asked.

Francesca nodded. "I confirmed it with him when he left me here after our stroll in the park." She was quite certain of the exchange; she clearly recalled feeling rather sick in her stomach when they had spoken of it. She hadn't wanted to see him again — not so quickly, anyway — but what could she do? Her mother had issued the invitation.

"He's probably just running late," said Hyacinth, Francesca's youngest sister. "I'm not surprised. His sort is always late."

Francesca turned on her instantly. "What is that supposed to mean?"

"I've heard all about his reputation."

160

"What has his reputation to do with anything?" Francesca asked testily. "And anyway, what would you know of it? He left England years before you made your bow."

Hyacinth shrugged, jabbing a needle into her extremely untidy embroidery. "People still speak of him," she said carelessly. "The ladies swoon like idiots at the mere mention of his name, if you must know."

"There's no other way to swoon," put in Eloise, who, although Francesca's elder by precisely one year, was still unmarried.

"Well, rake he may be," Francesca said archly, "but he has always been punctual to a fault." She never could countenance others speaking ill of Michael. She might sigh and moan and belabor his faults, but it was entirely unacceptable that Hyacinth, whose knowledge of Michael was based entirely on rumor and innuendo, would make such a sweeping judgment.

"Believe what you will," Francesca said sharply, because there was no way she was going to allow Hyacinth to have the last word, "but he would never be late to a supper here. He holds Mother in far too high regard."

"What about his regard for you?" Hyacinth said.

Francesca glared at her sister, who was

161

smirking into her embroidery. "He —" No, she wasn't going to do this. She wasn't going to sit here and get into an argument with her younger sister, not when something might actually be wrong. Michael was, for all his wicked ways, faultlessly polite and considerate to the bone, or at least he had always been so in her presence. And he would never have arrived for supper — she glanced up at the mantel clock — over thirty minutes late. Not, at least, without sending word.

She stood, briskly smoothing down her dove gray skirts. "I am going to Kilmartin House," she announced.

"By yourself?" Violet asked.

"By myself," Francesca said firmly. "It is my home, after all. I hardly think that tongues will wag if I stop by for a quick visit."

"Yes, yes, of course," her mother said. "But don't stay too long."

"Mother, I am a widow. And I do not plan to spend the night. I merely intend to inquire as to Michael's welfare. I shall be just fine, I assure you."

Violet nodded, but from her expression, Francesca could see that she would have liked to have said more. It had been like this for years — Violet wanted to resume her role of mother hen to her young widowed daughter, but she held back, attempting to respect her independence.

She didn't always manage to resist interfering, but she tried, and Francesca was grateful for the effort.

"Do you want me to accompany you?" Hyacinth asked, her eyes lighting up.

"No!" Francesca said, surprise making her tone a bit more vehement than she'd intended it. "Why on earth would you want to?"

Hyacinth shrugged. "Curiosity. I'd like to meet the Merry Rake."

"You've met him," Eloise pointed out.

"Yes, but that was ages ago," Hyacinth said with a dramatic sigh, "before I understood what a rake was."

"You don't understand that now," Violet said sharply.

"Oh, but I —"

"You do *not*," Violet repeated, "understand what a rake is."

"Very well." Hyacinth turned to her mother with a sickly sweet smile. "I don't know what a rake is. I also don't know how to dress myself or wash my own teeth."

"I did see Polly helping her on with her evening gown last night," Eloise murmured from the sofa.

"No one can get into an evening gown on her own," Hyacinth shot back.

"I'm leaving," Francesca announced, even though she was quite certain no one was listening to her.

"What are you doing?" Hyacinth demanded.

Francesca stopped short until she realized that Hyacinth wasn't speaking to her.

"Just examining your teeth," Eloise said sweetly.

"Girls!" Violet exclaimed, although Francesca couldn't imagine that Eloise took too kindly to the generalization, being seven and twenty as she was.

And indeed she didn't, but Francesca took Eloise's irritation and subsequent rejoinder as an opportunity to slip out of the room and ask a footman to call up the carriage for her.

The streets were not very crowded; it was early yet, and the *ton* would not be heading out for parties and balls for at least another hour or two. The carriage moved swiftly through Mayfair, and in under a quarter of an hour Francesca was climbing the front steps of Kilmartin House in St. James's. As usual, a footman opened the door before she could even lift the knocker, and she hurried inside.

"Is Kilmartin here?" she asked, realizing with a small jolt of surprise that it was the first time she had referred to Michael as such. It was strange, she realized, and good, really, how naturally it had come to her lips. It was probably past time that they all grew used to the change. He was the earl now, and he'd never be plain Mr. Stirling again.

"I believe so," the footman replied. "He came in early this afternoon, and I was not made aware of his departure."

Francesca frowned, then gave a nod of dismissal before heading up the steps. If Michael was indeed at home, he must be upstairs; if he were down in his office, the footman would have noticed his presence.

She reached the second floor, then strode down the hall toward the earl's suite, her booted feet silent on the plush Aubusson carpet. "Michael?" she called out softly, as she approached his room. "Michael?"

There was no response, so she moved closer to his door, which she noticed was not quite all the way closed. "Michael?" she called again, only slightly louder. It wouldn't do to bellow his name through the house. Besides, if he was sleeping, she didn't wish to wake him. He was probably still tired from his long journey and had been too proud to indicate as such when Violet had invited him to supper.

Still nothing, so she pushed the door open a few additional inches. "Michael?"

She heard something. A rustle, maybe. Maybe a groan.

"Michael?"

"Frannie?"

It was definitely his voice, but it wasn't like anything she'd ever heard from his lips.

"Michael?" She rushed in to find him huddled in his bed, looking quite as sick as she'd ever seen another human being. John, of course, had never been sick. He'd merely gone to bed one evening and woken up dead.

So to speak.

"Michael!" she gasped. "What is wrong with you?"

"Oh, nothing much," he croaked. "Head cold, I imagine."

Francesca looked down at him with dubious eyes. His dark hair was plastered to his forehead, his skin was flushed and mottled, and the level of heat radiating from the bed quite took her breath away.

Not to mention that he smelled sick. It was that awful, sweaty, slightly putrid smell, the sort that, if it had a color, would

166

surely be vomitous green. Francesca reached out and touched his forehead, recoiling instantly at the heat of it.

"This is *not* a head cold," she said sharply.

His lips stretched into a hideous approximation of a smile. "A really bad head cold?"

"Michael Stuart Stirling!"

"Good God, you sound like my mother."

She didn't particularly feel like his mother, especially not after what had happened in the park, and it was almost a bit of a relief to see him so feeble and unattractive. It took the edge off whatever it was she'd been feeling earlier that afternoon.

"Michael, what is wrong with you?"

He shrugged, then buried himself deeper under the covers, his entire body shaking from the exertion of it.

"Michael!" She reached out and grabbed his shoulder. None too gently, either. "Don't you dare try your usual tricks on me. I know exactly how you operate. You always pretend that nothing matters, that water rolls off your back —"

"It does roll off my back," he mumbled. "Yours as well. Simple science, really."

"Michael!" She would have smacked

him if he weren't so ill. "You will not attempt to minimize this, do you understand
me? I insist that you tell me right now what
is wrong with you!"

"I'll be better tomorrow," he said.

"Oh, *right*," Francesca said, with all the
sarcasm she could muster, which was, in
truth, quite a bit.

"I will," he insisted, restlessly shifting
positions, every movement punctuated
with a groan. "I'll be fine for tomorrow."

Something about the phrasing of his
words struck Francesca as profoundly odd.
"And what about the day after that?" she
asked, her eyes narrowing.

A harsh chuckle emerged from somewhere under the covers. "Why, then I'll be
sick as a dog again, of course."

"Michael," she said again, dread forcing
her voice low, "what is wrong with you?"

"Haven't you guessed?" He poked his
head back out from under the sheet, and
he looked so ill she wanted to cry. "I have
malaria."

"Oh, my God," Francesca breathed, actually backing up a step. "Oh, my God."

"First time I've ever heard you blaspheme," he remarked. "Probably ought to
be flattered it's over me."

She had no idea how he could be so flip

at such a time. "Michael, I —" She reached out, then didn't reach out, unsure of what to do.

"Don't worry," he said, huddling closer into himself as his body was wracked with another wave of shudders. "You can't catch it from me."

"I can't?" She blinked. "I mean, of course I can't." And even if she could, that ought not have stopped her from nursing him. He was Michael. He was . . . well, it seemed difficult precisely to define what he was to her, but they had an unbreakable bond, they two, and it seemed that four years and thousands of miles had done little to diminish it.

"It's the air," he said in a tired voice. "You have to breathe the putrid air to catch it. It's why they call it malaria. If you could get it from another person, we lot would have infected all of England by now."

She nodded at his explanation. "Are you . . . are you . . ." She couldn't ask it; she didn't know how.

"No," he said. "At least they don't think so."

She felt herself sag with relief, and she had to sit down. She couldn't imagine a world without him. Even while he'd been gone, she'd always known he was *there*, sharing the same planet with her, walking the same earth. And even in those early days following John's death, when she'd hated him for leaving her, even when she'd been so angry with him that she wanted to cry — she had taken some comfort in the knowledge that he was alive and well, and would return to her in an instant, if ever she asked it of him.

He was here. He was alive. And with John gone . . . Well, she didn't know how anyone could expect her to lose them both.

He shivered again, violently.

"Do you need medicine?" she asked, snapping to attention. "Do you *have* medicine?"

"Took it already," he chattered.

But she had to do *some*thing. She wasn't self-hating enough to think that there had been anything she could have done to prevent John's death — even in the worst of her grief she hadn't gone down *that* road — but she had always hated that the whole thing had happened in her absence. It was, in truth, the one momentous thing John had ever done without her. And even if Michael was only sick, and not dying, she was not going to allow him to suffer alone.

"Let me get you another blanket," she

said. Without waiting for his reply, she rushed through the connecting door to her own suite and pulled the coverlet off her bed. It was rose pink and would most likely offend his masculine sensibilities once he reached a state of sensibility, but that, she decided, was *his* problem.

When she returned to his room, he was so still she thought he'd fallen asleep, but he managed to rouse himself enough to say thank you as she tucked the blanket over him.

"What else can I do?" she asked, pulling a wooden chair to the side of his bed and sitting down.

"Nothing."

"There must be something," she insisted. "Surely we're not meant to merely wait this out."

"We're meant," he said weakly, "to merely wait this out."

"I can't believe that's true."

He opened one eye. "Do you mean to challenge the entire medical establishment?"

She ground her teeth together and hunched over in her chair. "Are you certain you don't need more medicine?"

He shook his head, then moaned at the exertion of it. "Not for another few hours."

"Where is it?" she asked. If the only thing she could truly do was to locate the medication and be ready to dispense it, then by God, she would at least do that.

He moved his head slightly to the left. Francesca followed the motion toward a small table across the room, where a medicinal bottle sat atop a folded newspaper. She immediately rose and retrieved it, reading the label as she walked back to her chair. "Quinine," she murmured. "I've heard of that."

"Miracle medicine," Michael said. "Or so they say."

Francesca looked at him dubiously.

"Just look at me," he said with a lopsided — and feeble — grin. "Proof positive."

She inspected the bottle again, watching the powder shift as she tilted it. "I remain unconvinced."

One of his shoulders attempted to move in a blithe gesture. "I'm not dead."

"That's not funny."

"No, it's the *only* funny thing," he corrected. "We've got to take our laughter where we can. Just think, if I died, the title would go to — how does Janet always put it — that —"

"Awful Debenham side of the family," they finished together, and Francesca couldn't believe it, but she actually smiled.

He could always make her smile.

She reached out and took his hand. "We will get through this," she said.

He nodded, and then he closed his eyes.

But just when she thought he was asleep, he whispered, "It's better with you here."

The next morning Michael was feeling somewhat refreshed, and if not quite his usual self, then at least a damn sight better than he'd been the night before. Francesca, he was horrified to realize, was still in the wooden chair at his bedside, her head tilted drunkenly to the side. She looked uncomfortable in every way a body *could* look uncomfortable, from the way she was perched in the chair to the awkward angle of her neck and the strange spiral twist of her torso.

But she was asleep. Snoring, even, which he found rather endearing. He'd never pictured her snoring, and sad to say, he had imagined her asleep more times than he cared to count.

He supposed it had been too much to hope that he could hide his illness from her; she was far too perceptive and certainly far too nosy. And even though he would have preferred that she didn't worry over him, the truth was, he'd been comforted by her presence the night before. He shouldn't have been, or at least he shouldn't have allowed himself to be, but he just couldn't help it.

He heard her stir and rolled to his side to get a better look. He had never seen her wake up, he realized. He wasn't certain why he found that so strange; it wasn't as if he'd been privy to many of her private moments before. Maybe it was because in all of his daydreams, in all of his fantasies, he'd never quite pictured this — the low rumbling from deep in her throat as she shifted position, the small sigh of sound when she yawned, or even the delicate ballet of her eyelids as they fluttered open.

She was beautiful.

He'd known that, of course, had known that for years, but never before had he felt it quite so profoundly, quite so deeply in his bones.

It wasn't her hair, that rich, lush wave of chestnut that he was rarely so privileged as to see down. And it wasn't even her eyes, so radiantly blue that men had been moved to write poetry — much, Michael recalled, to John's everlasting amusement. It wasn't even in the shape of her face or the structure of her bones; if that were the case, he'd have been obsessed with the loveliness of all the Bridgerton girls; such peas in a pod they were, at least on the outside.

It was something in the way she moved.

Something in the way she breathed.

Something in the way she merely *was*.

And he didn't think he was ever going to get over it.

"Michael," she murmured, rubbing the sleep from her eyes.

"Good morning," he said, hoping she'd mistake the roughness in his voice for exhaustion.

"You look better."

"I feel better."

She swallowed and paused before she said, "You're used to this."

He nodded. "I wouldn't go so far as to say that I don't mind the illness, but yes, I'm used to it. I know what to do."

"How long will this continue?"

"It's hard to say. I'll get fevers every other day until I just . . . stop. A week in total, maybe two. Three if I'm fiendishly unlucky."

"And then what?"

He shrugged. "Then I wait and hope it never happens again."

"It can do that?" She sat up straight.

"Just never come back?"

"It's a strange, fickle disease."

Her eyes narrowed. *"Don't* say it's like a woman."

"Hadn't even occurred to me until you brought it up."

Her lips tightened slightly, then relaxed as she asked, "How long has it been since your last . . ." She blinked. "What do you call them?"

He shrugged. "I call them attacks. Certainly feels like one. And it's been six months."

"Well, that's good!" She caught her lower lip between her teeth. "Isn't it?"

"Considering it had only been three before that, yes, I think so."

"How often has this happened?"

"This is the third time. All in all, it's not too bad compared with what I've seen."

"Am I meant to take solace in that?"

"I do," he said bluntly. "Model of Christian virtue that I am."

She reached out abruptly and touched his forehead. "You're much cooler," she remarked.

"Yes, I will be. It's a remarkably consistent disease. Well, at least when you're in the midst of it. It would be nice if I knew when I might expect an onset."

"And you'll really have another fever in a day's time? Just like that?"

"Just like that," he confirmed.

She seemed to consider that for a few moments, then said, "You won't be able to hide this from your family, of course."

He actually tried to sit up. "For God's sake, Francesca, *don't* tell my mother and —"

"They're expected any day now," she cut in. "When I left Scotland, they said they would be only a week behind me, and knowing Janet, that really means only three days. Do you truly expect them not to notice that you're rather conveniently —"

"Inconveniently," he cut in acerbically.

"Whichever," she said sharply. "Do you really think they won't notice that you're sick as death every other day? For heaven's sake, Michael, do credit them with a bit of intelligence."

"Very well," he said, slumping back against the pillows. "But no one else. I have no wish to become the freak of London."

"You're hardly the first person to be stricken with malaria."

"I don't want anyone's pity," he bit off. "Most especially yours."

She drew back as if struck, and of course

177

he felt like an ass.

"Forgive me," he said. "That came out wrong."

She glared at him.

"I don't want your pity," he said repentantly, "but your care and your good wishes are most welcome."

Her eyes didn't meet his, but he could tell that she was trying to decide if she believed him.

"I mean it," he said, and he didn't have the energy to try to cover the exhaustion in his voice. "I am glad you were here. I have been through this before."

She looked over sharply, as if she were asking a question, but for the life of him, he didn't know what.

"I have been through this before," he said again, "and this time was . . . different. Better. Easier." He let out a long breath, relieved to have found the correct word. "Easier. It was easier."

"Oh." She shifted in her chair. "I'm . . . glad."

He glanced over at the windows. They were covered with heavy drapes, but he could see glimmers of sunlight peeking in around the sides. "Won't your mother be worried about you?"

"Oh, *no!*" Francesca yelped, jumping to

her feet so quickly that her hand slammed into the bedside table. "Ow ow *ow*."

"Are you all right?" Michael inquired politely, since it was quite clear she'd done herself no real harm.

"Oh . . ." She was shaking her hand out, trying to stem the pain. "I'd forgotten all about my mother. She was expecting me back last night."

"Didn't you send her a note?"

"I did," she said. "I told her you were ill, but she wrote back and said she would stop by in the morning to offer her assistance. What time is it? Do you have a clock? Of course you have a clock." She turned frantically to the small mantel clock over the fireplace.

It had been John's room; it still was John's room, in so many ways. Of course she'd know where the clock was.

"It's only eight," she said with a relieved sigh. "Mother never rises before nine unless there is an emergency, and hopefully she won't count this as one. I tried not to sound too panicked in my note."

Knowing Francesca, it would have been worded with all the coolheaded calmness she was known for. Michael smiled. She'd probably lied and said she'd hired a nurse.

"There's no need to panic," he said.

She turned to him with agitated eyes. "You said you didn't want anyone to know you had malaria."

His lips parted. He had never dreamed that she would hold his wishes quite so close to her heart. "You would keep this from your mother?" he asked softly.

"Of course. It is your decision to tell her, not mine."

It was really quite touching, rather tender even —

"I think you're insane," she added sharply.

Well, maybe tender wasn't quite the right word.

"But I will honor your wishes." She planted her hands on her hips and regarded him with what could only be described as vexation. "How could you even think I would do otherwise?"

"I have no idea," he murmured.

"Really, Michael," she grumbled. "I do not know what is wrong with you."

"Swampy air?" he tried to joke.

She shot him A Look. Capitalized.

"I'm going back to my mother's," she said, pulling on her short gray boots. "If I don't, you can be sure she will show up here with the entire faculty of the Royal College of Physicians in tow."

He lifted a brow. "Is that what she did whenever you took ill?"

She let out a little sound that was half snort, half grunt, and all irritation. "I will be back soon. Don't go anywhere."

He lifted his hands, gesturing somewhat sarcastically to the sickbed.

"Well, I wouldn't put it past you," she muttered.

"Your faith in my superhuman strength is touching."

She paused at the door. "I swear, Michael, you make the most annoying deathly ill patient I have ever met."

"I live to entertain you!" he called out as she was walking down the hall, and he was quite certain that if she'd had something to throw at the door, she would have done so. With great vigor.

He settled back down against his pillows and smiled. He might make an annoying patient, but she was a crotchety nurse.

Which was just fine with him.

Chapter 9

. . . it is possible that our letters have crossed in the mail, but it does seem more likely that you simply do not wish to correspond. I accept that and wish you well. I shan't bother you again. I hope you know that I am listening, should you ever change your mind.

*— from the Earl of Kilmartin
to the Countess of Kilmartin,
eight months after his arrival in India*

It wasn't easy hiding his illness. The *ton* didn't present a problem; Michael simply turned down all of his invitations, and Francesca put it about that he wished to settle in at his new home before taking his place in society.

The servants were more difficult. They talked, of course, and often to servants from other households, so Francesca had had to make sure that only the most loyal retainers were privy to what went on in Michael's sickroom. It was tricky, especially since she wasn't even officially living at Kilmartin House, at least not until Janet and Helen arrived, which Francesca fervently hoped was soon.

But the hardest part, the people who were the most fiendishly curious and difficult to keep in the dark, had to be Francesca's family. It had never been easy maintaining a secret within the Bridgerton household, and keeping one from the whole lot of them was, to put it simply, a bloody nightmare.

"Why do you go over there every day?" Hyacinth asked over breakfast.

"I live there," Francesca replied, taking a bite of a muffin, which any reasonable person would have taken as a sign that she did not wish to converse.

Hyacinth, however, had never been known to be reasonable. "You live here," she pointed out.

Francesca swallowed, then took a sip of tea, the delay intended to preserve her composed exterior. "I sleep here," she said coolly.

"Isn't that the definition of where you live?"

Francesca slathered more jam on her

muffin. "I'm eating, Hyacinth."

Her youngest sister shrugged. "So am I, but it doesn't prevent me from carrying on an intelligent conversation."

"I'm going to kill her," Francesca said to no one in particular. Which was probably a good thing, as there was no one else present.

"Who are you talking to?" Hyacinth demanded.

"God," Francesca said baldly. "And I do believe I have been given divine leave to murder you."

"Hmmph," was Hyacinth's response. "If it was that easy, I'd have asked permission to eliminate half the *ton* years ago."

Francesca decided just then that not all of Hyacinth's statements required a rejoinder. In fact, few of them did.

"Oh, Francesca!" came Violet's voice, thankfully interrupting the conversation. "There you are."

Francesca looked up to see her mother entering the breakfast room, but before she could say a word, Hyacinth piped up with, "Francesca was just about to kill me."

"Excellent timing on my part, then," Violet said, taking her seat. She turned to Francesca. "Are you planning to go over to Kilmartin House this morning?"

Francesca nodded. "I live there."

"I think she lives here," Hyacinth said, adding a liberal dose of sugar to her tea.

Violet ignored her. "I believe I will accompany you."

Francesca nearly dropped her fork. "Why?"

"I should like to see Michael," Violet said with a delicate shrug. "Hyacinth, will you please pass me the muffins?"

"I'm not sure what his plans are today," Francesca said quickly. Michael had had an attack the night before — his fourth malarial fever, to be precise, and they were hoping it would be the last of the cycle. But even though he would be much recovered by now, he would still most likely look dreadful. His skin — thank God — wasn't jaundiced, which Michael had told her was often a sign that the sickness was progressing to its fatal stage, but he still had that awful sickly air to him, and Francesca knew that if her mother caught one glimpse of him she would be horrified. And furious.

Violet Bridgerton did not like to be kept in the dark. Especially when it pertained to a matter about which one could use the term "life and death" without being accused of hyperbole.

185

"If he's not available I will simply turn around and go home," Violet said. "Jam please, Hyacinth."

"I'll come, too," Hyacinth said.

Oh, *God*. Francesca's knife skittered right across her muffin. She was going to have to drug her sister. It was the only solution.

"You don't mind if I come along, too, do you?" Hyacinth asked Violet.

"Didn't you have plans with Eloise?" Francesca said quickly.

Hyacinth stopped, thought, blinked a few times. "I don't think so."

"Shopping? At the milliner?"

Hyacinth took another moment to run through her memory. "No, in fact I'm quite certain I don't. I just purchased a new bonnet last week. Lovely one, actually. Green, with the most cunning ecru trim." She glanced down at her toast, regarded it for a moment, then reached for the marmalade. "I'm weary of shopping," she added.

"No woman is ever weary of shopping," Francesca said, a touch desperately.

"This woman is. Besides, the earl —" Hyacinth cut herself off, turning to her mother. "May I call him Michael?"

"You'll have to ask him," Violet replied,

taking a bite of eggs.

Hyacinth turned back to Francesca. "He's been back in London an entire week, and I haven't even seen him. My friends have been asking me about him, and I don't have anything to say."

"It's not polite to gossip, Hyacinth," Violet said.

"It isn't gossip," Hyacinth retorted. "It's the honest dissemination of information."

Francesca actually felt her chin drop. "Mother," she said, shaking her head, "you really should have stopped at seven."

"Children, you mean?" Violet asked, sipping at her tea. "Sometimes I do wonder."

"Mother!" Hyacinth exclaimed.

Violet just smiled at her. "Salt?"

"It took her eight tries to get it right," Hyacinth announced, thrusting the salt cellar at her mother with a decided lack of grace.

"And does that mean that you, too, hope to have eight children?" Violet inquired sweetly.

"*God* no," Hyacinth said. With great feeling. And neither she nor Francesca could quite resist a chuckle after that.

"It's not polite to blaspheme, Hyacinth," Violet said, in much the same tone she'd used to tell her not to gossip.

"Why don't we stop by shortly after noon?" Violet asked Francesca, once the moment of levity had petered out.

Francesca glanced up at the clock. That would give her barely an hour to make Michael presentable. And her mother had said *we*. As in more than one person. As in she was actually going to bring Hyacinth, who had the capacity to turn any awkward situation into a living nightmare.

"I'll go now," Francesca blurted out, standing up quickly. "To see if he's available."

To her surprise, her mother stood also. "I will walk you to the door," Violet said. Firmly.

"Er, you will?"

"Yes."

Hyacinth started to rise.

"Alone," Violet said, without even giving Hyacinth a glance.

Hyacinth sat back down. Even she was wise enough not to argue when her mother was combining her serene smile with a steely tone.

Francesca allowed her mother to precede her out of the room, and they walked in silence until they reached the front hall, where she waited for a footman to retrieve her coat.

"Is there something you wish to tell me?" Violet asked.

"I don't know what you mean."

"I think you do."

"I assure you," Francesca said, giving her mother her most innocent look, "I don't."

"You have been spending a great deal of time at Kilmartin House," Violet said.

"I live there," Francesca pointed out, for what felt like the hundredth time.

"Not right now you don't, and I worry that people will talk."

"No one has said a word about it," Francesca returned. "I haven't seen a thing in the gossip columns, and if people were talking about it, I'm sure that one of us would have heard by now."

"Just because people are keeping quiet today doesn't mean they will do so tomorrow," Violet said.

Francesca let out an irritated exhale. "It's not as if I'm a never-married virgin."

"Francesca!"

Francesca crossed her arms. "I'm sorry to speak so frankly, Mother, but it is true."

The footman arrived just then with Francesca's coat and informed her that the carriage would be in front momentarily. Violet waited until he stepped outside to await its arrival, then turned to Francesca and asked, "What, precisely, is your relationship to the earl?"

Francesca gasped. "Mother!"

"It is not a silly question," Violet said.

"It is the silliest — no, quite the stupidest — question I have ever heard. Michael is my cousin!"

"He was your husband's cousin," Violet corrected.

"And he was my cousin as well," Francesca said sharply. "And my friend. Good heavens, of all people . . . I can't even imagine . . . Michael!"

But the truth was, she *could* imagine. Michael's illness had kept it all at bay; she'd been so busy caring for him and keeping him well that she'd managed to avoid thinking about that jolting moment in the park, when she'd looked at him and something had sparked to life within her.

Something she had been quite certain had died inside of her four years earlier.

But hearing her *mother* bring it up . . . Good God, it was mortifying. There was no way, no earthly way that she could feel an attraction to Michael. It was wrong. It was really wrong. It was . . . well, it was just *wrong*. There wasn't another word that described it better.

"Mother," Francesca said, keeping her voice carefully even, "Michael has not been feeling well. I told you that."

"Seven days is quite a long time for a head cold."

"Perhaps it is something from India," Francesca said. "I don't know. I think he is almost recovered. I have been helping him get settled here in London. He has been gone a very long time and as you've noted, he has many new responsibilities as the earl. I thought it my duty to help him with all of this." She looked at her mother with a resolute expression, rather pleased with her speech. But Violet just said, "I will see you in an hour," and walked away.

Leaving Francesca feeling very panicked indeed.

Michael was enjoying a few moments of peace and quiet — not that he'd been bereft of quiet, but malaria did little to allow a body peace — when Francesca burst through his bedroom door, wild-eyed and out of breath.

"You have two choices," she said, or rather, heaved.

"Only two?" he murmured, even though he hadn't a clue what she was talking about.

"Don't make jokes."

He hauled himself into a sitting position. "Francesca?" he asked gingerly, since it was his experience that one should always proceed with caution when a female was in a state. "Are you quite all —"

"My mother is coming," she said.

"Here?"

She nodded.

It wasn't an ideal situation but hardly something deserving of Francesca's feverish demeanor. "Why?" he inquired politely.

"She thinks —" She stopped, catching her breath. "She thinks — Oh, heavens, you won't believe it."

When she didn't expound upon this any further, he widened his eyes and held out his hands in an impatient gesture, as if to say — *Care to elaborate?*

"She thinks," Francesca said, shuddering as she turned to him, "that we are conducting an affair."

"After only a week back in London," he murmured thoughtfully. "I'm faster than I imagined."

"How can you joke about this?" Francesca demanded.

"How can you not?" he returned. But of course she could never laugh about such a thing. To her it was unthinkable. To him it was . . .

Well, something else entirely.

"I am horrified," she declared.

Michael just offered her a smile and a shrug, even though he was starting to feel a little pricked. Naturally, he did not expect Francesca to think of him in such a manner, but a reaction of horror didn't exactly make a fellow feel *good* about his manly prowess.

"What are my two choices?" he asked abruptly.

She just stared at him.

"You said I have two choices."

She blinked, and would have looked rather adorably befuddled if he weren't a bit too annoyed with her ire to credit her with anything that charitable. "I . . . don't recall," she finally said. "Oh, my heavens," she moaned. "What am I to do?"

"Settling down might be a good beginning," he said, sharply enough to make her head jerk back in his direction. "Stop and think, Frannie. This is *us*. Your mother will realize how foolish she's being once she takes the time to think about it."

"That's what I told her," she replied fervently. "I mean, for goodness' sake. Can you imagine?"

He could, actually, which had always been a bit of a problem.

"It is the most unfathomable thing," Francesca muttered, pacing across the room. "As if I —" She turned, gesturing to him with overblown motions. "As if *you* —" She stopped, planted her hands on her hips, then clearly gave up on trying to hold still and began to pace anew. "How could she even consider such a thing?"

"I don't believe I have ever seen you quite so put out," Michael commented.

She halted in her tracks and stared at him as if he were an imbecile. With two heads.

And maybe a tail.

"You really ought to endeavor to calm down," he said, even though he knew his words would have the exact opposite effect. Women hated to be told to calm down, especially women like Francesca.

"Calm down?" she echoed, turning on him as if possessed by an entire spectrum of furies. "Calm *down?* Good God, Michael, are you still feverish?"

"Not at all," he said coolly.

"Do you understand what I'm saying to you?"

"Quite," he bit off, about as politely as any man could after having his manhood impugned.

"It's insane," she said. "Simply insane. I mean, look at you."

Really, she might as well just grab a knife and apply it to his ballocks. "You know, Francesca," he said with studied mildness, "there are a lot of women in London who would be rather pleased to be, how did you say it, conducting an affair with me."

Her mouth, which had been hanging open after her latest outburst, snapped shut.

He lifted his brows and leaned back against his pillows. "Some would call it a privilege."

She glared at him.

"*Some* women," he said, knowing full well he should never bait her about such a subject, "might even engage in physical battle just for the mere opportunity —"

"Stop!" she snapped. "Good heavens, Michael, such an inflated view of your own prowess is not attractive."

"I'm told it's deserved," he said with a languid smile.

Her face burned red.

He rather enjoyed the sight. He might love her, but he hated what she did to him, and he was not so big of heart that he didn't occasionally take a bit of satisfaction in seeing her so tortured.

It was only a fraction of what *he* felt on a day-to-day basis, after all.

"I have no wish to hear about your amorous exploits," Francesca said stiffly.

"Funny, you used to ask about them all the time." He paused, watching her squirm. "What was it you always asked me?"

"I don't —"

"Tell me something wicked," he said, using his best trying-to-sound-as-if-he'd-just-thought-of-it voice, when of course he never forgot anything she said to him. "Tell me something wicked," he said again, more slowly this time. "That was it. You rather liked me when I was wicked. You were always so curious about my exploits."

"That was before —"

"Before what, Francesca?" he asked.

There was an odd pause before she spoke. "Before this," she muttered. "Before now, before everything."

"I'm supposed to understand that?"

Her answer was merely a glare.

"Very well," he said, "I suppose I should get ready for your mother's visit. It shouldn't be too much of a problem."

Francesca regarded him dubiously. "But you look terrible."

"I knew there was a reason I loved you

so well," he said dryly. "One really needn't worry about falling into the sin of vanity with you about."

"Michael, be serious."

"Sadly, I am."

She scowled at him.

"I can rise to my feet now," he told her, "exposing you to parts of my body I would imagine you'd rather not see, or you can leave and await my glorious presence downstairs."

She fled.

Which puzzled him. The Francesca he knew didn't flee anything.

Nor, for that matter, would she have departed without at least making an attempt to get the last word.

But most of all, he couldn't believe she had let him get away with calling himself glorious.

Francesca never did have to suffer a visit from her mother. Not twenty minutes after she left Michael's bedchamber, a note arrived from Violet informing her that her brother Colin — who had been traveling in the Mediterranean for months — had just returned to London, and Violet would have to postpone her visit. Then, later that evening, much as Francesca had predicted at the onset of Michael's attack, Janet and Helen arrived in London, assuaging Violet's concerns about Francesca and Michael and their lack of a chaperone.

The mothers — as Francesca and Michael had long since taken to calling them — were thrilled at Michael's unexpected appearance, although one look at his sickly features propelled both of them into maternal tizzies of concern that had forced Michael to take Francesca aside and beg her not to leave him alone with either of the two ladies. In truth, the timing of their arrival was rather fortuitous, as Michael had a comparatively healthy day in their presence before being struck by another raging fever. Francesca had taken them aside before the next expected attack and explained the nature of the illness, so by the time they saw the malaria in all its horrible glory, they were prepared.

And unlike Francesca, they were more agreeable — no, downright eager — to keep his malady a secret. It was difficult to imagine that a wealthy and handsome earl might not be considered an excellent catch by the unmarried ladies of London, but malaria was never a mark in one's favor when looking for a wife.

And if there was one thing Janet and

Helen were determined to see before the year was out, it was Michael standing at the front of a church, his ring firmly on the finger of a new countess.

Francesca was actually relieved to sit back and listen to the mothers harangue him about getting married. At least it took their attention off of *her*. She had no idea how they would react to her own marital plans — she rather imagined they would be happy for her — but the last thing she wanted was two more matchmaking mamas attempting to pair her up with every poor pathetic bachelor on the Marriage Mart.

Good heavens, she had enough to put up with, with her *own* mother, who was surely not going to be able to resist the temptation to meddle once Francesca made clear her desire to find a husband this year.

And so Francesca moved back to Kilmartin House, and the entire Stirling household turned itself into a little cocoon, with Michael declining all invitations with the promise that he would be out and about once he settled in from his long journey. The three ladies did occasionally go out in society, and although Francesca had expected questions about the new earl, even she was unprepared for the volume and frequency.

Everyone, it seemed, was mad for the Merry Rake, especially now that he'd shrouded himself with mystery.

Oh, and inherited an earldom. Mustn't forget that. Or the hundred thousand pounds that went with it.

Francesca shook her head as she thought about it. Truly Mrs. Radcliffe herself couldn't have devised a more perfect hero. It was going to be a madhouse once he was recovered.

And then, suddenly, he was.

Very well, Francesca supposed it wasn't that sudden; the fevers had been steadily decreasing in severity and duration. But it did seem that one day he still looked wan and pale, and the next he was his regular hale and hearty self, prowling about the house, eager to escape into the sunshine.

"Quinine," Michael said with a lazy shrug when she remarked upon his changed appearance at breakfast. "I'd take the stuff six times a day if it didn't taste so damned foul."

"Language, please, Michael," his mother murmured, spearing a sausage with her fork.

"Have you tasted the quinine, Mother?" he asked.

"Of course not."

"Taste it," he suggested, "and then we'll see how *your* language compares."

Francesca chuckled under her napkin.

"*I* tasted it," Janet announced.

All eyes turned to her. "You did?" Francesca asked. Even she hadn't been so daring. The smell alone had been enough for her to keep the bottle firmly corked at all times.

"Of course," Janet replied. "I was curious." She turned to Helen. "It really is foul."

"Worse than that awful concoction Cook made us take last year for the, er . . ." Helen gave Janet a look that clearly meant *you know what I mean*.

"Much worse," Janet affirmed.

"Did you reconstitute it?" Francesca asked. The powder was meant to be mixed with purified water, but she supposed that Janet might have simply put a bit on her tongue.

"Of course. Aren't I supposed to?"

"Some people like to mix it with gin," Michael said.

Helen shuddered.

"It could hardly be worse than on its own," Janet said.

"Still," Helen said, "if one is going to

201

mix it with spirits, one might at least choose a nice whisky."

"And spoil the whisky?" Michael queried, helping himself to several spoonfuls of eggs.

"It can't be that bad," Helen said.

"It is," Michael and Janet said in unison.

"It's true," Janet added. "I can't imagine ruining a fine whisky that way. Gin would be a happy medium."

"Have you even tasted gin?" Francesca asked. It was not, after all, considered a suitable spirit for the upper classes, most especially women.

"Once or twice," Janet admitted.

"And here I thought I knew everything about you," Francesca murmured.

"I have my secrets," Janet said airily.

"This is a very odd conversation for the breakfast table," Helen stated.

"True enough," Janet agreed. She turned to her nephew. "Michael, I am most pleased to see you up and about and looking so fine and healthy."

He inclined his head, thanking her for the compliment.

She dabbed the corners of her mouth daintily with her napkin. "But now you must attend to your responsibilities as the earl."

He groaned.

"Don't be so petulant," Janet said. "No one is going to hang you up by your thumbs. All I was going to say is that you must go to the tailor and make sure you have proper evening clothes."

"Are you certain I can't donate my thumbs instead?"

"They're lovely thumbs," Janet replied, "but I do believe they'd better serve all of humanity attached to your hands."

Michael met her eyes with a steady stare. "Let's see. I have on my schedule today — my first since rising from my sickbed, I might add — a meeting with the prime minister concerning my assumption of my seat in parliament, a meeting with the family solicitor so that I might review the state of our financial holdings, and an interview with our primary estate manager, who I'm told has come down to London with the express purpose of discussing the state of all seven of our family properties. At which point, might I inquire, do you wish me to squeeze in a visit to the tailor?"

The three ladies were speechless.

"Perhaps I should inform the prime minister that I shall have to move him until Thursday?" he asked mildly.

"When did you make all of these appointments?" Francesca asked, a bit ashamed that she was so surprised at his diligence.

"Did you think I'd spent the last fortnight staring at the ceiling?"

"Well, no," she replied, although in truth she didn't know what she'd thought he'd been doing. Reading, she supposed. That's what she would have done.

When no one said anything further, Michael pushed back his chair. "If you ladies will excuse me," he said, setting his napkin down, "I believe we have established that I have a busy day ahead of me."

But he'd not even risen from his seat before Janet said quietly, "Michael? The tailor."

He froze.

Janet smiled at him sweetly. "Tomorrow would be perfectly acceptable."

Francesca rather thought she heard his teeth grind.

Janet just tilted her head ever so slightly to the side. "You do need new evening clothes. Surely you would not dream of missing Lady Bridgerton's birthday ball?"

Francesca quickly forked a bite of eggs into her mouth so that he wouldn't catch her grinning. Janet was devious in the extreme. Her mother's birthday party was the one event that Michael would feel positively obligated to attend. Anything else he could shrug off without a care.

But Violet?

Francesca didn't *think* so.

"When is it?" he sighed.

"April eleventh," Francesca said sweetly. "Everyone will be there."

"Everyone?" he echoed.

"All the Bridgertons."

He brightened visibly.

"And everyone else," she added with a shrug.

He looked at her sharply. "Define 'everyone.'"

Her eyes met his. "Everyone."

He slumped in his seat. "Am I to get no reprieve?"

"Of course you are," Helen said. "You did, in fact. Last week. We called it malaria."

"And here I was looking forward to health," he muttered.

"Fear not," Janet said. "You will have a fine time, I'm sure."

"And perhaps meet a lovely lady," Helen put in helpfully.

"Ah, yes," Michael murmured, "lest we forget the real purpose of my life."

"It's not such a bad purpose," Francesca said, unable to resist the small chance to tease him.

"Oh, really?" he asked, swinging his head around to face her. His eyes settled on hers with startling accuracy, leaving Francesca with the extremely unpleasant sensation that perhaps she shouldn't have provoked him.

"Er, really," she said, since she couldn't back down now.

"And what are *your* purposes?" he asked sweetly.

Out of the corner of her eye, Francesca could see Janet and Helen watching the exchange with avid and unconcealed curiosity.

"Oh, this and that," Francesca said with a blithe wave of her hand. "Presently, just to finish my breakfast. It is most delicious, wouldn't you agree?"

"Coddled eggs with a side portion of meddling mothers?"

"Don't forget your cousin as well," she said, kicking herself under the table as soon as the words left her lips. Everything about his demeanor screamed not to provoke him, but she just couldn't help it.

There was little in this world she enjoyed more than provoking Michael Stirling, and moments like this were simply too delicious to resist.

"And how will you be spending your

season?" Michael asked, tilting his head slightly into an obnoxiously patient expression.

"I imagine I'll begin by going to my mother's birthday party."

"And what will you be doing there?"

"Offering my felicitations."

"Is that all?"

"Well, I won't be inquiring after her age, if that's what you're asking," Francesca replied.

"Oh, no," Janet said, followed by Helen's equally fervent, "Don't do that."

All three ladies turned to Michael with identical expectant expressions. It was his turn to speak, after all.

"I'm leaving," he said, his chair scraping along the floor as he stood.

Francesca opened her mouth to say something provoking, since it was always her first inclination to tease him when he was in such a state, but she found herself without words.

Michael had changed.

It wasn't that he'd been irresponsible before. It was just that he'd been without responsibilities. And it hadn't really occurred to her how well he might rise to the occasion once he returned to England.

"Michael," she said, her soft voice instantly gaining his attention, "good luck with Lord Liverpool."

His eyes caught hers, and something flashed there. A hint of appreciation, maybe of gratitude.

Or maybe it was nothing so precise. Maybe it was just a wordless moment of understanding.

The sort she'd had with John.

Francesca swallowed, uncomfortable with this sudden realization. She reached for her tea with a slow and deliberate movement, as if her control over her body might extend to her mind as well.

What had just happened?

He was just Michael, wasn't he?

Just her friend, just her longtime confidant.

Wasn't that all?

Wasn't it?

Chapter 10

. . . .
— nothing more than hatchmarks,
caused by the tapping of
the Countess of Kilmartin's
pen against paper, two weeks after
the receipt of the Earl of Kilmartin's
third missive to her

"Is he here?"

"He's not here."

"Are you certain?"

"I'm quite certain."

"But he is coming?"

"He said he was."

"Oh. But when is he coming?"

"I'm sure I don't know."

"You don't?"

"No, I don't."

"Oh. Right. Well . . . Oh, look! I see my daughter. Lovely seeing you, Francesca."

Francesca rolled her eyes — not an affectation she espoused except under the most severe of circumstances — as she watched Mrs. Featherington, one of the *ton*'s most notorious gossips, toddle off toward her daughter Felicity, who was chatting amiably with a handsome, albeit untitled, young man at the edge of the ballroom.

The conversation would have been amusing if it hadn't been the seventh — no eighth, mustn't forget her own mother — time she had been subjected to it. And the conversation was always the same, truly down to the very word, save for the fact that not everyone knew her well enough to use her given name.

Once Violet Bridgerton had let it be known that the elusive Earl of Kilmartin would be making his reappearance at her birthday party — Well, Francesca was quite sure she would never be safe from interrogation again, at least not from anyone with any attachment to an unmarried female.

Michael was the catch of the season, and he hadn't even shown up yet.

"Lady Kilmartin!"

She looked up. Lady Danbury was coming her way. A more crotchety and outspoken old lady had never graced the ballrooms of London, but Francesca rather liked her, so she just smiled as the countess approached, noticing that the partygoers on either side of her quickly fled to parts unknown.

"Lady Danbury," Francesca said, "how nice to see you this evening. Are you enjoying yourself?"

Lady D thumped her cane against the ground for no apparent reason. "I'd enjoy myself a dashed sight more if someone would tell me how old your mother is."

"I wouldn't dare."

"Pfft. What's the fuss? It's not as if she's as old as I am."

"And how old are *you*?" Francesca asked, her tone as sweet as her smile was sly.

Lady D's wrinkled face cracked into a smile. "Heh heh heh, clever one you are. Don't think I'm going to tell *you*."

"Then surely you will understand if I exercise the same loyalty toward my mother."

"Hmmph," Lady Danbury grunted by way of a response, thumping her cane against the floor for emphasis. "What's the use of a birthday party if no one knows what we're celebrating?"

"The miracle of life and longevity?"

Lady Danbury snorted at that, then asked, "Where's that new earl of yours?"

My, she was blunt. "He's not *my* earl," Francesca pointed out.

"Well, he's more yours than anyone else's."

That much was probably true, although Francesca wasn't about to confirm it with Lady Danbury, so she just said, "I imagine his lordship would take exception to being labeled as anyone's but his own."

"His lordship, eh? That's rather formal, don't you think? Thought the two of you were friends."

"We are," Francesca said. But that did not mean she would bandy about his given name in public. Truly, it wouldn't do to stir up any rumors. Not if she needed to keep her reputation pristine in her search for a husband of her own. "He was my husband's closest confidant," she said pointedly. "They were like brothers."

Lady Danbury looked disappointed with Francesca's bland characterization of her relationship with Michael, but all she did was pinch her lips as she scanned the crowd. "This party needs some livening up," she muttered, tapping her cane again.

"Do try not to say that to my mother," Francesca murmured. Violet had spent weeks on the arrangements, and truly, no one could find exception with the party.

The lighting was soft and romantic, the music pure perfection, and even the food was good — no small achievement at a London ball. Francesca had already enjoyed two éclairs and had spent the time since plotting how to make her way back to the table of refreshments without appearing a complete glutton.

Except that she kept getting waylaid by inquisitive matrons.

"Oh, it's not your mother's fault," Lady D said. "She's not to blame for the overpopulation of dullards in our society. Good God, she bred eight of you, and not an idiot in the lot." She gave Francesca a pertinent glance. "That's a compliment, by the way."

"I'm touched."

Lady Danbury's mouth clamped together into a frighteningly serious line. "I'm going to have to do something," she said.

"About what?"

"The party."

An awful sensation took hold in Francesca's stomach. She'd never known Lady Danbury to actually ruin someone else's fête, but the old lady was clever enough to do some serious damage if she put her mind to it. "What, exactly, do you plan to do?" Francesca asked, trying to keep her voice free of panic.

"Oh, don't look at me like I'm about to kill your cat."

"I don't have a cat."

"Well, *I* do, and I assure you, I'd be mad as Hades if anyone tried to harm him."

"Lady Danbury, what on *earth* are you talking about?"

"Oh, I don't know," the old lady said with an irritated wave of her hand. "You can be sure that if I did, I'd have done it already. But I certainly wouldn't cause a scene at your mother's party." She lifted her chin sharply in the air and gifted Francesca with a disdainful sniff. "As if I would do anything to hurt your dear mama's feelings."

Somehow that did little to assuage Francesca's apprehension. "Right. Well, whatever you do, please be careful."

"Francesca Stirling," Lady D said with a sly smile, "are you worried for my welfare?"

"You, I have no qualms about whatsoever," Francesca replied pertly, "it's the rest of us for whom I tremble."

Lady Danbury let out a cackle of laughter. "Well said, Lady Kilmartin. I do believe you deserve a reprieve. From me," she added, in case Francesca didn't grasp her meaning.

"You *are* my reprieve," Francesca muttered.

But Lady D obviously didn't hear her as she looked out over the crowd, because she sounded quite singleminded as she declared, "I do believe I shall go pester your brother."

"Which one?" Not that they all couldn't use a bit of torture.

"That one." She pointed toward Colin. "Hasn't he just returned from Greece?"

"Cyprus, actually."

"Greece, Cyprus, it's all the same to me."

"Not to them, I imagine," Francesca murmured.

"Who? You mean the Greeks?

"Or the Cypriots."

"Pfft. Well, if one of them chooses to show up tonight they can feel free to explain the difference. Until then, I shall wallow in my ignorance." And with that, Lady Danbury thumped her cane against the floor one last time before turning toward Colin and bellowing, "Mr. Bridgerton!"

Francesca watched with amusement as her brother tried desperately to pretend that he hadn't heard her. She was rather pleased that Lady D had chosen to torture Colin a bit — he undoubtedly deserved it — but now that she was on her own again, she realized that Lady Danbury had provided her with a rather effective defense against the multitude of matchmaking mamas who saw her as their only link to Michael.

Good God, she could see three of them approaching already.

Time to escape. Now. Francesca quickly turned on her heel and started walking toward her sister Eloise, who was easy to spot by the bright green of her dress. In truth, she would have much rather bypassed Eloise entirely and headed straight out the door, but if she was serious about this marriage business, then she had to circulate and let it be known she was in the market for a new husband.

Not that anyone was likely to care one way or another until Michael finally showed his face. Francesca could have announced her plan to move to dark Africa and take up cannibalism, and all anyone would have said was, "And will the earl be accompanying you?"

"Good evening!" Francesca said, joining the small group around her sister. It was all family — Eloise was chatting amiably with their two sisters-in-law, Kate and Sophie.

"Oh, hullo, Francesca," Eloise said. "Where's —"

"Don't *you* start."

"What's wrong?" Sophie asked, eyes all concern.

"If one more person asks me about Michael, I swear my head will explode."

"That would certainly change the tenor of the evening," Kate remarked.

"Not to mention the cleaning duties of the staff," Sophie added.

Francesca actually growled.

"Well, where *is* he?" Eloise demanded. "And don't look at me like —"

"— I'm trying to kill your cat?"

"I don't have a cat. What the devil are you talking about?"

Francesca just sighed. "I don't know. He said he would be here."

"If he's smart, he's probably hiding in the hall," Sophie said.

"Good God, you're probably right." Francesca could easily see him bypassing the ballroom entirely and ensconcing himself in the smoking saloon.

Away, in other words, from all females.

"It's still early," Kate put in helpfully.

"It doesn't feel early," Francesca grumbled. "I wish he'd just get here, so that people would stop asking me about him."

Eloise actually laughed, fiendish turncoat that she was. "Oh, my poor delusional Francesca," she said, "once he arrives the questions will redouble. They'll simply change from 'Where is he?' to 'Tell us more.' "

"I fear she's right," Kate said.

"Oh, God," Francesca groaned, looking for a wall to sag against.

"Did you just blaspheme?" Sophie asked, blinking in surprise.

Francesca sighed. "I seem to be doing quite a bit of it lately."

Sophie gave her a kindly look, then suddenly exclaimed, "You're wearing blue!"

Francesca looked down at her new evening gown. She was quite pleased with it actually, not that anyone had noticed besides Sophie. It was one of her favorite shades of blue, not quite royal and not quite marine. The gown was elegantly simple, with a neckline adorned with a softly draped swath of lighter blue silk. She felt like a princess in it, or if not a princess, then at the very least, not quite so much the untouchable widow.

"Are you out of mourning, then?" Sophie asked.

"Well, I've been out of mourning for a few years now," Francesca mumbled. Now that she had finally shrugged off her grays and lavenders, she felt a little silly for having clung to them for so long.

"We knew you were out and about," Sophie said, "but you never changed your clothing, and — Well, it's of no matter. I'm just so pleased to see you in blue!"

"Does this mean that you will consider remarrying?" Kate asked. "It *has* been four years."

Francesca winced. Trust Kate to get right to the point. But she couldn't keep her plans a secret forever, not if she wanted to meet with any success, so all she said was, "Yes."

For a moment no one spoke. And then of course, they spoke all at once, offering congratulations and advice and various other bits of nonsense that Francesca wasn't positive she wished to hear. But it was all said with the best and most loving of intentions, so she just smiled and nodded and accepted their good wishes.

And then Kate said, "We shall have to set this about, of course."

Francesca was aghast. "I beg your pardon?"

"The blue dress is an excellent signal of

your intentions," Kate explained, "but do you really think the men of London are perceptive enough to grasp it? Of course not," she said, answering her own question before anyone else could. "I could dye Sophie's hair to black, and most of them wouldn't notice a thing."

"Well, Benedict would notice," Sophie pointed out loyally.

"Yes, well, he's your husband, and besides that, he's a painter. He's trained to actually notice things. Most men —" Kate cut herself off, looking rather irritated with the turn in the conversation. "You do see my point, don't you?"

"Of course," Francesca murmured.

"The fact of the matter," Kate continued, "is that most of humanity has more hair than wit. If you wish for people to be aware that you are on the Marriage Mart, you shall have to make it quite clear. Or rather, we shall have to make it clear for you."

Francesca had horrible visions of her female relatives, chasing down men until the poor fellows ran screaming for the doors. "What, precisely, do you mean to do?"

"Oh, goodness, don't cast up your dinner."

"Kate!" Sophie exclaimed.

"Well, you must admit that she looked as if she were about to."

Sophie rolled her eyes. "Well, yes, but you needn't have remarked upon it."

"I enjoyed the comment," Eloise put in helpfully.

Francesca speared her with a glare, since she was feeling the need to give *some*one a dirty look, and it was always easiest to do so with one's blood relatives.

"We shall be masters of tact and discretion," Kate said.

"Trust us," Eloise added.

"Well, I certainly can't stop you," Francesca said.

She noticed that even Sophie did not contradict her.

"Very well," she said. "I am off to obtain one last éclair."

"I think they're gone," Sophie said, giving her a sympathetic look.

Francesca's heart sank. "The chocolate biscuits?"

"Gone as well."

"What's left?"

"The almond cake."

"The one that tasted like dust?"

"That's the one," Eloise put in. "It was the only dessert Mother didn't sample ahead of time. I warned her, of course, but no one ever listens to me."

Francesca felt herself deflate. Pathetic as she was, the promise of a sweet was the only thing keeping her going just then.

"Cheer up, Frannie," Eloise said, her chin lifting a notch as she looked out over the crowd. "I see Michael."

And sure enough, there he was. Standing on the other side of the room, looking sinfully elegant in his black evening kit. He was surrounded by women, which didn't surprise Francesca in the least. Half were the sorts who were pursuing him for marriage, either for themselves or their daughters.

The other half, Francesca noted, were young and married, and clearly pursuing him for something else entirely.

"I'd forgotten how handsome he was," Kate murmured.

Francesca glared at her.

"He's very tanned," Sophie added.

"He was in India," Francesca said. "Of course he's tanned."

"You're rather short of temper this evening," Eloise said.

Francesca schooled her features into an impassive mask. "I'm just weary of being asked about him, that's all. He's not my favorite topic of conversation."

"Did the two of you have a falling out?" Sophie inquired.

"No, of course not," Francesca replied, realizing belatedly that she'd given the wrong impression. "But I have done nothing but speak of him all evening. At this point I would be quite delighted to comment on the weather."

"Hmmm."

"Yes."

"Right. Of course."

Francesca had no idea who'd said what, especially when she realized that all four of them were just standing there staring at Michael and his bevy of women.

"He *is* handsome." Sophie sighed. "All that delicious black hair."

"Sophie!" Francesca exclaimed.

"Well, he is," Sophie said defensively. "And you didn't say anything to Kate when she made the same comment."

"You're both married," Francesca muttered.

"Does that mean *I* might comment upon his good looks?" Eloise asked. "Spinster that I am."

Francesca turned to her sister in disbelief. "Michael is the last man you'd want to marry."

"Why is that?" This came from Sophie,

but Francesca noticed that Eloise was listening closely for her answer as well.

"Because he's a terrible rake," Francesca said.

"Funny," Eloise murmured. "You flew quite off the handle when Hyacinth said the same thing a fortnight ago."

Trust Eloise to remember *every*thing. "Hyacinth didn't know what she was talking about," Francesca said. "She never does. And besides, we were talking about his punctuality, not his marriageability."

"And what renders him so unmarriageable?" Eloise asked.

Francesca leveled a serious stare at her older sister. Eloise was mad if she thought she should set her cap for Michael.

"Well?" Eloise prodded.

"He could never remain faithful to one woman," Francesca said, "and I doubt you'd be willing to put up with infidelities."

"No," Eloise murmured, "not unless he'd be willing to put up with severe bodily injury."

The four ladies fell silent at that, continuing their shameless perusal of Michael and his companions. He leaned down and murmured something in one of their ears, causing the lady in question to titter and blush, hiding her mouth behind her hand.

"He's quite a flirt," Kate said.

"A certain air about him," Sophie confirmed. "Those women haven't a chance."

He smiled at one of his companions then, a slow, liquid grin that caused even the Bridgerton women to sigh.

"Haven't we something better to do besides spy on Michael?" Francesca asked, disgusted.

Kate, Sophie, and Eloise looked at each other, blinking.

"No."

"No."

"I guess not," Kate concluded. "Not just now, anyway."

"You should go and talk to him," Eloise said, nudging Francesca with her elbow.

"Why on earth?"

"Because he's *here*."

"So are a hundred other men," Francesca replied, "all of whom I'd rather marry."

"I only see three I'd even consider promising to obey," Eloise muttered, "and I'm not even certain about them."

"Be that as it may," Francesca said, not wanting to grant Eloise the point, "my purpose here is to find a husband, so I hardly see how dancing attendance on Michael will be of any benefit."

"And I thought we were here to wish Mother a happy birthday," Eloise murmured.

Francesca glared at her. She and Eloise were the closest of all the Bridgertons in age — exactly one year apart. Francesca would have given her life for Eloise, of course, and there was certainly no other woman who knew more of her secrets and inner thoughts, but half the time she could have happily strangled her sister.

Including right now. Especially right now.

"Eloise is right," Sophie said to Francesca. "You should go over and greet Michael. It's only polite, considering his long stay abroad."

"It's not as if we haven't been living in the same house for over a week," Francesca said. "We've more than said our greetings."

"Yes, but not in public," Sophie replied, "and not at your family's home. If you don't go over and speak with him, everyone will comment upon it tomorrow. They will think there is a rift between the two of you. Or worse, that you do not accept him as the new earl."

"Of course I accept him," Francesca

said. "And even if I didn't, what would it matter? The line of succession was hardly in doubt."

"You need to show everyone that you hold him in high esteem," Sophie said. Then she turned to Francesca with a quizzical expression. "Unless, of course, you don't."

"No, of course I do," Francesca said with a sigh. Sophie was right. Sophie was always right when it came to matters of propriety. She should go and greet Michael. He deserved an official and public welcome to London, as ludicrous as it seemed, given that she had spent the last few weeks nursing him through his malarial fevers. She just didn't relish fighting her way through his throng of admirers.

She'd always found Michael's reputation amusing. Probably because she felt rather removed from it all, above it, even. It had been a bit of an inside joke between the three of them — her, John, and Michael. He'd never taken any of the women seriously, and so she hadn't, either.

But now she wasn't watching from her comfortable, secure position as a happily married lady. And Michael was no longer just the Merry Rake, a ne'er-do-well who maintained his position in society through wit and charm.

He was an earl, and she was a widow, and she suddenly felt rather small and powerless.

It wasn't his fault, of course. She knew that, just as she knew . . . well, just as she knew that he'd make someone a terrible husband someday. But somehow she couldn't quite block her ire, if not with him then with the gaggle of giggling females around him.

"Francesca?" Sophie asked. "Do you want one of us to go with you?"

"What? No. No, of course not." Francesca drew herself up straight, embarrassed to have been caught woolgathering by her sisters. "I can see to Michael," she said firmly.

She took two steps in his direction, then turned back to Kate, Sophie, and Eloise. "After I see to myself," she said.

And with that, she turned to make her way to the ladies' retiring room. If she was going to have to smile and be polite amidst Michael's simpering women, she might as well do it without feeling she had to hop from foot to foot.

But as she departed, she heard Eloise's low murmur of, "Coward."

It took all of Francesca's fortitude not to turn around and impale her sister with a scathing retort.

Well, that and the fact that she rather feared Eloise was right.

And it was mortifying to think that she might have turned coward over Michael, of all people.

Chapter 11

. . . I have heard from Michael. Three times, actually. I have not yet responded. You would be disappointed in me, I'm sure. But I —

— from the Countess of Kilmartin to her deceased husband, ten months after Michael's departure for India, crumpled with a muttered, "This is madness," and tossed in the fire

Michael had spotted Francesca the moment he'd entered the ballroom. She was standing at the far side of the room, chatting with her sisters, wearing a blue gown and new hairstyle.

And he noticed the instant she left as well, exiting through the door in the northwest wall, presumably to go to the ladies' retiring room, which he knew was just down the hall.

Worst of all, he was quite certain he

would be equally aware of her return, even though he was conversing with about a dozen other ladies, all of whom thought he was giving their little gathering his full attention.

It was like a sickness with him, a sixth sense. He couldn't be in a room with Francesca and not know where she was. It had been like this since the moment they'd met, and the only thing that made it bearable was that she hadn't a clue.

It was one of the things he had most enjoyed about India. She wasn't there; he never had to be *aware* of her. But she'd haunted him still. Every now and then he'd catch a glimpse of chestnut hair that caught the candlelight as hers did, or someone would laugh, and for a split second it sounded like hers. His breath would catch, and he would look for her, even though he *knew* she wasn't there.

It was hell, and usually worthy of a stiff drink. Or a night spent with his latest paramour.

Or both.

But that was over, and now he was back in London, and he was surprised by how easy it was to fall into his old role as the devil-may-care charmer. Nothing much had changed in town; oh, some of the faces were different, but the aggregate sum of the *ton* was the same. Lady Bridgerton's birthday fête was much as he had anticipated, although he had to admit that he was a little taken aback at the level of curiosity aroused by his reappearance in London. It seemed the Merry Rake had become the Dashing Earl, and within the first fifteen minutes of his arrival, he had been accosted by no fewer than eight — no make that nine, mustn't forget Lady Bridgerton herself — society matrons, all eager to court his favor and, of course, introduce him to their lovely and unattached daughters.

He wasn't quite sure if it was amusing or hell.

Amusing, he decided, for now at least. By next week he had no doubt it would be hell.

After another fifteen minutes of introductions, reintroductions, and only slightly veiled propositions (thankfully by a widow and not one of the debutantes or their mothers), he announced his intention to locate his hostess and excused himself from the crowd.

And then there she was. Francesca. Halfway across the room, of course, which meant that he'd have to make his way through the punishing crowd if he wanted to speak with her. She looked breathtakingly lovely in a deep blue gown, and he realized that for all her talk about buying herself a new wardrobe, this was the first he'd seen her out of her half-mourning colors.

Then it hit him again. She was finally out of mourning. She would remarry. She would laugh and flirt and wear blue and find a husband.

And it would probably all happen in the space of a month. Once she made clear her intention to remarry, the men would be beating down her door. How could anyone *not* want to marry her? She might not have been as youthful as the other women looking for husbands, but she had something the younger debutantes lacked — a sparkle, a vivacity, a gleam of intelligence in her eyes that brought something extra to her beauty.

She was still alone, standing in the doorway. Amazingly, no one else seemed to have noticed her entrance, so Michael decided to brave the crowds and make his way to her.

But she saw him first, and although she did not exactly smile, her lips curved, and her eyes flashed with recognition, and as she walked to him, his breath caught.

It shouldn't have surprised him. And yet it did. Every time he thought he knew everything about her, had unwillingly memorized every last detail, something inside her flickered and changed, and he felt himself falling anew.

He would never escape her, this woman. He would never escape her, and he could never have her. Even with John gone, it was impossible, quite simply wrong. There was too much there. Too much had happened, and he would never be able to shake the feeling that he had somehow stolen her.

Or worse, that he had wished for this. That he had wanted John gone and out of the way, wanted the title and Francesca and everything else.

He closed the distance between them, meeting her halfway. "Francesca," he murmured, making his voice smooth and personable, "it is a delight to see you."

"And you as well," she replied. She smiled then, but it was in an amused sort of fashion, and he had the unexpected sense that she was mocking him. But there seemed little to be gained by pointing this out; it would only demonstrate how attuned he was to her every expression. And so he just said, "Have you been enjoying yourself?"

"Of course. Have you?"

"Of course."

She quirked a brow. "Even in your present state of solitude?"

"I beg your pardon?"

She shrugged carelessly. "The last I saw of you, you were surrounded by women."

"If you saw me, why didn't you come over to save me?"

"Save you?" she said with a laugh. "Anyone could see that you were enjoying yourself."

"Is that so?"

"Oh, please, Michael," she said, giving him a pointed glance. "You live to flirt and seduce."

"In that order?"

She shrugged. "You're not the Merry Rake for nothing."

He felt his jaw clamping together. Her comment rankled, and then the fact that it did rankled some more.

She studied his face, closely enough to make him want to squirm with discomfort, and then her own erupted into a smile. "You don't like it," she said slowly, almost breathless with the realization. "Oh, my heavens, you don't like it."

She looked as if she'd just experienced an epiphany of biblical proportions, but as the whole thing was at his expense, all he could do was scowl.

Then she laughed, which made it even worse. "Oh, my," she said, actually holding her hand to her belly in mirth. "You feel like a fox at a hunt, and you don't like it one bit. Oh, this is simply too much. After all the women you've chased . . ."

She had it all wrong, of course. He didn't much care one way or another that the society matrons had labeled him the season's biggest catch and were pursuing him accordingly. That was just the sort of thing it was easy to maintain a sense of humor over.

He didn't care if they called him the Merry Rake. He didn't care if they thought him a worthless seducer.

But when Francesca said the same thing . . .

It was like acid.

And the worst of it was, he had no one to blame but himself. He had cultivated this reputation for years, spent countless hours teasing and flirting, and then making sure Francesca saw, so she would never guess the truth.

And maybe he had done it for himself,

too, because if he was the Merry Rake, at least he was *some*thing. The alternative was to be nothing but a pathetic fool, hopelessly in love with another man's wife. And hell, he was *good* at being the man who could seduce with a smile. He might as well have something in life he could succeed at.

"You can't say I didn't warn you," Francesca said, sounding very pleased with herself.

"It's not so bad surrounding oneself with beautiful women," he said, mostly to irritate her. "Even better when it comes about so effortlessly."

It worked, because her face pinched just a bit around the mouth. "I'm sure it's more than delightful, but you must be careful not to forget yourself," she said sharply. "These are not your usual women."

"I wasn't aware I had usual women."

"You know exactly what I mean, Michael. Others may have called you a complete rogue, but I know you better than that."

"Oh, really?" And he almost laughed. She thought she knew him so well, but she knew nothing. She'd never know the full truth.

"You had standards four years ago," she

continued. "You never seduced anyone who would be irreparably hurt by your actions."

"And what makes you think I'm about to start now?"

"Oh, I don't think you'd do anything like that on purpose," she said, "but before, you never even associated with young women looking for marriage. There wasn't even the possibility that you might make a misstep and accidentally ruin one of them."

The vague, prickling sense of irritation that had been simmering within him began to grow and boil. "Who do you think I am, Francesca?" he asked, his entire body stiff with something he couldn't quite put his finger on. He hated that she thought this of him, *hated* it.

"Michael —"

"Do you really think me so dim that I might *accidentally* ruin a young lady's reputation?"

Her lips parted, then quivered slightly before she replied. "Not dim, Michael, of course not. But —"

"Careless, then," he bit off.

"No, not that, either. I just think —"

"What, Francesca?" he asked ruthlessly. "What *do* you think of me?"

"I think you are one of the finest men I know," she said softly.

Damn. Trust her to unman him with a single sentence. He stared at her, just stared at her, trying to figure out what the *hell* she'd meant by that.

"I do," she said with a shrug. "But I also think you're foolish, and I think you can be fickle, and I think you're going to break more hearts this spring than I'll be able to count."

"It isn't your job to count them," he said, his voice quiet and hard.

"No, it isn't, is it?" She looked over at him and smiled wryly. "But I'm going to end up doing it all the same, won't I?"

"And why is that?"

She didn't seem to have an answer to that, and then, just when he was sure she would say no more, she whispered, "Because I won't be able to stop myself."

Several seconds passed. They just stood there, their backs to the wall, looking for all the world as if they were just watching the party. Finally, Francesca broke the silence and said, "You should dance."

He turned to her. "With you?"

"Yes. Once, at least. But you should also dance with someone eligible, someone you might marry."

Someone he might marry. Anyone but her.

"It will signal to society that you are at least open to the possibility of matrimony," Francesca added. When he made no comment, she asked, "Aren't you?"

"Open to matrimony?"

"Yes."

"If you say so," he said, somewhat flippantly. He had to be cavalier. It was the only way he could mask the bitterness sweeping over him.

"Felicity Featherington," Francesca said, motioning toward a very pretty young lady about ten yards away. "She'd be an excellent choice. Very sensible. She won't fall in love with you."

He looked down at her sardonically. "Heaven forbid I find love."

Francesca's lips parted and her eyes grew very wide. "Is that what you want?" she asked. "To find love?"

She looked delighted by the prospect. Delighted that he might find the perfect woman.

And there it was. His faith in a higher power reaffirmed. Truly, moments of this ironic perfection could not come about by accident.

"Michael?" Francesca asked. Her eyes

were bright and shining, and she clearly wanted something for him, something wonderful and good.

And all he wanted was to scream.

"I have no idea," he said caustically. "Not a single, bloody clue."

"Michael . . ." She looked stricken, but for once, he didn't care.

"If you will excuse me," he said sharply, "I believe I have a Featherington to dance with."

"Michael, what is wrong?" she asked. "What did I say?"

"Nothing," he said. "Nothing at all."

"Don't be this way."

As he turned to her, he felt something wash over him, a numbness that somehow slid a mask back over his face, enabled him to smile smoothly and regard her with his legendary heavy-lidded stare. He was once again the rake, maybe not so merry, but every bit the urbane seducer.

"What way?" he asked, his lips twisting with the perfect mix of innocence and condescension. "I'm doing exactly what you asked of me. Dance with a Featherington, didn't you say? I'm following your instructions to the letter."

"You're angry with me," she whispered.

"Of course not," he said, but they both

241

knew his voice was too easy, too suave. "I've merely accepted that you, Francesca, know best. Here I've been listening to my own mind and conscience all this time, but to what avail? Heaven knows where I'd be if I'd listened to you years ago."

Her breath gasped across her lips and she drew back. "I need to go," she said.

"Go, then," he said.

Her chin lifted a notch. "There are many men here."

"Very many."

"I need to find a husband."

"You should," he agreed.

Her lips pressed together and then she added, "I might find one tonight."

He almost gave her a mocking smile. She always had to have the last word. "You might," he said, at the very second he knew she thought the conversation had concluded.

By then she was just far enough away that she couldn't yell back one last retort. But he saw the way she paused and tensed her shoulders, and he knew she'd heard him.

He leaned back against the wall and smiled. One had to take one's simple pleasures where one could.

The next day Francesca felt perfectly

242

horrid. And worse, she couldn't quell an extremely annoying quiver of guilt, even though Michael was the one who'd spoken so insultingly the night before.

Truly, what had she said to provoke such an unkind reaction on his part? And what right did he have to act so badly toward her? All she had done was express a bit of joy that he might want to find a true and loving marriage rather than spend his days in shallow debauchery.

But apparently she'd been wrong. Michael had spent the entire night — both before and after their conversation — charming every woman at the party. It had gotten to the point where she had thought she might be ill.

But the worst of it was, she couldn't seem to stop herself from counting his conquests, just as she'd predicted the night before. *One, two, three,* she'd murmured, watching him enchant a trio of sisters with his smile. *Four, five, six* — there went two widows and a countess. It was disgusting, and Francesca was disgusted with herself for having been so mesmerized.

And then every now and then, he'd look at her. Just look at her with a heavy-lidded, mocking stare, and she couldn't help but think that he knew what she was doing, that he was moving from woman to woman just so that she could round her count up to the next dozen or so.

Why had she said that? What had she been thinking?

Or had she been thinking not at all? It seemed the only explanation. She certainly hadn't intended to tell him that she wouldn't be able to stop herself from tallying his broken hearts. The words had whispered over her lips before she'd even realized she was thinking them.

And even now, she wasn't sure what it meant.

Why did she care? Why on earth did she care how many ladies fell under his spell? She'd never cared before.

It was only going to get worse, too. The women were mad for Michael. If the rules of society were reversed, Francesca thought wryly, their drawing room at Kilmartin House would be overflowing with flowers, all addressed to the Dashing Earl.

It was still going to be dreadful. She would be inundated with visitors today, of that she was certain. Every woman in London would call upon her in hopes that Michael might stroll through the drawing room. Francesca was going to have to en-

dure countless questions, occasional innuendo, and —

"Good heavens!" She stopped short,
peering into the drawing room with dubious eyes. "What is all this?"

Flowers. Everywhere.

It was her nightmare come true. Had
someone changed the rules of society and
forgotten to tell her?

Violets, irises, and daisies. Imported tulips. Hothouse orchids. And roses. Roses
everywhere. Of every color. The smell was
almost overwhelming.

"Priestley!" Francesca called out, spying
her butler across the room, setting a tall
vase of snapdragons on a table. "What are
all these flowers?"

He gave the vase one last adjustment,
twisting one pink stalk so that it faced
away from the wall, then turned and
walked toward her. "They are for you, my
lady."

She blinked. "Me?"

"Indeed. Would you care to read the
cards? I have left them on the arrangements so that you would be able to identify
each sender."

"Oh." It seemed all she could say. She
felt rather like a simpleton, with her hand
over her opened mouth, glancing back and

forth at all the flowers.

"If you'd like," Priestley continued, "I could remove each card and note on the back which arrangement I took it from. Then you could read through them all at once." When Francesca didn't reply, he suggested, "Perhaps you would like to remove yourself to your desk? I would be happy to bring you the cards."

"No, no," she said, still feeling terribly distracted by all this. She was a widow, for heavens sake. Men weren't supposed to bring her flowers. Were they?

"My lady?"

"I . . . I . . ." She turned to Priestley, straightening her spine as she forced her mind back to clarity. Or tried. "I will just, ah, have a look at . . ." She turned to the nearest bouquet, a lovely and delicate arrangement of grape hyacinths and stephanotis. "A pale comparison to your eyes," the card read. It was signed by the Marquess of Chester.

"Oh!" Francesca gasped. Lord Chester's wife had died two years earlier. Everyone knew he was looking for a new bride.

Barely able to contain the oddly giddy feeling rising within her, she inched down toward an arrangement of roses and picked up the card, trying very hard not to appear too eager in front of the butler. "I wonder who this is from," she said with studied casualness.

A sonnet. From Shakespeare, if she remembered correctly. Signed by Viscount Trevelstam.

Trevelstam? They'd only been introduced but once. He was young, very handsome, and it was rumored that his father had squandered away most of the family fortune. The new viscount would have to marry someone wealthy. Or so everyone said.

"Good heavens!"

Francesca turned to see Janet behind her.

"What is this?" she asked.

"I do believe those were my exact words upon entering the room," Francesca murmured. She handed Janet the two cards, then watched her carefully as her eyes scanned the neatly handwritten lines.

Janet had lost her only child when John had died. How would she react to Francesca being wooed by other men?

"My goodness," Janet said, looking up. "You seem to be this season's Incomparable."

"Oh, don't be silly," Francesca said, blushing. Blushing? Good God, what was wrong with her? She didn't blush. She hadn't even blushed during her first season, when she really had been an Incomparable. "I'm far too old for that," she mumbled.

"Apparently not," Janet said.

"There are more in the hall," Priestley said.

Janet turned to Francesca. "Have you looked through all the cards?"

"Not yet. But I imagine —"

"That they're more of the same?"

Francesca nodded. "Does that bother you?"

Janet smiled sadly, but her eyes were kind and wise. "Do I wish you were still married to my son? Of course. Do I want you to spend the rest of your life married to his memory? Of course not." She reached out and clasped one of Francesca's hands in her own. "You are a daughter to me, Francesca. I want you to be happy."

"I would never dishonor John's memory," Francesca assured her.

"Of course not. If you were the sort who would, he'd never have married you in the first place. Or," she added with a sly look, "I would never have allowed him to."

"I would like children," Francesca said.

Somehow she felt the need to explain it, to make sure that Janet understood that what she truly wanted was to be a mother, not necessarily a wife.

Janet nodded, turning away as she dabbed at her eyes with her fingertips. "We should read the rest of the these cards," she said, her brisk tone signaling that she'd like to move on, "and perhaps prepare ourselves for an onslaught of afternoon calls."

Francesca followed her as she sought out an enormous display of tulips and plucked the card free. "I rather think the callers will be women," Francesca said, "inquiring after Michael."

"You may be right," Janet replied. She held the card up. "May I?"

"Of course."

Janet scanned the words, then looked up and said, "Cheshire."

Francesca gasped, "As in the Duke of?"

"The very one."

Francesca actually placed her hand over her heart. "My word," she breathed. "The Duke of Cheshire."

"You, my dear, are clearly the catch of the season."

"But I —"

"What the devil is this?"

It was Michael, catching a vase he'd

249

nearly overturned and looking extremely cross and put out.

"Good morning, Michael," Janet said cheerfully.

He nodded at her, then turned to Francesca and grumbled, "You look as if you're about to pledge allegiance to your sovereign lord."

"And that would be you, I imagine?" she shot back, quickly dropping her hand to her side. She hadn't even realized it was still over her heart.

"If you're lucky," he muttered.

Francesca just gave him a look.

He smirked right back in return. "And are we opening a flower shop?"

"No, but clearly we could," Janet replied. "They're for Francesca," she added helpfully.

"Of course they're for Francesca," he muttered, "although, good God, I don't know who would be idiot enough to send roses."

"I like roses," Francesca said.

"Everyone sends roses," he said dismissively. "They're trite and old, and" — he motioned to Trevelstam's yellow ones — "who sent this?"

"Trevelstam," Janet answered.

Michael let out a snort and swung

around to face Francesca. "You're not going to marry *him,* are you?"

"Probably not, but I fail to see what —"

"He hasn't two shillings to rub together," he stated.

"How would you know?" Francesca asked. "You haven't even been back a month."

Michael shrugged. "I've been to my club."

"Well, it may be true, but it is hardly his fault," Francesca felt compelled to point out. Not that she felt any great loyalty to Lord Trevelstam, but still, she did try to be fair, and it was common knowledge that the young viscount had spent the last year trying to repair the damage his profligate father had done to the family fortunes.

"You're not marrying him, and that's final," Michael announced.

She *should* have been annoyed by his arrogance, but the truth was, she was mostly just amused. "Very well," she said, lips twitching. "I'll select someone else."

"Good," he grunted.

"She has many to choose from," Janet put in.

"Indeed," Michael said caustically.

"I'm going to have to find Helen," Janet said. "She won't want to miss this."

"I hardly think the flowers are going to fly out the window before she rises," Michael said.

"Of course not," Janet replied sweetly, giving him a motherly pat on the arm.

Francesca quickly swallowed a laugh. Michael would hate that, and Janet knew it.

"She does adore her flowers, though," Janet said. "May I take one of the arrangements up to her?"

"Of course," Francesca replied.

Janet reached for Trevelstam's roses, then stopped herself. "Oh, no, I had better not," she said, turning back around to face Michael and Francesca. "He might stop by, and we wouldn't want him to think we'd banished his flowers to some far corner of the house."

"Oh, right," Francesca murmured, "of course."

Michael just grunted.

"Nevertheless, I'd better go tell her about this," Janet said, and she turned and hurried up the stairs.

Michael sneezed, then glared at a particularly innocuous display of gladiolas. "We're going to have to open a window," he grumbled.

"And freeze?"

"I'll wear a coat," he ground out.

Francesca smiled. She wanted to grin. "Are you jealous?" she asked coyly.

He swung around and nearly leveled her with a dumbstruck expression.

"Not over *me*," she said quickly, almost blushing at the thought. "My word, not *that*."

"Then what?" he asked, his voice quiet and clipped.

"Well, just — I mean —" She motioned to the flowers, a clear display of her sudden popularity. "Well, we're both after much the same goal this season, aren't we?"

He just stared at her blankly.

"Marriage," she said. Good heavens, he was particularly obtuse this morning.

"Your point?"

She let out an impatient breath. "I don't know if you had thought about it, but I'd naturally assumed you would be the one to be relentlessly pursued. I never dreamed that I would . . . Well . . ."

"Emerge as a prize to be won?"

It wasn't the nicest way of putting it, but it wasn't exactly inaccurate, so she just said, "Well, yes, I suppose."

For a moment he said nothing, but he was watching her strangely, almost wryly, and then he said, his voice quiet, "A man would have to be a fool not to want to marry you."

Francesca felt her mouth form a surprised oval. "Oh," she said, quite at a loss for words. "That's . . . that's . . . quite the nicest thing you could have said to me just now."

He sighed and ran his hand through his hair. She decided not to tell him that he'd just deposited a streak of yellow pollen into the black strands.

"Francesca," he said, looking tired and weary and something else.

Regretful?

No, that was impossible. Michael wasn't the sort to regret anything.

"I would never begrudge you this. You . . ." He cleared his throat. "You should be happy."

"I —" It was the strangest moment, especially after their tense words the night before. She hadn't the faintest clue how to reply, and so she just changed the subject and said, "Your turn will come."

He looked at her quizzically.

"It already has, really," she continued. "Last night. I was besieged with far more admirers for your hand than for my own. If women could send flowers, we'd be completely awash with them."

He smiled, but the sentiment didn't quite reach his eyes. He didn't look angry, just . . . hollow.

And she was struck by what a strange observation that was.

"Er, last night," he said, reaching up and tugging at his cravat. "If I said anything to upset you . . ."

She watched his face. It was so dear to her, and she knew every last detail of it. Four years, it seemed, did little to smudge a memory. But something was different now. He'd changed, but she wasn't sure how.

And she wasn't sure why.

"Everything is fine," she assured him.

"Nonetheless," he said gruffly, "I'm sorry."

But for the rest of the day, Francesca wondered if he knew exactly what he was apologizing for. And she couldn't escape the feeling that she wasn't sure, either.

Chapter 12

. . . rather ridiculous writing to you, but I suppose after so many months in the East, my perspective on death and the afterlife has slid into something that would have sent Vicar MacLeish screaming for the hills. So far from England, it is almost possible to pretend that you are still alive and able to receive this note, just like the many I sent from France. But then someone calls out to me, and I am reminded that I am Kilmartin and you are in a place unreachable by the Royal Mail.

> *— from the Earl of Kilmartin*
> *to his deceased cousin, the previous*
> *earl, one year and two months*
> *after his departure for India,*
> *written to completion and*
> *then burned slowly over a candle*

It wasn't that he *enjoyed* feeling like an ass,

Michael reflected as he swirled a glass of brandy at his club, but it seemed that lately, around Francesca at least, he couldn't quite avoid acting like one.

There she had been at her mother's birthday party, so damned *happy* for him, so delighted that he had uttered the word *love* in her presence, and he had simply snapped.

Because he knew how her mind worked, and he knew that she was already thinking madly ahead, trying to select the perfect woman for him, and the truth was . . .

Well, the truth was just too pathetic for words.

But he'd apologized, and although he could swear up and down that he wasn't going to behave like an idiot again, he would probably find himself apologizing again sometime in the future, and she would most likely just chalk it all up to a cranky nature on his part, never mind that he'd been a model of good humor and equanimity when John had been alive.

He downed his brandy. Bugger it all.

Well, he'd be done with this nonsense soon. She'd find someone, marry the bloke, and move out of the house. They would remain friends, of course — Francesca wasn't the sort to allow otherwise —

but he wouldn't see her every day over the breakfast table. He wouldn't even see her as often as he had before John's death. Her new husband would not permit her to spend so much time in his company, cousinly relationship or no.

"Stirling!" he heard someone call out, followed by the usual slight cough which preceded, "Kilmartin, I mean. So sorry."

Michael looked up to see Sir Geoffrey Fowler, an acquaintance of his from his days at Cambridge. "Nothing of it," he said, motioning to the chair across from him.

"Splendid to see you," Sir Geoffrey said, taking a seat. "I trust your journey home was uneventful."

The pair exchanged the most basic of pleasantries until Sir Geoffrey got to the point. "I understand that Lady Kilmartin is looking for a husband," he said.

Michael felt as if he'd been punched. Never mind the atrocious floral display in his drawing room; it still sounded rather distasteful coming from someone's lips.

Someone young, reasonably handsome, and obviously in the market for a wife.

"Er, yes," he finally replied. "I believe she is."

"Excellent." Sir Geoffrey rubbed his

hands together in anticipation, leaving Michael with the overwhelming desire to smack his face.

"She will be quite choosy," Michael said peevishly.

Sir Geoffrey didn't seem to care. "Will you dower her?"

"What?" Michael snapped. Good God, he was now her nearest male relative, wasn't he? He'd probably have to give her away at her wedding.

Hell.

"Will you?" Sir Geoffrey persisted.

"Of course," Michael bit off.

Sir Geoffrey sucked in his breath appreciatively. "Her brother offered to do so as well."

"The Stirlings will care for her," Michael said stiffly.

Sir Geoffrey shrugged. "It appears the Bridgertons will as well."

Michael felt his teeth grinding to powder.

"Don't look so dyspeptic," Sir Geoffrey said. "With a double dowry, she'll be off your hands in no time. I'm sure you're eager to be rid of her."

Michael cocked his head, trying to decide which side of Sir Geoffrey's nose could better take a punch.

"She's got to be a burden on you," Sir Geoffrey continued blithely. "The clothes alone must cost a fortune."

Michael wondered what the legal ramifications were for strangling a knight of the realm. Surely nothing he couldn't live with.

"And then when *you* marry," Sir Geoffrey continued, obviously unaware that Michael was flexing his fingers and measuring his neck, "your new countess won't want her in the house. Can't have two hens in charge of the household, right?"

"Right," Michael said tightly.

"Very well, then," Sir Geoffrey said, standing up. "Good to speak with you, Kilmartin. I must be off. Need to go tell Shively the news. Not that I want the competition, of course, but this isn't likely to stay a secret for very long, anyway. I might as well be the one to let it out."

Michael frosted him with a glare, but Sir Geoffrey was too excited with his gossip to notice. Michael looked down at his glass. Right. He'd drunk it all. Damn.

He signaled to a waiter to bring him another, then sat back with every intention of reading the newspaper he'd picked up on the way in, but before he could even scan the headlines, he heard his name yet again. He made the minimum effort required to hide his irritation and looked up.

Trevelstam. Of the yellow roses. Michael felt the newspaper crumple between his fingers.

"Kilmartin," the viscount said.

Michael nodded. "Trevelstam." They knew each other; not closely, but well enough so that a friendly conversation was not unexpected. "Have a seat," he said, motioning to the chair across from him.

Trevelstam sat, setting his half-sipped drink on the table. "How do you fare?" he asked. "Haven't seen you much since your return."

"Well enough," Michael grunted. Considering that he was being forced to sit with some ninny who wanted to marry Francesca's dowry. No, make that her double dowry. The way gossip spread, Trevelstam had probably already heard the news from Sir Geoffrey.

Trevelstam was slightly more sophisticated than Sir Geoffrey — he managed to make small talk for a full three minutes, asking about Michael's trip to India, the voyage back, et cetera et cetera et cetera. But then, of course, he got down to his true purpose.

"I called upon Lady Kilmartin this afternoon," he said.

"Did you?" Michael murmured. He hadn't returned home since leaving that morning. The last thing he had wanted was to be present for Francesca's parade of suitors.

"Indeed. She's a lovely woman."

"That she is," Michael said, glad his drink had arrived.

Then not so glad when he realized it had arrived two minutes earlier and he had already drunk it.

Trevelstam cleared his throat. "I'm sure you are aware that I intend to court her."

"I'm certainly aware of it now." Michael eyed his glass, trying to determine if there might be a few drops of brandy left after all.

"I wasn't certain whether I should inform you or her brother of my intentions."

Michael was quite certain that Anthony Bridgerton, Francesca's eldest brother, was quite capable of weeding out unsuitable marriage prospects, but nonetheless he said, "I am quite sufficient."

"Good, good," Trevelstam murmured, taking another sip of his drink. "I —"

"Trevelstam!" came a booming voice. "And Kilmartin, too!"

It was Lord Hardwick, big and beefy, and if not yet drunk, not exactly sober either.

"Hardwick," both men said, acknowledging his arrival.

Hardwick grabbed a chair, scraping it along the floor until it found a place at the table. "Good to see you, good to see you," he huffed. "Capital night, don't you think? Most excellent. Most excellent, indeed."

Michael had no idea what he was talking about, but he nodded, anyway. Better that than actually to ask him what he meant; Michael was quite certain he lacked the patience to listen to an explanation.

"Thistleswaite's over there setting bets on the Queen's dogs, and, oh! Heard about Lady Kilmartin, too. Good talk tonight," he said, nodding approvingly. "Good talk, indeed. Hate when it's quiet here."

"And how are the Queen's dogs faring?" Michael inquired.

"Out of mourning, I understand."

"The dogs?"

"No, Lady Kilmartin!" Hardwick chortled. "Heh heh heh. Good one, there, Kilmartin."

Michael signaled for another drink. He was going to need it.

"Wore blue the other night, she did,"

Hardwick said. "Everyone saw."

"She looked quite lovely," Trevelstam added.

"Indeed, indeed," Hardwick said. "Good woman. I'd go after her myself if I weren't already shackled to Lady Hardwick."

Small favors and all that, Michael decided.

"She mourned the old earl for how long?" Hardwick asked. "Six years?"

As the "old earl" had been but twenty-eight at the time of his death, Michael found the comment somewhat offensive, but there seemed little point in attempting to change Lord Hardwick's customary bad judgment and behavior at this late stage in his life — and from the size and ruddiness of him, he was clearly going to keel over at any time. Right now, in fact, if Michael was lucky.

He glanced across the table. Still alive. Damn.

"Four years," he said succinctly. "My cousin died four years ago."

"Four, six, whatever," Hardwick said with a shrug. "It's still a bloody long time to black the windows."

"I believe she was in half-mourning for some time," Trevelstam put in.

"Eh? Really?" Hardwick took a swig of

his drink, then wiped his mouth rather sloppily with a handkerchief. "All the same for the rest of us when you think about it. She wasn't looking for a husband 'til now."

"No," Michael said, mostly because Hardwick had actually stopped talking for a few seconds.

"The men are going to be after her like bees to honey," Hardwick predicted, drawing out the *bees* until it sounded like it ended with four Zs. "Bees to honey, I tell you. Everyone knows she was devoted to the old earl. Everyone."

Michael's drink arrived. Thank God.

"And there's been no whiff of scandal attached to her name since he died," Hardwick added.

"I should say not," Trevelstam said.

"Not like some of the widows out and about," Hardwick continued, taking another swig of his liquor. He chuckled lewdly and elbowed Michael. "If you know what I mean."

Michael just drank.

"It's like . . ." Hardwick leaned in, his jowls jiggling as his expression grew salacious. "It's like . . ."

"For God's sake, man, just spit it out," Michael muttered.

"Eh?" Hardwick said.

Michael just scowled.

"I'll tell you what it's like," Hardwick said with a leer. "It's like you're getting a virgin who knows what to do."

Michael stared at him. "What did you just say?" he asked, very quietly.

"I said —"

"I'd take care not to repeat that if I were you," Trevelstam quickly interjected, casting an apprehensive glance at Michael's darkening visage.

"Eh? It's no insult," Hardwick grunted, gulping down the rest of his drink. "She's been married, so you know she ain't untouched, but she hasn't gone and —"

"Stop *now*," Michael ground out.

"Eh? Everyone is saying it."

"Not in my presence," Michael bit off. "Not if they value their health."

"Well, it's better than saying she ain't like a virgin." Hardwick chortled. "If you know what I mean."

Michael lunged.

"Good God, man," Hardwick yelped, falling back onto the floor. "What the hell is wrong with you?"

Michael wasn't certain how his hands had come to be around Hardwick's neck, but he realized he rather liked them there. "You will never," he hissed, "utter her name again. Do you understand me?"

Hardwick nodded frantically, but the motion cut off his air even further, and his cheeks began to purple.

Michael let go and stood up, wiping his hands against each other as if attempting to rub away something foul. "I will not countenance Lady Kilmartin being spoken of in such disrespectful terms," he bit off. "Is that clear?"

Hardwick nodded. And so did a number of the onlookers.

"Good," Michael grunted, deciding now was a good time to get the hell out. Hopefully Francesca would already be in bed when he got home. Either that or out. Anything as long as he didn't have to see her.

He walked toward the exit, but as he stepped out of the room and into the hall, he heard his name being uttered yet again. He turned around, wondering what man was idiot enough to pester him in such a state.

Colin Bridgerton. Francesca's brother. Damn.

"Kilmartin," Colin said, his handsome face decorated with his customary half smile.

"Bridgerton."

Colin motioned lightly to the now overturned table. "That was quite a show in there."

Michael said nothing. Colin Bridgerton had always unnerved him. They shared the same sort of reputation — that of the devil-may-care rogue. But whereas Colin was the darling of the society mamas, who cooed over his charming demeanor, Michael had always been (or at least until he'd come into the title) treated with a bit more caution.

But Michael had long suspected there was quite a bit of substance under Colin's ever-jovial surface, and perhaps it was because they were alike in so many ways, but Michael had always feared that if anyone were to sense the truth of his feelings for Francesca, it would be this brother.

"I was having a quiet drink when I heard the commotion," Colin said, motioning to a private salon. "Come join me."

Michael wanted nothing more than to get the hell out of the club, but Colin was Francesca's brother, which made them relations of a sort, requiring at least the pretense of politeness. And so he gritted his teeth and walked into the private salon, fully intending to take his drink and leave in under ten minutes.

"Pleasant night, don't you think?" Colin

said, once Michael was pretending to be comfortable. "Aside from Hardwick and all that." He sat back in his chair with careless grace. "He's an ass."

Michael gave him a terse nod, trying not to notice that Francesca's brother was watching him as he always did, his shrewd gaze carefully overlaid with an air of charming innocence. Colin cocked his head slightly to the side, rather as if, Michael thought acerbically, he were angling for a better look into his soul.

"Damn it all," Michael muttered under his breath, and he rang for a waiter.

"What was that?" Colin asked.

Michael turned slowly back to face him. "Do you want another drink?" he asked, his words as clear as he could manage, considering they had to squeeze through his clenched teeth.

"I believe I will," Colin replied, all friendliness and good cheer.

Michael didn't believe his façade for a moment.

"Do you have any plans for the remainder of the evening?" Colin asked.

"None."

"Neither do I, as it happens," Colin murmured.

Damn. Again. Was it really too much to

wish for one bloody hour of solitude?

"Thank you for defending Francesca's honor," Colin said quietly.

Michael's first impulse was to growl that he didn't need to be thanked; it was his place as well as any Bridgerton's to defend Francesca's honor, but Colin's green eyes seemed uncommonly sharp that evening, so he just nodded instead. "Your sister deserves to be treated with respect," he finally said, making sure that his voice was smooth and even.

"Of course," Colin said, inclining his head.

Their drinks arrived. Michael fought the urge to down his in one gulp, but he did take a large enough sip for it to burn down his throat.

Colin, on the other hand, let out an appreciative sigh and sat back. "Excellent whisky," he said with great appreciation. "Best thing about Britain, really. Or one of them at least. One just can't get anything like it in Cyprus."

Michael just grunted a response. It was all that seemed necessary.

Colin took another drink, clearly savoring the brew. "Ahhh," he said, setting his glass down. "Almost as good as a woman."

Michael grunted again, raising his glass to his lips.

And then Colin said, "You should just marry her, you know."

Michael nearly choked. "I beg your pardon?"

"Marry her," Colin said with a shrug. "It seems simple enough."

It was probably too much to hope that Colin was speaking of anyone but Francesca, but Michael took one desperate stab, anyway, and said, in quite the chilliest tone he could muster, "To whom, might I ask, do you refer?"

Colin lifted his eyebrows. "Do we really need to play this game?"

"I can't marry Francesca," Michael sputtered.

"Why not?"

"Because —" He cut himself off. Because there were a hundred reasons he couldn't marry her, none of which he could speak aloud. So he just said, "She was married to my cousin."

"Last I checked, there was nothing illegal in that."

No, but there was everything immoral. He'd wanted Francesca for so long, loved her for what felt like an eternity — even when John had been living. He had de-

271

ceived his cousin in the basest way possible; he would not compound the betrayal by stealing his wife.

It would complete the ugly circle that had led to his being the Earl of Kilmartin, a title that was never supposed to have been his. *None* of it was supposed to be his. And except for those damned boots he'd forced Reivers to toss in a wardrobe, Francesca was the only thing left of John's that he *hadn't* made his own.

John's death had given him fabulous wealth. It had given him power, prestige, and the title of earl.

If it gave him Francesca as well, how could he possibly hang onto the thread of hope that he hadn't somehow, even if only in his dreams, wished for this to happen?

How could he live with himself then?

"She has to marry someone," Colin said.

Michael looked up, aware that he'd been silent with his thoughts for some time. And that Colin had been watching him closely all the while. He shrugged, trying to maintain a cavalier mien, even though he suspected it wouldn't fool the man across the table. "She'll do what she wants," he said. "She always does."

"She might marry hastily," Colin murmured. "She wants to have children before she's too old."

"She's not too old."

"No, but she might think she is. And she might worry that others will think she is, as well. She didn't conceive with your cousin, after all. Well, not successfully."

Michael had to clutch the end of the table to keep from rising. He could have had Shakespeare at his side to translate, and still not have been able to explain why Colin's remark infuriated him so.

"If she chooses too hastily," Colin added, almost offhandedly, "she might choose someone who would be cruel to her."

"Francesca?" Michael asked derisively. Maybe some other woman would be that foolish, but not his Francesca.

Colin shrugged. "It could happen."

"Even if it did," Michael countered, "she would never remain in such a marriage."

"What choice would she have?"

"This is *Francesca,*" Michael said. Which really should have explained it all.

"I suppose you're right," Colin acceded, sipping at his drink. "She could always take refuge with the Bridgertons. We would certainly never force her to return to a cruel spouse." He set his glass down on the table and sat back. "Besides, the point is moot, anyway, is it not?"

There was something strange in Colin's tone, something hidden and provoking. Michael looked up sharply, unable to resist the impulse to search the other man's face for clues to his agenda. "And why is that?" he asked.

Colin took another sip of his drink. Michael noticed that the volume of liquid in the glass never seemed to go down.

Colin toyed with his glass for several moments before looking up, his gaze settling on Michael's face. To anyone else, it might have seemed a bland expression, but there was something in Colin's eyes that made Michael want to squirm in his seat. They were sharp and piercing, and although different in color, shaped precisely like Francesca's.

It was damned eerie, that.

"Why is the point moot?" Colin murmured thoughtfully. "Well, because you so clearly don't wish to marry her."

Michael opened his mouth for a quick retort, then slammed it shut when he realized — with more than considerable shock — that he'd been about to say, "Of course I do."

And he did.

He wanted to marry her.

He just didn't think he could live with his conscience if he did.

"Are you quite all right?" Colin asked.

Michael blinked. "Perfectly so, why?"

Colin's head tilted slightly to the side. "For a moment there, you looked . . ." He gave his head a shake. "It's nothing."

"What, Bridgerton?" Michael nearly snapped.

"Surprised," Colin said. "You looked rather surprised. Bit odd, I thought."

Dear God, one more moment with Colin Bridgerton, and the bloody bastard would have all of Michael's secrets laid open and bare. Michael pushed his chair back. "I need to be going," he said abruptly.

"Of course," Colin said genially, as if their entire conversation had consisted of horses and the weather.

Michael stood, then gave a curt nod. It wasn't a terribly warm farewell, considering that they were relations of a sort, but it was the best he could do under the circumstances.

"Think about what I said," Colin murmured, just when Michael had reached the door.

Michael let out a harsh laugh as he pushed through the door and into the hall.

As if he'd be able to think about anything else.

For the rest of his life.

 *Chapter 13*

. . . all at home is pleasant and well, and Kilmartin thrives under Francesca's careful stewardship. She continues to mourn John, but then of course, so do we all, as, I'm sure, do you. You might consider writing to her directly. I know that she misses you. I do pass along all of your tales, but I am certain you would relate them to her in a different fashion than you do to your mother.

— from Helen Stirling to her son, the Earl of Kilmartin, two years after his departure for India

The rest of the week passed in a supremely annoying blur of flowers, candy, and one appalling display of poetry, recited aloud, Michael recalled with a shudder, on his front steps.

Francesca, it seemed, was putting all the fresh-faced debutantes to shame. The number of men vying for her hand might not have been doubling every day, but it certainly felt like it to Michael, who was constantly tripping over some lovesick swain in the hall.

It was enough to make a man want to vomit. Preferably on the lovesick swain.

Of course he had his admirers as well, but as it was not suitable for a lady to call upon a gentleman, he generally only had to deal with them when he chose to do so, and not when they took it upon themselves to stop by unannounced and for no apparent reason other than to compare his eyes to —

Well, to whatever one would compare your average gray eyes. It was a stupid analogy, anyway, although Michael had been forced to listen to more than one man rhapsodize over Francesca's eyes.

Good God, didn't any of them have an original thought in his head? Forget that *everyone* made mention of her eyes; at the very least one of them could have had the creativity to compare them to something other than the water or the sky.

Michael snorted with disgust. Anyone who took the time to really look at Francesca's eyes would have realized that they were quite their own color.

As if the sky could even compare.

Furthermore, Francesca's nauseating parade of suitors was made all the more difficult to bear by Michael's complete inability to stop thinking about his recent conversation with her brother.

Marriage to Francesca? He had never even let himself think about such a notion.

But now it gripped him with a fervor and intensity that left him reeling.

Marriage to Francesca. Good God. Everything about it was wrong.

Except he wanted it so badly.

It was hell watching her, hell speaking to her, hell living in the same house. He'd thought it was difficult before — loving someone who could never be his — but this . . .

This was a thousand times worse.

Colin knew.

He had to know. Why would he have suggested it if he didn't?

Michael had held on to his sanity all these years for one reason and one reason only: No one knew he was in love with Francesca.

Except, apparently, he was to be denied even that last shred of dignity.

But now Colin knew, or at least he damn

well suspected, and Michael couldn't quite quash this rising sense of panic within his chest.

Colin knew, and Michael was going to have to do something about it.

Dear God, what if he told Francesca?

That question was foremost in his mind, even now, as he stood slightly off to the side at the Burwick ball, nearly a week after his momentous meeting with Colin.

"She looks beautiful tonight, doesn't she?"

It was his mother's voice at his ear; he had forgotten to pretend that he wasn't watching Francesca. He turned to Helen and gave her a little bow. "Mother," he murmured.

"Doesn't she?" Helen persisted.

"Of course," he agreed, quickly enough so she might think he was just being polite.

"Green suits her."

Everything suited Francesca, but he wasn't about to tell his mother that, so he just nodded and made a murmur of agreement.

"You should dance with her."

"I'm sure I will," he said, taking a sip of his champagne. He *wanted* to march across the ballroom and forcibly remove her from her annoying little crowd of admirers, but he couldn't very well show such emotion in front of his mother. So he concluded with, "*After* I finish my drink."

Helen pursed her lips. "Her dance card will surely be filled by then. You should go now."

He turned to his mother and smiled, just the sort of devilish grin designed to take her mind off of whatever it was that had her so fixated. "Now why would I do that," he queried, setting his champagne flute down on a nearby table, "when I can dance with you instead?"

"You rascal," Helen said, but she didn't protest when he led her out on the floor.

Michael knew he'd pay for this tomorrow; already the society matrons were circling him for the kill, and there was nothing they liked better than a rake who doted upon his mother.

The dance was a lively one, which didn't allow for much conversation. And as he twisted and turned, dipped and bowed, he kept catching glances of Francesca, radiant in her emerald gown. No one seemed to notice that he was watching her, which suited him just fine, except that as the music reached its penultimate crescendo, Michael was forced to make one final turn away from her.

And when he turned back to face her again, she was gone.

He frowned. That didn't seem right. He supposed she could have darted out to the ladies' retiring room, but, pathetic fool that he was, he'd been watching her closely enough that he knew that she had done that just twenty minutes earlier.

He completed his dance with his mother, bade her farewell, then ambled casually over to the north side of the room, where he'd last seen Francesca. He had to move quickly, lest someone tried to waylay him. But he kept his ears open as he moved through the crowds. No one, however, seemed to be speaking of her.

When he reached her previous location, however, he noticed French doors, presumably to the back garden. They were curtained and closed, of course; it was only April, and not warm enough to be letting the night air in, even with a crowd of three hundred heating up the room. Michael was instantly suspicious; he'd lured too many women out to gardens himself not to be aware of what could happen in the dark of the night.

He slipped outside, making his exit unobtrusive. If Francesca was indeed out in the back garden with a gentleman, the last thing he wanted was a crowd trailing in his wake.

The rumble of the party seemed to pulsate through the glass doors, but even with that, the night felt quiet.

Then he heard her voice.

And it sliced his gut.

She sounded happy, he realized, more than content to be in the company of whatever man had lured her out into the dark. Michael couldn't make out her words, but she was definitely laughing. It was a musical, tinkling sound, and it ended in a soul-searing, flirtatious murmur.

Michael put his hand back on the knob. He should leave. She wouldn't want him here.

But he was rooted to the spot.

He'd never — ever — spied on her with John. Not once had he listened in on a conversation that wasn't meant to include him. If he stumbled within earshot, he had always removed himself immediately. But now — it was different. He couldn't explain it, but it was different, and he could not force himself to leave.

One more minute, he swore to himself. That was all. One more minute to assure that she was not in a dangerous situation, and —

"No, no."

Francesca's voice.

His ears pricked up and he took a few steps in the direction of her voice. She didn't sound upset, but she *was* saying no. Of course, she could be laughing about a joke, or maybe some inane piece of gossip.

"I really must — *No!*"

And that was all it took for Michael to move.

Francesca knew that she shouldn't have come outside with Sir Geoffrey Fowler, but he had been polite and charming, and she was feeling a trifle warm in the crowded ballroom. It was the sort of thing she'd never have done as an unmarried debutante, but widows weren't held to quite the same standards, and besides, Sir Geoffrey had said that he would leave the door ajar.

All had been perfectly pleasant for the first few minutes. Sir Geoffrey made her laugh, and he made her feel beautiful, and it was almost heartbreaking to realize how much she'd missed that. And so she had laughed and flirted, and allowed herself to melt into the moment. She wanted to feel like a woman again — maybe not in the fullest sense of the word, but still, was it so wrong to enjoy the heady intoxication of knowing that she was desired?

Maybe they were all after her now infamous double dowry, maybe they wanted the alignment with two of Britain's most notable families — Francesca was both a Bridgerton and a Stirling, after all. But for one lovely evening, she was going to let herself believe it was all about *her*.

But then Sir Geoffrey had moved closer. Francesca had backed up as discreetly as she was able, but he took another step in her direction, and then another, and before she knew it, her back was against a fat-trunked tree, and Sir Geoffrey's hands were planted against the bark, each uncomfortably close to her head.

"Sir Geoffrey," Francesca said, endeavoring to remain polite as long as she possibly could, "I'm afraid there has been a misunderstanding. I believe I would like to return to the party." She kept her voice light and friendly, not wishing to provoke him into something she would regret.

His head dipped an inch closer to hers. "Now, why would you want to do that?" he murmured.

"No, no," she said, ducking to the side as he came in closer, "people will be missing me." Dash it all, she was going to have to stamp on his foot, or worse, unman him in the manner her brothers had taught her back when she was a green girl. "Sir Geoffrey," she said, trying one last time for civility, "I really must —"

And then his mouth, wet and mushy and entirely unwelcome, landed on hers.

"— No!" she managed to squeal.

But he was quite determined to mash her with his lips. Francesca twisted this way and that, but he was stronger than she had realized, and he clearly had no intention of letting her escape. Still struggling, she maneuvered her leg so that she might jam her knee up into his groin, but before she could do that, Sir Geoffrey seemed to . . . quite simply . . . disappear.

"Oh!" The surprised sound flew from her lips of its own accord. There was a flurry of movement, a noise that sounded rather sickeningly like knuckles on flesh, and one very heartfelt cry of pain. By the time Francesca had any idea what was going on, Sir Geoffrey was sprawled on the ground, swearing most vehemently, and a large man loomed over him, his boot planted firmly on Sir Geoffrey's chest.

"Michael?" Francesca asked, unable to believe her eyes.

"Say the word," Michael said, in a voice

she had never dreamed could cross his lips, "and I will crush his ribs."

"No!" Francesca said quickly. She'd not have felt the least bit guilty for kneeing Sir Geoffrey between the legs, but she didn't want Michael to *kill* the man.

And from the look on Michael's face, she was quite certain he would have happily done so.

"That's not necessary," she said, hurrying to Michael's side and then backing up when she saw the feral gleam in his eyes. "Er, perhaps we could just ask him to leave?"

For a moment Michael did nothing but stare at her. Hard, in the eyes, and with an intensity that robbed her of the ability to breathe. Then he ground his boot down into Sir Geoffrey's chest. Not too very much harder, but enough to make the supine man grunt with discomfort.

"Are you certain?" Michael bit off.

"Yes, please, there's no need to hurt him," Francesca said. Good heavens, this would be a nightmare if anyone caught them thus. Her reputation would be tarnished, and heaven knew what they'd say about Michael, attacking a well-respected baronet. "I shouldn't have come out here with him," she added.

"No, you shouldn't have done," Michael said harshly, "but that hardly gives him leave to force his attentions on you." Abruptly, he removed his boot from Sir Geoffrey's chest and hauled the quivering man to his feet. Grabbing him by his lapels, he pinned him against the tree and then jerked his own body forward until the two men were nearly nose to nose.

"Doesn't feel so good to be trapped, does it?" Michael taunted.

Sir Geoffrey said nothing, just stared at him in terror.

"Do you have something to say to the lady?"

Sir Geoffrey shook his head frantically.

Michael slammed his head back against the tree. "Think harder!" he growled.

"I'm sorry!" Sir Geoffrey squeaked.

Rather like a girl, Francesca thought dispassionately. She'd known he wouldn't make a good husband, but that clinched it.

But Michael was not through with him. "If you ever step within ten yards of Lady Kilmartin again, I will personally disembowel you."

Even Francesca flinched.

"Am I understood?" Michael ground out.

Another squeak, and this time Sir Geoffrey sounded like he might cry.

"Get out of here," Michael grunted, shoving the terrified man away. "And while you're at it, endeavor to leave town for a month or so."

Sir Geoffrey looked at him in shock.

Michael stood still, dangerously so, and then shrugged one insolent shoulder. "You won't be missed," he said softly.

Francesca realized she was holding her breath. He was terrifying, but he was also magnificent, and it shook her to her very core to realize that she'd never seen him thus.

Never dreamed he could *be* like this.

Sir Geoffrey ran off, heading across the lawn to the back gate, leaving Francesca alone with Michael, alone and, for the first time since she'd known him, without a word to say.

Except, perhaps, "I'm sorry."

Michael turned on her with a ferocity that nearly sent her reeling. "Don't apologize," he bit off.

"No, of course not," she said, "but I should have known better, and —"

"*He* should have known better," he said savagely.

It was true, and Francesca was certainly not going to take the blame for her attack, but at the same time, she thought it best not to feed his anger any further, at least not right now. She'd never seen him like this. In truth, she'd never seen anyone like this — wound so tightly with fury that he seemed as if he might snap into pieces. She'd thought he was out of control, but now, as she watched him, standing so still she was afraid to breathe, she realized that the opposite was true.

Michael was holding onto his control like a vise; if he hadn't, Sir Geoffrey would be lying in a bloody heap right now.

Francesca opened her mouth to say something more, something placating or even funny, but she found herself without words, without the ability to do anything but watch him, this man she'd thought she knew so well.

There was something mesmerizing about the moment, and she couldn't take her eyes off of him. He was breathing hard, obviously still struggling to control his anger, and he was, she realized with curiosity, not entirely *there*. He was staring at some far off horizon, his eyes unfocused, and he looked almost . . .

In pain.

"Michael?" she whispered.

No reaction.

"Michael?" This time, she reached out and touched him, and he flinched, whipping around so quickly that she stumbled backward.

"What is it?" he asked gruffly.

"Nothing," she stammered, not certain what it was she'd meant to say, not even certain if she'd *had* something to say other than his name.

He closed his eyes for a moment, then opened them, clearly waiting for her to say more.

"I believe I will go home," she said. The party no longer held appeal; all she wanted to do was cocoon herself where all was safe and familiar.

Because Michael was suddenly neither of those things.

"I will make your apologies inside," he said stiffly.

"I'll send the carriage back for you and the mothers," Francesca added. The last she'd looked, Janet and Helen were enjoying themselves immensely. She didn't want to cut their evening short.

"Shall I escort you through the back gate, or would you rather go through the ball?"

"The back gate, I think," she said.

And he did, the full distance to the carriage, his hand burning at her back the entire way. But when she reached the carriage, instead of accepting his assistance to climb up, she turned to him, a question suddenly burning on her lips.

"How did you know I was in the garden?" she inquired.

He didn't say anything. Or maybe he would have done, just not quickly enough to suit her.

"Were you watching me?" she asked.

His lips curved, not quite into a smile, not even into the beginnings of a smile. "I'm always watching you," he said grimly.

And she was left with *that* to ponder for the rest of the evening.

Chapter 14

. . . Did Francesca say that she misses me? Or did you merely infer it?

> — *from the Earl of Kilmartin to his mother, Helen Stirling, two years and two months after his departure for India*

Three hours later, Francesca was sitting in her bedroom back at Kilmartin House when she heard Michael return. Janet and Helen had come home quite a bit earlier, and when Francesca had (somewhat purposefully) run into them in the hall, they'd informed her that Michael had chosen to round out his evening with a visit to his club.

Most likely to avoid *her*, she'd decided, even though there was no reason for him to expect to see her at such a late hour. Still, she had left the ball earlier that evening with the distinct impression that Michael did not desire her company. He had defended her honor with all the valor and purpose of a true hero, but she couldn't help but feel that it was done almost reluctantly, as if it was something he *had* to do, not something he wanted to do.

And even worse, that she was someone whose company he had to endure, rather than the cherished friend she had always told herself she was.

That, she realized, hurt.

Francesca told herself that when he returned to Kilmartin House she would leave well enough alone. She would do nothing but listen at the door as he tramped down the hallway to his bedchamber. (She was honest enough with herself to admit that she was not above — and in fact fundamentally unable to resist — eavesdropping.) Then she would scoot over to the heavy oak door that connected their rooms (locked on both sides since her return from her mother's; she certainly didn't fear Michael, but proprieties were proprieties) and then listen there a few minutes longer.

She had no idea what she'd be listening for, or even why she felt the need to hear his footsteps as he moved about his room, but she simply had to do it. Something had changed tonight. Or maybe nothing had changed, which might have been worse. Was it possible that Michael had never been the man she'd thought he was? Could she have been so close to him for so long, counted him as one of her dearest friends, even when they'd been estranged, and still not *known* him?

She'd never dreamed that Michael might have secrets from her. From *her!* Everyone else, maybe, but not her.

And it left her feeling rather off balance and untidy. Almost as if someone had come up to Kilmartin House and shoved a pile of bricks under the south wall, setting the entire world at a drunken slant. No matter what she did, no matter what she thought, she still felt as if she were sliding. To where, she didn't know, and she didn't dare hazard a guess.

But the ground was most definitely no longer firm beneath her feet.

Her bedroom faced the front of Kilmartin House, and when all was quiet she could hear the front door close, provided the person closing it did so with enough force. It didn't need to be slammed, but —

Well, whatever firmness it required, Michael evidently was exercising it, because she heard the telltale thunk beneath her feet, followed by a low rumble of voices,

295

presumably Priestley chatting with him as he took his coat.

Michael was home, which meant she could finally just go to bed and at least pretend to sleep. He was home, which meant that it was time to declare the evening officially over. She should put this behind her, move on, maybe pretend nothing had happened . . .

But when she heard his footsteps coming up the stairs, she did the one thing she never would have expected herself to do —

She opened her door and dashed out into the hall.

She had no idea what she was doing. Not even a clue. By the time her bare feet touched the runner carpet, she was so shocked at her own actions that she found herself somewhat frozen and out of breath.

Michael looked exhausted. And surprised. And heartstoppingly handsome with his cravat slightly loosened and his midnight hair falling in wavy locks over his forehead. Which left her wondering — When had she begun to notice how handsome he was? It had always been something that had simply been *there*, that she knew in an intellectual sense but never really took note of.

But now . . .

Her breath caught. Now his beauty seemed to fill the air around her, swirling about her skin, leaving her shivery and hot, all at the same time.

"Francesca," Michael said, her name more of a tired statement than anything else.

And of course she had nothing to say. It was so unlike her to do something like this, to rush in without thinking about what she was planning, but she didn't particularly feel like herself that evening. She was so unsettled, so off balance, and the only thought in her head (if indeed there had been any) before dashing out her door was that she had to *see* him. Just catch a glimpse and maybe hear his voice. If she could convince herself that he really *was* the person she thought she knew, then maybe she was still the same, too.

Because she didn't feel the same.

And it shook her to the core.

"Michael," she said, finally finding her voice. "I . . . Good evening."

He just looked at her, raising one brow at her remarkably meaningless statement.

She cleared her throat. "I wanted to make sure you were, er . . . all right." The ending sounded a little weak, even to her ears, but it was the best adjective she could come up with on such short notice.

"I'm fine," he said gruffly. "Just tired."

"Of course," she said. "Of course, of course."

He smiled, but entirely without humor. "Of course."

She swallowed, then tried to smile, but it felt forced. "I didn't thank you earlier," she said.

"For what?"

"For coming to my aid," she replied, thinking that ought to be obvious. "I would have . . . Well, I would have defended myself." At his wry glance, she added, somewhat defensively, "My brothers showed me how."

He crossed his arms and looked down at her in a vaguely paternalistic manner. "In that case, I'm sure you would have rendered him a soprano in no time."

She pinched her lips together. "Regardless," she said, deciding not to comment upon his sarcasm, "I very much appreciated not having to, er . . ." She blushed. Oh, God, she hated when she blushed.

"Knee him in the ballocks?" Michael finished helpfully, one corner of his mouth curving into a mocking smile.

"Indeed," she ground out, quite convinced that her cheeks had gone from pink straight to crimson, skipping all shades of rose, fuchsia, and red along the way.

"You're quite welcome," he said abruptly, giving her a nod that was meant to indicate the end of the conversation. "Now, if you will excuse me."

He moved as if heading for his bedroom door, but Francesca wasn't quite ready (and she was certain that the devil himself only knew why) to end the conversation. "Wait!" she called out, gulping when she realized that now she was going to have to *say* something.

He turned around, slowly and with a strange sense of deliberation. "Yes?"

"I . . . I just . . ."

He waited while she floundered, then finally said, "Can it wait until morning?"

"No! Wait!" And this time she reached out and grabbed his arm.

He froze.

"Why are you so angry with me?" she whispered.

He just shook his head, as if he couldn't quite believe her question. But he did not take his eyes off of her hand on his arm. "What are you talking about?" he asked.

"Why are you so angry with me?" she repeated, and she realized that she hadn't even realized she'd felt this way until the words had left her lips. But something wasn't right between them, and she had to know why.

"Don't be ridiculous," he muttered. "I'm not angry with you. I'm merely tired, and I want to go to bed."

"You are. I'm sure you are." Her voice was rising with conviction. Now that she'd said it, she knew it was true. He tried to hide it, and he'd become quite accomplished at apologizing when it slipped to the fore, but there was anger inside of him, and it was directed at her.

Michael placed his hand over hers. Francesca gasped at the heat of the contact, but then all he did was lift her hand off of his arm and allow it to drop. "I'm going to bed," he announced.

And then he turned his back on her. Walked away.

"No! You can't go!" She dashed after him, unthinking, unheedful . . .

Right into his bedroom.

If he hadn't been angry before, he was now. "What are you doing here?" he demanded.

"You can't just dismiss me," she protested.

He stared at her. Hard. "You are in my bedchamber," he said in a low voice. "I suggest you leave."

"Not until you explain to me what is going on."

Michael held himself perfectly still. His every muscle had frozen into a hard, stiff line, and it was a blessing, really, because if he'd allowed himself to move — if he'd felt even capable of moving — he would have lunged at her. And what he would do when he caught her was anyone's guess.

He'd been pushed to the edge. First by her brother, and then by Sir Geoffrey, and now by Francesca herself, standing in front of him without a bloody clue.

His world had been overturned by a single suggestion.

Why don't you just marry her?

It dangled before him like a ripe apple, a wicked possibility that shouldn't be his to take.

John, his conscience pounded. *John. Remember John.*

"Francesca," he said, his voice hard and controlled, "it is well past midnight, and you are in the bedchamber of a man to whom you are not married. I suggest you leave."

But she didn't. Damn her, she didn't even move. She just stood there, three feet past the still-open doorway, staring at him as if she'd never seen him before.

He tried not to notice that her hair was loose. He tried not to see that she was wearing her nightclothes. They were demure, yes, but still meant to be removed, and his gaze kept dipping to the silken hem, which brushed the top of her foot, allowing him a tantalizing peek at her toes.

Good God, he was staring at her toes. Her *toes*. What had his life come to?

"Why are you angry with me?" she asked again.

"I'm not," he snapped. "I just want you to get the h—" He caught himself at the last moment. "To get out of my room."

"Is it because I wish to remarry?" she asked, her voice choked with emotion. "Is that it?"

He didn't know how to answer, so he just glared at her.

"You think I'm betraying John," she said accusingly. "You think I should spend my days mourning your cousin."

Michael closed his eyes. "No, Francesca," he said wearily, "I would never —"

But she wasn't listening. "Do you think I don't mourn him?" she demanded. "Do you think I don't think about him each and every day? Do you think it feels *good* to know that when I marry, I'll be making a mockery of the sacrament?"

He looked at her. She was breathing hard, caught up in her anger and maybe her grief as well.

"What I had with John," she said, her entire body shaking now, "I'm not going to find with any of the men sending me flowers. And it feels like a desecration — a selfish desecration that I'm even considering remarrying. If I didn't want a baby so . . . so *damned* much . . ."

She broke off, maybe from overemotion, maybe just at the shock of having actually cursed aloud. She just stood there, blinking, her lips parted and quivering, looking as if she might break at the merest touch.

He should have been more sympathetic. He should have tried to comfort her. And he would have done both of those things, if they had been in any other room besides his bedchamber. But as it was, it was all he could do just to control his breathing.

And himself.

She looked back up at him, her eyes huge and heartstoppingly blue, even in the candlelight. "You don't know," she said, turning away. She walked to a long, low bureau of drawers. She leaned heavily against it, her fingers biting the wood.

"You just don't know," she whispered, her back still to him.

And somehow that was more than he could take. She had barged her way in here, demanding answers when she didn't even understand the questions. She'd invaded his bedchamber, pushed him to the limit, and now she was just going to *dismiss* him? Turn her back on him and tell him *he* didn't know?

"Don't know what?" he demanded, just before he crossed the room. His feet were silent but swift, and before he knew it he was right behind her, close enough to touch, close enough to grab what he wanted and —

She whirled around. "You —"

And then she stopped. Didn't make another sound. Did nothing but allow her eyes to lock onto his.

"Michael?" she whispered. And he didn't know what she meant. Was it a question? A plea?

She stood there, stock still, the only sound her breath over her lips. And her eyes never left his face.

His fingers tingled. His body burned. She was close. As close as she'd ever stood to him. And if she were anyone else, he would have sworn that she wanted to be kissed.

Her lips were parted, her eyes were unfocused. And her chin seemed to tilt up, as if she were waiting, wishing, wondering when he would finally bend down and seal her fate.

He felt himself say something. Her name, maybe. His chest grew tight, and his heart pounded, and suddenly the impossible became the inevitable, and he realized that this time there was no stopping. This time it wasn't about his control or his sacrifice or his guilt.

This time was for him.

And he was going to kiss her.

When she thought about it later, the only excuse she could come up with was that she didn't know he was right behind her. The carpet was soft and thick, and she hadn't heard his footsteps over the roaring of blood in her ears. She didn't know all that, she *couldn't* have, because then she *never* would have whirled around, intending for all the world to silence him with a scathing retort. She was going to say something horrid and cutting, and intended to make him feel guilty and awful, but when she turned . . .

He was right there.

Close, so close. Mere inches away. It had

been years since anyone had stood so close to her, and never, *ever* Michael.

She couldn't speak, couldn't think, couldn't do anything but breathe as she stared at his face, realizing with an awful intensity that she wanted him to kiss her.

Michael.

Good God, she wanted Michael.

It was like a knife slicing through her. She wasn't supposed to feel this. She wasn't supposed to want *anyone*. But Michael . . .

She should have walked away. Hell, she should have run. But something rooted her to the spot. She couldn't take her eyes off of his, couldn't help but moisten her lips, and when his hands settled on her shoulders, she didn't protest.

She didn't even move.

And maybe, just maybe she even leaned in a little, something within her recognizing this moment, this subtle dance between man and woman.

It had been so long since she'd swayed into a kiss, but it seemed that there were some things a body did not forget.

He touched her chin, raised her face just the barest hint.

Still, she didn't say no.

She stared at him, licked her lips, and waited . . .

Waited for the moment, the first touch, because as terrifying and wrong as it was, she knew it would feel like perfection.

And it did.

His lips touched hers in the barest, softest hint of a caress. It was the sort of kiss that seduced with subtlety, sent tingles through her body and left her desperate for more. Somewhere in the hazy back recesses of her mind, she knew that this was wrong, that it was more than wrong — it was insane. But she couldn't have moved if the fires of hell were licking at her feet.

She was mesmerized, transfixed by his touch. She couldn't quite bring herself to make another move, to invite him in any other manner than the soft sway of her body, but neither did she make any attempt to break the contact.

She just waited, breath baited, for him to do something more.

And he did. His hand found the small of her back and splayed there, his fingers tempting her with their intoxicating heat. He didn't exactly pull her toward him, but the pressure was there, and the space between them whispered away until she could feel the gentle scrape of his evening clothes through the silk of her dressing gown.

And she grew hot. Molten.

Wicked.

His lips grew more demanding, and hers parted, allowing him greater exploration. He took full advantage, his tongue swooping in in a dangerous dance, teasing and tempting, stoking her desire until her legs grew weak, and she had no choice but to grasp onto his upper arms, to hold him, to touch him of her own accord, to acknowledge that she was there in the kiss, too, that she was taking part.

That she wanted this.

He murmured her name, his voice hoarse with desire and need and something more, something pained, but all she could do was hold onto him, and let him kiss her, and God help her, kiss him back.

Her hand moved to his neck, reveling in the soft heat of his skin. His hair was slightly long these days and curled onto her fingers, thick and crisp, and — Oh, God, she just wanted to sink into it.

His hand slid up her back, leaving a trail of fire in its wake. His fingers caressed her shoulder, slid down her arm, and then over to her breast.

Francesca froze.

But Michael was too far gone to notice; he cupped her, moaning audibly as he squeezed.

"No," she whispered. This was too much, it was too intimate.

It was too . . . *Michael.*

"Francesca," he murmured, his lips trailing along her cheek to her ear.

"No," she said, and she wrenched herself free. "I can't."

She didn't want to look at him, but she couldn't *not* do it. And when she did, she was sorry.

His chin was dipped, and his face was slightly turned, but he was still staring at her, his eyes searing and intense.

And she was burned.

"I can't do this," she whispered.

He said nothing.

The words came faster, but not in greater numbers. "I can't. I can't. I can't . . . I . . . I —"

"Then go," he bit off. "Now."

She ran.

She ran to her bedroom, and then the next day she ran to her mother.

And then the day after that, she ran all the way to Scotland.

Chapter 15

... I am pleased that you are thriving in India, but I do wish you would consider returning home. We all miss you, and you do have responsibilities that cannot be fulfilled from abroad.

— from Helen Stirling to her son, the Earl of Kilmartin, two years and four months after his departure for India

Francesca had always been a rather good liar, and, Michael reflected as he read the short letter she'd left for Helen and Janet, she was even better when she could avoid face-to-face contact and do it in writing.

An emergency had arisen at Kilmartin, Francesca had written, describing the outbreak of spotted fever among the sheep in admirable detail, and it required her immediate attention. They weren't to worry, she assured them, she'd be back soon, and she promised to bring down some of Cook's splendid raspberry jam, which, as they all knew, was unmatched by any confection in London.

Never mind that Michael had never heard of a sheep contracting spotted fever, or any other farm animal for that matter. Where, one had to wonder, did the sheep show their spots?

It was all very neat, and all very easy, and Michael wondered if Francesca had even arranged for Janet and Helen to be out of town for the weekend just so that she could make her escape without having to make her farewells face to face.

And it *was* an escape. There was no doubting that. Michael didn't believe for one minute that there was an emergency up at Kilmartin. If that had been the case, Francesca would have felt duty bound to inform him of it. She might have been running the estate for years, but he was the earl, and she wasn't the sort to usurp or undermine his position now that he was back.

Besides, he had kissed her, and more than that, he had seen her face after he'd kissed her.

If she could have run to the moon, she would have done so.

Janet and Helen hadn't seemed too terribly concerned that she was gone, although they did chatter on (and on and on) about how they missed her company.

Michael just sat in his study, pondering methods of self-flagellation.

He had kissed her. *Kissed* her.

Not, he thought wryly, the best course of action for a man attempting to hide his true feelings.

Six years, he'd known her. Six years, and he'd kept everything beneath the surface, played his role to perfection. Six years, and he'd gone and ruined the whole thing with one simple kiss.

Except there hadn't been anything simple about it.

How was it possible that a kiss could exceed his every fantasy? And with six years to fantasize, he'd imagined some truly superior kisses.

But this . . . it was more. It was better. It was . . .

It was Francesca.

Funny how that changed everything. You could think about a woman every day for years, imagine what she might feel like in your arms, but it never, ever matched the real thing.

And now he was worse off than ever before. Yes, he'd kissed her; yes, it had been quite the most spectacular kiss of his life.

But yes, it was also all over.

And it wasn't going to happen again.

Now that it had finally happened, now that he had tasted perfection, he was in more agony than ever before. Now he knew exactly what he was missing; he understood with painful clarity just what it was that would never be his.

And nothing would ever be the same.

They would never be friends again. Francesca was not the sort of woman who could treat an intimacy lightly. And as she hated awkwardness of any kind, she would go out of her way to avoid his presence.

Hell, she'd gone all the way to Scotland just to be rid of him. A woman couldn't make her feelings much clearer than that.

And the note she'd penned to him — Well, it was far less conversational than the one she'd left for Janet and Helen.

It was wrong. Forgive me.

What the hell she thought she needed forgiveness for was beyond him. *He* had kissed *her*. She might have entered his bedchamber against his wishes, but he was man enough to know that she had not done so with the expectation that he might maul her. She had been concerned because she thought he was angry with her, for God's sake.

She had acted rashly, but only because she cared for him and valued their friendship.

And now he had gone and ruined *that*.

He still wasn't quite certain how it had happened. He'd been looking at her; he couldn't take his eyes off of her. The moment was seared in his brain — her pink silk dressing robe, the way her fingers had pinched together as she spoke to him. Her hair had been loose, hanging over one shoulder, and her eyes had been huge and wet with emotion.

And then she had turned away.

That was when it had happened. That was when everything had changed. Something had risen within him, something he couldn't possibly identify, and his feet had moved. Somehow he found himself across the room, inches away, close enough to touch, close enough to take.

Then she had turned back.

And he was lost.

There was no stopping himself at that point, no listening to reason. Whatever fist of control he'd kept wrapped around his desire for years had simply evaporated, and he had to kiss her.

It had been as simple as that. There had been no choice involved, no free will. Maybe if she'd said no, maybe if she'd backed up and walked away. But she did neither of those things; she just stood there, her breath the only sound between them, and waited.

Had she waited for the kiss? Or had she waited for him to come to his senses and step away?

It was no matter, he thought harshly, crumpling a piece of paper between his fingers. The floor around his desk was now littered with crumpled pieces of paper. He was in a destructive mood, and the sheets were easy targets. He picked up a creamy white card sitting on his blotter and glanced at it before readying his fingers for the kill. It was an invitation.

He stopped, then took a closer look. It was for tonight, and he'd probably answered in the affirmative. He was quite certain Francesca had planned to go; the hostess was a longtime friend of hers.

Maybe he should drag his pathetic self upstairs and dress for the evening. Maybe he should go out, find himself a wife. It probably wouldn't cure what ailed him, but it had to be done sooner or later. And it had to be better for the soul than sitting around and drinking behind his desk.

He stood, eyeing the invitation again. He sighed. He really didn't want to spend the evening socializing with a hundred people who were going to ask after Francesca. With his luck, the party would be full of Bridgertons, or even worse, Bridgerton females, who looked fiendishly alike with their chestnut hair and wide smiles. None held a candle to Francesca, of course — her sisters were almost too friendly, too sunny and open. They lacked Frannie's sense of mystery, the ironic twinkle that colored her eyes.

No, he didn't want to spend the evening among polite company.

And so he decided to take care of his problems as he had so many times before.

By finding himself a woman.

Three hours later, Michael was at the front door to his club, his mood stunningly foul.

He'd gone to La Belle Maison, which was, if one wanted to be honest about it, nothing but a brothel, but as far as brothels went, it was classy and discreet, and one could be assured that the women were clean and there of their own free will. Michael had been an occasional guest during the years he'd lived in London; most men of his acquaintance had visited La Belle, as they liked to call it, at one point or another. Even John had gone, before he'd married Francesca.

He'd been greeted with great warmth by the madam, treated like a prodigal son. He had a reputation, she explained; and they'd missed his presence. The women had always adored him, frequently remarking that he was one of the few who seemed to care for their pleasure as well as his own.

For some reason, the flattery just left a sour taste in his mouth. He didn't feel like a legendary lover just then; he was sick of his rakish reputation and didn't much care if he pleased anyone that night. He just wanted a woman who might make his mind a delirious blank, even if only for a scant few minutes.

They had just the girl for him, the madam cooed. She was new and in great demand, and he would love her. Michael just shrugged and allowed himself to be led to a petite blond beauty that he was assured was the "very best."

He started to reach out for her, but then

his hand dropped. She wasn't right. She was too blond. He didn't want a blond.

Quite all right, he was told, and out emerged a ravishing brunette.

Too exotic.

A redhead?

All wrong.

Out they came, one after another, but they were too young, too old, too buxom, too slight, and then finally he'd selected one at random, determined to just close his damned eyes and get it over with.

He'd lasted two minutes.

The door had shut behind him and he'd felt sick, almost panicked, and he realized he couldn't do it.

He couldn't make love to a woman. It was appalling. Emasculating. Hell, he might as well have grabbed a knife and eunuched himself.

Before, he had taken his pleasure with women to blot out *one* woman. But now that he'd tasted her, even with one fleeting kiss, he was ruined.

And so instead he'd come here, to his club, where he didn't have to worry about seeing anyone of the female persuasion. The aim, of course, was to wipe Francesca's face from his mind, and he was rather hoping that alcohol would work where the delectable girls of La Belle Maison had not.

"Kilmartin."

Michael looked up. Colin Bridgerton.

Damn.

"Bridgerton," he grunted. Damn damn damn. Colin Bridgerton was the last person he wanted to see right now. Even the ghost of Napoleon, come down to slice a rapier through his gullet, would have been preferable.

"Sit down," Colin said, motioning to the chair across from him.

There was no getting out of it; he could have lied and said he was meeting someone, but he still would have no excuse for not sitting with Colin to share a quick drink while he was waiting. And so Michael just gritted his teeth and sat, hoping that Colin had another engagement that would require his presence in — oh, about three minutes.

Colin picked up his tumbler, regarded it with curious diligence, then swirled the amber liquid around several times before taking a small sip. "I understand that Francesca has returned to Scotland."

Michael gave a grunt and a nod.

"Surprising, wouldn't you think? With the season still so young."

"I don't pretend to know her mind."

"No, no, of course you wouldn't," Colin said softly. "No man of any intelligence would pretend to know a female mind."

Michael said nothing.

"Still, it's only been . . . what . . . a fortnight since she came down?"

"Just over," Michael bit off. Francesca had returned to London the precise day that he had done.

"Right, of course. Yes, you'd know that, wouldn't you?"

Michael shot Colin a sharp look. What the hell was he getting at?

"Ah, well," Colin said, lifting one of his shoulders into a careless shrug. "I'm sure she'll be back soon. Not likely to find a husband up in Scotland, after all, and that is her aim for this spring, is it not?"

Michael nodded tersely, eyeing a table across the room. It was empty. So empty. So joyfully, blessedly empty.

He could picture himself a very happy man at that table.

"Not feeling very conversational this evening, are we?" Colin asked, breaking into his (admittedly tame) fantasies.

"No," Michael said, not appreciating the vague hint of condescension in the other man's voice, "*we* are not."

Colin chuckled, then took the last sip of his drink. "Just testing you," he said, leaning back in his chair.

"To see if I have spontaneously divided into two separate beings?" Michael bit off.

"No, of course not," Colin said with a suspiciously easy grin. "I can see that quite clearly. I was merely testing your mood."

Michael arched a brow in a most forbidding manner. "And you found it . . . ?"

"Rather as usual," Colin answered, undeterred.

Michael did nothing but scowl at him as the waiter arrived with their drinks.

"To happiness," Colin said, lifting his glass in the air.

I am going to strangle him, Michael decided right then and there. *I am going to reach across the table and wrap my hands around his throat until those annoying green eyes pop right out of his head.*

"No toast to happiness?" Colin asked.

Michael let out an incoherent grunt and downed his glass in one gulp.

"What are you drinking?" Colin asked conversationally. He leaned over and peered at Michael's glass. "Must be jolly good stuff."

Michael fought the urge to clock him over the head with his now empty tumbler.

"Very well," Colin said with a shrug, "I shall toast to my own happiness, then." He took a sip, leaned back, then touched his lips to the glass again.

Michael glanced at the clock.

"Isn't it a good thing I have nowhere to be?" Colin mused.

Michael let his glass drop down onto the table with a loud *thunk*. "Is there a point to any of this?" he demanded.

For a moment it looked like Colin, who could, by all accounts, talk anyone under the table when he so chose, would remain silent. But then, just when Michael was ready to give up on any guise of politeness and simply get up and leave, he said, "Have you decided what you're going to do?"

Michael held himself very still. "Meaning?"

Colin smiled, with just enough condescension that Michael wanted to punch him. "About Francesca, of course," he said.

"Didn't we just confirm that she has left the country?" Michael said carefully.

Colin shrugged. "Scotland's not so very far away."

"It's far enough," Michael muttered. Certainly far enough to make it abundantly clear that she didn't want anything to do with him.

"She'll be all alone," Colin said on a sigh.

Michael just narrowed his eyes and stared at him. Hard.

"I still think you should —" Colin broke himself off, quite on purpose, Michael was convinced. "Well, you know what I think," Colin finally finished, taking a sip of his drink.

And Michael just gave up on being polite. "You don't know a damned thing, Bridgerton."

Colin raised his brows at the snarl in Michael's voice. "Funny," he murmured, "I hear that very thing all day long. Usually from my sisters."

Michael was familiar with this tactic. Colin's neat sidestep was exactly the sort of maneuver he himself employed with such facility. And it was for probably this reason that his right hand had formed a fist under the table. Nothing had the power to irritate like the reflection of one's own behavior in someone else.

But oh God, Colin's face was so close.

"Another whisky?" Colin asked, effectively ruining Michael's lovely vision of blackened eyes.

Michael was in the perfect mood to drink himself into oblivion, but *not* in the company of Colin Bridgerton, so he just let out a terse, "No," and pushed his chair back.

"You do realize, Kilmartin," Colin said, his voice so soft it was almost chilling, "that there is no reason you can't marry her. None at all. Except, of course," he added, almost as an afterthought, "the reasons you manufacture for yourself."

Michael felt something tearing in his chest. His heart, probably, but he was growing so used to the feeling it was a wonder he still noticed it.

And Colin, damn his eyes, just wouldn't shut up.

"If you don't want to marry her," Colin said thoughtfully, "then you don't want to marry her. But —"

"She might say no," Michael heard himself say. His voice sounded rough, choked, foreign to his ears.

Dear God, if he'd jumped on the table and declared his love for Francesca, he couldn't have made it any more clear.

Colin's head tilted a fraction of an inch to the side, just enough to acknowledge that he'd heard the subtext in Michael's words. "She might," he murmured. "In fact, she probably will. Women often do, the first time you ask."

"And how many times have you proposed marriage?"

Colin smiled slowly. "Just once, actually. This afternoon, as a matter of fact."

It was the one thing — truly, the only thing — that Colin could have said to completely diffuse Michael's churning emotions. "I beg your pardon?" Michael asked, his jaw dropping in shock. This was Colin Bridgerton, the eldest of the unmarried Bridgerton brothers. He'd practically created a profession of avoiding marriage.

"Indeed," Colin said mildly. "Thought it was about time, although I suppose honesty is owed here, so I should probably admit that she did not force me to ask twice. If it makes you feel any better, however, it did take several minutes to wheedle the *yes* out of her."

Michael just stared.

"Her first reaction to my query was to fall to the pavement in surprise," Colin admitted.

Michael fought the impulse to look around to see if he'd somehow been trapped in a theatrical farce without his knowledge. "Er, is she well?" he asked.

"Oh, quite," Colin said, picking up his drink.

Michael cleared his throat. "Might I inquire as to the identity of the lucky lady?"

"Penelope Featherington."

The one who doesn't speak? Michael almost blurted out. Now there was an odd match if ever he'd seen one.

"Now you *really* look surprised," Colin said, thankfully with good humor.

"I did not realize you'd hoped to settle down," Michael hastily improvised.

"Neither did I," Colin said with a smile. "Funny how that works out."

Michael opened his mouth to congratulate him, but instead he heard himself asking, "Has anyone told Francesca?"

"I became engaged *this afternoon,*" Colin reminded him, somewhat bemusedly.

"She'll want to know."

"I expect she will. I certainly tormented her enough as a child. I'm sure she will wish to devise some sort of wedding-related torture for me."

"Someone needs to tell her," Michael said forcefully, ignoring Colin's stroll through his childhood memories.

Colin leaned back in his seat with a casual sigh. "I imagine my mother will pen her a note."

"Your mother will be quite busy. It won't be the first thing on her agenda."

"I couldn't speculate."

Michael frowned. "Someone should tell her about it."

"Yes," Colin said with a smile, "someone should. I'd go myself — It's been an age since I've been up to Scotland. But of course I'm going to be a touch busy here in London, seeing as how I'm getting married. Which is, of course, the entire reason for this discussion, is it not?"

Michael shot him an annoyed glance. He hated that Colin Bridgerton thought he was cleverly manipulating him, but he didn't see how he could disabuse him of that notion without admitting that he desperately wanted to travel to Scotland to see Francesca.

"When is the wedding to be?" he asked.

"I'm not entirely sure yet," Colin said. "Soon, I would hope."

Michael nodded. "Then Francesca will need to be informed right away."

Colin smiled slowly. "Yes, she will, won't she?"

Michael scowled.

"You don't have to marry her while you're up there," Colin said, "just inform her of my impending nuptials."

Michael revisited his earlier fantasy of strangling Colin Bridgerton and found the image even more tantalizing than before.

"I'll see you later," Colin said as Michael headed for the door. "Perhaps a month or so?"

Meaning that he fully expected Michael *not* to be in London anytime soon.

Michael swore under his breath, but he did nothing to contradict him. He might hate himself for it, but now that he had an excuse to go after Francesca, he couldn't resist making the trip.

The question was, would he be able to resist *her?*

And more to the point, did he even want to?

Several days later, Michael was standing at the front door of Kilmartin, his childhood home. It had been years since he'd stood here, more than four, to be precise, and he couldn't quite halt the catch in his throat when he realized that all of *this* — the house, the lands, the legacy — was his. Somehow it hadn't sunk in, perhaps in his brain, but not in his heart.

Springtime didn't seem to have arrived in the border counties of Scotland yet, and the air, while not biting, held a chill that

had him rubbing his gloved hands together. The air was misty and the skies
were gray, but there was something in the
atmosphere that called to him, reminding
his weary soul that *this,* not London and
not India, was home.

But his sense of place was little comfort
as he prepared for what lay ahead. It was
time to face Francesca.

He had rehearsed this moment a thousand times since his conversation with
Colin Bridgerton back in London. What
he'd say to her, how he'd make his case.
And he rather thought he'd figured it out.
Because before he convinced Francesca,
he'd had to convince himself.

He was going to marry her.

He'd have to get her to agree, of course;
he couldn't very well force her into marriage. She'd probably come up with countless reasons why it was a mad idea, but in
the end, he'd convince her.

They would marry.

Marry.

It was the one dream he'd never per-
mitted himself to consider.

But the more he thought about it, the
more it made sense. Forget that he loved
her, forget that he'd loved her for years.
She didn't need to know any of that; telling

her would only make her feel awkward and then he'd feel like a fool.

But if he could present it to her in practical terms, explain why it made *sense* that they marry, he was sure he could warm her to the idea. She might not understand the emotions, not when she didn't feel them herself, but she had a cool head, and she understood sense.

And now that he'd finally allowed himself to imagine a life with her, he couldn't let it go. He *had* to make it happen. He had to.

And it would be good. He might not ever have all of her — her heart, he knew, would never be his — but he'd have most of her, and that would be enough.

It was certainly more than he had now.

And even half of Francesca — Well, that would be ecstasy.

Wouldn't it?

 *Chapter 16*

... but as you have written, Francesca is managing Kilmartin with admirable skill. I do not mean to shirk my duties, and I assure you, had I not such an able stand-in, I would return immediately.

> — *from the Earl of Kilmartin*
> *to his mother, Helen Stirling,*
> *two years and six months*
> *after his departure for India,*
> *written with a muttered,*
> *"She never answered my question."*

Francesca didn't like to think of herself as a coward, but when her choices were that and fool, she chose coward. Gladly.

Because only a fool would have remained in London — in the same house, even — as Michael Stirling after experiencing his kiss.

It had been . . .

No, Francesca wouldn't think about it.

When she thought about it, she inevitably ended up feeling guilty and ashamed, because she wasn't supposed to feel like this about Michael.

Not Michael.

She hadn't planned to feel desire for *anyone*. Truly, the most she'd been hoping for with a husband was a mild, pleasant sensation — a kiss that felt nice against the lips but left her unaffected everywhere else.

That would have been enough.

But now . . . But this . . .

Michael had kissed her. He'd kissed her, and worse, she'd kissed him back, and since then all she could do was imagine his lips on hers, then imagine them everywhere else. And at night, when she was alone in her enormous bed, the dreams became more vivid, and her hand would creep down her body, only to halt before it reached its final destination.

She wouldn't — No, she couldn't fantasize about Michael. It was wrong. She would have felt terrible for feeling this kind of desire about anyone, but Michael . . .

He was John's cousin. His best friend. Her best friend, too. And she shouldn't have kissed him.

But, she thought with a sigh, it had been magnificent.

And that was why she'd had to choose coward over fool and run to Scotland. Because she had no faith in her ability to resist him again.

She'd been at Kilmartin for nearly a week now, trying to immerse herself in the regular, everyday life of the family seat. There was always much to do — accounts to review, tenants to visit — but she didn't find the same satisfaction she usually did in such tasks. The regularity of it should have been soothing, but instead, it just made her restless, and she couldn't force herself to focus, to center her mind on any one thing.

She was jittery and distracted, and half the time she felt as if she didn't know what to do with herself — in the most literal and physical sense. She couldn't seem to sit still, and so she had taken to leaving Kilmartin for hours on end, strapping on her most comfortable boots and trekking across the countryside until she was exhausted.

Not that it made her sleep any better at night, but still, at least she was trying.

And right now she was trying with great vigor, having just hauled herself up Kilmartin's biggest hill. Breathing hard from the exertion, she glanced up at the darkening sky, trying to gauge both the time and the likelihood that it would rain.

Late, and probably.

She frowned. She should head home.

She didn't have far to go, just down the hill and across one grassy field. But by the time she reached Kilmartin's stately front portico, it had begun to sprinkle, and her face was lightly dusted with misty droplets. She removed her bonnet and shook it out, thankful that she'd remembered to don it before leaving — she wasn't always that diligent — and was just heading upstairs to her bedchamber, where she thought she might indulge herself in some chocolate and biscuits, when Davies, the butler, appeared before her.

"My lady?" he said, clearly desiring her attention.

"Yes?"

"You have a visitor."

"A visitor?" Francesca felt her brow furrow in thought. Most everyone who came calling up at Kilmartin had already removed to Edinburgh or London for the season.

"Not precisely a visitor, my lady."

Michael. It had to be. And she couldn't say she was surprised, not exactly. She had thought he might follow her, although she'd assumed he'd do it right away or not at all. Now, after the passage of a sennight, she'd reckoned she might be safe from his attentions.

Safe from her own response to them.

"Where is he?" she asked Davies.

"The earl?"

She nodded.

"Waiting for you in the rose drawing room."

"Has he been here long?"

"No, my lady."

Francesca nodded her dismissal and then forced her feet to carry her down the hall to the drawing room. She shouldn't be dreading this quite so intensely. It was just Michael, for heaven's sake.

Except she had a sinking feeling that he would never be *just Michael* ever again.

Still, it wasn't as if she hadn't gone over what she might say a million times in her head. But all of her platitudes and explanations sounded rather inadequate now that she was faced with the prospect of actually uttering them aloud.

How nice to see you, Michael, she could say, pretending that nothing had happened.

Or — *You must realize that nothing will change* — even though, of course, everything had changed.

Or she could make good humor her guide and open with something like — *Can you believe the silliness of it all?*

Except that she rather doubted either of them had found it silly.

And so she just accepted that she was going to have make it all up as she went along, and she stepped through the doorway into Kilmartin's famed and lovely rose drawing room.

He was standing by the window — watching for her, perhaps? — and didn't turn when she entered. He looked travelworn, with slightly wrinkled clothing and ruffled hair. He wouldn't have ridden all the way to Scotland — only a fool or a man chasing someone to Gretna would do that. But she had traveled with Michael often enough to know that he'd probably joined the driver in front for a fair bit of the trip. He'd always hated closed carriages for long journeys and had more than once sat in the drizzle and rain rather than remain penned in with the rest of the passengers.

She didn't say his name. She could have done, she supposed. She wasn't buying herself very much time; he would turn around soon enough. But for now she just wanted to take the time to acclimate herself to his presence, to make sure that her breathing was under control, that she wasn't going to do something truly foolish like burst into tears, or, just as likely, erupt with silly, nervous laughter.

"Francesca," he said, without even turning around.

He'd sensed her presence, then. Her eyes widened, although she shouldn't have been surprised. Ever since he'd left the army he'd had an almost catlike ability to sense his surroundings. It was probably what had kept him alive during the war. No one, apparently, could attack him from behind.

"Yes," she said. And then, because she thought she should say more, she added, "I trust you had a pleasant journey."

He turned. "Very much so."

She swallowed, trying not to notice how handsome he was. He'd quite taken her breath away in London, but here in Scotland he seemed changed. Wilder, more elemental.

Far more dangerous to her soul.

"Is anything amiss in London?" she asked, hoping there was some sort of practical purpose to his visit. Because if there wasn't, then he had come just for *her,* and that scared the very devil out of her.

"Nothing amiss," he said, "although I do bear news."

She tilted her head, waiting for his reply.

"Your brother has become betrothed."

"Colin?" she asked in surprise. Her brother had been so committed to his life as a bachelor that she wouldn't have been shocked if he'd told her that the lucky fellow was actually her younger brother Gregory, even though he was nearly ten years Colin's junior.

Michael nodded. "To Penelope Featherington."

"To Penel— oh, my, that *is* a surprise. But lovely, I should say. I think she will suit him tremendously."

Michael took a step toward her, his hands remaining clasped behind his back. "I thought you would want to know."

And he couldn't have penned a letter? "Thank you," she said. "I appreciate your thoughtfulness. It's been a long time since we've had a wedding in the family. Not since —"

Mine, they both realized she'd been about to say.

The silence hung in the room like an unwanted guest, and then finally she broke it with, "Well, it has been a long time. My mother must be delighted."

"She is quite," Michael confirmed. "Or so your brother told me. I didn't have an opportunity to converse with her myself."

Francesca cleared her throat, then tried to feign comfort with the strange tableau by giving a little wave with one of her hands as she asked, "Will you stay long?"

"I haven't decided," he said, taking another step in her direction. "It depends."

She swallowed. "On what?"

He'd halved the distance between them. "On you," he said softly.

She knew what he meant, or at least she thought she did, but the last thing she wanted to do just then was acknowledge what had transpired in London, so she backed up a step — which was as far as she could go without actually fleeing the room — and pretended to misunderstand. "Don't be silly," she said. "Kilmartin is yours. You may come and go as you please. I have no control over your actions."

His lips curved into a wry smile. "Is that what you think?" he murmured.

And she realized he'd halved the distance between them yet again.

"I'll have a room readied for you," she said hastily. "Which would you like?"

"It doesn't matter."

"The earl's bedchamber, then," she said,

well aware that she was babbling now. "It's only right. I'll move down the hall. Or, er, to another wing," she added, mumbling.

He took another step toward her. "That may not be necessary."

Her eyes flew to his. What was he suggesting? Surely he didn't think that a single kiss in London would give him leave to avail himself of the connecting door between the earl's and countess's bedchambers?

"Shut the door," he said, nodding at the open doorway behind her.

She glanced backward, even though she knew exactly what she'd see there. "I'm not sure —"

"I am," he said. And then, in a voice that was velvet over steel he said, "Shut it."

She did. She was fairly certain it was a bad idea, but she did it anyway. Whatever he planned to say to her, she didn't particularly care to have overheard by a fleet of servants.

But once her fingers left the doorknob she scooted around him and into the room, setting a more comfortable distance — and an entire seating group — between them.

He looked amused by her actions, but he

did not mock her for them. Instead, he merely said, "I have given matters a great deal of thought since you left London."

As had she, but there seemed little point in mentioning it.

"I hadn't meant to kiss you," he said.

"No!" she said, too loudly. "I mean, no, of course not."

"But now that I have . . . Now that *we* have . . ."

She winced at his use of the plural. He wasn't going to allow her to pretend that she hadn't been a willing participant.

"Now that it is done," he said, "I'm sure you understand that everything is changed."

She looked up at him then; she'd been quite intently focusing on the pink-and-cream fleur-de-lis pattern on the damask-covered sofa. "Of course," she said, trying to ignore the way her throat was beginning to tighten.

His fingers wrapped around the mahogany edge of a Hepplewhite chair. Francesca glanced down at his hands; his knuckles had gone white.

He was nervous, she realized with surprise. She hadn't expected that. She didn't know that she had ever seen him nervous before. He was always such a model of urbane elegance, his charm easy and smooth, his wicked wit always a whisper from his lips.

But now he looked different. Stripped down. Nervous. It made her feel . . . not better, precisely, but maybe not so much like the only fool in the room.

"I have given the matter a great deal of thought," he said.

He was repeating himself now. This was very strange.

"And I have come to a conclusion that surprised even me," he continued, "although now that I have reached it, I am quite convinced it is the best course of action."

With his every word, she felt more in control, less ill at ease. It wasn't that she *wanted* him to feel badly — well, maybe she did; it was only fair after how *she'd* spent the last week. But there was something rather relieving in the knowledge that the awkwardness was not one-sided, that he'd been as disturbed and shaken as she.

Or if not, at least that he had not been unaffected.

He cleared his throat, then moved his chin slightly, stretching his neck. "I believe," he said, his gaze suddenly settling on hers with remarkable clarity, "that we should be married."

What?

Her lips parted.

What?

And then, finally, she said it. *"What?"*

Not *I beg your pardon*. Not even the more succinct *Excuse me*. Just *What?*

"If you listen to my arguments," he said, "you will see that it makes sense."

"Are you mad?"

He drew back slightly. "Not at all."

"I can't marry you, Michael."

"Why not?"

Why not? Because . . . Because . . . "Because I can't!" she finally burst out. "For heaven's sake, you of all people ought to understand the insanity of such a suggestion."

"I will allow that on first reflection, it seems highly irregular, but if you simply listen to my arguments, you will see the sense in it."

She gaped at him. "How can it make sense? I can't think of anything that makes *less* sense!"

"You won't have to move," he said, ticking the items off on his fingers, "and you will retain your title and position."

Convenient, both items, but hardly

reason enough to marry *Michael,* who . . .
well . . . *Michael.*

"You will be able to enter into the marriage knowing that you will be treated with
care and respect," he added. "It could take
months to reach the same conclusion
about another man, and even then, could
you really be certain? Early impressions
can be deceiving, after all."

She searched his face, trying to see if
there was anything, *anything* behind his
words. There had to be some sort of
reason for this, because she just couldn't
grasp that he was proposing. It was mad. It
was . . .

Good God, she wasn't sure what it was.
Was there a word to apply to something
that quite simply removed the earth from
beneath one's feet?

"I will give you children," he said softly.
"Or at least, I will try."

She blushed. She felt it in an instant, her
cheeks turning a furiously hot pink. She
didn't want to imagine herself in bed with
him. She'd spent the last week desperately
trying not to do that.

"What will you gain?" she whispered.

He appeared momentarily startled by
her query, but he quickly recovered and
said, "I will have a wife who has been run-

ning my estates for years. I am certainly not so proud that I would not take advantage of your superior knowledge."

She nodded. Just once, but it was enough to signal for him to continue.

"I already know you and trust you," he said. "And I am secure in the knowledge that you will not stray."

"I can't think about this right now," she said, bringing her hands to her face. Her head was spinning with it all, and she had the horrible sensation that it would never quite recover.

"It makes sense," Michael said. "You need only consider —"

"No," she said, desperately searching for a resolute tone. "It would never work. You know that." She turned away, not wanting to look at him. "I can't believe you would even consider it."

"I couldn't either," he admitted, "when the idea first came to me. But once it did, I couldn't let it go, and I soon realized it made perfect sense."

She pressed her fingers into her temples. For God's sake, why did he keep carping on about sense? If he uttered the word one more time she thought she might scream.

And how could he be so calm? She wasn't certain how she thought he *ought* to act; she'd certainly never imagined *this* moment. But something about his bloodless recitation of a proposal gnawed at her. He was so cool, so collected. A bit nervous, perhaps, but with his emotions completely even and unengaged.

Whereas she felt as if her world might spin right off its axis.

It wasn't fair.

And for that moment at least, she hated him for making her feel that way.

"I'm going upstairs," she said abruptly. "I'll have to talk with you about it in the morning."

She almost made it. She was more than halfway to the door when she felt his hand on her arm, his grasp gentle and yet holding her with unrelenting strength.

"Wait," he said, and she could not move.

"What do you want?" she whispered. She wasn't looking at him, but she could see his face in her mind, the way his midnight hair fell over his forehead, his heavy-lidded eyes, framed with lashes so long they could make an angel weep.

And his lips. Most of all, she could see his lips, perfectly shaped, finely molded, perpetually curved into that devilish expression of his, as if he *knew* things, understood the world in a way that more

346

innocent mortals never would.

His hand traveled up her arm until it reached her shoulder, and then one of his fingers traced a feather-light line down the side of her neck.

His voice, when it came, was low and husky, and she felt it right in the very center of her being.

"Don't you want another kiss?"

Chapter 17

. . . yes, of course. Francesca is a wonder. But you already knew that, didn't you?

> — *from Helen Stirling to her son,*
> *the Earl of Kilmartin,*
> *two years and nine months*
> *after his departure for India*

Michael wasn't certain when it had become apparent to him that he would have to seduce her. He'd tried to appeal to her mind, to her innate sense of the practical and wise, and it wasn't working.

And it couldn't be about emotion, because that, he knew, was one-sided.

So it would have to be passion.

He wanted her — Oh, God, he wanted her. With an intensity he hadn't even imagined before he'd kissed her the week previous in London. But even as his blood raced with desire and need and, yes, love, his mind was sharp and calculating, and he knew that if he was to bind her to him, he would need to do it with this. He would have to claim her in a way she could not deny. He couldn't just try to convince her with words and thoughts and ideas. She could attempt to talk herself out of that, pretend the feelings weren't there.

But if he made her his, left his imprint on her in the most physical way possible, he would be with her always.

And she would be his.

She slipped out from beneath his fingers, edging backward until she'd put a few paces between them.

"Don't you want another kiss, Francesca?" he murmured, moving toward her with predatory grace.

"It was a mistake," she said, her voice shaky. She scooted back a few inches farther, stopping only when she bumped into the edge of a table.

He moved forward. "Not if we marry."

"I can't marry you, you know that."

He took her hand, idly rubbed the skin with his thumb. "And why is that?"

"Because I . . . you . . . you're you."

"True," he said, lifting her hand to his mouth and kissing her palm. Then he flicked his tongue along her wrist, just because he could. "And for the first time in a very long while," he said, glancing up at her through his lashes, "there is no one I'd rather be just now."

"Michael . . ." she whispered, arching backwards.

But she wanted him. He could hear it in her breath.

"Michael no, or Michael yes?" he murmured, kissing the inside of her elbow.

"I don't know," she moaned.

"Fair enough." He moved higher, nudging at her chin until she had no choice but to loll back.

And he had no choice but to make love to her neck.

He kissed her slowly, thoroughly, sparing no inch of skin his sensual onslaught. He moved up to the line of her jaw, then over to her earlobe, then back down to the edge of her bodice, grasping it between his teeth. He heard Francesca gasp, but she didn't tell him to stop, so he just pulled and pulled and pulled until one breast popped free.

God, he loved current women's fashions.

"Michael?" she whispered.

"Shhh." He didn't want to have to answer any questions. He didn't want her thinking enough to ask one.

He ran his tongue along the underside of her breast, tasting the salty-sweet essence of her skin, then reached out and cupped her. He'd touched her through her dress the first time they'd kissed, and he'd thought that was heaven, but nothing compared to the feel of her, hot and bare, in his hand.

"Oh, my," she moaned. "Oh . . ."

He blew lightly on her nipple. "Shall I kiss you?" He looked up. He knew he was taking a chance with this, waiting for her answer. He probably shouldn't even have posed the question, but even though his intent was to seduce, he couldn't quite bring himself to do it without at least one affirmative word from her.

"Shall I?" he murmured again, sweetening the deal with one light flick of his tongue across her nipple.

"Yes!" she burst out. "Yes, for God's sake, yes!"

He smiled. Slowly, languidly, savoring the moment. And then, after letting her quiver with anticipation for one second longer than was probably fair, he leaned in and took her into his mouth, pouring years and years of desire onto the one breast, centering it wickedly onto one innocent nipple.

She wasn't going to stand a chance.

"Oh, my God!" she gasped, grasping the edge of the table for purchase as her entire body arched back. "Oh, my God. Oh, Michael. Oh, my God."

He took advantage of her passion to slide his hands around her hips and lift her up until she was seated on the table, her legs parting for him as he stepped into their feminine cradle.

Satisfaction raced through his veins, even as his body screamed for its own pleasure. He loved that he could do this to her, make her scream and moan and cry out with desire. She was so strong, always so cool and composed, and yet right now she was simply and purely his, a slave to her own needs, captive to his expert touch.

He kissed, he licked, he nibbled, he tugged. He tortured her until he thought she might explode. Her breath was loud and gasping, and her moans had grown more and more incoherent.

And all the while his hands were moving silently up her legs, first grasping her ankles, then her calves, pushing her skirts up and up, until they settled in a rumpled pool above her knees.

And it was only then that he pulled away and gave her a hint of a reprieve.

She looked at him, her eyes glazed, her lips pink and parted. She didn't say anything; he didn't think she *could* say anything. But he saw the questions in her eyes. She might be beyond speech, but she was several minutes away from total insanity.

"I thought it would be cruel to torture it any longer," he said, lightly taking her nipple between his thumb and forefinger.

She groaned.

"You like that." It was a statement, and not a particularly sophisticated one, but this was Francesca, not some nameless woman he was tupping while he closed his eyes and imagined her face. And every time she mewled with pleasure his heart raced with joy. "You like it," he said again, smiling with satisfaction.

"Yes," she whispered. "Yes."

He leaned in until his lips were brushing her ear. "You'll like this, too."

"What?" she asked, surprising him with her query. He'd thought she was too far gone to question him aloud.

He nudged her skirts a little higher, just enough so that there was no danger of them falling off her lap. "You want to hear it, don't you?" he murmured, sliding his hands until they were just above her knees. He squeezed her thighs gently, circling against her skin with his thumbs. "You want to know."

She nodded.

He moved toward her again, lightly touching his lips to hers, close enough to feel her, yet far enough to speak. "You were always so curious," he murmured. "You asked so many questions."

He slid his lips along her cheek to her ear, whispering all the way. "Michael," he said, softening his voice to mimic hers, "tell me something naughty. Tell me something wicked."

She blushed. He couldn't see it, but he could feel it, sense the hot rush of blood to her skin.

"But I never told you what you wanted to hear, did I?" he asked, lightly nipping at her earlobe. "I always left you outside the bedroom door."

He paused, not because he expected an answer, just because he wanted to hear her breathe.

"Did you wonder?" he whispered. "Did you leave me and wonder what I hadn't told you?" He leaned in, just so she'd feel his lips move whisper-light against her ear. "Did you want to know," he whispered, "what I did when I was wicked?"

He wouldn't make her answer; it

wouldn't be fair. But he couldn't stop his own mind from racing back in time, remembering the countless times he'd teased her with hints of his exploits.

He had never been the one to bring them up, however; she had *always* asked.

"Do you want me to tell you?" he murmured. He felt her jerk slightly in surprise, and he chuckled. "Not about them, Francesca. You. Only you."

She turned, causing his lips to slide along her cheek. He drew back so he could see her face, and her question was clear in her eyes.

What do you mean?

He moved his hands, exerting just enough pressure on her thighs to spread them open one more wicked inch. "Do you want me to tell you what I'm going to do now?" He leaned down, running his tongue along her nipple, which had grown hard and taut in the cool air of the late afternoon. "To you?" he added.

She swallowed convulsively. He decided to take that as a yes.

"There are so many choices," he said huskily, sliding his hands up her legs another few inches. "I scarcely know where to start."

He stopped to look at her for a moment.

She was breathing hard, her lips parted and plump from his kisses. And she was mesmerized, completely under his spell.

He dipped closer once again, to her other ear, so he could make sure his words fell hot and moist upon her soul. "I think, however, that I would have to start where you need me most. First I'd kiss you . . ." — he pressed his thumbs into the soft flesh of her inner thighs — ". . . *here*."

He held silent, just for a second, just long enough for her to shiver with desire. "Would you like that?" he murmured, his question intended to torment and tease. "Yes, I can see that you would.

"But that wouldn't be enough," he mused, "for either of us. So clearly, I would then have to kiss you *here*." His thumbs inched up until they reached the hot crevice between her legs and her torso, and then he pressed gently, so she would know exactly what he was talking about. "I think you would enjoy a kiss right there," he added, "almost as much" — he slid along the crease, down, down, closer to the very center of her, but not quite all the way — "as I would like to kiss you."

Her breath came a little faster.

"I'd have to take my time there," he murmured, "switch, perhaps, from my lips to my tongue. Run it along the edge right here." He used one fingernail to show her what he meant. "And all the while, I would be pushing you farther and farther open. Like that, maybe?"

He drew back, as if to examine his handiwork. The sight of her was stunningly erotic. She was perched on the edge of the table, her legs open to him, although not nearly enough for what he wanted to do. The skirt of her dress still hung down between her thighs, shielding her from his view, but somehow that made her almost more tempting. He didn't need to see her, he realized, not yet, anyway. Her position was sultry enough, made even more wicked by her breast, still bared to his gaze, its nipple pink and taut and begging for more.

But nothing, nothing could have speared him with more desire than the sight of her face. Parted lips, eyes darkened to cobalt with passion. Every breath she took seemed to call to him —

Take me.

And it was almost enough to force him to abandon his wicked seduction and plunge into her right then and there.

But no — he had to do this slowly. He had to tease her and torture her, bring her to the very heights of ecstasy and then keep her there as long as he could. He had to make sure they both understood that this was something they could never, *ever* live without.

But still, it was hard — no, *he* was hard, and it was so damned difficult to exercise restraint.

"What do you think, Francesca?" he murmured, giving her thighs one last squeeze. "I don't think we've opened you enough, do you?"

She made a sound. He would never know how to describe it, but it set him afire.

"Maybe," he said softly, "more like this." And he pushed, slowly, inexorably, until she was spread wide. Her skirt went taut over her thighs, and he tsk tsked at it, murmuring, "That can't be comfortable. Let me help you with that."

He hooked his fingers over the hem, and slid it up until it pooled about her waist.

And she was completely exposed.

He couldn't see her yet, not with his eyes still focused inexorably on her face. But the knowledge of her position made them both shiver, he with desire, she with anticipation, and he had to steel his shoulders just to maintain his control. It wasn't his time yet. It would be soon, to be sure; he was quite certain he'd perish if he didn't make her his that night.

But for now, this was still about Francesca. And what he could make her feel.

He put his lips to her ear. "You're not cold, are you?"

Her only answer was her shivering breath.

He brought one finger to her womanly center and began to stroke. "I would never allow you to remain cold," he whispered. "That would be so ungentlemanly of me."

His strokes slid into circles, slow and hot against her flesh.

"If we were out of doors," he mused, "I would offer my coat. But here" — he slid one fingertip inside, just enough to make her gasp — "I can only offer my mouth."

She made another incoherent sound, this one barely more than strangled cry.

"Yes," he said wickedly, "that is what I would do to you. I'd kiss you right here, right where it would pleasure you the most."

She could do nothing but breathe.

"I believe I would start with my lips," he murmured, "but then I would have to use my tongue so I could explore you more deeply." He used his fingers to tickle her, demonstrating what he planned to do with his mouth. "Rather like this, I think, but it would be much hotter." He ran his tongue along the inside of her ear. "And wetter."

"Michael," she moaned.

She'd said his name. And nothing more. She was getting closer to the brink.

"I'd taste everything," he whispered. "Every last drop of you. And then, just when I was sure I'd explored you completely, I'd part you further." He spread her with his fingers, pulling her open in the most wicked way possible. Then he tickled her flesh with his fingernail. "Just in case I'd missed some secret corner."

"Michael," she moaned again.

"Who knows how long I'd kiss you?" he murmured. "I might not be able to stop." He moved his face down a little, so that he could nuzzle her neck. "You might not want me to stop." He paused, then slid another finger inside of her. He whispered, "Do you want me to stop?"

He was playing with fire every time he asked her a question, every time he gave her a chance to say no. If he were colder, more calculating, he would just press on with his seduction, and he could sweep her away before she could even begin to consider her actions. She'd be lost on her wave of passion, and before she knew it he would be inside of her, and she would be, finally and indelibly, his.

But something in him could never be quite that ruthless, not with Francesca. And he needed her approval, even if it was nothing more than a nod or a moan. She'd probably regret this later, but even so, he didn't want her to be able to say, even to herself, that she hadn't been thinking, that she hadn't said yes.

And *he* needed the yes. He had loved her for years, dreamed about touching her for so damned long. And now that the moment was finally here, he just didn't know if he could bear it if she didn't really want it. There were only so many ways a man's heart could break, and he had a feeling his couldn't survive another puncture.

"Do you want me to stop?" he whispered again, and this time he did stop. He didn't remove his hands, but he didn't move them either, just held still and allowed her a moment of quiet in which to make her answer. And he pulled his head back, just far enough so that she had to look at him. Or if not that, then at least he would be looking at her.

"No," she whispered, not quite raising her eyes to his.

His heart jumped in his chest. "Then I had better get to doing everything I talked about," he murmured.

And he did. He sank to his knees and he kissed her. He kissed her as she shuddered, he kissed her as he moaned. He kissed her when she grabbed his hair and pulled, and he kissed her when she let go, her hands scrambling wildly for purchase.

He kissed her in every way he'd promised he would, and he kissed her until she almost climaxed.

Almost.

He should have done it, should have followed through, but he just couldn't manage it. He had to have her. He'd wanted this for so long, wanted to make her scream his name and shudder in his arms. But when it happened, for the first time at least, he wanted to be inside her. He wanted to feel her around him, and he wanted to . . .

Hell, he just wanted it this way, and if it meant he was out of control, so be it.

Hands shaking, he tore open his breeches, finally allowing his manhood to spring free.

"Michael?" she whispered. Her eyes had

been closed, but when he moved and left her she'd opened them. She looked down at him, her eyes widening. There was no mistaking what was about to happen.

"I need you," he said hoarsely. And when she did nothing but stare at him, he said it again. "I need you now."

But not on the table. Even he wasn't that talented, so he picked her up, shuddering with delight as she wrapped her legs around him, and set her down on the plush carpet. It wasn't a bed, but there was no way he was going to make it to a bed, and frankly, he didn't think either of them would care. He pushed her skirts back up to her waist, and he covered her.

And entered her.

He'd thought to go slowly, but she was so wet and ready for him, that he just slid inside, even as she gasped at the intrusion.

"Did that hurt?" he grunted.

She shook her head. "Don't stop," she moaned. "Please."

"Never," he vowed. "Never."

He moved, and she moved beneath him, and they were both already so aroused that it was a mere moment later that they both exploded.

And he, who had slept with countless women, suddenly realized that he'd been nothing but a green boy.

Because it had *never* been like this.

That had been his body. *This* was his soul.

 *Chapter 18*

. . . absolutely.

*— from Michael Stirling
to his mother, Helen,
three years after
his departure for India*

The following morning was, to the best of
Francesca's recollection, quite the worst of
recent memory.

All she wanted to do was cry, but even
that seemed beyond her. Tears were for the
innocent, and that was an adjective that
she could never again use to describe herself.

She hated herself this morning, hated
that she'd betrayed her heart, her every last
principle, all for a spot of wicked passion.

She hated that she had felt desire for a
man other than John, and *really* hated that
the desire had gone beyond anything she'd
felt with her husband. Her marriage bed

had been one of laughter and passion, but nothing, *nothing* could have prepared her for the wicked thrill she had felt when Michael had placed his lips to her ear and told her all the naughty things he wanted to do with her.

Or for the explosion that had followed, when he'd made good on his promises.

She hated that this had all happened, and she hated that it had happened with Michael, because somehow that made it all seem triply wrong.

And most all, she hated *him* because he'd asked her permission, because every step of the way, even as his fingers had teased her mercilessly, he had made sure she was willing, and now she could never claim that she'd been swept away, that she'd been powerless against the force of her own passion.

And now it was the morning after, and Francesca realized that she could no longer differentiate between coward and fool, at least not as the terms pertained to herself.

She clearly was both, quite possibly with an *immature* thrown in for bad measure.

Because all she wanted to do was run.

She could face up to the consequences of her actions.

Truly, that was what she *should* do.

But instead, just like before, she fled.

She couldn't really leave Kilmartin; she'd just got there, after all, and unless she was prepared to carry her northward flight straight past the Orkney Islands into Norway, she was stuck where she was.

But she *could* leave the house, which was precisely what she did at the first streaks of dawn, and this after her pathetic performance the night before, when she'd stumbled out of the rose drawing room some ten minutes after her intimacies with Michael, mumbling incoherencies and apologies, only to barricade herself in her bedroom for the rest of the evening.

She didn't want to face him yet.

Heaven above, she didn't think she *could*.

She, who had always prided herself on her cool and level head, had been reduced to a stammering idiot, muttering to herself like a bedlamite, terrified to face the one man she quite obviously couldn't avoid forever.

But if she could avoid him for one day, she told herself, that was something. And as for tomorrow — Well, she could worry about tomorrow some other time. Tomorrow, maybe. For now all she wanted to do was run from her problems.

Courage, she was now quite certain, was

a vastly overrated virtue.

She wasn't sure where she wanted to go; anywhere that could be termed *out* would probably do, any spot where she could tell herself that the odds of running into Michael were slim indeed.

And then, because she was quite convinced that no higher power was inclined to show her benevolence ever again, it began to rain an hour into her hike, starting first as a light sprinkle but quickly developing into a full-fledged downpour. Francesca huddled under a wide-limbed tree for shelter, resigned to wait out the rain, and then finally, after twenty minutes of shifting her weight from foot to foot, she just sat her bottom down onto the damp earth, cleanliness be hanged.

She was going to be here for some time; she might as well be comfortable, since she wasn't going to be either warm or dry.

And of course, that was how Michael found her, just short of two hours later.

Good God, it figured he'd look for her. Couldn't a man be counted on to behave like a cad when it truly mattered?

"Is there room for me under there?" he called out over the rain.

"Not for you *and* your horse," she grumbled.

"What was that?"

"No!" she yelled.

He didn't listen to her, of course, and nudged his mount under the tree, loosely tying the gelding to a low branch after he'd hopped down.

"Jesus, Francesca," he said without preamble. "What the hell are you doing out here?"

"And good day to you, too," she muttered.

"Do you have any idea how long I've been looking for you?"

"About as long as I've been huddled under the tree, I imagine," she retorted. She supposed she should be glad that he'd come to rescue her, and her shivering limbs were just itching to leap onto his horse and ride away, but the rest of her was still in a foul mood and quite willing to be contrary just for the sake of being, well, contrary.

Nothing could put a woman in worse spirits than a nice bout of self-derision.

Although, she thought rather peevishly, *he* was certainly not blameless in the debacle that was last night. And if he assumed that her litany of panicked, after-the-fact *I'm sorrys* the night before meant that she'd absolved him of guilt, he was quite mistaken.

"Well, let's go, then," he said briskly, nodding toward his mount.

She kept her gaze fixed over his shoulder. "The rain is letting up."

"In China, perhaps."

"I'm quite fine," she lied.

"Oh, for God's sake, Francesca," he said in short tones, "hate me all you want, but don't be an idiot."

"It's too late for that," she said under her breath.

"Maybe so," he agreed, demonstrating annoyingly superior hearing, "but I'm damned cold, and I want to go home. Believe what you will, but right now I have a far greater desire for a cup of tea than I do for you."

Which should have reassured her, but instead all she wanted to do was hurl a rock at his head.

But then, perhaps just to prove that her soul wasn't immediately headed for a toasty locale, the rain did let up, not all the way, but enough to lend a hint of truth to her lie.

"The sun will be out in no time," she said, motioning to the drizzle. "I'm fine."

"And do you plan to lie in the middle of the field for six hours until your dress dries off?" he drawled. "Or do you just prefer a slow, lingering case of lung fever?"

She looked him straight in the eye for the first time. "You are a horrible man," she said.

He laughed. "Now *that* is the first truthful thing you've said all morning."

"Is it possible you don't understand that I wish to be alone?" she countered.

"Is it possible you don't understand that I wish for you *not* to die of pneumonia? Get on the horse, Francesca," he ordered, in much the same tone she imagined he'd used on his troops in France. "When we are home you may feel free to lock yourself in your room — for a full two weeks, if it so pleases you — but for now, can we just get the hell out of the rain?"

It was tempting, of course, but even more than that, damned irritating because he was speaking nothing but sense, and the last thing she wanted just now was for him to be *right* about anything. Especially because she had a sinking feeling she needed more than two weeks to get past what had happened the evening before.

She was going to need a lifetime.

"Michael," she whispered, hoping she might be able to appeal to whichever side of him took pity on pathetic, quivering females, "I can't be with you right now."

"For a twenty-minute ride?" he snapped. And then, before she had the presence of mind to even yelp in irritation, he'd hauled her to her feet, and then off her feet, and then onto his horse.

"Michael!" she shrieked.

"Sadly," he said in a dry voice, "not said in the same tones I heard from you last night."

She smacked him.

"I deserved that," he said, mounting the horse behind her, and then doing a devilish wiggle until she was forced by the shape of the saddle to settle partially onto his lap, "but not as much as you deserve to be horsewhipped for your foolishness."

She gasped.

"If you wanted me to kneel at your feet, begging for your forgiveness," he said, his lips scandalously close to her ear, "you shouldn't have behaved like an idiot and run off in the rain."

"It wasn't raining when I left," she said childishly, letting out a little "Oh!" of surprise when he spurred the horse into motion.

Then, of course, she wished she had something else to hold onto for balance besides his thighs.

Or that his arm wasn't wrapped quite so

tightly around her, or so high on her ribcage. Good God, her breasts were practically sitting on his forearm.

And never mind that she was nestled quite firmly between his legs, with her backside butted right up against —

Well, she supposed the rain was good for one thing. He had to be shriveled and cold, which was going a long way in her imagination toward keeping her own traitorous body in check.

Except that she'd seen him the night before, seen Michael in a way she'd never thought to see him, of all people, in all of his splendid male glory.

And that was the worst part of all. A phrase like *splendid male glory* ought to be a joke, to be uttered with sarcasm and a cunningly wicked smile.

But with Michael, it fit perfectly.

He'd fit perfectly.

And she'd lost whatever shreds of sanity she'd still possessed.

They rode on in silence, or if not precisely silence, they at least did not speak. But there were other sounds, far more dangerous and unnerving. Francesca was acutely aware of every breath he took, low and whispering across her ear, and she could swear she could hear his heart beating against her back. And then —

"Damn."

"What is it?" she asked, trying to twist around to see his face.

"Felix has gone lame," he muttered, leaping down from the saddle.

"Is he all right?" she inquired, accepting his wordless offer to help her dismount as well.

"He'll be fine," Michael said, kneeling in the rain to inspect the gelding's front left leg. His knees sank instantly into the muddy earth, ruining his riding breeches. "He can't carry the both of us, however. Couldn't even manage just you, I fear." He stood, scanning the horizon, determining just where on the property they were. "We'll have to make for the gardener's cottage," he said, impatiently pushing his sodden hair from his eyes. It slid right back over his brow.

"The gardener's cottage?" Francesca echoed, even though she knew perfectly well what he was talking about. It was a small, one-room structure, uninhabited since the current gardener, whose wife had recently been delivered of twins, had moved into a larger dwelling on the other side of Kilmartin. "Can't we go home?" she asked, a little desperately. She didn't

374

need to be alone with him, trapped in a cozy little cottage with, if she remembered correctly, a rather large bed.

"It will take us over an hour on foot," he said grimly, "and the storm is growing worse."

He was right, drat it all. The sky had taken on a queer, greenish hue, the clouds touched with that strange light that preceded a storm of exquisite violence. "Very well," she said, trying to swallow her apprehension. She didn't know which frightened her more — the thought of being stuck out of doors in the storm or trapped inside a small cottage with Michael.

"If we run, we can be there in just a few minutes," Michael said. "Or rather, you can run. I'll have to lead Felix. I don't know how long it will take for him to make the journey."

Francesca felt her eyes narrowing as she turned to him. "You didn't do this on purpose, did you?"

He turned to her with a thunderous expression, matched rather terrifyingly by the streak of lightning that flashed through the sky.

"Sorry," she said hastily, immediately regretting her words. There were certain things one *never* accused a British gentleman of, the foremost of which was deliberate injury to an animal, for *any* reason. "I apologize," she added, just as a clap of thunder shook the earth. "Truly, I do."

"Do you know how to get there?" he yelled over the storm.

She nodded.

"Can you start a fire while you wait for me?"

"I can try."

"Go, then," he said curtly. "Run and get yourself warm. I'll be there soon enough."

She did, although she wasn't quite sure whether she was running to the cottage or away from him.

And considering the fact that he'd be mere minutes behind her, did it really matter?

But as she ran, her legs aching and her lungs burning, the answer to that question didn't seem terribly important. The pain of the exertion took over, matched only by the sting of the rain against her face. But it all felt strangely appropriate, as if she deserved no more.

And, she thought miserably, she probably didn't.

By the time Michael pushed open the door to the gardener's cottage, he was soaked to the bone and shivering like a madman. It had taken far longer than he had anticipated to lead Felix to the gardener's cottage, and then, of course, he'd been faced with the task of finding a decent spot to tie the injured gelding, since he couldn't very well leave him under a tree in an electrical storm. He'd finally managed to fashion a makeshift stall in what used to be a chicken shed, but the end result was that by the time he made it into the cottage, his hands were bleeding and his boots were dotted with a foul substance that the rain had inexplicably not managed to wash off.

Francesca was kneeling by the fireplace, attempting to spark a flame. From the sound of her mutterings, she wasn't meeting with much success.

"Dear heavens!" she exclaimed. "What happened to you?"

"I had trouble finding a place to tie Felix," he explained gruffly. "I had to build him a shelter."

"With your own two hands?"

"I had no other tools," he said with a shrug.

She glanced nervously out the window. "Will he be all right?"

"I hope so," Michael replied, sitting

down on a three-legged stool to remove his boots. "I couldn't very well slap his rump and send him home on that injured leg."

"No," she said, "of course not." And then her face took on a horrified expression, and she jumped to her feet, exclaiming, "Will *you* be all right?"

Normally, he'd have welcomed her concern, but it would have been far easier to milk it if he knew what the devil she was talking about. "I beg your pardon?" he asked politely.

"The malaria," she said, with a touch of urgency. "You're soaked, and you've just had an attack. I don't want you to —" She stopped, clearing her throat and visibly squaring her shoulders. "My concern does not mean that I am more charitably inclined to you than I was an hour ago, but I do not wish for you to suffer a relapse."

He thought briefly about lying to gain her sympathies, but instead he just said, "It doesn't work that way."

"Are you certain?"

"Quite. Chills don't bring on the disease."

"Oh." She took a bit of time to digest that information. "Well, in that case . . ." Her words trailed off, and her lips tightened unpleasantly. "Carry on, then," she finally said.

Michael gave her an insolent salute and then went back to work on his boots, giving the second one a firm yank before gingerly picking up both by the tops and setting them down near the door. "Don't touch those," he said absently, moving over to the fireplace. "They're filthy."

"I couldn't get the fire started," she said, still standing awkwardly near the hearth. "I'm sorry. I haven't much experience in that area, I'm afraid. I did find some dry wood in the corner, though." She motioned to the grate, where she'd set down a couple of logs.

He set to work igniting a flame, his hands still stinging a bit from the scrapes he'd incurred clearing the bramble out of the chicken shed for Felix. He welcomed the pain, actually. Minor as it was, it still gave him something to think about other than the woman standing behind him.

She was angry.

He should have expected that. He did expect it, in truth, but what he didn't expect was how much it would sting his pride, and, in all honesty, his heart. He had known, of course, that she wouldn't suddenly declare her undying love for him after one episode of relentless passion, but he'd been just enough of a fool that a tiny little piece of him had hoped for such an outcome, all the same.

Who would have thought, after all his years of bad behavior, that he'd emerge such a hopeless romantic?

But Francesca would come around, he was fairly certain of that. She'd have to. She'd been compromised — quite thoroughly, he thought with some measure of satisfaction. And while she'd not been a virgin, that still meant something to a principled woman like Francesca.

He was left with a decision — did he wait out her anger, or did he needle and push until she accepted the inevitability of the situation? The latter was sure to leave him bruised and gasping, but he rather thought it presented a greater chance of success.

If he left her alone, she would think the problem into oblivion, maybe find a way to pretend nothing had ever happened.

"Did you get it started?" he heard her ask from across the room.

He fanned a spark for a few more seconds, then let out a satisfied exhale when tiny orange flames began to flicker and lick. "I'll have to nurse it along for a little while longer," he said, turning around to look at her. "But yes, it should be going strong quite soon."

"Good," she said succinctly. She took a few steps backward until she was butted up against the bed. "I'll be right here."

He couldn't help but crack a wry smile at that. The cottage held a single room. Where else did she think she was going to go?

"You," she said, with much the air of an unpopular governess, "can remain over there."

He followed the line of her pointed finger to the opposite corner. "Really?" he drawled.

"I think it's best."

He shrugged. "Fine."

"Fine?"

"Fine." And then he stood and began to strip off his clothing.

"What are you doing?" she gasped.

He smiled to himself, keeping his back to her. "Keeping to my corner," he said, tossing the words lightly over his shoulder.

"You are taking your clothes off," she said, somehow managing to sound shocked and haughty at the same time.

"I suggest you do the same," he said, frowning as he noticed a streak of blood on his sleeve. Damn, but his hands really were a mess.

"I most certainly will not," Francesca said.

"Hold this, will you?" he said, tossing her his shirt. She shrieked as it hit her in the chest, which brought him no small measure of satisfaction.

"Michael!" she exclaimed, hurling the garment back at him.

"Sorry," he said in his most unrepentant voice. "Thought you might like to use it as a cloth to wipe up."

"Put your shirt back on," she ground out.

"And freeze?" he asked, lifting one arrogant brow. "Malaria or no, I have no wish to catch a chill. Besides, it's nothing you haven't seen before." And then, over her gasp, he added, "No, wait. I do beg your pardon. You haven't seen it. I didn't manage to get anything more than my trousers off last night, did I?"

"Get out," she said, her voice low and furious.

He just chuckled and cocked his head toward the window, which was thrumming with the sound of the rain against the glass. "I don't think so, Francesca. You're stuck with me for the duration, I'm afraid."

As if to prove his point, the small cottage shook down to its foundations with the force of thunder.

"You might want to turn around," Michael said conversationally. Her eyes widened slightly in incomprehension, so he added, "I'm about to remove my breeches."

She let out a little grunt of outrage, but she turned.

"Oh, and get off the blanket," he called out, peeling off his sodden clothing. "You're soaking it."

For a second he thought she would plant her bottom even more firmly against it, just to defy him, but her good sense must have won out, because she stood and yanked the coverlet from the bed, shaking off whatever drops she'd left behind.

He walked over — it took only four steps with his lengthy stride — and pulled the other blanket off for himself. It wasn't as substantial as the one she held, but it would do. "I'm covered," he called out, once he was safely back in his corner.

She turned around. Slowly, and with only one eye open.

Michael fought the urge to shake his head at her. Truly, this all seemed rather after the fact, given what had transpired the night before. But if it made her feel better to grasp at the shreds of her maidenly virtue, he was willing to allow her the boon . . . for the rest of the morning, at least.

"You're shivering," he said.

"I'm cold."

"Of course you are. Your dress is soaked."

She didn't say anything, just shot him a look that told him she did not plan to remove her clothing.

"Do what you wish, then," he said, "but at least come sit near the fire."

She looked hesitant.

"For God's sake, Francesca," he said, his patience growing thin, "I hereby vow not to ravish you. At least not this morning, and not without your permission."

For some reason that made her cheeks burn with even greater ferocity, but she must have still held him and his word in some regard, because she crossed the room and sat near the fire.

"Warmer?" he asked, just to provoke her.

"Quite."

He stoked the fire for the next few minutes, carefully tending it to ensure that the flames would not die out, stealing glances at her profile from time to time. After a while, once her expression had softened a bit, he decided to press his luck, and he said, quite softly, "You never did answer my question last night."

She didn't turn. "What question was that?"

"I believe I asked you to marry me."

"No, you didn't," she replied, her voice quite calm, "you informed me that you believed we should be married and then proceeded to explain why."

"Is that so?" he murmured. "How remiss of me."

"*Don't* take that as an invitation to make your proposal right now," she said sharply.

"You'd have me waste this fabulously romantic moment?" he drawled.

He couldn't be sure, but he thought her lips might have tightened with the barest hint of contained humor.

"Very well," he said, in his most magnanimous tone, "I won't ask you to marry me. Forget that a gentleman would insist upon it, after what happened —"

"If you were a gentleman," she cut in, "it wouldn't have happened."

"There were two of us there, Francesca," he reminded her softly.

"I know," she said, and her tone was

so bitter, he regretted having provoked her.

Unfortunately, once he'd made the decision not to taunt her further, he was left with nothing to say. Which didn't seem to speak well of him, but there it was. So he held silent, pulling the woolen blanket more tightly around his barely clad body, surreptitiously eyeing her from time to time, trying to determine if she was becoming overchilled.

He'd hold his tongue, forked though it may be, to spare her feelings, but if she were endangering her health . . . well, then, all bets were off.

But she wasn't shivering, nor did she show any signs of feeling excessively cold, save for the way she was holding up various sections of her skirt toward the fire, vainly attempting to dry the fabric. Every now and then she looked as if she might speak, but then she'd just close her mouth again, wetting her lips with her tongue and letting out little sighs.

And then, without even looking at him, she said, "I will consider it."

He quirked a brow, waiting for her to elaborate.

"Marrying you," she clarified, still keeping her eyes on the fire. "But I won't give you an answer now."

"You might be carrying my child," he said softly.

"I am very much aware of that." She wrapped her arms around her bent knees and hugged. "I will give you an answer once I have that answer."

Michael's nails bit into his palms. He'd made love to her in part to force her hand — he couldn't get around that unsavory fact — but not in an attempt to impregnate her. He'd thought to bind her to him with passion, not with an unplanned pregnancy.

And now she was essentially telling him that the only way she would marry him was for the sake of a baby.

"I see," he said, thinking his voice uncommonly calm, given the hot rush of fury surging through his blood.

Fury he probably had no right to feel, but it was there nevertheless, and he was not enough of a gentleman to ignore it.

"It's too bad I promised not to ravish you this morning, then," he said dangerously, unable to resist a predatory smile.

Her head whipped around to face him.

"I could — how do they say it," he mused, lightly scratching his jawline, "seal the deal. Or at the very least, enjoy myself immensely while I try."

"Michael —"

"But how nice for me," he cut in, "that according to my watch" — he was near enough to where his coat lay on the table to pluck his pocketwatch out into the open — "we've only five minutes to noon."

"You wouldn't," she whispered.

He felt little humor, but he smiled all the same. "You leave me little choice."

"Why?" she asked, and he really didn't know what she was asking, but he answered her, anyway, with the one bit of truth he couldn't escape:

"Because I have to."

Her eyes widened.

"Will you kiss me, Francesca?" he asked.

She shook her head.

She was only five feet from him, and they were both sitting on the floor. He crawled closer, his heart racing when she didn't scoot away. "Will you let me kiss you?" he whispered.

She didn't move.

He leaned toward her.

"I told you I wouldn't seduce you without your permission," he said, his voice husky, his words falling mere inches from her lips.

Still, she didn't move.

"Will you kiss me, Francesca?" he asked again.

She swayed.

And he knew she was his.

 *Chapter 19*

. . . I do believe Michael might be considering a return home. He does not say so directly in his letters, but I cannot discount a mother's intuition. I know that I should not pull him away from all his successes in India, but I think that he misses us. Wouldn't it be lovely to have him home?

> — *from Helen Stirling*
> *to the Countess of Kilmartin,*
> *nine months prior to the*
> *Earl of Kilmartin's return*
> *from India*

As she felt his lips touch hers, Francesca could only wonder at the loss of her sanity. Once again, Michael had asked her permission. Once again, he had given her the opportunity to slide away, to reject him and keep herself at a safe distance.

But once again, her mind had been completely enslaved by her body, and she simply was not strong enough to deny the quickening of her breath, or the pounding of her heart.

Or the slow, hot tingle of anticipation she felt as his large, strong hands slid down her body, moving ever closer to the heart of her femininity.

"Michael," she whispered, but they both knew that her plea was not one of rejection. She wasn't asking him to stop — she was begging him to continue, to feed her soul as he had the night before, to remind her of all the reasons she loved being a woman, and to teach her the heady bliss of her own sensual power.

"Mmmm," was his only response. His fingers kept busy with the buttons on her frock, and even though the fabric was still damp and awkward, he divested her of it in record time, leaving her clad only in her thin cotton chemise, made almost transparent by the rain.

"You are so beautiful," he whispered, gazing down at the outline of her breasts, clearly defined under the white cotton. "I can't — I don't —"

He didn't say anything more, which she found puzzling, and she looked at his face. These weren't just words to him, she realized with a jolt of surprise. His throat was working with some emotion she didn't think she'd ever seen on him before.

"Michael?" she whispered. His name was a question, although she wasn't quite sure what she was asking.

And he, she was fairly certain, didn't know how to answer. At least not with words. He scooped her into his arms and then carried her to the bed, stopping at the edge of the mattress to peel away her chemise.

This was where she could stop, Francesca reminded herself. She could end it here. Michael wanted her — badly, she could see quite visibly. But he would stop if she just said the word.

But she couldn't. No matter how hard her brain argued for reason and clarity, her lips could do nothing but sway toward his, leaning in for a kiss, desperate to prolong the contact.

She wanted this. She wanted him. And even though she knew it was wrong, she was too wicked to stop.

He'd made her wicked.

And she wanted to revel in it.

"No," she said, the word crossing her lips with awkward bluntness.

His hands froze.

"I will do it," she said.

His eyes found hers, and she found herself drowning in those quicksilver depths. There were a hundred questions there, not one of which she was prepared to answer. But there was one thing she knew for herself, even if she would never speak the words aloud. If she was going to do this, if she was unable to refuse her own desire, then by God, she would do this in every way. She would take what she wanted, steal what she needed, and at the end of the day, if she managed to come to her senses and put an end to the madness, she would have had one erotic afternoon, one sizzling interlude during which she was in charge.

He'd awakened the wanton within her, and she wanted her revenge.

With one hand on his chest, she pushed him back onto the bed, and he stared up at her with fiery eyes, his lips parted with desire as he watched her in disbelief.

She took a step back, then reached down and lightly grasped the hem of her chemise. "Do you want me to take it off?" she whispered.

He nodded.

"Say it," she demanded. She wanted to know if he was beyond words. She wanted to know if she could reduce him to madness, enslave him to his needs, the way he'd done to her.

"Yes," he gasped, the word coming out hoarse and ripped.

Francesca was no innocent; she'd been married for two years to a man with healthy and active desires, a man who had taught her to celebrate the same in herself. She knew how to be brazen, understood how it could whip up her own urgency, but nothing could have prepared her for the electrical charge of this moment, for the decadent thrill of stripping for Michael.

Or the staggering rush of heat she felt when she raised her gaze to his, and watched him watching her.

This was power.

And she loved it.

With deliberate slowness, she edged the hem up, starting just above her knees, and then sliding up her thighs until she'd nearly reached her hips.

"Enough?" she teased, licking her lips into a sultry half-smile.

He shook his head. "More," he demanded.

Demanded? She didn't like that. "Beg me," she whispered.

"More," he said, more humbly.

She gave him a nod of approval, but just

before she let him see the thatch of her womanhood she turned around, wiggling the chemise up and over her bottom, then across her back and finally over her head.

His breath was coming hot and heavy over his lips; she could hear every whisper of it, almost feel it caressing her back. But still she didn't turn around. Instead she let out a slow, seductive moan and slid her hands up the sides of her body, curving slightly to the back as she passed over her derrière, then moving to the front when she reached her breasts. And then, even though she knew he couldn't see her, she squeezed.

He would know what she was doing.

And it would drive him wild.

She heard rustling on the bed, heard the wooden frame creak and groan, and she let out one sharp command:

"Don't move."

"Francesca," he moaned, and his voice was closer. He must've sat up, must've been seconds away from reaching for her.

"Lie down," she said in soft warning.

"Francesca," he said again, but now there was a hint of desperation in his voice.

It made her smile. "Lie down," she repeated, still not looking at him.

She heard him panting, knew that he

hadn't moved, that he was still trying to decide what to do.

"Lie down," she said, one last time. "If you want me."

For a second there was silence, and then she heard him settle back against the bed. But she also heard his breath, now tinged with a dangerously ragged edge.

"There you go," she whispered.

She taunted him a little more, running her hands lightly over her skin, her nails skimming the surface, raising goosebumps all along their path. "Mmmm," she moaned, the sound a deliberate tease. "Mmmm."

"Francesca," he whispered.

She moved her hands to her belly, then slid them down, not deeply to touch herself — she wasn't certain she was wicked enough to do that — but just enough cover her mound, leaving him in the dark, wondering just what it was her fingers were doing.

"Mmmm," she murmured again. "Ohhhh."

He made a sound, guttural, primitive, and entirely inarticulate. He was nearing his breaking point; she wouldn't be able to push him much further.

She looked over her shoulder, licking her

lips as she glanced at him. "You should take those off," she said, letting her gaze fall to his still-covered groin. He'd not undressed entirely when he'd removed his wet clothing, and his manhood strained furiously against the fabric. "You don't look very comfortable," she added, infusing her voice with just the barest hint of coy innocence.

He grunted something and then practically tore off his undergarments.

"Oh my," Francesca said, and even though she'd planned the words as a part of her teasing seduction, she found that she very much meant them. He looked huge and powerful, and she knew she was playing a dangerous game, pushing him to his very limits.

But she couldn't stop. She was glorying in her power over him, and she couldn't possibly stop.

"Very nice," she purred, letting her gaze roam up and down his body, settling directly upon his manhood.

"Frannie," he said, "enough."

She let her eyes level onto his. "You answer to *me*, Michael," she said with soft authority. "If you want me, you can have me. But I'm in charge."

"Fr—"

"Those are my terms."

He held still, then settled back slightly in acquiescence. But he did not lie down. He was sitting, leaning back slightly, his hands on the mattress behind him for support. His every muscle was straining, and his eyes held a feline air, as if he were poised to pounce.

He was, she realized, with a shiver of desire, simply magnificent.

And hers for the taking.

"What should I do now?" she wondered aloud.

"Come here," he answered gruffly.

"Not quite yet," she sighed, turning toward him until her body was in profile. She saw his gaze drop to the hardened tips of her breasts, saw his eyes darken as he licked his lips. And she felt herself tauten even more, as the mental image of his tongue on her sent a new rush of heat through her body.

She brought one hand to her breast, curving around the underside, pushing herself up, like some delectable offering. "Is this what you want?" she whispered.

His voice was nothing but a growl. "You know what I want."

"Mmm, yes," she murmured, "but what about in the meantime? Aren't things sweeter when we're forced to wait for them?"

"You have no idea," he said roughly.

She looked down at her breast. "I wonder what would happen if I do . . . this," she said, and then she moved her fingers to her nipple, rolling it about, her body twitching as the motion sent shivers down to the very center of her being.

"Frannie," Michael groaned. She glanced up at him. His lips were parted, and his eyes were glazed with desire.

"I like it," Francesca said, almost in wonderment. She'd never touched herself this way, never even thought to until this very moment, with Michael as her captive audience. "I like it," she said again, then brought her other hand to her other breast and pleasured them in unison. She pushed them up and together, her hands making a sultry corset.

"Oh, my God," Michael moaned.

"I had no idea I could do this," she said, arching her back.

"I can do it better," he gasped.

"Mmm, you probably could," she acceded. "You've had lots of practice, haven't you?" And she shot him a look, one of sophisticated elegance, as if she were comfortable with the fact that he'd seduced scores of women. And the strange truth was, until this very moment, she rather thought she had been.

But now . . .

Now he was hers. Hers to tempt and hers to enjoy, and as long as she had him exactly where she wanted him, she wasn't going to think of those other women. They weren't here in this room. It was just her, and Michael, and the sizzling heat rising between them.

She edged closer to the bed, batting his hand away when he reached toward her. "If I let you touch one, will you make me a promise?" she murmured.

"Anything."

"Nothing more," she said, her tone slightly officious. "You may do what I allow you and nothing more."

He nodded jerkily.

"Lie back," she ordered.

He did as she asked.

She climbed onto the bed, not allowing their bodies to touch in any way. Raising herself onto all fours, she let herself to sway above him, and then softly she said, "One hand, Michael. You may use one hand."

With a groan that sounded as if it were ripped from his throat, he reached for her, his hand large enough to grasp her entire breast. "Oh, my God," he gasped, his body jerking as he squeezed her. "Both hands, please," he begged.

She couldn't resist him. That one simple touch was reducing her to pure flame, and even as she wanted to exert her power over him, she couldn't say no. Nodding because she could barely speak, she arched her back, and then suddenly both of his hands were on her, kneading, caressing, whipping her already heightened senses into a frenzy.

"The tip," she whispered. "Do what I did."

He smiled stealthily, giving her the impression that she might no longer be quite as much in charge as she thought, but he did as she commanded, his fingers torturing her nipples.

And as promised, he was better at it than she was.

Her body bucked, and she almost lost the strength to hold herself up. "Take me in your mouth," she ordered, but her voice was not so authoritative any longer. She was begging him, and they both knew it.

But she wanted it. Oh, how she wanted it. John, for all his ebullience in bed, had never loved her breasts the way Michael had done the night before. He'd never suckled her, never shown her how lips and teeth could make her entire body squirm. Francesca hadn't even known that a man and woman could do such a thing.

But now that she did, she couldn't stop fantasizing about it.

"Come lower," Michael said softly, "if you want me to remain lying down."

Still on her hands and knees, she leaned down, allowing one breast to swing achingly close to his mouth.

He did nothing at first, forcing her to swing lower and lower, until her nipple was brushing lightly across his lips.

"What do you want, Francesca?" he asked, his breath hot and moist over her.

"You know," she whispered.

"Say it again."

She wasn't in charge anymore. She knew it, but she was past caring. His voice held the soft edge of authority, but she was too far gone to do anything but obey.

"Take me in your mouth," she said again.

His head snapped up and his lips nipped her, tugging her down until she was in a position for him to have his leisurely way with her. He tickled and teased, and she felt herself sinking deeper into his spell, losing her will and her strength, wanting nothing but to lie down on her back and allow him to do whatever he wanted to her.

"Now what?" he asked politely, not releasing her from his lips. "More of this? Or" — he swirled his tongue in a particularly wicked fashion — "something else?"

"Something else," she gasped, and she wasn't sure if it was because she wanted something else or because she didn't think she could stand one more minute of what he was doing just then.

"You're in charge," he said, his voice holding the barest hint of mocking. "I'm yours to command."

"I want . . . I want . . ." She was breathing too hard to finish the sentence. Or maybe she just didn't know what she wanted.

"Shall I offer you a few selections?"

She nodded.

He trailed one finger down the center of her belly to her womanhood. "I could touch you here," he said in a devilish whisper, "or if you'd prefer, I could kiss you."

Her body tightened at the thought.

"But that presents new questions," he said. "Do you lie back and allow me to kneel between your legs, or do you remain above me and lower yourself onto my mouth?"

"Oh, my God!" She didn't know. She just didn't know that such things were possible.

"Or," he said thoughtfully, "you could take me into your mouth. I'm quite certain I would enjoy it, although I must say, it's not really in the tenor of the interlude."

Francesca felt her lips part with shock, and she couldn't help but peer down at his manhood, large and ready for her. She had kissed John there once or twice, when she'd felt particularly daring, but to take it into her mouth?

It was too scandalous. Even in her present state of debauchery.

"No," Michael said with an amused smile. "Another time, perhaps. I can tell you'll be a most cunning pupil."

Francesca nodded, unable to believe what she was promising.

"So for now," he said, "those are our options, or . . ."

"Or what?" she asked, her voice more of a harsh whisper.

His hands settled on her hips. "Or we could just proceed right to the main course," he said commandingly, exerting a gentle but steady pressure on her, guiding her down toward the evidence of his desire. "You could ride me. Have you ever done that?"

She shook her head.

"Do you want to?"

She nodded.

One of his hands left her hips and found the back of her head, pulling her down until they were nose to nose. "I'm not a gentle pony," he said softly. "I promise you, you will have to work to keep your seat."

"I want it," she whispered.

"Are you ready for me?"

She nodded.

"Are you certain?" he whispered, his lips curving just enough to taunt her. She wasn't sure what he was asking, and he knew it.

She just looked at him, her eyes widening in question.

"Are you wet?" he murmured.

Her cheeks grew hot — as if they weren't already burning, but she nodded.

"Are you sure?" he mused. "I should probably check, just to make certain."

Francesca's breath caught as she watched his hand curve around her thigh, moving toward her center. He moved slowly, deliberately, drawing out the torture of anticipation. And then, just when she thought she might scream at it all, he touched her, one finger lazily drawing circles against her soft flesh.

"Very nice," he purred, his words echoing her own.

"Michael," she gasped.

But he was enjoying his position too much to allow her to rush things along. "I'm not sure," he said. "You're ready here, but what about . . . here?"

Francesca nearly screamed as one finger slipped inside of her.

"Oh, yes," he murmured. "And you like it, too."

"Michael . . . Michael . . ." It was all she could say.

Another finger slid into place next to the first. "So warm," he whispered. "The very heart of you."

"Michael . . ."

His eyes caught hers. "Do you want me?" he asked, his voice stark and direct.

She nodded.

"Now?"

She nodded again, this time with more vigor.

His fingers slid out, and his hands found her hips again, guiding her down . . . down . . . until she could feel the tip of him at her opening. She tried to move her body down onto him, but he held her in place. "Not too fast," he whispered.

"Please . . ."

"Let me move you," he said, and his hands gently pushed at her hips, edging her down until she felt herself being stretched open by him. He felt huge, and it was all so different in this position.

"Good?" he asked.

She nodded.

"More?"

She nodded again.

And he continued the torture, holding himself still, but moving her body down atop his, each impossible inch of him sliding into her, stealing her breath, her voice, her very ability to think.

"Slide up and down," he commanded.

Her eyes flew to his.

"You can do it," he said softly.

She did, testing the motion, moaning at the pleasure of the friction, then gasping as she realized that she was sliding farther down onto him, that he wasn't yet entirely embedded within her body.

"Take me to the hilt," he said.

"I can't." And she couldn't. She couldn't possibly. She knew she had done so the night before, but this was different. He couldn't possibly fit.

His hands tightened on her, and his hips arched slightly up, and then in one mind-numbing jolt, she found herself seated directly atop him, skin to skin.

And she could barely breathe.

"Oh, my God," he groaned.

She just sat there, rocking back and forth, unsure of what to do.

His breath was coming in fits and starts, and his body began to writhe under hers. She grasped his shoulders in an attempt to hold on, to keep her seat, and as she did, she began to move up and down, to take control, to seek pleasure for herself.

"Michael, Michael," she moaned, her body beginning to sway from side to side, unable to hold itself up, unable to maintain strength against the hot tide of desire sweeping across her.

He just grunted, his body bucking beneath her. As promised, he wasn't gentle, and he wasn't tame. He forced her to work for her pleasure, to hold on tight, to move with him, and then against him, and then . . .

A scream ripped from her throat.

And the world quite simply fell apart.

She didn't know what to do, didn't know what to say. She let go of his shoulders as her body straightened and then arched, every muscle growing impossibly taut.

And beneath her, he exploded. His face contorted, his body lifted them both off the bed, and she knew that he was pouring himself into her. Her name was on his lips, over and over, decreasing in volume until it was the barest of whispers. And when he was done, all he said was, "Lie with me."

She did. And she slept.

For the first time in days, she slept deeply and truly.

And she never knew that he laid awake the whole time, his lips at her temple, his hand against her hair.

Whispering her name.

Whispering other words as well.

 # Chapter 20

. . . Michael will do what he wishes. He always does.

> *— from the Countess of Kilmartin to Helen Stirling, three days after the receipt of Helen's missive*

The days that followed brought Francesca no peace. When she thought about it rationally — or at least as rationally as she was able — it seemed as if she should have found some answers, should have sensed some sort of logic in the air, something that might tell her what to do, how to act, what sort of choice she needed to make.

But, no. Nothing.

She'd made love to him twice.

Twice.

To Michael.

That alone should have dictated her decisions, convinced her to accept his proposal. It should have been clear. She had lain with him. She might be pregnant, although that did seem a remote possibility, given that it had taken her a full two years to conceive with John.

But even without such consequences, her decision should have been obvious. In her world, in her society, the sort of intimacies in which she'd engaged meant only one thing.

She must marry him.

And yet she couldn't quite summon the *yes* to her lips. Every time she thought she'd convinced herself that it was what she had to do, a little voice inside of her argued for caution, and she stopped, unable to move forward, too scared to delve into her feelings and try to figure out why she felt so paralyzed.

Michael didn't understand, of course. How could he, when she didn't understand herself?

"I shall call upon the vicar tomorrow morning," he'd murmured at her ear as he helped her mount a fresh horse outside the gardener's cottage. She had awakened alone sometime in the late afternoon, a brief note from him on the pillow beside her, explaining that he was taking Felix back to Kilmartin and would return shortly with a new mount.

But he had only brought one horse, forcing her once again to share the saddle, this time perched behind him.

"I'm not ready," she'd said, a sudden rush of panic filling her chest. "Don't go see him. Not yet."

His face had darkened, but he didn't allow his temper to rise any further. "We will discuss it later," he'd said.

And they'd ridden home in silence.

She tried to escape to her room once they reached Kilmartin, mumbling something about needing to bathe, but he caught her hand, his grip firm and unyielding, and she found herself alone with him, back in the rose drawing room of all places, the door shut firmly behind them.

"What is all this about?" he asked.

"What do you mean?" she stalled, trying desperately not to look at the table behind him. It was the one upon which he'd perched her the night before, then done unspeakable things to her.

And the memory alone was enough to make her shiver.

"You know what I mean," he said impatiently.

"Michael, I —"

"Will you marry me?" he demanded.

412

Dear God, she wished he hadn't just come out and said it. It was all so much easier to avoid when the words weren't right there, hanging between them.

"I — I —"

"Will you marry me?" he repeated, and this time the words were hard, with more of an edge to them.

"I don't know," she finally answered. "I need more time."

"Time for what?" he snapped. "For me to try a little harder to get you pregnant?"

She flinched as if struck.

He advanced upon her. "Because I'll do it," he warned. "I'll take you right now, and then again tonight, and then three times tomorrow if that's what is required."

"Michael, stop . . ." she whispered.

"I have lain with you," he said, his words stark and yet strangely urgent. "Twice. You are no innocent. You know what that means."

And it was *because* she was no innocent — and no one would ever expect her to be — that she was able to say, "I know. But that doesn't matter. Not if I don't conceive."

Michael hissed a word she never dreamed he'd say in her presence.

"I need time," she said, hugging her

arms against her body.

"Why?"

"I don't know. To think. To muddle through. I don't know."

"What the devil is there left to think about?" he bit off.

"Well, for one thing, about whether you'll make a good husband," she snapped back, finally goaded into anger.

He drew back. "What the hell is that supposed to mean?"

"Your past behavior, to start with," she replied, narrowing her eyes. "You haven't exactly been the model of Christian rectitude."

"This, coming from the woman who ordered me to strip off my clothing earlier this afternoon?" he taunted.

"Don't be ugly," she said in a low voice.

"Don't push my temper."

Her head began to pound, and she pressed her fingers to her temples. "For God's sake, Michael, can't you let me think? Can't you give me just a little time to think?"

But the truth was, she was terrified to think. Because what would she learn? That she was a wanton, a hussy? That she had felt a primitive thrill with this man, a soaring, scandalous sensation that had never

414

been there with her husband, whom she'd loved with every inch of her heart?

She'd found pleasure with John, but nothing like this.

She'd never even dreamed *this* existed.

And yet she'd found it with Michael.

Her friend, too. Her confidant.

Her lover.

Dear God, what did that make her?

"Please," she finally whispered. "Please. I need to be alone."

Michael stared at her for the longest time, long enough so that she wanted to squirm under his scrutiny, but finally he just swore under his breath and stalked from the room.

She collapsed onto the sofa and let her head hang in her hands. But she didn't cry.

She didn't cry. Not one single tear. And for the life of her, she didn't understand why not.

He would never understand women.

Michael swore viciously as he yanked off his boots, hurling the offending footwear against the door to his wardrobe.

"My lord?" came his valet's tentative voice, poking out through the opened door to the dressing room.

"Not now, Reivers," Michael snapped.

"Right," the valet said quickly, scurrying across the room to gather up the boots. "I'll just take these. You'll want them cleaned."

Michael cursed again.

"Er, or perhaps burned." Reivers gulped.

Michael just looked at him and growled.

Reivers fled, but fool that he was, he forgot to close the door behind him.

Michael kicked it shut, cursing again when he failed to find satisfaction in the slam.

Even the little pleasures in life were denied to him now, it seemed.

He paced restlessly across the deep burgundy carpet, pausing only occasionally at the window.

Forget understanding *women*. He'd never pretended to have that ability. But he thought he'd understood Francesca. At least well enough to safely tell himself that she would marry any man with whom she'd lain twice.

Once, maybe not. *Once* she could call a mistake. But twice —

She would never allow a man to take her twice unless she held him in some regard.

But, he thought with a twisted grimace, apparently not.

Apparently she was willing to use him for her own pleasure — and she had. Dear God, she had. She had assumed the lead, taken what she'd wanted, relinquishing control only when the flames between them spiraled into an inferno.

She had used him.

And he would never have thought she had it in her.

Had she been like this with John? Had she taken charge? Had she —

He stopped, his feet freezing into place on the carpet.

John.

He had forgotten about John.

How was that possible?

For years, every time he'd seen Francesca, every time he'd leaned in for one intoxicating whiff of her, John had been there, first in his thoughts, and then in his memory.

But since the moment she'd entered the rose drawing room last night, when he heard her footsteps behind him and whispered the words, "Marry me," to himself, he'd forgotten about John.

His memory would never disappear. He was too dear, too important — to both of them. But somewhere along the way, somewhere along the way to Scotland, to be precise, Michael finally allowed himself to think —

I could marry her. I could ask her. I really could.

And as he granted himself permission, it felt less and less like he was stealing her from his cousin's memory.

Michael hadn't asked to be placed in this position. He had never looked up to the heavens and wished himself the earldom. He had never even truly wished for Francesca, just accepted that she could never be his.

But John had died. He had *died*.

And it was nobody's fault.

John had died, and Michael's life had been changed in every way imaginable except one.

He still loved Francesca.

God, how he loved her.

There was no reason they couldn't marry. No laws, no customs, nothing but his own conscience, which had, quite suddenly, grown silent on the matter.

And Michael finally allowed himself to ponder, for the very first time, the one question he had never asked himself.

What would John think of all this?

And he realized that his cousin would have given his blessing. John's heart was that big, his love for Francesca — and Michael — that true. He would have wanted Francesca to be loved and cherished the way that Michael loved and cherished her.

And he would have wanted Michael to be happy.

The one emotion Michael had never truly thought he could apply to himself.

Happy.

Imagine that.

Francesca had been waiting for Michael to knock upon her door, but when the rap came, she still jumped with surprise.

Her shock was much greater when she opened the door and found she had to lower her gaze considerably. A full foot, to be precise. Michael wasn't on the other side of her door. It was just one of the housemaids, carrying a supper tray for her.

Eyes narrowing suspiciously, Francesca poked her head into the hall, looking this way and that, fully expecting Michael to be lurking in some darkened corner, just waiting for the right moment to pounce.

But he was nowhere.

"His lordship thought you might be hungry," the maid said, setting the tray down on Francesca's escritoire.

Francesca scanned the contents for a

note, a flower, something to indicate Michael's intentions, but there was nothing.

And there was nothing for the rest of the night, and nothing the next morning, either.

Nothing but a breakfast tray, and another bob and curtsy from the housemaid, with another, "His lordship thought you might be hungry."

Francesca had asked for time to think, and that appeared to be exactly what he was giving her.

And it was horrible.

Granted, it would probably have been worse if he'd disregarded her wishes and not allowed her to be alone. Clearly, she could not be trusted in his presence. And she didn't particularly trust him, either, with his sultry looks and whispered questions.

Will you kiss me, Francesca? Will you let me kiss you?

And she couldn't refuse, not when he was standing so close, his eyes — his amazing, silver, heavy-lidded eyes — watching her with such smoldering intensity.

He mesmerized her. That could be the only explanation.

She dressed herself that morning, donning a serviceable day dress which would serve her well out of doors. She didn't want to remain cooped up in her room, but neither did she wish to roam the halls of Kilmartin, holding her breath as she turned each corner, waiting for Michael to appear before her.

She supposed he could find her outside if he really wanted to, but at least he would have to expend a bit of effort to do it.

She ate her breakfast, surprised that she had an appetite under such circumstances, and then slipped out of her room, shaking her head at herself as she peered stealthily down the hall, acting like nothing so much as a burglar, eager to make a clean escape.

This was what she'd been reduced to, she thought grumpily.

But she didn't see him as she made her way down the hall, and she didn't see him on the stairs, either.

He wasn't in any of the drawing rooms or salons, and indeed, by the time she reached the front door, she couldn't help but frown.

Where was he?

She didn't wish to see him, of course, but it did seem rather anticlimactic after all of her worrying.

She placed her hand on the knob.

She *should* run. She should hurry out

now, while the coast was clear and she could make her escape.

But she paused.

"Michael?" She only mouthed the word, which shouldn't have counted for anything. But she couldn't shake the feeling that he was there, that he was watching her.

"Michael?" she whispered, looking this way and that.

Nothing.

She gave her head a shake. Good God, what had become of her? She was growing far too fanciful. Paranoid, even.

With one last glance behind her, she left the house.

And never did see him, watching her from under the curved staircase, his face touched with the smallest, and truest, of smiles.

Francesca had remained out of doors as long as she was able, finally giving in to a mixture of weariness and cold. She had wandered the grounds for probably six or seven hours, and she was tired, and hungry, and eager for nothing so much as a cup of tea.

And she couldn't avoid her house forever.

So she slipped back in as quietly as she'd left, planning to make her way up to her room, where she could dine in private. But before she could make it to the bottom of the stairs, she heard her name.

"Francesca!"

It was Michael. Of course it was Michael. She couldn't expect him to leave her alone forever.

But the strange thing was — she wasn't quite certain whether she was annoyed or relieved.

"Francesca," he said again, coming to the doorway of the library, "come join me."

He sounded affable — too affable, if that were possible, and furthermore, Francesca was suspicious at his choice of rooms. Wouldn't he have wanted to draw her into the rose drawing room, where she'd be assaulted by memories of their torrid encounter? Wouldn't he at least have chosen the green salon, which had been decorated in a lush, romantic style, complete with cushioned divans and overstuffed pillows?

What was he doing in the library, which had to be, she was quite certain, the least likely room at Kilmartin in which one might stage a seduction?

"Francesca?" he said again, by now

looking amused at her indecision.

"What are you doing in there?" she asked, trying not to sound suspicious.

"Having tea."

"Tea?"

"Leaves boiled in water?" he murmured. "Perhaps you've tried it."

She pursed her lips. "But in the library?"

He shrugged. "It seemed as good a place as any." He stepped aside and swooshed his arm in front of him, indicating that she should enter. "As *innocent* a place as any," he added.

She tried not to blush.

"Did you have a pleasant walk?" he asked, his voice perfectly conversational.

"Er, yes."

"Lovely day out."

She nodded.

"I imagine the ground is still a bit soggy in places, though."

What was he up to?

"Tea?" he asked.

She nodded, her eyes widening when he poured for her. Men *never* did that.

"Had to fend for myself from time to time in India," he explained, reading her thoughts perfectly. "Here you go."

She took the delicate china cup and sat, allowing the warmth of the tea to seep through the china and onto her hands. She blew lightly on it, then took a taste, testing the temperature.

"Biscuit?" He held out a plate laden with all sorts of baked delights.

Her stomach rumbled, and she took one without speaking.

"They're good," he offered. "I ate four while I was waiting for you."

"Were you waiting long?" she asked, almost surprised by the sound of her own voice.

"An hour or so."

She sipped at her tea. "It's still quite hot."

"I had the pot refilled every ten minutes," he said.

"Oh." Such thoughtfulness was, if not precisely surprising, then still unexpected.

One of his brows quirked, but only slightly, and she wasn't sure whether he'd done it on purpose. He was always in such control of his expressions; he'd have been a master gambler, had he had the inclination. But his left brow was different; Francesca had noticed years ago that it sometimes moved when he clearly thought he was keeping his face perfectly impassive. She'd always thought of it as her own little secret, her private window into the workings of his mind.

Except now she wasn't sure she wanted such a window. It implied a closeness with which she wasn't quite comfortable any longer.

Not to mention that she'd clearly been deluded when she'd thought she might ever understand the workings of his mind.

He plucked a biscuit off the tray, idly regarded the dollop of raspberry jam in its center, then popped it into his mouth.

"What is this about?" she asked, unable to contain her curiosity any longer. She felt rather like prey, being fattened up for the kill.

"The tea?" he inquired, once he'd swallowed. "Mostly about tea, if you must know."

"*Michael.*"

"I thought you might be cold," he explained with a shrug. "You were gone quite some time."

"You know when I left?"

He looked at her sardonically. "Of course."

And she wasn't surprised. That was the only thing that surprised her, actually — that she wasn't surprised.

"I have something for you," he said.

Her eyes narrowed. "You do?"

426

"Is that so remarkable?" he murmured, and he reached down onto the seat beside him.

Her breath caught. *Not a ring. Please, not a ring. Not yet.*

She wasn't ready to say yes.

And she wasn't ready to say no, either.

But instead, he set upon the table a small posy of flowers, each bloom more delicate than the last. She'd never been good with flowers, hadn't bothered to learn the names, but there was a stalky white one, and a bit of purple, and something that was almost blue. And it had all been tied rather elegantly with a silver ribbon.

Francesca just stared at it, unable to decide what to make of such a gesture.

"You can touch it," he said, a hint of amusement playing along his voice. "It shan't pass along disease."

"No," she said quickly, reaching out for the tiny bouquet, "of course not. I just . . ." She brought the blooms to her face and inhaled, then set them down, her hands retreating quickly to her lap.

"You just what?" he asked softly.

"I don't really know," she replied. And she didn't. She had no idea how she'd meant to complete that sentence, if indeed she had ever intended to. She looked down at the small bouquet, blinking several times before asking, "What is this?"

"I call them flowers."

She looked up, her eyes meeting his fully and deeply. "No," she said, *"what is this?"*

"The gesture, you mean?" He smiled. "Why, I'm courting you."

Her lips parted.

He took a sip of his tea. "Is it such a surprise?"

After all that had passed between them? *Yes.*

"You deserve no less," he said.

"I thought you said you intended to —" She broke off, blushing madly. He'd said he meant to take her until she became pregnant.

Three times today, as a matter of fact. Three times, he'd vowed, and they were still quite at zero and . . .

Her cheeks burned, and she couldn't help but feel the memory of him between her legs.

Dear God.

But — thank heavens — his expression remained innocent, and all he said was, "I've rethought my strategies."

She took a frenetic bite of her biscuit.

Any excuse to bring her hands to her face and hide a bit of her embarrassment.

"Of course I still plan to pursue my options in that area," he said, leaning forward with a sultry gaze. "I'm only a man, after all. And you, as I believe we've more than made clear, are very much a woman."

She jammed the rest of the biscuit into her mouth.

"But I thought you deserved more," he finished, sitting back with a mild expression, as if he hadn't just seared her with innuendo. "Don't you think?"

No, she didn't think. Not anymore, at least. It was a bit of a problem, that.

Because as she sat there, furiously stuffing food into her mouth, she couldn't take her eyes off his lips. Those magnificent lips, smiling languidly at her.

She heard herself sigh. Those lips had done such magnificent things to her.

To all of her. Every last inch.

Good God, she could practically feel them now.

And it left her squirming in her seat.

"Are you all right?" he asked solicitously.

"Quite," she somehow managed to say, gulping at her tea.

"Is your chair uncomfortable?"

She shook her head.

"Is there anything I can get for you?"

"Why are you doing this?" she finally burst out.

"Doing what?"

"Being so nice to me."

His brows lifted. "Shouldn't I be?"

"No!"

"I shouldn't be nice." It wasn't a question as he said it, rather an amused statement.

"That's not what I meant," she said, shaking her head. He'd befuddled her, and she hated it. There was nothing she valued more than a cool and clear head, and Michael had managed to steal that from her with a single kiss.

And then he'd done more.

So much more.

She was never going to be the same.

She was never going to be *sane*.

"You look distressed," he said.

She wanted to strangle him.

He cocked his head and smiled.

She wanted to kiss him.

He held up the teapot. "More?"

God yes, and that was the problem.

"Francesca?"

She wanted to jump across the table and onto his lap.

"Are you quite all right?"

It was growing difficult to breathe.

"Frannie?"

Every time he spoke, every time he moved his mouth, even just to breathe, her eyes settled on his lips.

She felt herself licking her own.

And she knew that he knew — with all of his experience, all of his seductive prowess — exactly what she was feeling.

He could reach for her now and she wouldn't refuse.

He could touch her and she'd go up in flames.

"I have to go," she said, but her words were breathless and lacking in conviction. And it didn't help that she couldn't seem to wrench her gaze from his own.

"Important matters to attend to in your bedchamber?" he murmured, his lips curving.

She nodded, even though she knew he was mocking her.

"Go then," he encouraged, but his voice was mild and in fact sounded like nothing so much as a seductive purr.

Somehow she managed to move her hands to the edge of the table. She gripped the wood, telling herself to push away, to do something, to move.

But she was frozen.

"Would you prefer to stay?" he murmured.

She shook her head. Or at least she thought she did.

He stood and came to the back of her chair, leaning down to whisper in her ear, "Shall I help you to rise?"

She shook her head again and nearly jumped to her feet, his nearness somewhat paradoxically breaking the spell he'd cast over her. Her shoulder bumped his chest, and she lurched back, terrified that further contact would cause her to do something she might regret.

As if she hadn't had enough of that already.

"I need to go upstairs," she blurted out.

"Clearly," he said softly.

"Alone," she added.

"I wouldn't dream of forcing you to endure my company for one moment longer."

She narrowed her eyes. Just what was he up to? And why the devil did she feel so disappointed?

"But perhaps . . ." he murmured.

Her heart leapt.

"— perhaps I should offer you a farewell kiss," he finished. "On the hand, of course. It would only be proper."

As if they hadn't discarded propriety back in London.

He took her fingers lightly in his own. "We are courting, after all," he said. "Aren't we?"

She stared down at him, unable to take her eyes off of his head as he bent down over her hand. His lips brushed her fingers. Once . . . twice . . . and then he was through.

"Dream of me," he said softly.

Her lips parted. She couldn't stop watching his face. He'd mesmerized her, held her soul captive. And she couldn't move.

"Unless you want more than a dream," he said.

She did.

"Will you stay?" he whispered. "Or will you go?"

She stayed. Heaven help her, she stayed.

And Michael showed her just how romantic a library could be.

 *Chapter 21*

. . . a brief note to let you know that I
have arrived safely in Scotland. I must
say, I am glad to be here. London was
stimulating as always, but I believe I
needed a bit of quiet. I feel quite more
focused and at peace here in the
country.

> — *from the Countess of Kilmartin*
> *to her mother, the dowager*
> *Viscountess Bridgerton, one day*
> *after her arrival at Kilmartin*

Three weeks later, Francesca still didn't
know what she was doing.

Michael had brought up the issue of
marriage twice more, and each time she'd
managed to dodge the question. If she
considered his proposal, she would actually have to think. She'd have to think
about him, and she'd have to think
about John, and worst of all, she'd have to

434

think about herself.

And she'd have to figure out just what it was she was doing. She kept telling herself she would marry him only if she became pregnant, but then she kept coming back to his bed, allowing him to seduce her at every turn.

But even that wasn't truly accurate any longer. She was delusional if she thought she required any seducing to make room for him in her bed. She'd become the wicked one, however much she tried to hide from the fact by telling herself that she was wandering the house at night in her bedclothes because she was restless, not because she was seeking his company.

But she always found him. Or if not, she placed herself in a position where he might find her.

And she never said no.

Michael was growing impatient. He hid it well, but she knew him well. She knew him better than she knew anyone left on this planet, and even though he insisted he was courting her, wooing her with romantic phrases and gestures, she could see the faint lines of impatience curling around his mouth. He would begin a conversation that she knew would lead to the subject of marriage, and she always dodged it before he mentioned the word.

He allowed her to get away with it, but his eyes would change, and his jaw would tighten, and then, when he took her — and he always did, after moments like those — it was with renewed urgency, and even a touch of anger.

But still, it wasn't quite enough to jolt her into action.

She couldn't say yes. She didn't know why; she just couldn't.

But she couldn't say no, either. Maybe she was wicked, and maybe she was a wanton, but she didn't want this to end. Not the passion, and not, she was forced to acknowledge, his company, either.

It wasn't just the lovemaking, it was the moments after, when she lay curled in his arms, his hand idly stroking her hair. Sometimes they were silent, but sometimes they talked, about anything and everything. He told her about India, and she told him of her childhood. She gave him her opinions about political matters, and he actually listened. And he told her devilish jokes that men were never supposed to tell women, and women certainly weren't supposed to enjoy.

And then, once the bed had stopped shaking with her mirth, his mouth would find hers, a smile embedded on his lips. "I love your laughter," he would murmur, and his hands would curl her to him. She'd sigh, still giggling, and they'd begin their passion anew.

And Francesca would, once again, be able to hold the rest of the world at bay.

And then she bled.

It started as it always did, just a few drops on the cotton of her chemise. She shouldn't have been surprised; her cycles may not have been regular, but they always arrived eventually, and she already knew that hers was not a terribly fertile womb.

But still, somehow she hadn't been expecting it. Not yet, anyway.

It made her cry.

Nothing dramatic, nothing that wracked her body and consumed her soul, but her breath caught when she saw the tiny drops of blood, and before she realized what she was doing, twin tears were trickling down her cheeks.

And she wasn't even sure why.

Was it because there would be no baby, or was it — God help her — because there would be no marriage?

Michael came to her room that night, but she sent him away, explaining that it wasn't the right time. His lips found her ear, and he reminded her of all the wicked things they could still do, blood or no, but she refused, and asked him to leave.

He looked disappointed, but he seemed to understand. Women could be squeamish about such things.

But when she woke in the middle of the night, she wished he was holding her.

Her menses didn't last long; it never did. And when Michael asked her discreetly if her time was through, she didn't lie. He'd have known if she had, anyway; he always did.

"Good," he said with a secret smile. "I've missed you."

Her lips parted to say that she'd missed him, too, but somehow she was afraid to say the words.

He nudged her toward the bed, and together they tumbled, their bodies a tangle of arms and legs as they fell.

"I dreamed of you," he said hoarsely, his hands pushing her skirt up to her waist. "Every night you came to me in dreams." One finger found her essence and dipped inside. "They were very, very good dreams," he finished, his voice hot and full of the devil.

She caught her lip between her teeth, her breath coming in short gasps as his finger slid out and caressed her right where he knew it would make her melt.

"In my dreams," he murmured, his lips hot at her ear, "you did unspeakable things."

She moaned at the sensation. He could ignite her body with a single touch, but she went up in flames when he spoke like this.

"New things," he murmured, spreading her legs wider. "Things I'm going to have to teach you . . . tonight, I think."

"Oh, God," she gasped. He'd moved his lips to her thigh, and she knew what was coming.

"But first a bit of the tried and true," he continued, his lips tickling their way up toward their destination. "We have all night to explore."

He kissed her then, just as he knew she liked it, holding her immobile with his powerful hands as his lips brought her closer and closer to the peaks of passion.

But before she reached the apex, he moved away, his hands tearing at the fastenings of his trousers. He swore when his fingers trembled, when the button didn't slip free on the first try.

And it gave Francesca just enough time to stop and think.

The one thing she truly didn't want to do.

But her mind was relentless, and it was unkind, and before she knew what she was doing, she'd scrambled from the bed, the word, "Wait!" flying from her lips, even as she flew across the room.

"What?" he gasped.

"I can't do this."

"You can't . . ." — he stopped, unable to finish the question without taking a heaving breath — ". . . *what?*"

He'd finally had success with his trousers, and they had fallen to the floor, leaving her with a stunning view of his arousal.

Francesca averted her eyes. She couldn't look at him. Not at his face, not at his . . . "I can't," she said, her voice shaking. "I shouldn't. I don't know."

"*I* know," he growled, stepping toward her.

"No!" she cried out, hurrying toward the door. She'd played with fire for weeks, tempting the fates, and she'd won her gamble. If there was ever a time to escape, this was it. And as hard as it was to leave, she knew that she must. She wasn't this sort of woman. She couldn't be.

"I can't do this," she said, her back now

flat against the hard wood of the door. "I can't. I . . . I . . ."

I want to, she thought. Even as she knew she shouldn't, she couldn't escape the fact that she wanted to, anyway. But if she told him that, would he make her change her mind? He could do it, too. She knew he could. One kiss, one touch, and all of her resolve would be lost.

He just swore and yanked his trousers back up.

"I don't know who I am any longer," she said. "I'm not this sort of woman."

"*What* sort of woman?" he snapped.

"A wanton," she whispered. "Fallen."

"Then marry me," he shot back. "I offered to make you respectable from the beginning, but *you* refused."

He had her there, and she knew it. But logic didn't seem to have a place in her heart these days, and all she could think was — How could she marry him? How could she marry *Michael?*

"I wasn't supposed to feel this for another man," she said, barely able to believe that she'd spoken the words aloud.

"Feel *what?*" he asked urgently.

She swallowed, forcing herself to bring her eyes to his face. "The passion," she admitted.

His face took on a strange expression, almost one of disgust. "Right," he drawled. "Of course. It's a damned good thing you have me here to service you."

"No!" she cried out, horrified by the derision lacing his voice. "That's not it."

"Isn't it?"

"No." But she didn't know what was.

He took a ragged breath and turned away from her, his body taut with tension. She watched his back with terrible fascination, unable to take her eyes off of him. His shirt was loose, and even though she couldn't see his face, she knew his body, every last curve of it. He looked desolate, hardened.

Worn out.

"Why do you stay?" he asked in a low voice, leaning on the edge of the mattress with the flats of both hands.

"Wh–what?"

"Why do you stay?" he repeated, his words rising in volume but never losing control. "If you hate me so much, why do you stay?"

"I don't hate you," she said. "You know I —"

"I don't know a damned thing, Francesca," he bit off. "I don't even know you any longer." His shoulders tensed as his fingers bit into the mattress. She could see one of his hands; the knuckles had gone white.

"I don't hate you," she said again, as if saying it twice would somehow turn her words into solid things, palpable and real, that she could force him to hold on to. "I don't. I don't hate you."

He said nothing.

"It's not you, it's me," she said, pleading with him now — for what, she wasn't certain. Maybe for him not to hate *her*. That was the one thing she didn't think she could bear.

But all he did was laugh. It was a horrible sound, bitter and low. "Oh, Francesca," he said, condescension lending his words a brittle flavor. "If I had a pound for every time I've said *that* . . ."

Her mouth settled into a grim line. She didn't like to be reminded of all the women who had gone before her. She didn't want to know about them, didn't even want to recall their existence.

"Why do you stay?" he asked again, finally turning around to face her.

She nearly reeled at the fire in his eyes. "Michael, I —"

"Why?" he demanded, fury pounding his voice into a harsh rumble. His face had tightened into deep, angry lines, and her hand instinctively reached for the door-knob.

"Why do you stay, Francesca?" he persisted, moving toward her with the predatory grace of a tiger. "There is nothing for you here at Kilmartin, nothing but *this*."

She gasped as his hands landed hard on her shoulders, let out a soft cry of surprise as his lips found hers. It was a kiss of anger, of brutal desperation, but still, her traitorous body wanted nothing more than to melt into him, to let him do what he wished, turn all of his wicked attentions on her.

She wanted him. Dear God, even like this, she wanted him.

And she feared she would never learn to say no.

But he wrenched himself away. *He* did it. Not her.

"Is that what you want?" he asked, his voice ragged and hoarse. "Is that all?"

She did nothing, didn't even move, just looked at him with wild eyes.

"Why do you stay?" he demanded, and she knew it was the last time he'd ask.

She didn't have an answer.

He gave her several seconds. He waited

for her to speak until the silence rose between them like a gorgon, but every time she opened her mouth, no sound emerged, and she couldn't do anything but stand there, shaking as she watched his face.

With a vicious curse, he turned away. "Leave," he ordered. "Now. I want you out of the house."

"Wh–what?" She couldn't believe it, couldn't believe that he would actually toss her out.

He didn't look at her as he said, "If you can't be with me, if you can't give all of yourself to me, then I want you gone."

"Michael?" It was just a whisper, barely that.

"I can't bear this halfway existence," he said, his voice so low she wasn't certain she'd heard correctly.

All she could manage to say was, "Why?"

At first she didn't think he was going to respond. His posture became impossibly taut, and then he began to shake.

Her hand rose to cover her mouth. Was he crying? Could he be . . .

Laughing?

"Oh, God, Francesca," he said, his voice punctuated with derisive laughter. "Now there's a good one. Why? *Why?* Why?" He gave each one a different tenor, as if he were testing out the word, asking it to different people.

"Why?" he asked again, this time with increased volume as he turned around to face her. "*Why?* It's because I love you, damn me to hell. Because I've always loved you. Because I loved you when you were with John, and I loved you when I was in India, and God only knows I don't deserve you, but I love you, anyway."

Francesca sagged against the door.

"How's that for a witty little joke?" he mocked. "I love *you*. I love *you*, my cousin's wife. I love *you*, the one woman I can never have. I love *you*, Francesca Bridgerton Stirling, who —"

"Stop," she choked out.

"Now? Now that I've finally gotten started? Oh, I don't think so," he said grandly, waving one of his arms through the air like a showman. He leaned in close — painfully, uncomfortably close. And his smile was terrifying as he asked, "Are you scared yet?"

"Michael —"

"Because I haven't nearly begun," he said, his voice skipping over hers. "Do you want to know what I was thinking when you were married to John?"

"No," she said desperately, shaking her head.

He opened his mouth to say more, his eyes still flashing with his contemptuous passion, but then something happened. Something changed. It was in his eyes. They were so angry, so inflamed, and then they simply . . .

Stopped.

Turned cold. Weary.

Then he closed them. He looked exhausted.

"Go," he said. "Now."

She whispered his name.

"Go," he repeated, ignoring her plea. "If you're not mine, I don't want you anymore."

"But I —"

He walked to the window, leaning heavily on the sill. "If this is to end, you will have to do it. You will have to walk away, Francesca. Because now . . . after everything . . . I'm just not strong enough to say goodbye."

She stood motionless for several seconds, and then, just when she was sure the tension between them would tighten and snap her in two, her feet somehow found purchase, and she ran from the room.

She ran.

And she ran.

And she ran.

She ran blindly, without thinking.

She ran outside, into the night, into the rain.

She ran until her lungs burned. She ran until she had no balance, was tripping and sliding in the mud.

She ran until she could run no longer, and then she just sat, finding comfort and shelter in the gazebo John had erected for her years earlier, after throwing up his arms and announcing that he'd given up trying to get her to curb her lengthy hikes, and this way at least she'd have a place outside to call her own.

She sat there for hours, shivering in the cold, but not feeling a thing. And all she could wonder was —

Just what was it she was running from?

Michael had no memory of the moments that followed her departure. It could have been one minute, it could have been ten. All he knew was that he seemed to wake up when he realized he'd nearly put his fist through the wall.

And yet somehow he barely noticed the pain.

"My lord?"

It was Reivers, popping his head in to inquire about the commotion.

"Get out," Michael growled. He didn't want to see anyone, didn't want to hear anyone even breathe.

"But maybe some ice for —"

"Get out!" Michael roared, and it felt as if his body were growing huge and monsterish as he turned. He wanted to hurt someone. He wanted to claw at the air.

Reivers fled.

Michael dug his fingernails into his palms, even as his right fist was beginning to swell. Somehow the motion seemed the only way to keep the devil inside at bay, to prevent him from tearing the room apart with his very fingers.

Six years.

He stood there, stock still, with only one thought in his head.

Six bloody years.

He'd held this inside for six years, scrupulously kept his feelings off of his face when he watched her, never told a soul.

Six years he'd loved her, and it had all come to *this*.

He'd laid his heart on the table. He'd practically handed her a knife and asked her to slice it open.

Oh, no, Francesca, you can do better than

that. Hold steady there, you can easily make a few more cuts. And while you're at it, why don't you take these pieces here and dice them up?

Whoever had said it was a good thing to speak the truth was an ass. Michael would have given anything, both his bloody feet, even, to have made this all go away.

But that was the thing about words.

He laughed miserably.

You couldn't take them back.

Spread it on the floor now. There you go, stamp it down. No, harder. Harder than that, Frannie. You can do it.

Six years.

Six bloody years, all lost in a single moment. All because he'd thought he might actually have the right to feel happy.

He should have known better.

And for the grand finale, just set the whole bloody thing aflame. Brava, Francesca!

There went his heart.

He looked down at his hands. His nails had carved half-moons into his palms. One had even broken the skin.

What was he going do? What the *hell* was he going to do now?

He didn't know how to live his life with her knowing the truth. For six years, his every thought and action had revolved around making sure she didn't know. All men had some guiding principle in their lives, and that had been his.

Make sure Francesca never finds out.

He sat in his chair, barely able to contain his own maniacal laughter.

Oh, Michael, he thought, the chair shaking beneath him as he let his head fall into his hands. *Welcome to the rest of your life.*

His second act, as it happened, opened far sooner than he'd expected, with a soft knock on his door about three hours later.

Michael was still sitting in his chair, his only concession to the passage of time the movement of his head from his hands to the seat back. He'd been leaning like that for some time now, his neck uncomfortable but unmoving, his eyes staring sightlessly at some random spot on the ecru silk fabric covering the wall.

He felt removed, set apart, and when he heard the knock, he didn't even recognize the sound at first.

But it came again, no less timid than the first, but still persistent.

Whoever it was, he wasn't going away.

"Enter!" he barked.

He was a she.

Francesca.

He should have risen. He wanted to. Even after everything, he didn't hate her, didn't wish to offer his disrespect. But she had wrenched everything from him, every last drop of strength and purpose, and all he could manage was a slight lifting of his brows, accompanied by a tired, "What?"

Her lips parted, but she didn't say anything. She was wet, he realized, almost idly. She must have gone outside. Silly fool, it was cold out.

"What is it, Francesca?" he asked.

"I'll marry you," she said, so quietly he more read the words on her lips than did he hear them. "If you'll still have me."

And you'd have thought he'd jump from his chair. Rise, at least, unable to tamp down the joy spreading through his body. You'd have thought he might stride across the room, a man of purpose and resolve, to sweep her from her feet, rain kisses on her face, and lay her on the bed, where he might seal the bargain in the most primitive manner possible.

But instead he just sat there, too heart-weary to do anything other than ask, "Why?"

She flinched at the suspicion in his voice, but he didn't feel particularly charitable at the moment. After what she'd done to him, she could suffer a bit of discomfort herself.

"I don't know," she admitted. She was standing very still, her arms straight at her sides. She wasn't rigid, but he could tell she was trying very hard not to move.

If she did, he suspected, she'd run from the room.

"You'll have to do better than that," he said.

Her lower lip caught between her teeth. "I don't know," she whispered. "Don't make me figure it out."

He lifted one sardonic brow.

"Not yet, at least," she finished.

Words, he thought, almost dispassionately. He'd had his words, and now these were hers.

"You can't take it back," he said in a low voice.

She shook her head.

He rose slowly to his feet. "There will be no backing out. No cold feet. No changed minds."

"No," she said. "I promise."

And that was when he finally let himself believe her. Francesca did not give promises lightly. And she never broke her vows.

He was across the room in an instant, his hands at her back, his arms around her, his mouth raining desperate kisses on her face.

"You will be mine," he said. "This is it. Do you understand?"

She nodded, arching her neck as his lips slid down the long column to her shoulder.

"If I want to tie you to the bed, and keep you there until you're heavy with child, I'll do it," he vowed.

"Yes," she gasped.

"And you won't complain."

She shook her head.

His fingers tugged at her gown. It fell to the floor with stunning speed. "And you'll like it," he growled.

"Yes. *Oh, yes.*"

He moved her to the bed. He wasn't gentle or smooth, but she didn't seem to want that, and he fell upon her like a starving man. "You will be mine," he said again, grasping her bottom and pulling her toward him. "Mine."

And she was. For that night, at least, she was.

 *Chapter 22*

. . . I am sure you have everything well in hand. You always do.

> — *from the dowager Viscountess Bridgerton to her daughter, the Countess of Kilmartin, immediately upon the receipt of Francesca's missive*

The hardest part about planning a wedding with Michael, Francesca soon realized, was figuring out how to tell people.

As difficult as it had been for her to accept the idea, she couldn't imagine how everyone else might take it. Good God, what would Janet say? She'd been remarkably supportive of Francesca's decision to remarry, but surely she hadn't considered Michael as a candidate.

And yet even as Francesca sat at her desk, her pen hovering over paper for hours on end, trying to find the right words, something inside of her knew that she was doing the right thing.

She still wasn't sure *why* she'd decided to marry him. And she wasn't sure how she ought to feel about his stunning revelation of love, but somehow she knew she wished to be his wife.

That didn't, however, make it any easier to figure out how to tell everyone else about it.

Francesca was sitting in her study, penning letters to her family — or rather, crumpling the paper of her latest misfire and tossing it on the floor — when Michael entered with the post.

"This arrived from your mother," he said, handing her an elegantly appointed cream-colored envelope.

Francesca slid her letter opener under the flap and removed the missive, which was, she noted with surprise, a full four pages long. "Good heavens," she murmured. Her mother generally managed to say what she needed to say with one sheet of paper, two at the most.

"Is anything amiss?" Michael asked, perching himself on the edge of her desk.

"No, no," Francesca said distractedly. "I just . . . Good heavens!"

He twisted and stretched a bit, trying to

get a look at the words. "What is it?"

Francesca just waved a shushing hand in his direction.

"Frannie?"

She flipped to the next page. "Good heavens!"

"Give me that," he said, reaching for the paper.

She turned quickly to the side, refusing to relinquish it. "Oh, my God," she breathed.

"Francesca Stirling, if you don't —"

"Colin and Penelope got married."

Michael rolled his eyes. "We already knew —"

"No, I mean they moved up the wedding date by . . . well, goodness, it must have been by over a month, I would think."

Michael just shrugged. "Good for them."

Francesca looked up at him with annoyed eyes. "Someone might have *told* me."

"I imagine there wasn't time."

"But that," she said with great irritation, "is not the worst of it."

"I can't imagine —"

"*Eloise* is getting married as well."

"Eloise?" Michael asked with some surprise. "Was she even being courted by anyone?"

"No," Francesca said, quickly flipping to the third sheet of her mother's letter. "It's someone she's never met."

"Well, I imagine she's met him now," Michael said in a dry voice.

"I can't believe no one *told* me."

"You *have* been in Scotland."

"Still," she said grumpily.

Michael just chuckled at her annoyance, drat the man.

"It's as if I don't exist," she said, irritated enough to shoot him her most ferocious glare.

"Oh, I wouldn't say —"

"Oh, yes," she said with great flair, *"Francesca."*

"Frannie . . ." He sounded quite amused now.

"Has someone told Francesca?" she said, doing a rather fine group impression of her family. "Remember her? Sixth of eight? The one with the blue eyes?"

"Frannie, don't be daft."

"I'm not daft, I'm just ignored."

"I rather thought you liked being a bit removed from your family."

"Well, yes," she grumbled, "but that's beside the fact."

"Of course," he murmured.

She glared at him for his sarcasm.

"Shall we prepare to leave for the wedding?" he inquired.

"As if I *could*," she said with great huff. "It's in three days' time."

"My felicitations," Michael said admiringly.

Her eyes narrowed suspiciously. "What is that supposed to mean?"

"One can't help but feel a great respect for any man who manages to get the deed done with such swiftness," he said with a shrug.

"Michael!"

He positively leered at her. "I did."

"I haven't married you yet," she pointed out.

He grinned. "The deed I was referring to wasn't marriage."

She felt her face go red. "Stop it," she muttered.

His fingers tickled along her hand. "Oh, I don't think so."

"Michael, this is not the time," she said, yanking her hand away.

He sighed. "It starts already."

"What does *that* mean?"

"Oh, nothing," he said, plopping down in a nearby chair. "Just that we're not even wed, and already we're an old married couple."

She gave him an arch look, then turned back to her mother's letter. They did sound like an old married couple, not that she wished to give him the satisfaction of her agreement. She supposed it was because unlike most newly affianced pairs, they had known each other for years. He was, despite the amazing changes of the past few weeks, her very best friend.

She stopped. Froze.

"Is something wrong?" Michael asked.

"No," she said, giving her head a little shake. Somehow, in the midst of her confusion, she'd lost sight of that. Michael may have been the last person she'd have thought she'd marry, but that was for a good reason, wasn't it?

Who'd have thought she'd marry her best friend?

Surely that had to bode well for the union.

"Let's get married," he said suddenly.

She looked up questioningly. "Wasn't that already on the agenda?"

"No," he said, grasping her hand, "let's do it today."

"Today?" she exclaimed. "Are you mad?"

"Not at all. We're in Scotland. We don't need banns."

"Well, yes, but —"

He knelt before her, his eyes aglow. "Let's do it, Frannie. Let's be mad, bad, and rash."

"No one will believe it," she said slowly.

"No one is going to believe it, anyway."

He had a point there. "But my family . . ." she added.

"You just said they left you out of their festivities."

"Yes, but it was hardly on purpose!"

He shrugged. "Does it matter?"

"Well, yes, if one really thinks about —"

He yanked her to his feet. "Let's go."

"Michael . . ." And she didn't know why she was dragging her feet, except maybe that she felt she ought. It was a wedding, after all, and such haste was a bit unseemly.

He quirked a brow. "Do you really want a lavish wedding?"

"No," she said, quite honestly. She'd done that once. It didn't seem appropriate the second time around.

He leaned in, his lips touching her ear. "Are you willing to risk an eight-month baby?"

"Obviously I *was*," she said pertly.

"Let's give our child a respectable nine months of gestation," he said jauntily.

She swallowed uncomfortably. "Michael, you must be aware that I may not conceive. With John, it took —"

"I don't care," he cut in.

"I think you do," she said softly, worried about his response, but unwilling to enter into marriage without a clear conscience. "You've mentioned it several times, and —"

"To trap you into marriage," he interrupted. And then, with stunning speed, he had her back against the wall, his body pressed up against hers with startling intimacy. "I don't care if you're barren," he said, his voice hot against her ear. "I don't care if you deliver a litter of puppies."

His hand crept under her dress, sliding right up her thigh. "All I care about," he said thickly, one finger turning very, very wicked, "is that you're *mine*."

"Oh!" Francesca yelped, feeling her limbs go molten. "Oh, yes."

"Yes on this?" he asked devilishly, wiggling his finger just enough to drive her wild, "or yes on getting married today?"

"On this," she gasped. "Don't stop."

"What about the marriage?"

Francesca grabbed his shoulders for support.

"What about the marriage?" he asked again, quickly withdrawing his finger.

"Michael!" she wailed.

His lips spread into a slow, feral smile. "What about the marriage?"

"Yes!" she begged. "Yes! Whatever you want."

"Anything?"

"Anything," she sighed.

"Good," he said, and then, abruptly, he stepped away.

Leaving her slackjawed and rather mussed.

"Shall I retrieve your coat?" he inquired, adjusting his cuffs. He was the perfect picture of elegant manhood, not a hair out of place, utterly calm and composed.

She, on the other hand, was quite certain she resembled a banshee. "Michael?" she managed to ask, trying to ignore the extremely uncomfortable sensation he'd left down in her lower regions.

"If you want to finish," he said, in much the same tone he might have used while discussing grouse hunting, "you'll have to do so as the Countess of Kilmartin."

"I *am* the Countess of Kilmartin," she growled.

He gave her a nod of acknowledgment. "You'll have to do it as *my* Countess of Kilmartin," he corrected. He gave her a moment to respond, and when she did not, he asked again, "Shall I get your coat?"

She nodded.

"Excellent choice," he murmured. "Will you wait here or accompany me to the hall?"

She pried her teeth apart to say, "I'll come out to the hall."

He took her arm and guided her to the door, leaning down to murmur, "Eager little thing, aren't we?"

"Just get my coat," she ground out.

He chuckled, but the sound was warm and rich, and already she felt her irritation beginning to melt away. He was a rogue and scoundrel, and probably a hundred other things as well, but he was her rogue and scoundrel, and she knew he possessed a heart as fine and true as any man she could ever hope to meet. Except for . . .

She stopped short and jabbed one finger against his chest.

"There will be no other women," she said sharply.

He just looked at her with one arched brow.

"I mean it. No mistresses, no dalliances, no —"

"Good God, Francesca," he cut in, "do you really think I could? No, scratch that. Do you really think I *would?*"

She'd been so caught up in her own intentions that she hadn't really looked at his face, and she was stunned by the expression she saw there. He was angry, she realized, irked that she'd even asked. But she couldn't dismiss out of hand a decade of bad behavior, and she didn't think he had the right to expect her to, so she said, lowering her voice slightly, "You don't have the finest reputation."

"For God's sake," he grunted, yanking her out into the hall. "They were all just to get you out of my mind, anyway."

Francesca was shocked into stumbling silence as she followed him toward the front door.

"Any other questions?" he asked, turning to her with such a supercilious expression that one would have thought he'd been born to the earldom, rather than fallen into it by chance.

"Nothing," she squeaked.

"Good. Now let's go. I have a wedding to attend."

Later that night, Michael couldn't help but be pleased by the day's turn of events. "Thank you, Colin," he said rather jovially to himself as he undressed for bed, "and thank you, too, whomever you are, for marrying Eloise on a moment's notice."

Michael rather doubted that Francesca would have agreed to a rushed wedding if her two siblings hadn't up and gotten married without her.

And now she was his wife.

His wife.

It was almost impossible to believe.

It had been his goal for weeks, and she'd finally agreed the night before, but it wasn't until he'd slid the ancient gold band onto her finger that it had sunk in.

She was his.

Until death do they part.

"Thank you, John," Michael added, the levity leaving his voice. Not for dying, never for that. But rather for releasing him of the guilt. Michael still wasn't quite certain how it had come about, but ever since that fateful night, after he and Francesca had made love at the gardener's cottage, Michael had known, in his heart of hearts, that John would have approved.

He would have given his blessing and in his more fanciful moments, Michael liked to think that if John could have chosen a new husband for Francesca, he would have selected him.

Clad in a burgundy robe, Michael walked to the connecting door between his and Francesca's rooms. Even though they had been intimate since his arrival at Kilmartin, it was only today that he had moved into the earl's bedchamber. It was odd; in London, he hadn't been so worried about appearances. They'd taken residence in the official bedrooms of the earl and countess and simply made sure the entire household was aware that the connecting door was firmly locked from both sides.

But here in Scotland, where they were behaving in a manner deserving of gossip, he'd been careful to unpack his belongings in a room as far down the hall from Francesca's as was available. It didn't matter that one or the other of them had been sneaking back and forth the whole time; at least they gave the appearance of respectability.

The servants weren't stupid; Michael was quite sure they'd all known what was going on, but they adored Francesca, and they wanted her to be happy, and they would never breathe a word against her to anyone.

Still, it was rather nice to put all of that nonsense behind them.

He reached for the doorknob but didn't grasp it right away, stopping instead to listen for sounds in the next room. He didn't hear much. He didn't know why he'd thought he might; the door was solid and ancient and not inclined to give up secrets. Still, there was something about the moment that called to him, that begged for savoring.

He was about to enter Francesca's bedchamber.

And he had every right to be there.

The only thing that might have made it better would be if she had told him she loved him.

The omission left a small, niggling spot on his heart, but that was more than overshadowed by his newfound joy. He didn't want her to say words she did not feel, and even if she never loved him as a wife ought to love her husband, he knew that her feelings were stronger and more noble than what most wives felt for their husbands.

He knew that she cared for him, loved him deeply as a friend. And if anything were to happen to him, she would mourn him with every inch of her heart.

He really couldn't ask for more.

He might *want* more, but he already had so much more than he'd ever hoped for. He shouldn't be greedy. Not when, on top of everything, he had the passion.

And there was passion.

It was almost amusing how much it had surprised her, how much it continued to surprise her each and every day. He had used it to his advantage; he knew that and he wasn't ashamed. He'd used it that very afternoon, while trying to convince her to marry him right then and there.

And it had worked.

Thank God, it had worked.

He felt giddy, like a green boy. When the idea had come to him — to wed that day — it had been like a strange shot of electricity through his veins, and he'd barely been able to contain himself. It had been one of those moments when he knew he had to succeed, would have done anything to win her over.

Now, as he stood on the threshold of his marriage, he couldn't help but wonder if it would be different now. Would she feel different in his arms as his wife than she had as his lover? When he looked upon her face in the morning, would the air feel changed? When he saw her across a crowded room —

He gave his head a little shake. He was turning into a sentimental fool. His heart had always skipped a beat when he saw her across a crowded room. Anything more, and he didn't think the organ could take the strain.

He pushed open the door. "Francesca?" he called out, his voice soft and husky in the night air.

She was standing by the window, clad in a nightgown of deep blue. The cut was modest, but the fabric clung, and for a moment, Michael couldn't breathe.

And he knew — he didn't know how, but he knew — that it would always be like this.

"Frannie?" he whispered, moving slowly toward her.

She turned, and there was hesitation on her face. Not nervousness, precisely, but rather an endearing expression of apprehension, as if she, too, realized that it was all different now.

"We did it," he said, unable to keep a loopy smile off of his face.

"I still can't believe it," she said.

"Nor can I," he admitted, reaching out to touch her cheek, "but it's true."

"I —" She shook her head. "Never mind."

"What were you going to say?"

"It's nothing."

He took both of her hands and tugged her toward him. "It's not nothing," he murmured. "When it's you, and when it's me, it's never nothing."

She swallowed, shadows playing across the delicate lines of her throat, and she finally said, "I just . . . I wanted to say . . ."

His fingers tightened around hers, lending her encouragement. He wanted her to say it. He hadn't thought he needed the words, not yet, anyway, but dear God, how much he wanted to hear them.

"I'm very glad I married you," she finished, her voice matching the uncharacteristically shy expression on her face. "It was the right thing to do."

He felt his toes clench slightly, gripping the carpet as he tamped down his disappointment. It was more than he'd ever thought to hear from her, and yet so much less than he'd hoped.

And yet, even with that, she was still here in his arms, and she was his wife, and that, he vowed fiercely to himself, had to count for something.

"I'm glad, too," he said softly, and pulled her close. His lips touched hers, and it *was* different when he kissed her. There was a new sense of belonging, and lack of furtiveness and desperation.

He kissed her slowly, gently, taking the time to explore her, to relish every moment. His hands slid along the silk of her nightgown, and she moaned as the fabric bunched under his fingers.

"I love you," he whispered, deciding there was no use in holding the words to himself any longer, even if she wasn't inclined to say the same. His lips moved across her cheek to her ear, and he nibbled gently on her lobe before moving down her neck to the delectable hollow at the base of her throat.

"Michael," she sighed, swaying into him. "Oh, Michael."

He cupped her bottom and pressed her to him, a groan slipping across his lips as he felt her tight and warm against his arousal.

He'd thought he'd wanted her before, but this . . . this was different.

"I need you," he said hoarsely, dropping to his knees as his lips slid down the center of her, over the silk. "I need you so much."

She whispered his name, and she sounded confused as she looked down at him, at his position of supplication.

"Francesca," he said, and he had no idea why he was saying it, just that her name was the most important thing in the world right then. Her name, and her body, and the beauty of her soul.

"Francesca," he whispered again, burying his face against her belly.

Her hands settled on his head, fingers entwined in his hair. He could have remained like that for hours, on his knees before her, but then she dropped down, too, and she moved toward him, arching her neck as she kissed him. "I want you," she said. "Please."

Michael groaned, pulling her toward him, and then pulling her to her feet before tugging her toward the bed. In moments they were on the mattress, the soft down of it drawing them in, embracing them even as they embraced each other.

"Frannie," he said, his trembling fingers sliding her silk gown up and over her waist.

One of her hands cupped the back of his head, and she pulled him down for another kiss, this one deep and hot. "I need you," she said, her voice almost a groan of need. "I need you so much."

"I want to see all of you," he said, practically tearing the silk from her body. "I need to *feel* all of you."

Francesca was as eager as he was, and her fingers went to the sash on his robe, untying the loose knot before pushing it open, revealing the broad expanse of his chest. She touched the light dusting of hair, almost feeling a sense of wonder as her hand moved across his skin.

She'd never thought to be in this place, in this moment. This certainly wasn't the first time she'd seen him this way, touched him in this manner, but somehow it was different now.

He was her husband.

It was so hard to believe, and yet it felt so perfect and right.

"Michael," she murmured, tugging the robe over his shoulders.

"Mmmm?" was his reply. He was busy doing something delectable to the back of her knee.

She fell back against the pillows, completely forgetting what she'd been about to say, if there had been anything at all.

His hand wrapped lightly around the front of her thigh, then slid up toward her hip, to her waist, and then finally to the side of her breast. Francesca wanted to take part, wanted to be adventurous and touch him as he was touching her, but his caresses were making her languid and lazy, and all she could do was lie back and enjoy his ministrations, occasionally reaching out to trail her fingers along whichever part of his skin they were able to reach.

She felt cherished.

Worshipped.

Loved.

It was humbling.

It was exquisite.

It was sacred and seductive, and it took her breath away.

His lips followed the trail his hands had forged, sending tingles of desire up and across her belly, coming to rest in the flattened hollow between her breasts.

"Francesca," he murmured, kissing his way to her nipple. He teased it first with his tongue, then took it in his mouth, biting it gently.

The sensation was intense and immediate. Her body convulsed, and her fingers gripped frantically into the bedsheets, desperate for purchase in a world that had suddenly tilted right off its axis.

"Michael," she gasped, arching her back. His fingers had slipped between her legs, not that she needed anything more to ready her for his eventual entry. She wanted this, and she wanted him, and she wanted it to last forever.

"You feel so good," he said hoarsely, his breath hot on her skin. He moved then, positioning himself at her entrance. His face was over hers, nose to nose, and his eyes glowed hot and intense.

Francesca wiggled beneath him, the movement tipping her hips to welcome him more deeply. "Now," she said, the word a cross between an order and a plea.

He moved slowly, inching his way inside with tantalizing deliberation. She felt herself opening, stretching to greet him until their bodies touched, and she knew that he was embedded fully.

"Oh, my God," he grunted, his face stretched taut with passion. "I can't . . . I have to . . ."

She answered by arching her hips, pressing herself even more firmly against him.

He began to move within her, each stroke bringing a new wave of sensation that spread and burned through her body. She said his name, and then she could not speak, could do nothing but gasp for air as their movements grew more frenzied and desperate.

And then it came upon her, in a lightning wave of pleasure. Her body exploded, and she cried out, unable to contain the intensity of the experience. Michael thrust into her harder, and then again, and again. He called out as he climaxed, her name a prayer and a benediction on his lips, and then he collapsed atop her.

"I'm too heavy," he said, making a half-hearted attempt to move off of her.

"Don't," she said, stilling him with her hand. She didn't want him to move, not yet. Soon it would be hard to breathe, and he'd have to adjust, but for now there was something elemental in their position, something to which she wasn't ready to bid farewell.

"No," he said, and she could hear a smile in his voice, "I'll crush you." He slid off of her, but he didn't relinquish their closeness, and she found herself curled next to him like a nested spoon, her back warmed by his skin, her body held snugly in place by his arm under her breasts.

He murmured something against her neck, and she couldn't really understand the words, but that didn't matter; she knew what he'd said.

He nodded off soon after, his breath a slow and steady lullaby at her ear. But Francesca did not sleep. She was tired, she was drowsy, and she was sated, but she did not sleep.

It had been different tonight.

And she was left wondering why.

Chapter 23

. . . I am sure that Michael will be penning a letter as well, but as I count you as a dear, dear friend, I wanted to write to you myself to inform you that we have married. Are you surprised? I must confess that I was.

> — *from the Countess of Kilmartin to Helen Stirling,*
> *three days after her marriage to the Earl of Kilmartin*

"You look terrible."

Michael turned to Francesca with a somewhat dry expression. "And good morning to you, too," he remarked, turning his attention back to his eggs and toast.

Francesca slid into place across the breakfast table from him. It was two weeks into their marriage; Michael had risen early that morning, and when she'd awakened, his side of the bed had been cold.

"I'm not joking," she said, feeling her concern knit her brows into a wrinkled line. "You look quite pasty, and you're not even sitting up straight. You should go back to bed and get some rest."

He coughed, then coughed again, the second spasm wracking his body. "I'm fine," he said, although the words came out rather like a gasp.

"You're not fine."

He rolled his eyes. "Married a fortnight, and already —"

"If you didn't wish for a nagging wife, you shouldn't have married me," Francesca said, judging the distance across the table and deciding that she couldn't reach far enough to touch his forehead to check for fever.

"I'm fine," he said firmly, and this time he picked up his copy of *The London Times* — several days old but as current as they could expect in the Scottish border counties — and proceeded to ignore her.

Two could play at that game, Francesca decided, and she devoted her attention to the always challenging task of spreading jam on her muffin.

Except he coughed.

She shifted in her seat, trying not to say anything.

He coughed again, this time turning away from the table so that he could bend over a bit.

"M—"

He gave her a look of such ferocity that she shut her mouth.

She narrowed her eyes.

He inclined his head in an annoyingly condescending manner, then had the effect ruined when his body convulsed with another spasm.

"That's it," Francesca announced, rising to her feet. "You are going back to bed. Now."

"I'm fine," he grunted.

"You're not fine."

"I'm —"

"Sick," she interrupted. "You're sick, Michael. Diseased, ill, plague-ridden, you're sick. As a dog. I don't see how I could possibly make it any more clear."

"I haven't got the plague," he muttered.

"No," she said, coming around the table to grasp his arm, "but you do have malaria, and —"

"It's not malaria," he said, whacking his chest as he coughed again.

She pulled him to his feet, a task she couldn't have completed without at least a bit of assistance on his part. "How do you know that?" she asked.

"I just do."

She pursed her lips. "And you speak with the medical expertise that comes from —"

"Having had the disease for the better part of a year," he cut in. "It's not malaria."

She nudged him toward the door.

"Besides," he protested, "it's too soon."

"Too soon for what?"

"For another attack," he explained wearily. "I just had one in London, what was it — two months ago? It's too soon."

"Why is it too soon?" she asked, her voice strangely quiet.

"It just is," he muttered, but inside, he knew a different truth. It wasn't too soon; he'd known plenty of people who'd had their malarial attacks two months apart.

They'd all been sick. Really sick.

Quite a few of them had died.

If his attacks were coming closer together, did that mean the disease was winning?

Now there was irony for you. He'd finally married Francesca, and now he might be dying.

"It isn't malaria," he said again, this time with enough force to make her stop walking and look up at him.

"It isn't," he said.

She just nodded.

"It's probably a cold," he said.

She nodded again, but he got the distinct impression that she was placating him.

"I'll take you to bed," she said softly.

And he let her.

Ten hours later, Francesca was terrified. Michael's fever was rising, and although he was not delirious or incoherent, it was clear that he was very, very ill. He kept saying that it wasn't malaria, that it didn't *feel* like malaria, but every time she pressed him for details, he couldn't explain why — at least not to her satisfaction.

She didn't know much about the disease; the fashionable ladies' bookshops in London declined to carry medical texts. She'd wanted to ask her own doctor, or even seek an expert at the Royal College of Physicians, but she had made a promise to Michael that she would keep his illness a secret. If she ran around town making queries about malaria, eventually someone would want to know why. Thus, most of what she knew she had learned from Michael during the few short months he'd been back from India.

But it didn't seem right that the attacks were coming closer together. Not, she had to allow, that she possessed any medical knowledge upon which to base that assumption. When he'd fallen ill in London, he'd said that it had been six months since his last set of fevers, and three before that.

Why would the disease suddenly change course and attack again so quickly? It just didn't make sense. Not if he was getting better.

And he had to be getting better. He had to be.

She sighed, reaching out to touch his forehead. He was sleeping now, snoring slightly, as he tended to when he was congested. Or so he'd told her. They hadn't been married long enough for her to have gained that knowledge firsthand.

His skin was hot, although not burningly so. His mouth looked parched, so she spooned some tepid tea over his lips, tilting up his chin to try to help him swallow in his sleep.

Instead, he choked and came awake, spewing the water across the bed.

"Sorry," Francesca said, surveying the damage. At least it had been a small spoonful.

"What the devil are you doing to me?" he sputtered.

"I don't know," she admitted. "I haven't much experience nursing. You looked thirsty."

"Next time I'm thirsty, I'll tell you," he grumbled.

She nodded her agreement and watched as he tried to make himself comfortable again. "You wouldn't happen to be thirsty right now?" she asked in a mild voice.

"Just a bit," he said, his syllables slightly clipped.

Without a word, she held out the cup of tea. He downed it all in one long gulp.

"Would you like another cup?"

He shook his head. "Any more and I'm going to have to pi—" He broke off and cleared his throat. "Sorry," he mumbled.

"I have four brothers," she said. "Pay it no mind. Would you like me to fetch you the chamberpot?"

"I can do it myself."

He didn't look well enough to cross the room on his own, but she knew better than to argue with a man in that irritable a state. He would come to his senses when he tried to stand and fell right back down against the bed. No amount of argument or reason on her part would convince him otherwise.

"You're quite feverish," she said softly.

"It isn't malaria."

"I didn't say —"

"You were thinking it."

"What happens if it *is* malaria?" she asked.

"It's not —"

"But what if it is?" she cut in, and to her horror, her voice had that awful pitch to it, that roundish sound of terror it made just before it actually choked.

Michael looked at her for several seconds, his eyes grim. Finally, he just rolled over and said, "It's not."

Francesca swallowed. She had her answer now. "Do you mind if I leave?" she blurted out, standing up so quickly the blood rushed from her head.

He didn't say anything, but she could see him shrug under the covers.

"It's just for a walk," she explained haltingly, making her way to the door. "Before the sun goes down."

"I'll be fine," he grunted.

She nodded, even though he wasn't looking at her. "I'll see you soon," she said.

But he'd already fallen back asleep.

The air was misty and threatened more

precipitation, so Francesca grabbed a rain parasol and made her way to the gazebo. The sides were open to the elements, but it had a roof, and should the heavens open, she would remain at least nominally dry.

But with every step, it felt as if her breathing was growing more labored, and by the time she reached her destination, she was heaving with exertion, not from the walk, but just from keeping the tears at bay.

The minute she sat down, she stopped trying.

Each sob was huge, and hugely unladylike, but she didn't care.

Michael might be dying. For all she knew, he *was* dying, and she was going to be a widow twice over.

It had nearly killed her last time.

And she just didn't know if she was strong enough to go through it all again. She didn't know if she wanted to be strong enough.

It wasn't right, and it wasn't fair, damn it all, that she should have to lose two husbands when so many women got to hold onto one for an entire lifetime. And most of those women didn't even like their spouses, whereas *she,* who actually loved them both —

Francesca's breath caught.

She loved him? Michael?

No, no, she assured herself, she didn't *love* him. Not like that. When she'd thought it, when the word had echoed through her brain, she'd meant in friendship. Of course she loved Michael *that* way. She'd always loved him, right? He was her best friend, had been even back when John was alive.

She pictured him, saw his face, his smile.

She closed her eyes, remembered his kiss and the perfect feeling of his hand at the small of her back as they walked through the house.

And she finally figured out why everything had seemed different between them of late. It wasn't, as she'd originally supposed, just because they'd married. It wasn't because he was her husband, because she wore his ring on her finger.

It was because she loved him.

This thing between them, this bond — it wasn't just passion, and it wasn't wicked.

It was love, and it was divine.

And Francesca could not have been more surprised if John had materialized before her and started to dance an Irish reel.

Michael.

She loved Michael.

Not just as a friend, but as a husband and a lover. She loved him with the depth and intensity she'd felt for John. It was different, because they were different men, and she was different now, too, but it was also the same. It was the love of a woman for a man, and it filled every corner of her heart.

And by God, she didn't want him to die.

"You can't do this to me," she yelled, hanging over the side of the gazebo bench and looking up at the sky. A fat raindrop landed on the bridge of her nose, splashing into her eye.

"Oh, no you don't," she growled, wiping the moisture away. "Don't think you can —"

Three more drops, in rapid succession.

"Damn," Francesca muttered, followed by a "Sorry," aimed back up at the clouds.

She pulled her head back into the gazebo, taking refuge under the wooden roof as the rain grew in intensity.

What was she supposed to do now? Charge forth with all the single-minded purpose of an avenging angel, or have a good cry and feel sorry for herself?

Or maybe a little of both.

Ridgefield Library
Tel (203) 438-2282
www.ridgefieldlibrary.org

Borrowed Items 8/24/2021 13:33
XXXXXXXXXX8736

Item Title	Due Date
34010082920090	9/14/2021 23:59
Tom Clancy's Op-center State of siege	
34010102154076	9/14/2021 23:59
Murder list	
34010101191061	9/14/2021 23:59
When he was wicked	

Thank you for visiting
the Ridgefield Library!

www.ridgefieldlibrary.org

She looked out at the rain, which was now thundering down with enough force to strike fear in the heart of even the most determined of avenging angels.

Definitely a little of both.

Michael opened his eyes, surprised to discover that it was morning. He blinked a few times, just to verify this fact. The curtains were drawn shut, but not all the way, and there was a clear streak of light making a stripe along the carpet.

Morning. Well. He must have been really tired. The last thing he remembered was Francesca dashing out the door, stating her intention to go for a walk, despite the fact that any fool would have realized that it was going to rain.

Silly woman.

He tried to sit up, then quickly flopped back down on the covers. Damn, he felt like death. Not, he allowed, the finest metaphor under the circumstances, but he couldn't think of much else that would adequately describe the ache that permeated his body. He felt exhausted, nearly glued to the sheets. The mere thought of sitting up was enough to make him groan.

Damn, he was miserable.

He touched his forehead, trying to ascertain if he still had a fever, but if his brow was hot, then so was his hand; he couldn't tell a thing other than the fact that he was damned sweaty and certainly in need of a good bath.

He tried to sniff the air around him, but he was so congested that he ended up coughing.

He sighed. Well, if he stank, at least *he* didn't have to smell it.

He heard a soft sound at the door and looked up to see Francesca entering the room. She moved quietly on stockinged feet, clearly trying to avoid disturbing him. As she approached the bed, however, she finally looked at him and let out a little, "Oh!" of surprise.

"You're awake," she said.

He nodded. "What time is it?"

"Half eight. Not too late, really, except that you fell asleep last evening before the supper hour."

He nodded again, since he didn't really have anything pertinent to add to the conversation. And besides that, he was too tired to speak.

"How are you feeling?" she asked, sitting down beside him. "And would you like something to eat?"

"Like hell, and no, thank you."

Her lips curved slightly. "Something to drink?"

He nodded.

She picked up a small bowl that had been sitting on a nearby table. A saucer had been resting on top of it, presumably to keep the contents warm. "It's from last night," she said apologetically, "but I've had it covered, so it shouldn't be too dreadful."

"Broth?" he asked.

She nodded, holding a spoon to his lips. "Is it too cold?"

He sipped a little, then shook his head. It was barely lukewarm, but he didn't think he could stand anything overheated, anyway.

She fed him in silence for a minute or so, and then, once he said he'd had enough, she set the bowl back down, carefully replacing the lid, even though he imagined she would wish to order up a new bowl for his next meal. "Do you have a fever?" she whispered.

He tried to summon a devil-may-care smile. "I have no idea."

She reached out to touch his forehead.

"Didn't have time to bathe," he mumbled, apologizing for his slippery visage without actually uttering the word *sweat*

491

in her presence.

She made no sign of having heard his attempt at a joke, instead just furrowed her brow as she pressed her hand against him more closely. And then, surprising him with her swiftness, she stood and leaned over him, touching her lips to his forehead.

"Frannie?"

"You're hot," she said, barely breathing the words. "You're hot!"

He did nothing but blink.

"You still have a fever," she said excitedly. "Don't you understand? If you still have a fever, it can't be malaria!"

For a moment he couldn't breathe. She was right. He couldn't believe it had not occurred to him, but she was right. The malarial fevers always disappeared by morning. They hit again the next day, of course, often with horrible force, but they always dissipated, giving him a day's respite before once again laying him low.

"It's not malaria," she said again, her eyes suspiciously bright.

"I told you it wasn't," he said, but inside, he knew the truth — He hadn't been so sure.

"You're not going to die," she whispered, her lower lip catching in her teeth.

His eyes flew to hers. "Were you worried

I would?" he asked quietly.

"Of course I was," she returned, no longer trying to hide the choking sound in her voice. "My God, Michael, I can't believe you — Do you have any idea how I — Oh, for God's sake."

He had no idea what she'd just said, but he had a feeling it was good.

She stood, the back of her chair bumping against the wall. A cloth napkin had been sitting beside the broth; she snatched it up and used it to dab at her eyes.

"Frannie?" he murmured.

"You're such a *man,*" she said with a scowl.

He could do nothing but raise his eyebrows at that.

"You should know I —" But she stopped, broke herself off.

"What is it, Frannie?"

She shook her head. "Not yet," she said, and he got the impression she was talking more to herself than to him. "Soon, but not yet."

He blinked. "I beg your pardon?"

"I have to go out," she said, her words oddly curt and abrupt. "There's something I need to do."

"At half eight in the morning?"

"I'll be back soon," she said, hurrying toward the door. "Don't go anywhere."

"Well, damn," he tried to joke, "there go my plans to visit the King."

But Francesca was so distracted she didn't even bother to poke at his rather pathetic attempt at humor. "Soon," she said, the word coming out strangely like a promise. "I'll be back soon."

All he could do was shrug and watch the door as she shut it behind her.

Chapter 24

. . . I am not certain how to tell you this, and moreover, I am not certain how the news will be received, but Michael and I were married three days ago. I don't know how to describe the events leading up to the marriage, except to say that it simply felt like the right thing to do. Please know that this in no way diminishes the love I felt for John. He will always hold a special and cherished place in my heart, as do you . . .

— from the Countess of Kilmartin to the dowager Countess of Kilmartin, three days after her marriage to the Earl of Kilmartin

A quarter of an hour later, Michael was feeling remarkably better. Not well, of course; not by any stretch of the imagination could he have convinced himself — or anyone else for that matter — that he was his regular hale and hearty self. But the broth must have restored him a bit, as had the conversation, and when he got up to use the chamberpot, he found he was steadier on his legs than he would have thought. He followed this task with a bit of a makeshift bath, using a dampened cloth to wash the worst of the perspiration from his body. After donning a clean dressing gown, he felt almost human again.

He started to walk back to his bed, but he just couldn't bring himself to slide his body back between those sweaty sheets, so instead he rang for a servant and sat down in his leather wingbacked chair, turning it slightly so that he might gaze out the window.

It was sunny. That was a nice change. The weather had been dismal for both the weeks of his marriage. He hadn't particularly minded; when one spent as much time making love to one's wife as he had done, one didn't particularly care if the sun was shining.

But now, escaping his sickbed, he found that his spirits were buoyed by the sparkle of the sunlight on the dewy grass.

A movement out the window caught his eye, and he realized that it was Francesca, hurrying across the lawn. She was too far away to see clearly, but she was bundled up in her most serviceable coat, and was clutching something in her hand.

He leaned forward for a better look, but she disappeared from view, slipping behind a hedgerow.

Just then, Reivers entered the room. "You rang, my lord?"

Michael turned to face him. "Yes. Could you see to having someone come and change the sheets?"

"Of course, my lord."

"And —" Michael had been about to ask him to have a bath drawn as well, but for some reason the following words slipped out of his mouth instead: "Do you happen to know where Lady Kilmartin went? I saw her walking across the lawn."

Reivers shook his head. "No, my lord. She did not see fit to confide in me, although Davies did tell me that she asked him to ask the gardener to cut her some flowers."

Michael nodded his head as he mentally followed the chain of people. He really ought to have more respect for the sheer efficiency of servants' gossip. "Flowers, you say," he murmured. That must have been what she was holding as she crossed the lawn a few minutes earlier.

"Peonies," Reivers confirmed.

"Peonies," Michael echoed, leaning forward with interest. They were John's favorite bloom, and had been the centerpiece of Francesca's wedding bouquet. It was almost appalling that he remembered such a detail, but while he'd gone and gotten himself rippingly drunk as soon as John and Francesca had departed the party, he remembered the actual ceremony with blinding detail.

Her dress had been blue. Ice blue. And the flowers had been peonies. They'd had to get them from a hothouse, but Francesca had insisted upon it.

And suddenly he knew exactly where she was going, bundled up against the slight nip in the air.

She was going to John's grave.

Michael had visited the site once since his return. He'd gone alone, a few days after that extraordinary moment in his bedchamber, when he'd suddenly realized that John would have approved of his marrying Francesca. More than that, he almost thought John was up there somewhere, having a good chuckle over the whole thing.

And Michael couldn't help but wonder

— Did Francesca realize? Did she realize that John would have wanted this? For both of them?

Or was she still gripped by guilt?

Michael felt himself rise from his chair. He knew guilt, knew how it ate at one's heart, tore at one's soul. He knew the pain, and he knew the way it felt like acid in one's belly.

And he never wanted that for Francesca. Never.

She might not love him. She might not *ever* love him. But she was happier now than she had been before they'd married; he was sure of it. And it would kill him if she felt any shame for that happiness.

John would have wanted her to be happy. He would have wanted her to love and be loved. And if Francesca somehow didn't realize that —

Michael started pulling on his clothing. He might still be weak, and he might still be feverish, but by God he could make it down to the chapel graveyard. It would half kill him, but he would not allow her to sink into the same sort of guilty despair he'd suffered for so long.

She didn't have to love him. She didn't. He'd said those words to himself so many times during their brief marriage that he almost believed them.

She didn't have to love him. But she did have to feel free. Free to be happy.

Because if she wasn't happy . . .

Well, that *would* kill him. He could live without her love, but not without her happiness.

Francesca had known the ground would be damp, so she'd brought along a small blanket, the green and gold of the Stirling plaid making her smile wistfully as she spread it out over the grass.

"Hello, John," she said, kneeling as she carefully arranged the peonies at the base of his headstone. His grave was a simple affair, far less ostentatious than the monuments many of the nobility erected to honor their dead.

But it was what John would have wanted. She'd known him so well, been able to predict his words half the time.

He would have wanted something simple, and he would have wanted it here, in the far corner of the churchyard, closer to the rolling fields of Kilmartin, his favorite place in the world.

And so that was what she'd given him.

"It's a nice day," she said, sitting back on her bottom. She hiked up her skirts so that she could sit Indian-style, then carefully arranged them back over her legs. It wasn't the sort of position she could ever assume in polite company, but this was different.

John would have wanted her to be comfortable.

"It's been raining for weeks," she said. "Some days worse than others, of course, but never a day without at least a few minutes of moisture. You wouldn't have minded it, but I must confess, I've been longing for the sun."

She noticed that one of the stems wasn't quite where she wanted it, so she leaned forward and reset it into place.

"Of course, it hasn't really stopped me from going out," she said with a nervous laugh. "I seem to get caught out in the rain quite a bit lately. I'm not really certain what it is — I used to be more heedful of the weather."

She sighed. "No, I do know what it is. I'm just afraid to tell you. Silly of me, I know, but . . ." She laughed again, that strained noise that sounded all wrong from her lips. It was the one thing she'd never felt around John — nervous. From the moment they'd met, she'd felt so comfortable in his presence, so utterly at ease, both with him and herself.

But now . . .

Now she finally had cause for nerves.

"Something has happened, John," she said, her fingers plucking at the fabric of her coat. "I . . . started feeling something for someone that perhaps I shouldn't have done."

She looked around, half expecting some sort of divine sign from above. But there was nothing, just the gentle ruffle of wind against the leaves.

She swallowed, focusing her attention back on John's headstone. It was silly that a piece of rock might come to symbolize a man, but she had no idea where else to look when she spoke to his memory. "Maybe I shouldn't have felt it," she said, "or maybe I should have, and I just thought I shouldn't have. I don't know. All I know is it happened. I didn't expect it, but then, there it was, and . . . with . . ."

She stopped, her mouth curving into a smile that was almost rueful. "Well, I suppose you know who it was with. Can you imagine?"

And then something remarkable happened. In retrospect, she rather thought the earth should have moved, or a shaft of light come sparkling down from the heavens across the gravesite. But there was none of that. Nothing palpable, nothing audible or visible, just an odd sense of shifting within herself, almost as if something had finally nudged itself into place.

And she knew — truly, fully knew — that John could have imagined it. And more than that, he would have wanted it.

He would have wanted her to marry Michael. He would have wanted her to marry any man with whom she'd fallen in love, but she rather thought he'd be almost tickled that it had happened with Michael.

They were his two favorite people, and he would have liked knowing that they were together.

"I love him," she said, and she realized it was the first time she'd said it aloud. "I love Michael. I do, and John —" She touched his name, etched in the headstone. "I think you would approve," she whispered. "Sometimes I almost think you arranged the whole thing.

"It's so strange," she continued, tears now filling her eyes. "I spent so much time thinking to myself that I would never fall in love again. How could I possibly? And when anyone asked me what you would have wanted for me, of course I replied that you would wish for me to find someone else. But inside —" She smiled wistfully. "Inside I knew it wouldn't happen. I wasn't going to fall in love. I knew it. I absolutely *knew* it. So it didn't really matter what you wanted for me, did it?

"Except it did happen," she said softly. "It happened, and I never expected it. It happened, and it happened with Michael. I love him so much, John," she said, her voice breaking with emotion. "I kept trying to tell myself that I didn't, but when I thought he was dying, it was just too much, and I knew . . . oh God, I knew it, John. I need him. I love him. I can't live without him, and I just needed to tell you, to know that you . . . that you . . ."

She couldn't go on. There was too much inside of her, too many emotions, all desperately pushing to get out. She put her face in her hands and cried, not out of sorrow, and not out of joy, but just because she couldn't keep it inside.

"John," she gasped. "I love him. And I think this is what you would have wanted. I really do, but —"

And then, from behind her, she heard a noise. A footstep, a breath. She turned, but she already knew who it would be. She could feel him in the air.

"Michael," she whispered, staring at him

like he was a specter. He was pale and gaunt and had to lean on a tree for support, but to her he looked perfect.

"Francesca," he said, the word awkwardly passing over his lips. "Frannie."

She rose to her feet, her eyes never leaving his. "Did you hear me?" she whispered.

"I love you," he said hoarsely.

"But did you hear me?" she persisted. She had to know, and if he hadn't heard her, she had to tell him.

He nodded jerkily.

"I love you," she said. She wanted to go to him, she wanted to throw her arms around him, but somehow she was rooted to her spot. "I love you," she said again. "I love you."

"You don't have to —"

"No, I do. I have to say it. I have to tell you. I love you. I do. I love you so much."

And then the distance between them was gone, and his arms came around her. She buried her face against his chest, her tears soaking his shirt. She wasn't sure why she was crying, but she didn't really care. All she wanted was the warmth of his embrace.

In his arms she could feel the future, and it was wonderful.

Michael's chin came to rest on her head. "I didn't mean that you didn't need to say it," he murmured, "just that you didn't have to repeat it."

She laughed at that, even as the tears kept flowing, and both of their bodies shook.

"You have to say it," he said. "If you feel it, then you have to say it. I'm a greedy bastard, and I want it all."

She looked up at him, her eyes bright. "I love you."

Michael touched her cheek. "I have no idea what I did to deserve you," he said.

"You didn't have to do anything," she whispered. "You just had to be." She reached up and touched his cheek, the gesture a perfect mirror of his own. "It just took me a while to realize it, that's all."

He turned his face into her hand, then brought both of his up to cover it. He pressed a kiss against her palm, stopping just to inhale the scent of her skin. He'd tried so hard to convince himself that it didn't matter if she loved him, that having her as his wife was enough. But now . . .

Now that she'd said it, now that he knew, now that his heart had soared, he knew better.

This was heaven.

This was bliss.

This was something he'd never dared hope to feel, something he never could have dreamed existed.

This was love.

"For the rest of my life," he vowed, "I will love you. For the rest of my life. I promise you. I will lay down my life for you. I will honor and cherish you. I will —" He was choking on the words, but he didn't care. He just wanted to tell her. He just wanted her to know.

"Let's go home," she said softly.

He nodded.

She took his hand, gently pulling him away from the clearing, back toward the wooded area that lay between the churchyard and Kilmartin. Michael leaned into her tug, but before his feet lifted from the earth, he turned back toward John's grave and mouthed the words, *Thank you.*

And then he let his wife lead him home.

"I wanted to tell you later," she was saying. Her voice was still shaky with emotion, but she was starting to sound a bit more like her usual self. "I'd planned a big romantic gesture. Something huge. Something . . ." She turned to him, offering him a rueful smile. "Well, I don't know what, but it would have been grand."

He just shook his head. "I don't need that," he said. "All I need . . . I just need . . ."

And it didn't matter that he didn't know how to finish the sentence, because somehow she knew, anyway.

"I know," she whispered. "I need the exact same thing."

Epilogue

My dear nephew,

Although Helen insists that she was not surprised at the announcement of your marriage to Francesca, I shall own up to a less clever imagination and confess that to me, it came as a complete shock.

I implore you, however, not to confuse shock with lack of acceptance. It did not require much time or thought to realize that you and Francesca are an ideal match. I don't know how I did not see it before. I do not profess to understand metaphysics, and in truth, I rarely have patience for those who claim that they do, but there is an understanding between the two of you, a meeting of the minds and souls that exists on a higher plane.

You were, it is clear, born for each other.

These are not easy words for me to write. John still lives on in my heart, and I feel his presence every day. I mourn my son, and I shall always do so. I cannot tell you *what comfort it gives me to know that you and Francesca feel the same.*

I hope you will not think me self-important when I offer you my blessing.

And I hope you will not think me foolish when I also extend my thanks.

Thank you, Michael, for letting my son love her first.

— from Janet Stirling,
dowager Countess of Kilmartin,
to Michael Stirling, Earl
of Kilmartin, June 1824

Author's Note

Dear Reader,

I have subjected the characters of *When He Was Wicked* to more than their fair share of medical misfortune. Researching the conditions of both John and Michael was complicated; I had to make sure that their disease processes made scientific sense, while at the same time revealing only what was known by medical science in 1824 England.

John died of a ruptured cerebral aneurysm. Cerebral aneurysms are congenital weak spots in the walls of blood vessels within the brain. They may lie dormant for many years or they may rapidly enlarge and then rupture, leading to bleeding in the brain, which can be followed by unconsciousness, coma, and death. Headaches brought on by ruptured cerebral aneurysms are sudden and explosive but can be preceded by a lingering headache for some time prior to the actual rupture.

Nothing could have been done to save

him; even today approximately one-half of ruptured cerebral aneurysms lead to death.

During the 19th century, the only way to make a definitive diagnosis of a ruptured cerebral aneurysm was at autopsy. It is extremely unlikely, however, that an earl would have undergone a postmortem dissection; therefore, John's death would have remained a mystery to those who loved him. All Francesca would ever know was that her husband had a headache, lay down, and died.

The turning point in the treatment of cerebral aneurysms came with the widespread use of angiography in the 1950s. This technique, which consists of the injection of radiopaque dye into the vessels feeding the brain to give an X-ray picture of the vascular anatomy, was developed by Egas Moniz in Portugal in 1927. An interesting historical footnote: Moniz won the Nobel Prize for Medicine in 1949, but not for his work in the groundbreaking and life-saving field of angiography. Rather, he was honored for his discovery of the frontal lobotomy as a treatment for psychiatric illness.

As for malaria, it is an ancient disease. Throughout recorded history, it has been observed that exposure to warm, moist, humid air is associated with periodic fevers, weakness, anemia, kidney failure, coma, and death. The name of the disease comes from the Italian for "bad air," and reflects the belief of our ancestors that the air itself was to blame. In *When He Was Wicked*, Michael cites "putrid air" as the source of his illness.

Today we understand that malaria is in fact a parasitic disease. The hot, swampy conditions themselves are not to blame, but rather serve as breeding grounds for mosquitoes of the genus *Anopheles*, the vector of the infection. During an insect bite, female *Anopheles* mosquitoes unwittingly inject microscopic organisms into the hapless human host. These organisms are single-celled parasites of the genus *Plasmodium*. There are four species of *Plasmodium* that can infect people: *falciparum*, *vivax*, *ovale*, and *malariae*. Once in the bloodstream, these microorganisms are swept into the liver, where they multiply at a furious pace; within a week, tens of thousands of parasites are released back into the bloodstream, where they infect red blood cells and feed upon the oxygen-carrying hemoglobin inside. Every two or three days, through a synchronized process that is poorly understood, the offspring of these parasites erupt from the red cells, leading to high fevers and violent chills. In the case of *falciparum* malaria, the infected cells can become sticky, and glom onto the inside of blood vessels in the kidney and brain, leading to renal failure and coma — and death, if treatment is delayed.

Michael was fortunate. Although he did not know it, he suffered from *vivax* malaria, which can persist in patients' livers for decades but rarely kills its victims. The exhaustion and fevers caused by *vivax* malaria, however, are severe.

At the end of the book, both Michael and Francesca worry that a higher frequency of attacks might indicate that he was losing his battle with the disease. In truth, with *vivax* malaria, this would not have mattered. There is little rhyme or reason to when a *vivax* patient might suffer an episode of malarial fevers (except in the case of immunosuppression, such as cancer, pregnancy, or AIDS). In fact, some patients experience a complete cessation of fevers and remain healthy for the rest of their lives. I'd like to think that Michael was one of the lucky ones, but even if not, there is no reason to think that he did not live to a ripe old age. Furthermore, since malaria is strictly a blood borne disease, he could not have transmitted it to members of his family.

The cause of malaria would not be understood for decades after *When He Was Wicked* took place, but the fundamentals of treatment were already known: A cure could be achieved by consuming the bark of the tropical cinchona tree. This was usually mixed with water, yielding "quinine water." Quinine was first sold commercially in France in 1820, but its use was fairly widespread for some time prior.

Malaria has been mostly eradicated from the developed world, in large part because of mosquito control efforts. However, it remains a leading cause of death and disability among people who live in the developing world. Between 1 million and 3 million people die of *falciparum* malaria every year. That averages one death every thirty seconds. Most of the dead are in sub-Saharan Africa, and most are children under five years of age.

A portion of the proceeds of this book will be donated to malarial drug development research.

Sincerely,

Julia Q.

About the Author

Julia Quinn started writing her first book one month after finishing college and has been tapping away at her keyboard ever since.

The *New York Times* bestselling author of thirteen novels for Avon Books, she is a graduate of Harvard and Radcliffe Colleges and lives with her family in the Pacific Northwest.

Please visit her on the web at
www.juliaquinn.com.

The employees of Thorndike Press hope you have enjoyed this Large Print book. All our Thorndike and Wheeler Large Print titles are designed for easy reading, and all our books are made to last. Other Thorndike Press Large Print books are available at your library, through selected bookstores, or directly from us.

For information about titles, please call:

(800) 223-1244

or visit our Web site at:

www.gale.com/thorndike
www.gale.com/wheeler

To share your comments, please write:

Publisher
Thorndike Press
295 Kennedy Memorial Drive
Waterville, ME   04901